BOOKS

倍斯特出版事業有限公司
Best Publishing Ltd.

新制多益
閱讀滿分

神準5回全真試題 ✚ 解題策略

TOEIC

韋爾 ◎ 著

四大特色

1 循環必考字彙設計：**迅速累積關鍵實力**
文法和字彙題均精心設計，每句收錄數個官方循環必考字，巧取式記憶考點，事半功倍獲
取理想成績。

2 時事話題收錄：**翻新試題提供給考生最新資訊**
出題時加入一定比例的時事話題，提升考生靈活思緒和學習興趣，並於演練當下記誦時下常
見生活語彙。

3 就業力強化：**「職場」和「考用」大結合**
納入更多職場中常見主題，豐富化實際商用情境，即刻與就業市場接軌，
猛提升求職面試和商業書信撰寫實力。

4 試題效度和鑑別度提升：**協助考生突破各卡關的分數段**
讓考生確實理解並突破學習盲點，非僅靠語感和答題技巧應考，
精煉綜合答題能力。

作者序

　　時間過得很快，很快地這本書也完成了，甚至以驚人的速度進行著，然後又在短時間內出了一堆試題，接續寫這兩本新多益模擬試題真的頗耗腦力。在這本閱讀模擬試題中有著許多的更新和調整。第一部分是關於主題的篩選，主題的介紹還是根據官方試題分類，但是刪去了某些在聽力試題中已經出現過的主題，例如空服和地勤類的話題。在新制中，Part 5的文法、單字部分也減至剩30題，所以在這五回模擬試題中，總共有150題的文法、單字題，以不同類型的主題進行介紹且讓考生演練不重複的精選考題。在命題上還有調整的部分是，**刪除了甜頭題、仰賴記憶和背誦、技巧性答題的試題**（仰賴記憶背誦的試題，例如背誦了某些其後加上動名詞的慣用語，就能於幾秒內答題並畫卡，但完全不用看句子跟理解上、下文的試題某部分失去了意義（**這也是官方將單字、文法題比例降低的原因，以檢測出考生真正的實力**），當中還增加了新制的插入句子題（且比例增加很多），這類試題更難靠猜測去答對，甚至更需要了解上、下文意和邏輯才能進行答題，更全盤檢視考生能力（這類試題對多數考生來說，也代表著答題時間的拉長）。

　　在Part 5和Part 6中，也刪除了「**仰賴語感答題**」的試題和提高各選項字彙的難度等等。先就「語感」來說，語感確實是答題的利器，就如同有些小學跟國中在國外唸書的學生，回台就讀高中時，在寫學測或指考模擬試題時，一定能答對一定的題數，輕易就考到某個成績。某些部分英文好的學習者也是仰賴這點答題，但這無形中卻成了一些侷限，也造成有些考生卡在某個分數段或是總是考到接近900但卻未能獲取更高分的主因。當中的原因是，仰賴語感造成了答題僅憑感覺，但卻**不思考理解文意、了解上下文跟選出最合適的選項**，進而造成本來可能可以達到某個分數段，但卻因為這些因素而未能考取一定的分數。但是在四個選項都是同詞性且無法依文法技巧或語感答題時，更不該僅仰賴語感答題，或是腦海中覺得「順」就答題了，因為這其中還包含上、下文意等，而如果出題中有兩、三個選項是都符合的，考生更不該太快下決定，應該要盡快思考後選出最適合的答案。另外，選項字彙難度的提升，也會造成是需要思考後再答題的，而這些出題的改變和調整，都能讓考生在寫這五回試題中更完備自己，達到理想的成績。

　　主題內容的部分，包含了常見的新多益主題，但也增加了更多讓讀者感到興趣的主題，以增加學習效果，讓試題不是僅是答某個商業書信，淪

為千篇一律式的書信類答題或答題機器。而我一直認為這些試題不論是聽力和閱讀是需要融入情感等等的。例如：一個國際運輸的主題好了（很容易又是一個無趣的選出運輸上所碰到的問題的搭配），所以我把它改成是，在巧克力工廠工作的女助理，遇到一千個巧克力包裹都突然被拆開的情況，她該在倉庫中埋怨?或是等待主管回覆信件和提供解決辦法呢?還是她自己也能構思出可能的解決辦法並且回報給主管呢?這樣就將試題改成一個較有趣且貼近工作實境的話題，而非教科書或考試答題。在Part 7雙篇類的主題中，除了這篇之外，在其他篇也包含了其他更有趣或懸疑的話題，像是一位女性民眾在住家附近泳池遇到離奇事件，但警方卻判定為只是單純的溺水事件，最後她發現一些不尋常的事情並寫信給八卦日報...而真相會是?...。

在Part 7的單篇閱讀中，也包含了某些主題，加入了商業間諜的單篇書信，受聘於公司的女職員被高層分派了另一個新任務，偽裝成咖啡店店員與另一位在敵對公司擔任員工的Bob進行聯繫...最後女職員取得機密文件，並放置在某個指定地點，在某一篇的商業書信中，她不忘提醒女高階主管單獨去取時要特別注意安全...（越寫越替主角感到擔心，不過礙於篇幅，也沒辦法接續寫下去...）。除了有趣的商業書信外，還加入了新聞類主題和求職專欄以提升實用性和貼近生活層面。求職專欄也是單篇書信的組成，由公司人事部門回覆求職者的疑惑，有求職者覺得自己對於面試的工作是志在必得，但卻未獲錄取，原因是什麼呢?...除了這個求職話題外，也包含了談薪資和光暈效應等等的探討，跟考生實際的生活層面做了連結，例如在*What to Say in Every Job Interview*中就提到的談薪資黃金法則，Rule One: He who mentions a dollar figure first loses。光暈效應則包含了期許以進修、充電獲取更佳的學歷，而暫時離開職場，但這對於求職者來說真的會比較好嗎?還是在累積一定工作資歷後，更審慎地看待這件事情呢?...單篇閱讀還包含了計算和各式表格題搭配的考點，讓考生更出奇制勝。

　　在新制Part 7的閱讀中，另一項重要的變革是有三篇書信所組成的閱讀文章，這部分也加入了故事性的閱讀搭配新多益的常見考題。一位自稱是Poor Man的中年男子，覺得此生一直一無所成，某天突然看到冒險島的廣告，於是他寫信到公司進一步詢問相關的細節，公司女職員詼諧地回覆他，並告訴他不會這麼無禮地稱呼他為「Poor Man」並告知他要簽署

免責條款等，就這樣他的發財夢旅程開始展開了，而這會是一場詐騙嗎？還是他真的能成為富翁並凱旋歸來呢？（在 *Grinding it Out* 中，Ray Kroc 也曾於年輕時參加淘金…而人應該被某個年紀或框架限制住呢？還是像 Ray Kroc 一樣即使有年紀了，仍相信自己能夠獲取成功呢?…）Poor Man 的旅程中還包含了許多自嘲、笑點、奇幻和懸疑事件的發生，而最後的結果又會是如何呢？

　　最後要說的是，感謝公司又讓我出版了這本書，還有要特別感謝 **Christine Etzel**、外籍友人和編輯部提供的建議和協助修訂，才能有這本書的誕生和更完備的內容呈現給讀者。雖然寫作過程中無疑等同又少了許多出遊和與朋友相聚等的時間（應該要說完全沒有這些時間），也於最近又收到一些朋友的訊息關於我之前曾給過的一些英語學習或工作上的建議，但是我想就像是 *Getting There* 中啟發我很多的一句話，When you're much more interested in what you're doing than going out with friends, you've found your bliss，準備這項考試真的只是 a short stretch of life，不論是你是因為學校要求、工作升遷等因素準備這項考試，考到理想成績後也衷心地希望你也能找到心中的 bliss。像三篇多益閱讀中其中一篇的主角一樣，不斷朝自己的夢想前進（真的do X do Y or do Z to prove that you deserve that job）最終獲得電影試鏡的機會...。

韋爾 敬上

使用說明

INSTRUCTIONS

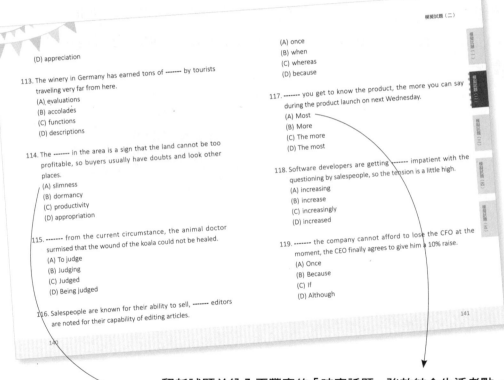

(D) appreciation

113. The winery in Germany has earned tons of ------- by tourists traveling very far from here.
    (A) evaluations
    (B) accolades
    (C) functions
    (D) descriptions

114. The ------- in the area is a sign that the land cannot be too profitable, so buyers usually have doubts and look other places.
    (A) slimness
    (B) dormancy
    (C) productivity
    (D) appropriation

115. ------- from the current circumstance, the animal doctor surmised that the wound of the koala could not be healed.
    (A) To judge
    (B) Judging
    (C) Judged
    (D) Being judged

116. Salespeople are known for their ability to sell, ------- editors are noted for their capability of editing articles.

140

(A) once
(B) when
(C) whereas
(D) because

117. ------- you get to know the product, the more you can say during the product launch on next Wednesday.
    (A) Most
    (B) More
    (C) The more
    (D) The most

118. Software developers are getting ------- impatient with the questioning by salespeople, so the tension is a little high.
    (A) increasing
    (B) increase
    (C) increasingly
    (D) increased

119. ------- the company cannot afford to lose the CFO at the moment, the CEO finally agrees to give him a 10% raise.
    (A) Once
    (B) Because
    (C) If
    (D) Although

141

- 翻新試題並納入更豐富的「時事話題」強效結合生活考點。
- 嚴守官方公佈的話題和出題，每句文法單字題均精心呈現，融入「4-7」個新多益必考字彙，學習一次掌握。
- 降低甜頭題、仰賴記憶性或背誦即能答對的試題，提高試題檢測考生能力的效度。
- 五回試題均為「精選試題」能於應考前重複練習。

更具鑑別度的 PART 6 出題

· 精心挑選各選項的單字且包含高階動詞的接續出題 **groom, thwarted, paralyzed, detained, tampered** 等高階動詞的考點。
· 包含更多「**答題技巧**」的掌握和理解，有效提升考生答題實力並篩選出最適合的答案。
· 更多新制題型中「**插入句**」的試題，潛移默化練就快速答這類試題的猛實力。

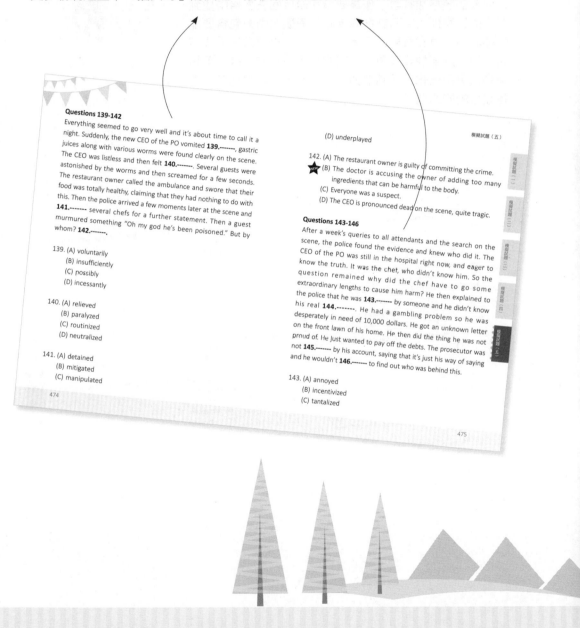

Questions 139-142

Everything seemed to go very well and it's about time to call it a night. Suddenly, the new CEO of the PO vomited **139.-------**, gastric juices along with various worms were found clearly on the scene. The CEO was listless and then felt **140.-------**. Several guests were astonished by the worms and then screamed for a few seconds. The restaurant owner called the ambulance and swore that their food was totally healthy, claiming that they had nothing to do with this. Then the police arrived a few moments later at the scene and **141.-------** several chefs for a further statement. Then a guest murmured something "Oh my god he's been poisoned." But by whom? **142.-------**.

139. (A) voluntarily
(B) insufficiently
(C) possibly
(D) incessantly

140. (A) relieved
(B) paralyzed
(C) routinized
(D) neutralized

141. (A) detained
(B) mitigated
(C) manipulated

474

(D) underplayed

模擬試題（五）

142. (A) The restaurant owner is guilty of committing the crime.
(B) The doctor is accusing the owner of adding too many ingredients that can be harmful to the body.
(C) Everyone was a suspect.
(D) The CEO is pronounced dead on the scene, quite tragic.

Questions 143-146

After a week's queries to all attendants and the search on the scene, the police found the evidence and knew who did it. The CEO of the PO was still in the hospital right now, and eager to know the truth. It was the chef, who didn't know him. So the question remained why did the chef have to go some extraordinary lengths to cause him harm? He then explained to the police that he was **143.-------** by someone and he didn't know his real **144.-------**. He had a gambling problem so he was desperately in need of 10,000 dollars. He got an unknown letter on the front lawn of his home. He then did the thing he was not proud of. He just wanted to pay off the debts. The prosecutor was not **145.-------** by his account, saying that it's just his way of saying and he wouldn't **146.-------** to find out who was behind this.

143. (A) annoyed
(B) incentivized
(C) tantalized

475

強化「**進階**」表格類題型的答題和閱讀表格資訊能力
一舉提升「**推測文意**」實力

· 最簡易的表格類答題，僅需要看完題目回去表格中找到
對應的答案即可。而許多較進階的考題，則會包含要能
濃縮表格訊息和掌握各個考點，有些表格題搭配「改寫
句」和「細節性資訊題」，就增加了考題的難度，書籍
中納入更多強化「**推測能力**」的試題，大幅強化考生答
各類型的閱讀題目。

Announcement/more to be announced		
item	note	Score
Golden eggs of a peacock	Per egg, has something related to history	100
Golden eggs of an ostrich	Per egg, has something related to geography	50
Silver feather of the eagle	Extremely rare, electrified stones	100
Gather a 7-colored stone	Can get yourself wet, monkeys	100
Consume raw snails for 50	Can generate **infestation**	10
Take down a giant spider	Fortune is associated	500
Get rare seaweed	A box, a **submerged** castle	50
Take down a giant snake	with wooden swords, diamonds	600

191. The word "**heightened**" in paragraph1, line 8, is closet in
meaning to
(A) composed
(B) reduced
(C) enhanced
(D) complicated

192. What is mentioned as the recent change for the guy?
(A) He was unfortunately injured when performing a difficult
task.
(B) He quit ordering drinks from the restaurant car to be
healthy.
(C) He bought the map and tried to get acquainted with it.
(D) He is physically ready to do the assignment.

193..The word "**infestation**" in the announcement, is closet in
meaning to
(A) production
(B) invasion
(C) visibility
(D) allocation

194. What can be inferred from the announcement?
(A) The silver feather of the eagle is easy to find.
(B) Wealth may be around the corner in a particular new
task.
(C) Four items have the same score.
(D) Nine new items are being added into the list.

195. The word "**submerged**" in the announcement, is closet in
meaning to
(A) serendipitous
(B) subsequent
(C) underwater
(D) underdeveloped

392

393

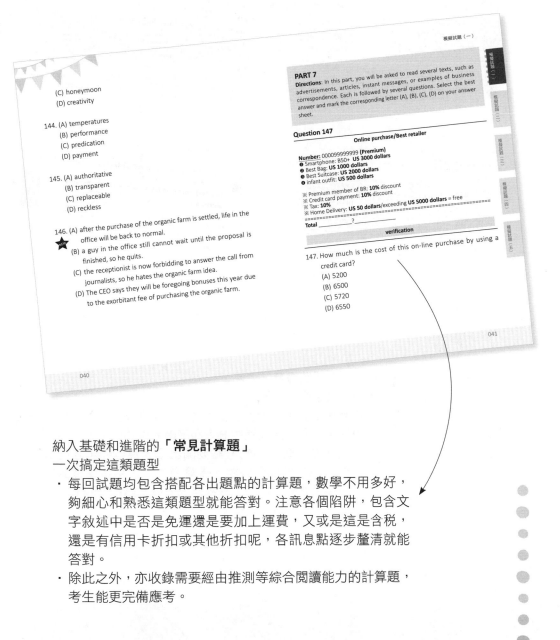

(C) honeymoon
(D) creativity

144. (A) temperatures
(B) performance
(C) predication
(D) payment

145. (A) authoritative
(B) transparent
(C) replaceable
(D) reckless

146. (A) after the purchase of the organic farm is settled, life in the office will be back to normal.
(B) a guy in the office still cannot wait until the proposal is finished, so he quits.
(C) the receptionist is now forbidding to answer the call from journalists, so he hates the organic farm idea.
(D) The CEO says they will be foregoing bonuses this year due to the exorbitant fee of purchasing the organic farm.

PART 7
Directions: In this part, you will be asked to read several texts, such as advertisements, articles, instant messages, or examples of business correspondence. Each is followed by several questions. Select the best answer and mark the corresponding letter (A), (B), (C), (D) on your answer sheet.

Question 147

Online purchase/Best retailer

Number: 000099999999 **(Premium)**
❶ Smartphone: B50+ **US 3000 dollars**
❷ Best Bag: **US 1000 dollars**
❸ Best Suitcase: **US 2000 dollars**
❹ infant outfit: **US 500 dollars**

※ Premium member of BR: **10%** discount
※ Credit card payment: **10%** discount
※ Tax: **10%**
※ Home Delivery: **US 50 dollars**/exceeding **US 5000 dollars** = free
===
Total _____?

verification

147. How much is the cost of this on-line purchase by using a credit card?
(A) 5200
(B) 6500
(C) 5720
(D) 6550

納入基礎和進階的「**常見計算題**」
一次搞定這類題型
・每回試題均包含搭配各出題點的計算題，數學不用多好，夠細心和熟悉這類題型就能答對。注意各個陷阱，包含文字敘述中是否是免運還是要加上運費，又或是這是含稅，還是有信用卡折扣或其他折扣呢，各訊息點逐步釐清就能答對。
・除此之外，亦收錄需要經由推測等綜合閱讀能力的計算題，考生能更完備應考。

(B) counterproductive

(C) flexible

(D) stationary

190. In which of the positions marked **(1)**, **(2)**, **(3)**, and **(4)** does the following sentence best belong? (the third letter)

"**Oh my god it was gold**"

(A) (1)

(B) (2)

(C) (3)

(D) (4)

Questions 191-195

Day 76

It was as authentic as it could be... because I even bit the gold.... it was real...**(1)** Since day one... I couldn't say I hadn't had the slightest doubt about the program thing. **(2)** Now without finishing all goals here and went on to find the real treasure on the island. We hit the lottery by finding it first. We were so happy and so angry at the same time. **(3)** The fake spider was **inflamed** due to the torch I threw at it a moment before... we had to move boxes of gold outside before the fire was too big. The smoke was so unbearable. **(4)** We could have died here by inhaling too much deleterious gas. We had to retreat and find something to extinguish the fire.

Day 77

Miraculously, the fire was put out. And we all knew that boxes of gold had to be equally split between 10 people. Still it was a great fortune, enough for any of us to use for the rest of our lives. Of course, I didn't want any confrontations with others. I gathered everyone here and told them that each of us would get 1/10 share of what we found. All of them agreed. We moved all of the boxes outside the cave and decided to **calculate** the amount of gold in those boxes. A real giant spider approached. Some of the guys said run... hurry... ran away... what a coward? Without a weapon, I had to run, too.

498

Day 78

We decided to regroup and launch an attack. By the time we got back to the original place, the giant spider was gone. So were boxes of gold. Who did that? The spider couldn't do that right? The ten of us went back to where we camped and were too exhausted. The wealth was just within reach, and now it was all gone. We had to start somewhere. We weren't in the mood to call the restaurant car. Then we saw several ostriches chasing by the cheetah and we grasped the chance to take a closer look at the nest. No golden ostrich eggs could be found, but there was something else. We moved several ostrich eggs to our jeep and then we found that it was like a floorboard thing. It's a gateway to the basement. Another new finding... good for us...

191. The word "**inflamed**" in paragraph1, line 6, is closet in meaning to

(A) terrified

(B) lit up

(C) led to

(D) unaware of

192. In which of the positions marked **(1)**, **(2)**, **(3)**, and **(4)** does the following sentence best belong?

"**The fake spider must have been made by a harmful substance.**"

(A) (1)

(B) (2)

(C) (3)

(D) (4)

499

靈活應答「**跨篇章**」考點

迅速突破某個分數關卡

· 在新制多益中包含了三篇的文章或信件類的搭配，出題考點中，為了更區隔中高階和高階考生等的能力，也會包含了單一題目中的考點要閱讀 2-3 篇信件後才能掌握全部訊息，進而答題。書籍中加入了更多這樣的練習，能夠充分提供考生檢視自己對於閱讀能力的掌握，一次性考到所設定的成績門檻。

更豐富的表格類出題設計
提升考生「綜合」答題實力
・表格類試題中包含了各類型的問法，提升對新制**「暗示性」**、
「推測類」、**「判斷類」**等題型的應對能力，更靈活面對不能
僅靠定位、死記或記憶性的題目。

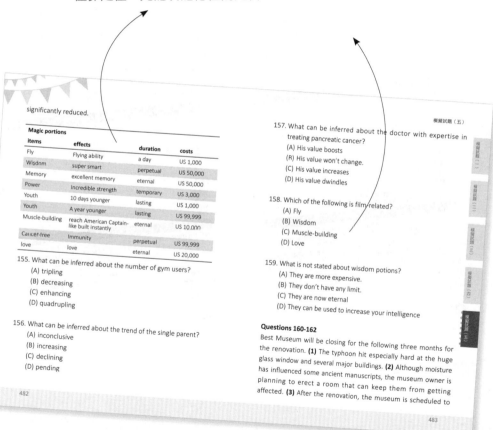

significantly reduced.

Magic portions

items	effects	duration	costs
Fly	Flying ability	a day	US 1,000
Wisdom	super smart	perpetual	US 50,000
Memory	excellent memory	eternal	US 50,000
Power	incredible strength	temporary	US 3,000
Youth	10 days younger	lasting	US 1,000
Youth	A year younger	lasting	US 99,999
Muscle-building	reach American Captain-like built instantly	eternal	US 10,000
Cancer-free	Immunity	perpetual	US 99,999
love	love	eternal	US 20,000

155. What can be inferred about the number of gym users?
(A) tripling
(B) decreasing
(C) enhancing
(D) quadrupling

156. What can be inferred about the trend of the single parent?
(A) inconclusive
(B) increasing
(C) declining
(D) pending

模擬試題（五）

157. What can be inferred about the doctor with expertise in treating pancreatic cancer?
(A) His value boosts
(B) His value won't change.
(C) His value increases
(D) His value dwindles

158. Which of the following is film-related?
(A) Fly
(B) Wisdom
(C) Muscle-building
(D) Love

159. What is not stated about wisdom potions?
(A) They are more expensive.
(B) They don't have any limit.
(C) They are now eternal
(D) They can be used to increase your intelligence

Questions 160-162
Best Museum will be closing for the following three months for the renovation. **(1)** The typhoon hit especially hard at the huge glass window and several major buildings. **(2)** Although moisture has influenced some ancient manuscripts, the museum owner is planning to erect a room that can keep them from getting affected. **(3)** After the renovation, the museum is scheduled to

「**中英對照**」設計
閱讀和備考更為便利

· 全書包含五回試題，每回試題後的解析均搭配中英對照，便於考生學習，大幅節省翻閱對照看的時間，並順道記憶選項中其他單字，事半功倍攻略新多益閱讀。

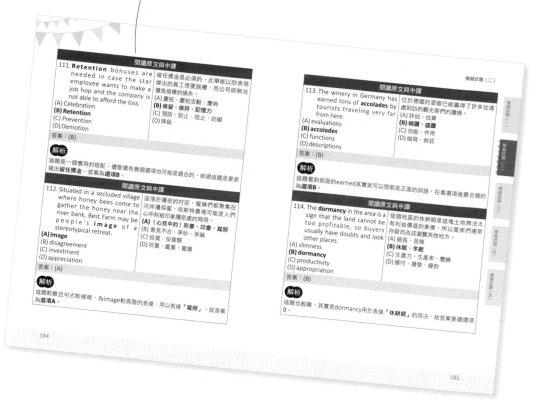

閱讀原文與中譯

111. **Retention** bonuses are needed in case the star employee wants to make a job hop and the company is not able to afford the loss.

(A) Celebration
(B) Retention
(C) Prevention
(D) Demotion

留任獎金是必須的，此舉能以防表現傑出的員工想要跳槽，而公司卻無法擔負這樣的損失。

(A) 慶祝、慶祝活動、慶典
(B) 保留、保持、記憶力
(C) 預防、防止、阻止、妨礙
(D) 降級

答案：(B)

解析

這題是一個慣用的搭配，儘管還有幾個選項也可能是適合的，部過這題是要表達出留任獎金，答案為**選項B**。

閱讀原文與中譯

112. Situated in a secluded village where honey bees come to gather the honey near the river bank, Best Farm may be people's **image** of a stereotypical retreat.

(A) image
(B) disagreement
(C) investment
(D) appreciation

座落於隱密的村莊，蜜蜂們都聚集在河岸邊採蜜，倍斯特農場可能是人們心中刻板印象處的寫照。

(A)（心目中的）形象、印象、寫照
(B) 意見不合、爭吵、爭論
(C) 投資、投資額
(D) 欣賞、鑑賞、賞識

答案：(A)

解析

這題較難且句式較複雜，為image較高階的表達，用以表達「**寫照**」，故答案為**選項A**。

閱讀原文與中譯

113. The winery in Germany has earned tons of **accolades** by tourists traveling very far from here.

(A) evaluations
(B) accolades
(C) functions
(D) descriptions

位於德國的酒窖已經贏得了許多從遠處到訪的觀光客們的讚揚。

(A) 評估、估算
(B) 稱讚、盛讚
(C) 功能、作用
(D) 描寫、敘述

答案：(B)

解析

這題看到前面的earned其實就可以預期是正面的詞語，在看選項後最合適的為**選項B**。

閱讀原文與中譯

114. The **dormancy** in the area is a sign that the land cannot be too profitable, so buyers usually have doubts and look other places.

(A) slimness
(B) dormancy
(C) productivity
(D) appropriation

這個地區的休耕期是這塊土地無法太有利益價值的象徵，所以買家們通常存疑而改成瀏覽其他地方。

(A) 細長、苗條
(B) 休眠、冬眠
(C) 生產力、生產率、豐饒
(D) 撥付、撥發、撥款

答案：(B)

解析

這題也較難，其實是dormancy用於表達「**休耕期**」的用法，故答案要選選項B。

Best Column

170. What is **NOT** stated about the "Job Column"?
 (A) Disclosing your health conditions falls into the category of the jeopardizing.
 (B) Be confident during the interview.
 (C) Be active during the interview.
 (D) You have to answer all the questions in the interview.

171. The word "**mentality**" in the letter, line 8, is closet in meaning to
 (A) adaptation
 (B) manipulation
 (C) attitude
 (D) benevolence

172. In which of the positions marked **(1)**, **(2)**, **(3)**, and **(4)** does the following sentence best belong?
 "**Also, you have to be careful about questions that trick you into answering things that can jeopardize the hire.**"
 (A) (1)
 (B) (2)
 (C) (3)
 (D) (4)

Questions 173-175
As to the question for asking for a raise. Just do that whenever you think you deserve it. Life is simply too short and you do need to have the guts to say that. (even if they say no, there is no harm in asking. You are doing a better job than those who don't ask.) Of course, you don't have to piss of your boss. **(1)** Do it under the right circumstance, not during the economic downturn or the **downsizing** period. **(2)** You also have to understand your salary in the job market and your salary is based on your expertise and contribution. You don't have to mistakenly think of asking for a promotion or a raise as an embarrassment. **(3)** That means you care about your growth and you have ambitions. **(4)** That also means you are not making a job hop, and you want to contribute more. You can also ask them that, if you do expect a higher salary, how much contribution requires to do in order for that to happen...

Best Column

173. What is **NOT** stated about the "Job Column"?
 (A) One has to surprise his or her boss to get the raise.
 (B) One has to pick the right moment to ask for a raise.
 (C) One's contribution to the job is related to the evaluation of the salary.
 (D) One needs to be brave enough to ask for a raise.

結合實際職場主題並規劃進 **PART 7** 單篇商業書信類文章中

・納入「求職專欄」，「考用」和「職場」的大結合，考生更能感受到效果，畢業不失業 !!!

目次
CONTENTS

- 餐廳結束營業和回饋
- 觀光所帶來的負面影響
- 求職專欄: 還是要聽懂面試官到底在問什麼
- 求職專欄: 迷惘期和找到自己要的

雙篇文章

- 歐洲之星 EuroStar 銷售大戰: 戴面罩的銷售、企劃案等同沒做功課
- 拍攝時程衝突: 被降為助理、力往狂瀾

三篇文章

- 商學院暑假閱讀書單和寫作比賽
- 拯救農田作物計劃: 大象的搶食、與西瓜、芒果和榴槤間的關係、解決辦法
- 電影公司招募: 徵才廣告、受挫後的努力、贏得試鏡機會

PART 5 單句填空

PART 6 短文填空

- 董事會對於執行長的表現甚感滿意
- 人事部門已經選擇了最終候選人並彙報給執行長
- 莓果的培植也讓觀光客跟動物間建立情感連結
- 觀光客不需要前往泰國即能與動物互動

PART 7 閱讀測驗

單篇文章

- 倍斯特漢堡：薯條、洋蔥圈、漢堡和飲料的銷售
- 海產的訂購
- 倍斯特國際氣球節：7 種類型可供選擇
- 商業書信：領取兩份薪資和新身分
- 倍斯特菁英大學：學校軟體能測出畢業後五年的個人成就和薪資所得
- 彈珠遊戲和賭博式玩法，真的划算嗎？
- 倍斯特遊樂園：鬼屋增添設施和更改政策
- 倍斯特電影公司的場勘和古堡篩選
- 求職專欄：關於狡詐的提問
- 求職專欄：關於加薪這件事

雙篇文章

- 倍斯特餐廳：抱怨信、富人朋友也不再去消費了、瘋狂大學生偽裝成員工

第三回模擬試題 題目

第三回模擬試題 解析

PART 5 單句填空

PART 6 短文填空

PART 7 閱讀測驗

單篇文章

- 倍斯特樂園：恐怖的萬聖節火車
- 商業書信：對於對手的商業宣傳噱頭毫無頭緒
- 倍斯特大學：對音樂和體育均優的學生進行招生
- 夜市射飛鏢：勞力換飛鏢、情人節心型氣球
- 倍斯特整形外科：男模特兒招募
- 倍斯特模特兒經紀公司：候選人實力均優，看來評審會有困擾
- 求職專欄：累積資歷後該回學校唸書嗎？
- 求職專欄： hygiene factor

雙篇文章
- 倍斯特購物中心：商店行竊、銀行貸款支付員工薪資、檢控官的來信
- 泳池事件：寫信給八卦日報、事件的真相

三篇文章
- 冒險島：連一擊都承受不住、隊上跑最慢的、厚重裝甲和教練的營救
- 冒險島：佈告欄公告：關於餐車的品項、商人就是想榨乾消費者、從雌性母獅身上取得幼獸的任務
- 冒險島：註冊的款項加上訓練費用是 7 萬美元、任務公告和對應的分數、沒有人成功取得水蜜蜂過

第四回模擬試題 題目

PART 5 單句填空

PART 6 短文填空

- 公司安全性考量和風險管理

- 數據科學家的分析和新鮮食材

- 新鮮食材的體驗和欲進行收購一間公司

- 致電另一間執行長並洽談可能性

PART 7 閱讀測驗

單篇文章

- 倍斯特服飾和鞋子舉行的聖誕折扣

- 花店的補償和以直升專機送花

- 商業書信：不用工作的咖啡店員

- 倍斯特科技公司於 2050 年研發出的魔法藥水

- 夜市撈金魚：包含七彩撈具和撈罕見金魚

- 倍斯特修復中心：注入靈魂的機器人，失去摯愛者的救星

- 倍斯特動物園：暫時性「生命互換鍵」

- 求職專欄：工作到底該做多久呢？

- 求職專欄：探索自我

雙篇文章

- 巧克力事件：該如何處裡一千個國際包裹都被打開呢？

- 遊戲愛好者的 AI 體驗：情感抽離和執行長檢視產品

三篇文章

- 冒險島：體格的變化、前往奪取罕見水果以及老鷹的阻撓、仍無法尋獲金羽毛的孔雀
- 冒險島：點了第一杯珍珠奶茶、連中心教練都沒有島上地圖、更多新任務的公告
- 冒險島：神秘的甕和購買吉普車、終於隱約見到七彩石頭、瀑布旁的機關

第五回模擬試題 題目

第五回模擬試題 解析

PART 5 單句填空

PART 6 短文填空

- 收購後，公司股價來到新高
- 升遷的晚宴以及餐廳鮮少製作的料理
- 新任命執行長的身體不適和警方到場盤查
- 檢控官對於嫌疑犯說法抱持懷疑的態度

PART 7 閱讀測驗

單篇文章

- 母親節蛋糕趕不及給客戶和退款
- 倍斯特森林：5 大特色
- 商業書信：鮑伯紅假髮的偽裝和機密文件的擺放

- 倍斯特科技中心：新增添愛情藥水和永久青春藥水
- 倍斯特博物館：颱風的襲擊、館內翻修和拍賣會的舉辦
- 四間銀行搶案都發生在同個時間點，狀況百出
- 求職專欄：根據黃金法則，先提到薪資的那方是輸家。
- 求職專欄：消除面試官的疑慮
- 套圈圈：在七種天然地形中的冒險性玩法，1.08 億畫素相機能窺見瓶中放多少錢

雙篇文章

- 數次與升遷擦身而過，還要繼續待嗎？、另一間挖角公司的意外劫機事件
- 性騷擾事件的控訴和公司的正視、招聘廣告

三篇文章

- 冒險島：所取的七彩石是贗品、猴子遞的神祕盒子、假的巨型蜘蛛和火炬
- 冒險島：好多黃金、令人難忍受的煙霧、1/10 份、真的巨型蜘蛛、被獵豹追逐的鴕鳥
- 冒險島：中了機關和金色鴕鳥蛋、幕後主嫌和島上地圖、金鴕鳥蛋的秘密、孔雀山谷、三種說法

- 【Part 5】納入了更多高階動詞、形容詞和名詞的單字出題，考生要多注意這方面的答題，而文法題則以基礎題為主。
- 【Part 6】考生要注意容易誤選的題目，並寫完後仔細琢磨各選項的出題，或是要注意必須要選出更合適的選項的題目。
- 【Part 7】的計算題要注意要加上含稅的費用和要注意是否是免運費，這些細節都影響到是否能答對。另外也要注意各類型的同義轉換。

模擬試題（一）

READING TEST

In this section, you must demonstrate your ability to read and comprehend English. You will be given a variety of texts and asked to answer questions about these texts. This section is divided into three parts and will take 75 minutes to complete.

Do not mark the answers in your test book. Use the answer sheet that is separately.

PART 5

Directions: In each question, you will be asked to review a statement that is missing a word or phrase. Four answer choices will be provided for each statement. Select the best answer and mark the corresponding letter (A), (B), (C), or (D) on the answer sheet.

101. Best Automobile ------- 11 million dollars from the investor last week, making it competitive enough to enter the global market.
    (A) prolonged
    (B) permitted
    (C) promoted
    (D) procured

102. Best Design hit the ------- with its innovative kitchen wares that can greatly reduce the preparation time for millions of housewives.
    (A) sensations
    (B) headlines
    (C) hotlines

(D) boards

103. A piece of software equipment priced at US 500 dollars is considered expensive in the eyes of the -------.
(A) devaluation
(B) dilemma
(C) dilettante
(D) expert

104. According to the rituals, rookie pilots are asked to ------- at the canteen before every dinner.
(A) supervise
(B) resemble
(C) authorize
(D) assemble

105. Best Furniture has surpassed its rival by launching the unprecedented furnishings that ------- consumers' expectations.
(A) downplay
(B) shorten
(C) exceed
(D) contemplate

106. Mass production of milk is worthy of praises but not during the time when the virus is ------- the globe.

(A) be devastated

(B) devastated

(C) devastating

(D) to devastate

107. Although the economy hits us all, Best Watch, a ------- of the Fashion Watch, has handed in impressive yields, contrary to what the sources said.

(A) supporter

(B) bystander

(C) parent

(D) subsidiary

108. Analysts are predicting that Best Automobile won't be the ------- after the huge merger because there seems to be lots of unresolved issues in the company.

(A) sponsor

(B) beneficiary

(C) spectator

(D) shareholder

109. ------- vendors had already stockpiled millions of clinical masks before the virus began to ravage people's lives.

(A) Hesitant

(B) Tolerable

(C) Unscrupulous

(D) Adjustable

110. Further down the supply chain, Best Drinks is backed up by ingredient ------- that help it to produce the best milk tea in town.
(A) underperformers
(B) arraignments
(C) suppliers
(D) contractors

111. Due to the economic downturn, executives in the conference have decided to cut ad ------- so that the cash flow for the next few months won't be an issue.
(A) expenditures
(B) readjustments
(C) motivations
(D) evaluations

112. Both insufficient tourists visiting in the areas and a significant change in consumer shopping habits have contributed to the significant drop in retailers' -------.
(A) interpretations
(B) revenues
(C) calculations
(D) evaluations

113. To encourage the use of the ------- shopping bag, several
    department stores are rewarding consumers using it during
    the festival with an additional 10% discount.
    (A) persuasive
    (B) extravagant
    (C) reusable
    (D) dominant

114. For the sake of the incident in the news, store workers are
    now pretty ------- about the intruders, especially during the
    night shift.
    (A) intimate
    (B) vigilant
    (C) capable
    (D) communicative

115. To ------- the attention of the lion, the circus performer uses
    the lingering scent of its favorite dishes.
    (A) distracted
    (B) distracting
    (C) distract
    (D) being distracted

116. Studying marine mammals ------- harder in good weather
    conditions, so the professor wants the students to cherish the
    moment.

(A) were

(B) are

(C) is

(D) was

117. The insurance company will not ------- the money to those who self-injury themselves.

(A) legitimize

(B) applause

(C) accuse

(D) compensate

118. In the kindergarten, teachers often underestimate children's ------- to explore new things in a new environment.

(A) curious

(B) curiosity

(C) curiously

(D) curry

119. One of the most exhilarating things in the office ------- the birthday present prepared by the CEO.

(A) was

(B) is

(C) are

(D) were

120. For customers who had ------- been turned down before can now receive the monetary compensations.
(A) subsequent
(B) previously
(C) later
(D) previous

121. In 2010, Best Cellphone began to lose ------- advantage to the rival company and the stock price dropped as well.
(A) their
(B) it
(C) its
(D) them

122. ------- to find outside investors to finance, Best Clothing has to make the cut of at least 10,000 workers, according to the report.
(A) Able
(B) Inability
(C) Capable
(D) Unable

123. Best Fitness Center, ------- memberships was few and far between last month, now surprisingly transcends one of the best fitness centers in town.
(A) who

(B) which
(C) where
(D) whose

124. The aquarium is not specifically aimed at ------- marine biologists because it needs to make money.
(A) to attract
(B) attracted
(C) being attracted
(D) attracting

125. The town is ------- reliant on the export to make money, so local residents have to think other ways to transport the goods.
(A) heavy
(B) heavily
(C) heavier
(D) more heavier

126. Remaining extremely ------- during confrontations is a good thing for the business deal.
(A) calmness
(B) calm
(C) calming
(D) calmed

127. Tourists in our garden can even visit our strawberry lab to test the freshness of the related product ------- they make a purchase.
(A) after
(B) before
(C) if
(D) although

128. During the period of the COVID-19 virus, Best Hotel admitted in the conference that the company encountered the greatest obstacle in 50 years, but it wanted to keep all employees -------.
(A) employ
(B) employment
(C) employing
(D) employed

129. Much of the time was spent ------- evidence that can prove the client is actually innocent.
(A) find
(B) finds
(C) finding
(D) found

130. The CEO of Best Kitchen is now ------- to get rid of lazy workers and employees who spread rumor about the company.

(A) determine

(B) determination

(C) determined

(D) determining

PART 6

Directions: In this part, you will be asked to read four English texts. Each text is missing a word, phrase, or sentence. Select the answer choice that correctly completes the text and mark the corresponding letter (A), (B), (C), or (D) on the answer sheet.

Questions 131-134

Best Zoo made its acquisition with one of the largest on-line retailers, DEF, so it now has a great deal of money to renovate the zoo, including the facility. However, from now on every penny spent is **131.-------** by the Finance Department and outside investors, according to the earlier report. The huge deficit was the main reason why Best Zoo **132.-------** sought out a buyout offer and outside investors. Any **133.-------** international travel will be turned down by the CEO, and that makes many executives who used to have **134.-------** trips and the benefit of staying in the luxurious hotels so hard to adjust. Plus, all executives are getting a pay cut of 30%, whereas employees at lower levels are getting a 10% increase in pay. This actually boosts the morale of the company, a reporter said.

131. (A) resumed
    (B) regulated
    (C) assembled
    (D) addressed

132. (A) unavoidably
    (B) understandably
    (C) desperately
    (D) independently

133. (A) superfluous
    (B) deterrent
    (C) skeptical
    (D) astonishing

134. (A) reserved
    (B) futile
    (C) fruitful
    (D) frequent.

Questions 135-138

After the adjustment, the CEO is pleased **135.-------** the result of the progress of the company, but the board has been waiting for the firm to actually do something. That's why the concept of a sustainable farm was brought up in the conference. With the sustainable farm, **136.-------**, and it can totally make the animals' meals more abundant and diversified. That means, all animals are able to consume food that is **137.-------** different nutrients. They are going to be healthy and robust. Animal doctors **138.-------** the new announcement, and they can also cook in the zoo with fresh vegetables handy in the organic farm. This is definitely a great step for all employees and animals.

135. (A) in
(B) on
(C) at
(D) with

136. (A) the company will be rewarded enormously by the government
(B) the export of the company will have a significant boost
(C) the company does not have to rely heavily on import of food and vegetables
(D) the board wants more documents to evaluate

137. (A) famous for
(B) interested in
(C) rich in
(D) exposed to

138. (A) are replaced with
(B) are content with

(C) are worried about

(D) are based on

Questions 139-142

Due to the building of the new organic farm, several executives have prepared the document with company attorneys to ABC architecture firm, and will take a good look at the land that is on the market. The land has to be **139.-------** and rich in minerals so that the organic farm can actually work. The company has also hired soil biologists who **140.-------** in the business for twenty years. They have narrowed the options down to four sites to check before the summer, but the CEO gave them the specific **141.-------** of July 30. **142.-------**. They will vote for the site of the organic farm out of final three options.

139. (A) popular
   (B) celebratory
   (C) unvarnished
   (D) cultivable

140. (A) has
   (B) had
   (C) have
   (D) have been

141. (A) arraignment

(B) deadline

(C) experiment

(D) challenge

142. (A) They have to prepare proposals with the CEO before that date in the conference with all foreign investors.

(B) The bidding was is getting increasingly fierce.

(C) These places are not the CEO's favorite.

(D) They have to cancel the meeting because something bad happens in the office.

Questions 143-146

The **143.-------** for the CEO is too short, so the CEO urges his subordinates to prepare the final presentation a week earlier than the original deadline. Now several executives groan during the lunch break because they are now working 24/7 with a 30% decrease in **144.-------**. The demanding new CEO certainly makes their lives less comfortable compared with the former CEO. But during this economy, they cannot be **145.-------** and hand in resignation letters. Not just yet, according to one of the executives in the company. He said that **146.-------.** He is hoping that all the effort will be rewarded in the year-end bonus, if there is going to be one...

143. (A) dedication

(B) promotion

(C) honeymoon

(D) creativity

144. (A) temperatures

(B) performance

(C) predication

(D) payment

145. (A) authoritative

(B) transparent

(C) replaceable

(D) reckless

146. (A) after the purchase of the organic farm is settled, life in the

NEW office will be back to normal.

(B) a guy in the office still cannot wait until the proposal is finished, so he quits.

(C) the receptionist is now forbidding to answer the call from journalists, so he hates the organic farm idea.

(D) The CEO says they will be foregoing bonuses this year due to the exorbitant fee of purchasing the organic farm.

PART 7

Directions: In this part, you will be asked to read several texts, such as advertisements, articles, instant messages, or examples of business correspondence. Each is followed by several questions. Select the best answer and mark the corresponding letter (A), (B), (C), (D) on your answer sheet.

Question 147

Online purchase/Best retailer

Number: 000099999999 **(Premium)**
❶ Smartphone: B50+ **US 3000 dollars**
❷ Best Bag: **US 1000 dollars**
❸ Best Suitcase: **US 2000 dollars**
❹ infant outfit: **US 500 dollars**

※ Premium member of BR: **10%** discount
※ Credit card payment: **10%** discount
※ Tax: **10%**
※ Home Delivery: **US 50 dollars**/exceeding **US 5000 dollars** = free
==
Total _____?_____

verification

147. How much is the cost of this on-line purchase by using a credit card?

(A) 5200

(B) 6500

(C) 5720

(D) 6550

Question 148

Mark 1:06 p.m.
Hi, Miss Lin. Unfortunately, the ticket is not refundable, so there is nothing I can do. I am sure the clerk had told you before you made the purchase.

Miss Lin 1:08 p.m.
Is it possible I put the photo on the website to see if someone is interested in going to the Museum for the next few days?

Mark 1:11 p.m.
Perhaps, other travelers who are museumgoers might purchase it. You can try it by trimming down the price and with a reason that why you'd like to sell it, instead of going to the place yourself.

Miss Lin 1:13 p.m.
I have to change the schedule due to some unforeseen reasons at work... that kind of reason?

Mark 1:15 p.m.
It wouldn't hurt to give it a try... now you have to excuse me.... customers are waiting...

148. At 1:11 p.m. why does Mark mention about "**trimming down the price and so on**"?

(A) The price was set too high for the museumgoers.

(B) That way, the ticket can be sold more quickly.

(C) The ticket is not refundable.

(D) The museum will be having the discounted price.

Questions 149-152

Dear Mary

Now it's time that you know the truth about Bob's true identity. **(1)** On the surface, he is currently working under the title of the manager of ABC Human Resources, but indeed he works for us. **(2)**

He has been feeding us with marketing strategies used by our opponent. **(3)** Last month, he brought us client data of ABC, and I have got to say that's quite valuable to us, and our engineers have been working on that part too so that some day we can totally **dominate** the market. **(4)** When you meet Bob, just act normally. It's not a big deal that he now knows that you know, got it? You have your new role by pretending to be a coffee clerk and approach him. I feel so relieved by telling you this.

Manager of CCC HR

149. What has Mary been requested to do?
    (A) to be an engineer
    (B) to be an HR
    (C) to be a manager
    (D) to be a barista

150. What is **NOT** mentioned about the letter?
    (A) Bob is an engineer.
    (B) Bob gave them information about the rival.
    (C) The manager has been keeping the secret for a long time.
    (D) Bob is a spy.

151. The word "**dominate**" in the letter, line 8, is closet in meaning to
    (A) formulate

(B) predominate

(C) eliminate

(D) translate

152. In which of the positions marked **(1)**, **(2)**, **(3)**, and **(4)** does the

⭐NEW following sentence best belong?

"**That's why we are always one step ahead of ABC Human Resources.**"

(A) (1)

(B) (2)

(C) (3)

(D) (4)

Questions 153-158

Best Elite Elementary School
Classification

Reading		
Animal	Group	Trait
Minke whale	A	endurance
Octopus	B	versatility
Swordfish	C	speed
Math/Chemistry/Physics		
Animal	Group	Trait
Raccoon	A	agileness
Octopus	B	reasoning/problem-solving

Parrot	C	mimicry
Cuckoo bird	D	cunning

Geography/History

Animal	Group	Trait
Dolphin	A	sense of direction/location
Elephant	B	memorization
Chimpanzee	C	reasoning

Note:

1. The classification is based entirely on the entrance exam taken twice before enrolling. The reading part is solely based on student's written scores, whereas GH involves both written grades and interactions with other kids in the computerized room where students are monitored by a group of professors. Students' MCP scores depend heavily on the test conducted by the Education Bureau as a reference.
2. Whatever they are, just be happy for them. All students are required to take the test every two years, so the group to which they are belonged might change from time to time.
3. If a student has shown a striking similarity in both animals (and it's quite possible), he or she has the right to choose the group of animal they are in.

153. How many tests do students have to take in a 6-year program in BEE School?
    (A) 2
    (B) 3
    (C) 4
    (D) 5

154. What is True about the categorization?
   (A) Students only have to take the admission test.
   (B) Students can use the money to change the animal group.
   (C) Students need more than paper test scores to get higher grades in GH.
   (D) Students cannot have the trait of more than one animal.

155. What is mentioned about the dolphin?
   (A) It swims slower than the swordfish.
   (B) It has nothing to do with direction.
   (C) It falls under the category of GH.
   (D) Its popularity is not greater than the chimpanzee.

156. What is **NOT** stated about the categorization of the octopus?
   (A) its trait irrelevant to problem-solving
   (B) its trait related to reasoning
   (C) its trait related to versatility
   (D) its trait unrelated to speed

157. Which of the following creature demonstrates the charade?
   (A) elephant
   (B) octopus
   (C) cuckoo bird
   (D) parrot

158. Which of the following subject contains more than three

categorizations?

(A) History

(B) Reading

(C) Chemistry

(D) Geography

Questions 159-162

The basketball toss is unlike what you have seen in the night market. You have to be qualified to play the game. Our machine has been set at the yard. You have to pass the labyrinth to get here, during which a flashlight and other devices cannot be used, so you can only depend on the lighting of the fireflies. Don't feel bad if you can't find us. It's not your fault. Our place only opens after midnight. You might even have a question of why people bother to come here. It's kind of romantic to be with your loved one or close friends to embark on a new adventure here. That's the main reason why we are so popular, and we have the greatest camp and other amazing dishes here.

Tossing in a special location	
Accumulated scores	Prizes
1,000	A box of coke
5,000	A stuffed animal
80,000	The latest smartphone
500,000	A Porsche

Note:

1. Recently, we have begun to work on having other ways to play the ball, including kicking under the water, walking against the current, and tossing a basketball ball in a desert-like environment.

159. When can people be seen playing the basketball toss?
    (A) during the dinner time
    (B) 5 p.m.
    (C) 3 a.m.
    (D) during lunch hour

160. If an avid basketball toss player has exchanged a car, what can be inferred about the scores he has collected?
    (A) 90,000
    (B) 80,000
    (C) 5,000
    (D) 500,050

161. What can be inferred about the maze?
    (A) It's crowded.
    (B) It's murky.
    (C) It's bright.
    (D) It's sunny.

162. What is **NOT** mentioned about "other ways" to play the game?
    (A) under the lake

(B) in the torrents

(C) under a sweltering hot weather condition

(D) under the ice

Questions 163-165

Best Restaurant is planning to close in May due to the COVID-19 virus. Although we would like to thank every supporter from the past by having a feast outside the restaurant, we eventually choose not to do the celebration. **(1)** A crowd gathering might make the outbreak of the virus **rampant**, and that is the last thing that we would like to see. **(2)** In return, we would like to give free masks to those in need and send good meals to the hospitals to thank for the hard work that has been done by nurses and doctors. **(3)** If you still have the coupons that you haven't used, you get to exchange the coupon with a free meal from our delivery boy. **(4)** If you still have other questions, please don't hesitate to let us know.

163. The word "**rampant**" in line 5, is closet in meaning to

(A) consistent

(B) romantic

(C) uncontrollable

(D) intervened

164. In which of the positions marked **(1)**, **(2)**, **(3)**, and **(4)** does the following sentence best belong?

"**The hot delicious meal will be sent to your doorstep.**"

(A) (1)
(B) (2)
(C) (3)
(D) (4)

165. What is the article mainly about?

    (A) the vaccine for the virus

    (B) the celebration with a great feast

    (C) the termination of the canteen

    (D) the fantastic meal for nurses and doctors

Questions 166-169

Often people craze for a view at the Best Train Station. That makes the train earn its fame and the crowd. **(1)** But recently, local residents have begun to see the **downside** of this sightseeing business. Flowers in the surroundings are not as beautiful as usual, and they are a few weeks late to blossom. **(2)** Too many crowds gathering here means more damage to the land. Lots of people camp here and barbecue. This has created more intolerant noise during the night. **(3)** The ecological loss is **incalculable**. Ecologists have now gathered here to put a stop to this. **(4)** Local residents support the movement and protest, even if that means less cash earned by every household which relies on the sightseeing money for monthly expenditures.

166. What is the article mainly about?

    (A) the fantastic view at the Train Station

    (B) flowers blossom incredibly

    (C) the disadvantages brought by the sightseeing boom

    (D) the loss for the local residents

167. The word "**downside**" in line 3, is closet in meaning to

    (A) harassment

    (B) downsize

    (C) disadvantage

    (D) situation

168. The word "**incalculable**" in line 8, is closet in meaning to

    (A) immeasurable

    (B) accusatory

    (C) untransferable

    (D) estimated

169. In which of the positions marked **(1)**, **(2)**, **(3)**, and **(4)** does the following sentence best belong?

    "**Some rare insects are missing, too.**"

    (A) (1)

    (B) (2)

    (C) (3)

    (D) (4)

Dear Susan,

It's great to have that kind of ambition, but having an overt ambition can do you more harm than good. You said that you felt like you had nailed the interview and couldn't think of any reason why you didn't get picked. **(1)** After doing some thinking, I come to understand why, and most twentysomethings answer those types of questions wrong. **(2)** Just answer that you will feel satisfied with the current position and you are ready to give all you to the company. **(3)** You don't have to say something like you are aiming for a position that exceeds your current position. **(4)** The point is that they don't know you, so you just have to keep that ambition to yourself. Even if you get hired, I feel a little bit concerned about your future in the company. You might encounter some hurdles that are totally **unnecessary**.

Best Column

170. What is **NOT** stated about the "Job Column"?
    (A) The columnist does not think in Susan's shoe.
    (B) Most twentysomethings answer some questions incorrectly.
    (C) Being too ambitious can have a bad consequence.
    (D) Susan didn't get the offer because of her lack of interview skills.

171. The word "**unnecessary**" in the letter, line 13, is closet in meaning to
     (A) complimentary
     (B) unessential
     (C) important
     (D) entertain

172. In which of the positions marked **(1)**, **(2)**, **(3)**, and **(4)** does the following sentence best belong?
     "**That can be the interviewer's job or those senior colleagues' future goals.**"
     (A) (1)
     (B) (2)
     (C) (3)
     (D) (4)

Questions 173-175

Dear Jason,

It can take quite some time to figure out what you would like to do in the future. Unless you major in medicine and other specialized majors, it's normal that you are encountering the period of "disorientation". **(1)** And to be honest, most twentysomethings do not know that, after graduating from the university. You don't have to be so hard on yourself to hurt your inner soul. However, you have to know that sooner. You can start that by having the first few jobs. **(2)** Through trial and error, you will understand things that you don't like and get to narrow down to things that you do want to do. **(3)** You aim for a job that's better suited to your personality and other aspects. As to the reason why you have to figure out that sooner, because before 30, most interviewers can tolerate that and the job hop. **(4)** And you don't know if it is what you want until you have worked in that position. But after 30, the reality sinks in. You might feel the cruelty if you are still **disoriented** in the sea of the job market and don't know where to land.

Best Column

173. What is **NOT** stated about the "Job Column"?
    (A) You can find the job closer to your ideal by taking a few attempts.
    (B) Interviewers are lenient for someone who is not 30.
    (C) Most twentysomethings do not know what they want.
    (D) The best job has already been taken by others.

174. The word "**disoriented**" in line 15, is closet in meaning to
    (A) certified
    (B) committed
    (C) designated
    (D) directionless

175. In which of the positions marked **(1)**, **(2)**, **(3)**, and **(4)** does the following sentence best belong?

"**You are young, still trying to figure out what you want**"

(A) (1)

(B) (2)

(C) (3)

(D) (4)

Questions 176-180

Proposal

Dear Manager,

I've drafted the proposal for the EuroStar. Participants will be required to wear a mask on the train to sell products, so they cannot rely on their appearance to **sway** the decision of the passengers. It will be more intriguing during the Halloween time, and it will be fairer to someone who is not naturally good-looking. The person who sells the most during the 2.5 hours period on the train will be the winner. What do you think of this proposal? Please let me know if there's something that needs to be modified.... Thanks.

Sincerely
Event planner, Cindy

Dear Cindy,

(1) I highly recommend that you to go to the storage room and get the copy of all our rivals' event plans from the past ten years, and study those files before you do the proposal in the future. **(2)** I will have your colleague Lucy to handle the event planning this year. **(3)** She seems well-prepared and knows what she is doing. **(4)** If you still have any questions, you can consult her and other colleagues as well. I won't be in the office for the following two weeks. I will be in Paris to have three meetings with Italian clients. That's all.

Mary Wang

176. What is **NOT** stated in the first letter?

    (A) Passengers have to sell items in less than 3 hours.

    (B) Passengers are asked to wear the mask.

    (C) Cindy will choose the winner based on her preference.

    (D) Cindy values fairness.

177. The word "**sway**" in paragraph1, line 3, is closet in meaning to

    (A) explain

    (B) organize

    (C) consider

    (D) influence

178. In which of the positions marked **(1)**, **(2)**, **(3)**, and **(4)** does the following sentence best belong?

    "**ABC Company did the same thing last year, and it seems that you didn't do the homework.**"

    (A) (1)

    (B) (2)

    (C) (3)

    (D) (4)

179. What can be inferred about Lucy?

    (A) She gets the copy of the rival company

    (B) She has been eyeing for the event planning for months.

    (C) She is the subordinate of Mary

(D) She will be in Europe for a few weeks.

180. Where can Cindy get the copy of rivals' event plans?

(A) in the office

(B) on the desk of Mary

(C) in the conference room

(D) in the storage room

Questions 181-185

Dear Jane,

Really sorry for the delay for the mail, but there seems to be a conflicting schedule in the photoshoot of the wedding and the event itself. Plus, according to your schedule, the photographer cannot do the photograph. He will be in Europe working with Best Magazine for the fashion shoot. And I don't know how you are going to respond to our client that their favorite photographer cannot do their wedding photograph. It's not that they are going to remarry for each other. Perhaps I should have assigned the assignment to someone more experienced. I totally overestimate your ability and let you be in charge of so many things. Therefore, I am **demoting** you to an assistant, and you now report to our new hire, Candy.

Branch manager

Dear manager,

I'm so sorry. I typed it wrong. **(1)** My bad. The dates of the shooting, so it will be fine. The photographer can still do the wedding photos. I'm dying to see how their wedding pics on the spot. **(2)** As for the demotion, could you please take it back?... I would really appreciate it and I promise I will be more attentive and meticulous. It's just the job has been really stressful for the past few weeks. I promise it won't happen again. Totally an unrelated topic, I have contacted the principal of Best Elite Primary School. **(3)** The school is more than happy to have your kids to study there. **(4)** If there is something that you would like me to do please let me know... Thanks...

Wedding editor

181. Where will the photographer be working at?

    (A) Europe

    (B) North America

    (C) South America

    (D) Asia

182. What can be inferred about Candy?

    (A) Her ability has been overestimated.

    (B) She will be the assistant.

    (C) She will be the superior of the branch manager

    (D) She is new to the company.

183. The word "**demoting**" in paragraph1, line 9, is closet in meaning to

    (A) degrading

    (B) managing

    (C) promoting

    (D) delaying

184. What is mentioned in the second letter?

    (A) The wedding editor has the association with the principal.

    (B) The job is too demanding for Candy.

    (C) The cameraman cannot do the photoshoot.

    (D) The manager doesn't want the kid in the first place.

185. In which of the positions marked **(1)**, **(2)**, **(3)**, and **(4)** does the following sentence best belong?

NEW

"**Your kids are in.**"

(A) (1)

(B) (2)

(C) (3)

(D) (4)

Questions 186-190

Dear all,

The following is the suggested reading list for your summer vacation. Our first two weeks in the next semester, we will be discussing all mentioned books. Students enrolled in this course will be asked to write a book report for at least three books. For those who are avid readers or who do not have any plan during the summer, you can work on the writing beforehand. You should write at least 1000 words for each report. Finally, for those who would like to get a higher grade for the first assignment, you are required to read through all and write no fewer than four book reports.

Dean

List of BOOKS
A *Rich Dad Poor Dad*
B *The Millionaire Next Door*
C *Millionaire Teacher*
D *The Richest Man in Babylon*
E *Millionaire Success Habits*
F *The Millionaire Fastlane*
G *Secrets of the Millionaire Mind*

Writing Contest

Enclosed is the English Writing Contest that is scheduled to take place after the mid-term. You can see the information on the poster yourself.

Poster

2020 English Writing Contest by Best Elite University

Requirements
1. Business majors
2. Sophomore
3. Have not received any school scholarship

Winning Prizes

title	money
The first place	US 5,000 dollars
Runner up	US 3,000 dollars
The third place	US 1,000 dollars

Note:

1. Students wanting to attend the contest are required to use the apps and make an on-line registration before October.

Dear all,

I'm so sorry for having emailed you guys the poster from last year. My bad. Enclosed is the update. Check out the information.

2021 English Writing Contest by Best Elite University

Requirements
1. Students in all departments
2. Junior and senior
3. Have not received any school scholarship

Winning Prizes

title	money
The first place	US 9,000 dollars
Runner up	US 6,000 dollars
The third place	US 3,000 dollars

Note:

1. Students wanting to attend the contest are required to use the apps and make an on-line registration before October.
2. Students getting the first place will participate in the National English Writing Contest, and the winner will be rewarded a signed contract with one of the top cellphone companies in the world.

186. What is enclosed with the letter?

(A) the information about the recommended readings

(B) the information about students

(C) The information about the money

(D) the information about the contest

187. What does the dean want the students to do during the summer vacation?

(A) fritter away the money

(B) seize the time to make money

(C) seize the time to read some books

(D) fritter away the time

188. What will the runner up of the 2020 be getting?

(A) US 5,000

(B) US 3,000

(C) US 1,000

(D) NT 90,000

189. What will the runner up of the 2021 be getting?

(A) NT 6,000

(B) NT 180,000

(C) NT 3,000

(D) NT 90,000

190. What will the first place be getting in addition to the money?

(A) a singing contract

(B) a termination

(C) a written contract

(D) a cellphone user manual

Questions 191-195

This place used to be immune from the ravage of elephants, but now with the habitat changes and many other things, elephants are the frequent visitors to the farmland. The financial loss is enormous. As we all know that local residents rely heavily on the sales of crops to live, coming up with the solution is urgent.

Enclosed is the estimated **monetary** loss for fruits and vegetables. You guys should take a look.

Fruits and vegetables	Estimated loss
Bananas	US 500,000 dollars
Mangos	US 1000,000 dollars
Watermelons	US 700,000 dollars
Durians	Zero
Cabbages	US 600,000 dollars

Reply

I know some of you might wonder do elephants consume watermelons? Perhaps some elephants do because watermelons contain sugary juice that can make them happy. The point is the place where they go, their powerful feet **crumble** these profitable crops. And as to those mangos, elephants are able to grab them just like they take away those bananas from your hands? I bet some of you haven't been to the camp to witness the feeding of elephants. However, local residents still have durians for sell. Perhaps their outer appearance protects them from getting harmed by a herd of elephants. Have you ever gotten hit by those durians? I bet the outer skin of elephants, even though it is strong and solid, cannot withstand those durians falling from the trees and hitting their body.

The following is the suggested methods for us to consider. Since we are just a small town, we cannot afford to spend a great deal of money on this. Even though we eventually get the fund from the city council, the money is still short for a project that is going to cost more than US 40,000 dollars.

Suggested methods

Items	Cost
1. Erect stone walls	US 50,000,000 dollars
2. Direct elephants to wild lands	US 50,000 dollars
3. Build a circus	US 8,000,000 dollars
4. Evacuate for a while	Zero
5. Transport elephants to another continent	US 600,000 dollars

191. What is enclosed with the letter?

   (A) the financial loss of losing star elephants

   (B) the reduction in profits in several fruits and vegetables

   (C) the list of crops damaged by the elephants

   (D) the profits brought by the elephants

192. The word "**monetary**" in paragraph1, line 6, is closet in meaning to

   (A) pecuniary

   (B) mortgaged

   (C) tremendous

   (D) universal

193. The word "**crumble**" in paragraph2, line 4, is closet in meaning to

   (A) animate

   (B) standardize

   (C) disintegrate

(D) transform

194. What is **NOT** stated about the reply?

(A) Some elephants have a penchant for watermelons.

(B) Mangos are ignored by the elephants.

(C) Durians have the protection on the outside.

(D) Elephants cannot stand those durians

195. Which of the following suggested method costs the least money?

(A) Item 1

(B) Item 2

(C) Item 3

(D) Item 4

Questions 196-200

Best Acting Agency for Recruitment

We would like to hire several candidates for the Halloween shoot, and requirements are as follows.
A. Candidates should be taller than 180 cm
B. Previous acting experience required
C. Submit the recording of self-introduction at least 10 minutes
D. Do not have the criminal record

Dear recruitment team,

This is Jason Lin. I went to the interview at your agency two years ago, but didn't get chosen. This year, I'm well-prepared. I even got signed by a modeling agency right after getting turned down. I've enclosed several stunning pics of me at the English Castle, where I was asked to portray a guy in a thriller, quite scary. Hope that you guys will not be scared by these pics. Furthermore, I also had the commercial for Bestland in which I **impersonated** the ghost at a haunted house. Finally, attached please also find my recording of the self-introduction and a few recommendation letters from previous superiors. Truly hope that I have the chance to work with you in the shoot.

Jason Lin

Dear Jason,

We have seen your portfolio, and we love it. You seem well-prepared. Glad that you didn't quit because of the first "no", and we admire your enthusiasm and continued trying. The rejection may sting, but it is just a part of the process. Along the way, you have gradually built the brand of yours by having the commercial and other things. Since you have passed the preliminary screening with work experience, we would like you to participate in our second interview at Studio 999. Make sure you bring your portfolio with you next Monday at 6 p.m. You might be asked to test your ability to perform on stage... That's all.

HR Department

196. From the recruitment, what is required to bring during the interview?

(A) The criminal record

(B) the height

(C) the recording

(D) the acting experience

197. What is **NOT** indicated about Jason Lin?

(A) He got the contract from a modeling agency.

(B) He did an acting in a thriller.

(C) He wants this opportunity badly.

(D) He rejected the offer from Bestland.

198. The word "**impersonated**" in paragraph2, line 6, is closet in meaning to

(A) animated

(B) implemented

(C) portrayed

(D) transformed

199. What is **NOT** stated in the reply?

(A) Jason has passed the first screening.

(B) Jason is persistent.

(C) Jason has to be there on time at 6 p.m.

(D) Jason have passed the second interview.

200. What industry is Jason planning to dabble and build a career?

(A) Music

(B) Film

(C) Advertising

(D) Modeling industry

模擬試題（一）

閱讀原文與中譯	
101. Best Automobile **procured** 11 million dollars from the investor last week, making it competitive enough to enter the global market. (A) prolonged (B) permitted (C) promoted **(D) procured**	倍斯特汽車於上週從投資者那裡獲得1千1百萬元的資金，使其足以具備有進入全球市場的競爭力。 (A) 延長、拉長；拖延 (B) 允許、許可、准許 (C) 晉升、促進、推銷 **(D) 取得、獲得**
答案：(D)	

解析

這題根據語意要選「**獲得**」，故答案要選選項D。

閱讀原文與中譯	
102. Best Design hit the **headlines** with its innovative kitchen wares that can greatly reduce the preparation time for millions of housewives. (A) sensations **(B) headlines** (C) hotlines (D) boards	倍斯特設計公司以其創新的廚具組上了新聞頭條，將替數百萬的家庭主婦大幅地縮短準備時間。 (A) 感覺、知覺、轟動的事件 **(B)（報紙等的）標題、大標題** (C) 熱線 (D) 董事會
答案：(B)	

解析

這題是一個常見的慣用表達**hit the headlines**，故答案要選**選項B**。

閱讀原文與中譯	
103. A piece of software equipment priced at US 500 dollars is considered expensive in the eyes of the **dilettante**. (A) devaluation (B) dilemma **(C) dilettante** (D) expert	在業餘者的眼中，一件定價在500美元的軟體設備被視為是昂貴的。 (A) 貶值 (B) 困境，進退兩難 **(C) 半吊子、業餘愛好者** (D) 專家

答案：(C)

 解析

這題也是一個高階字的使用，且未使用amateur而是**dilettante**，故答案要選**選項C**。

閱讀原文與中譯	
104. According to the rituals, rookie pilots are asked to **assemble** at the canteen before every dinner. (A) supervise (B) resemble (C) authorize **(D) assemble**	根據老規矩，菜鳥機師被要求要在每次晚餐期間於餐廳內集合。 (A) 監督、管理、指導 (B) 相似、類似 (C) 全權委託、批准、認可 **(D) 集合、召集、聚集**

答案：(D)

 解析

這題要選動詞且是「**集合**」這個語意的字，故答案為**選項D**。

105. Best Furniture has surpassed its rival by launching the unprecedented furnishings that **exceed** consumers' expectations. (A) downplay (B) shorten **(C) exceed** (D) contemplate	藉由推出超越消費者期盼史無前例的傢俱，倍斯特傢俱行已經超越其競爭對手。 (A) 將......輕描淡寫、貶低 (B) 使變短、縮短 **(C) 超過、勝過** (D) 思量、仔細考慮、注視

答案：(C)

這題that之後也要使用動詞... **exceed** one's expectations為常見的慣用表達，故答案為**選項C**。

106. Mass production of milk is worthy of praises but not during the time when the virus is **devastating** the globe. (A) be devastated (B) devastated **(C) devastating** (D) to devastate	牛奶的大量生產是值得稱讚的，但在病毒肆虐全球的期間卻恰好相反。

答案：(C)

這題依據語法要選devastating表達「**肆虐**」，故答案為**選項C**。

閱讀原文與中譯

107. Although the economy hits us all, Best Watch, a **subsidiary** of the Fashion Watch, has handed in impressive yields, contrary to what the sources said.

(A) supporter
(B) bystander
(C) parent
(D) subsidiary

儘管我們都受到經濟衝擊，倍斯特手錶，一間時尚手錶的子公司，已經交出了令人欽佩的利潤，這不同於其他消息所述。

(A) 支持者、擁護者
(B) 旁觀者
(C) 父母
(D) 輔助物、子公司

答案：(D)

 解析

這題句子中有同位語的表達且選項中的句意要選擇**「子公司」**，故答案為**選項D**。

閱讀原文與中譯

108. Analysts are predicting that Best Automobile won't be the **beneficiary** after the huge merger because there seems to be lots of unresolved issues in the company.

(A) sponsor
(B) beneficiary
(C) spectator
(D) shareholder

分析師預測倍斯特汽車不會是巨大合併後的受益者，因為公司似乎仍存在著許多未解的議題。

(A) 發起者、主辦者、倡議者
(B) 受益人、受惠者
(C) 觀眾、旁觀者、目擊者
(D) 股東

答案：(B)

 解析

這題依據語意要選**「受益人」**，故答案要選**選項B**。

閱讀原文與中譯	
109. **Unscrupulous** vendors had already stockpiled millions of clinical masks before the virus began to ravage people's lives. (A) hesitant (B) tolerable **(C) unscrupulous** (D) adjustable	在病毒開始摧毀人命之前，無恥的攤商已經囤積了百萬片的醫療用口罩。 (A) 遲疑的、躊躇的 (B) 可忍受的、可容忍的 **(C) 肆無忌憚的、不講道德的、無恥的** (D) 可調整的、可調節的

答案：(C)

這題也是較高階形容詞的考點，要選語意是表達「**無恥的**」，故答案為**選項 C**。

閱讀原文與中譯	
110. Further down the supply chain, Best Drinks is backed up by ingredient **suppliers** that help it to produce the best milk tea in town. (A) underperformers (B) arraignments **(C) suppliers** (D) contractors	在供應鏈之下，倍斯特飲料有著原料供應商的支持，幫助其生產小鎮上的最佳牛乳。 (A) 表現不佳者 (B) 傳訊、提訊、控告 **(C) 供應者、供應商** (D) 立契約者、承包人、承包商

答案：(C)

ingredient supplier是一個搭配且符合語意，故答案為**選項C**。

閱讀原文與中譯

111. Due to the economic downturn, executives in the conference have decided to cut ad **expenditures** so that the cash flow for the next few months won't be an issue.

(A) expenditures
(B) readjustments
(C) motivations
(D) evaluations

由於經濟衰退，會議室中的高階主管已經決定要刪減廣告支出，這樣一來接下來幾個月的現金流就不會是個問題。

(A) 消費、支出、用光
(B) 重新調整、重新適應
(C) 刺激、推動、動機
(D) 評估、估價、評價

答案：(A)

 解析

Cut ad expenditures也是一個搭配且符合語意，故答案為**選項A**。

閱讀原文與中譯

112. Both insufficient tourists visiting in the areas and a significant change in consumer shopping habits have contributed to the significant drop in retailers' **revenues**.

(A) interpretations
(B) revenues
(C) calculations
(D) evaluations

參訪此地的觀光客數的不足和消費購物習慣的顯著改變已經導致了零售商總收入的明顯下降。

(A) 解釋、口譯
(B) 稅收、收入、收益
(C) 計算、估計
(D) 評估、估價、評價

答案：(B)

 解析

這題是要表達出零售商**總收入**的明顯下降，故答案要選**選項B**。

113. To encourage the use of the **reusable** shopping bag, several department stores are rewarding consumers using it during the festival with an additional 10% discount. (A) persuasive (B) extravagant **(C) reusable** (D) dominant	為了鼓勵使用可重複利用的購物袋，幾間百貨公司獎勵在節慶期間使用的消費者享有額外10%的折扣。 (A) 勸誘的、有說服力的 (B) 奢侈的、浪費的 **(C) 可再度使用的、可多次使用的** (D) 佔優勢的、支配的、統治的

答案：(C)

這題依句意要選「**重複性使用的**」，故答案要選**選項C**。

114. For the sake of the incident in the news, store workers are now pretty **vigilant** about the intruders, especially during the night shift. (A) intimate **(B) vigilant** (C) capable (D) communicative	由於新聞事件的緣故，店裡的工人現在對於闖入者相當機警，尤其是在夜間值班期間。 (A) 親密的、熟悉的 **(B) 警戒的、警惕的** (C) 有能力的、能幹的、有才華的 (D) 暢談的、愛社交的、交際的

答案：(B)

這題依句意要選「**機警的**」，故答案要選**選項B**。

閱讀原文與中譯	
115. To **distract** the attention of the lion, the circus performer uses the lingering scent of its favorite dishes. (A) distracted (B) distracting **(C) distract** (D) being distracted	為了分散獅子的注意力，馬戲團的表演者使用了牠最喜愛餐點的氣味。

答案：(C)

 解析

這題依據語法要選**動詞**，故答案為**選項C**。

閱讀原文與中譯	
116. Studying marine mammals **is** harder in good weather conditions, so the professor wants the students to cherish the moment. (A) were (B) are **(C) is** (D) was	在天氣良好的時候要研究海洋哺乳類動物都有些難了，所以教授想要學生珍惜這個時刻。

答案：(C)

 解析

這題是動名詞當主詞，所以其後要加**單數動詞**，故答案要選**選項C**。

閱讀原文與中譯	
117. The insurance company will not **compensate** the money to those who self-injury themselves. (A) legitimize (B) applause (C) accuse **(D) compensate**	這間保險公司不會補償那些自我傷害的人金錢。 (A) 使……合法、宣布為合法、承認 (B) 鼓掌歡迎、喝采、稱讚 (C) 指控、控告、譴責 **(D) 補償、賠償、酬報**

答案：(D)

這題要選動詞且依句意要選**「補償」**，故答案為**選項D**。

閱讀原文與中譯	
118. In the kindergarten, teachers often underestimate children's **curiosity** to explore new things in a new environment. (A) curious **(B) curiosity** (C) curiously (D) curry	在幼稚園裡，老師通常低估了小孩在一個新環境會去探索新事物的好奇心。

答案：(B)

這題依語法要選名詞，故答案為**選項B**。

閱讀原文與中譯	
119. One of the most exhilarating things in the office **is** the birthday present prepared by the CEO. (A) was **(B) is** (C) are (D) were	在辦公室內，其中最令人感到振奮的事情是由執行長所準備的生日禮物。

答案：(B)

 解析

這題依據語法要選「**單數動詞**」，故答案為**選項B**。

閱讀原文與中譯	
120. For customers who had **previously** been turned down before can now receive the monetary compensations. (A) subsequent **(B) previously** (C) later (D) previous	對於先前受到拒絕的顧客現在可以收到金錢的補償了。 (A) 後來的、其後的、隨後的 **(B) 事先；以前** (C) 較晚的、更晚的 (D) 前的、以前的

答案：(B)

解析

這題的句子結構很完整了，所以空格僅有可能是要填**副詞**，故答案為**選項B**。

| 121. In 2010, Best Cellphone began to lose **its** advantage to the rival company and the stock price dropped as well.
(A) their
(B) it
(C) its
(D) them | 在2010年，面對著競爭對手，倍斯特手機開始失去了優勢，股價也因此而下跌。 |

答案：(C)

 解析

這題根據語法要使用**its**，故答案為**選項C**。

| 122. **Unable** to find outside investors to finance, Best Clothing has to make the cut of at least 10,000 workers, according to the report.
(A) Able
(B) Inability
(C) Capable
(D) Unable | 由於無法找到外部的投資客資助，倍斯特服飾必須要裁減至少一萬名工人，根據報導。 |

答案：(D)

 解析

able和unable後才是加上to的搭配，這題依據語法和句意要選選項D，故**答案為D**。

閱讀原文與中譯

123. Best Fitness Center, **whose** memberships was few and far between last month, now surprisingly transcends one of the best fitness centers in town.
(A) who
(B) which
(C) where
(D) whose

在上個月，倍斯特健身中心的會員還相當稀少，現在卻出奇地超越了小鎮上其中一間最棒的健身中心。

答案：(D)

 解析

根據空格後的membership得知要選**whose**才合乎語法，故答案為**選項D**。

閱讀原文與中譯

124. The aquarium is not specifically aimed at **attracting** marine biologists because it needs to make money.
(A) to attract
(B) attracted
(C) being attracted
(D) attracting

水族館並未特別將目標放在吸引海洋生物學家，因為它要將其用於獲利。

答案：(D)

 解析

At是介係詞，其後要加上Ving，故答案要選**選項D**。

125. The town is **heavily** reliant on the export to make money, so local residents have to think other ways to transport the goods. (A) heavy **(B) heavily** (C) heavier (D) more heavier	小鎮高度仰賴出口來賺錢，所以當地居民必須要思考以其他方式來運送貨物。

答案：(B)

 解析

這題依據語法要選「**副詞**」，故答案為**選項B**。

126. Remaining extremely **calm** during confrontations is a good thing for the business deal. (A) calmness **(B) calm** (C) calming (D) calmed	在爭執期間維持相當冷靜對於商業交易來說是件好事。

答案：(B)

 解析

這題依據語法要選「**形容詞**」，故答案為**選項B**。

閱讀原文與中譯	
127. Tourists in our garden can even visit our strawberry lab to test the freshness of the related product **before** they make a purchase. (A) after **(B) before** (C) if (D) although	在購買前，花園的觀光客甚至可以參訪我們的草莓實驗室以檢測相關商品的新鮮度。

答案：(B)

 解析

這題依據語意要選「**Before**」，故答案為**選項B**。

閱讀原文與中譯	
128. During the period of the COVID-19 virus, Best Hotel admitted in the conference that the company encountered the greatest obstacle in 50 years, but it wanted to keep all employees **employed**. (A) employ (B) employment (C) employing **(D) employed**	在新冠肺炎這段期間，倍斯特旅館在新聞記者會上坦承，公司遭遇了50年來最大的阻礙，但是會致力讓所有員工都能保有飯碗。

答案：(D)

 解析

這題依據語法要選「**employed**」，故答案為**選項D**。

129. Much of the time was spent **finding** evidence that can prove the client is actually innocent. (A) find (B) finds **(C) finding** (D) found	大多數時間都花費在尋找能夠證明客戶是真的清白的證據。

答案：(C)

 解析

這題依據語法要選「**finding**」，故答案為**選項C**。

130. The CEO of Best Kitchen is now **determined** to get rid of lazy workers and employees who spread rumor about the company. (A) determine (B) determination **(C) determined** (D) determining	倍斯特廚房的執行長決定要除掉懶惰的工人和散布公司傳聞的員工。

答案：(C)

 解析

這題依據語法要選「**determined**」，故答案為**選項C**。

PART 6　中譯和解析

Questions 131-134

Best Zoo made its acquisition with one of the largest on-line retailers, DEF, so it now has a great deal of money to renovate the zoo, including the facility. However, from now on every penny spent is **regulated** by the Finance Department and outside investors, according to the earlier report. The huge deficit was the main reason why Best Zoo **desperately** sought out a buyout offer and outside investors. Any **superfluous** international travels will be turned down by the CEO, and that makes many executives who used to have **frequent** trips and the benefit of staying in the luxurious hotels so hard to adjust. Plus, all executives are getting a pay cut of 30%, whereas employees at lower levels are getting a 10% increase in pay. This actually boosts the morale of the company, a reporter said.

倍斯特動物園與線上其中一間最大型的零售商DEF進行併購，所以現在有大量的資金能夠用於修繕動物園，包含園區設備。然而，從現在起，每分錢的花費都受到財務部門和外部投資人的控管，根據稍早之前的報導。預算赤字是倍斯特動物園迫切向外尋求收購提案和外部投資客的主因。任何多餘的國際性旅行都會被執行長拒絕，而這讓許多過去享有頻繁旅行和享有待在豪華旅館福利的高階主管難以調適。再說，所有高階主管都受到30%的減薪，而位在較低階層的員工們有著10%的薪資增幅。根據記者所述，這實際上提升了公司的士氣。

試題中譯與解析

131.	131.
(A) resumed	(A) 重新開始、繼續、恢復
(B) regulated	**(B) 管理、控制、校準、調整**
(C) assembled	(C) 集合、召集、聚集、收集
(D) addressed	(D) 向......致詞、對...說
132.	132.
(A) unavoidably	(A) 無可避免地
(B) understandably	(B) 可理解地
(C) desperately	**(C) 迫切地**
(D) independently	(D) 獨立地、自立地

133.	133.
(A) superfluous	**(A) 過剩的、多餘的、不必要的**
(B) deterrent	(B) 威懾的、遏制的
(C) skeptical	(C) 懷疑性的、懷疑論的
(D) astonishing	(D) 驚人的
134.	134.
(A) reserved	(A) 預定的
(B) futile	(B) 無益的、無效的、無用的
(C) fruitful	(C) 富有成效的、收益好的、（土地）肥沃的、富饒的
(D) frequent.	**(D) 頻繁的**

第**131**題，這題要選regulated，因為依文意的表達，是說每分所花費的錢都會由FD所**控管**，故答案為**選項B**。

第**132**題，這題要選**迫切地**，公司其實急著找尋buyout，故答案為**選項C**。

第**133**題，這題要小心誤選，但由句意要選superfluous，CEO會回絕那些不必要的旅行支出，故答案為**選項A**。

第**134**題，這題要選frequent，這些過慣好日子的高階管理人，過去享有**頻繁**的旅遊，故答案為**選項D**。

Questions 135-138

After the adjustment, the CEO is pleased **with** the result of the progress of the company, but the board has been waiting for the firm to actually do something. That's why the concept of a sustainable farm was brought up in the conference. With the sustainable farm, **the company does not have to rely heavily on import of food and vegetables**, and it can totally make the animals' meals more abundant and diversified. That means, all animals are able to consume food that is **rich in** different nutrients. They are going to be healthy and robust. Animal doctors **are content with** the new announcement, and they can also cook in the zoo with fresh vegetables handy in the organic farm. This is definitely a great step for all employees and animals.

在調整後，執行長對於公司的進步感到滿意，但是董事會正等待公司有實際的作為。這就是為什麼「永續農場」的概念於會議中被提出來。有了永續農場，公司不必高度仰賴進口蔬果，且此舉可以讓動物的肉食更豐富且多樣化。這也意謂著，所有動物都能夠攝取到富含各種營養素的食物。牠們將會是健康且健壯。動物醫生對於這項的新公告感到滿意，而他們也能以在有機農場中唾手可得的新鮮蔬果在動物園中進行烹飪。對於所有員工和動物們來說，這確實向前躍進了一大步。

試題中譯與解析	
135. (A) in (B) on (C) at **(D) with**	135. (A) in (B) on (C) at **(D) with**
136. (A) The company will be rewarded enormously by the government (B) The export of the company will have a significant boost **(C) The company does not have to rely heavily on import of food and vegetables** (D) The board wants more documents to evaluate	136. (A) 公司會收到政府高額的報酬。 (B) 公司的出口將會有顯著的增長。 **(C) 公司不需要高度仰賴進口的食物和蔬菜。** (D) 董事會想要更多文件以進行評估。
137. (A) famous for (B) interested in **(C) rich in** (D) exposed to	137. (A) ...以...聞名 (B) ...對...有興趣 **(C) 富含...** (D) 接觸、曝露
138. (A) are replaced with **(B) are content with** (C) are worried about (D) are based on	138. (A) 取代 **(B) 滿意** (C) 擔憂 (D) 以...為基礎

第135題，依句意要選be pleased with故要選with，故答案為**選項D**。
第136題，依句意要選C，因為有了有機農場後，公司就不需要仰賴進口了，故答案為**選項C**。
第137題，這題要選be rich in，所有動物都能夠攝取**富含**各種營養素的食物，故答案為**選項C**。
第138題，動物醫生對於這項的新公告感到**滿意**，這題要選be content with，故答案為**選項B**。

Questions 139-142

Due to the building of the new organic farm, several executives have prepared the document with company attorneys to ABC architecture firm, and will take a good look at the land that is on the market. The land has to be **cultivable** and rich in minerals so that the organic farm can actually work. The company has also hired soil biologists who **have been** in the business for twenty years. They have narrowed the options down to four sites to check before the summer, but the CEO gave them the specific **deadline** of July 30. **They have to prepare proposals with the CEO before that date in the conference with all foreign investors.** They will vote for the site of the organic farm out of final three options

由於新設有機農場的建造，幾個高階主管與公司的律師們已經準備好去ABC建築行的文件，並且好好審視在市場上所預售的土地。這塊土地必須要是可耕種且富含著礦物質的，這樣有機農場才能夠發揮成效。公司也雇用了在業界具有20年經驗的土壤生物學家。在夏季到來前，土壤生物學家已經將選擇篩選至四塊土地，但是執行長給了確切的截止日期7月30日。在與所有外國投資客們在會議室商談的日期前，他們必須要與執行長準備提案。他們將會在最後三個選項中進行投票以決定有機農場的位置。

試題中譯與解析	
139. (A) popular (B) celebratory (C) unvarnished **(D) cultivable**	139. (A) 流行的 (B) 興高采烈的、慶祝的 (C) 未塗漆的、無掩飾的 **(D) 可耕種的、可培養的**

140. (A) has (B) had (C) have **(D) have been**	140. (A) has (B) had (C) have **(D) have been**
141. (A) arraignment **(B) deadline** (C) experiment (D) challenge	141. (A) 傳訊、提訊、控告、指責 **(B) 截止期限、最後限期** (C) 實驗 (D) 挑戰
142. **(A) They have to prepare proposals with the CEO before that date in the conference with all foreign investors.** (B) The bidding war getting increasingly fierce. (C) These places are not the CEO's favorite. (D) They have to cancel the meeting because something bad happens in the office.	142. **(A) 在與所有外部的投資客的會議之前，他們必須要與執行長準備提案。They** (B) 競價戰變得異常激烈。 (C) 這些地方不是執行長所喜愛的。 (D) 他們必須要取消會議，因為辦公室發生了不好的事情。

第**139**題，依上、下文句意要選「可耕種的」cultivable，故答案為**選項D**。

第**140**題，依語法要選have been，故答案為**選項D**。

第**141**題，依句意要選截止日期deadline，故答案為**選項B**。

第**142**題，依句意要選A，故答案為**選項A**。

Questions 143-146

The **honeymoon** for the CEO is too short, so the CEO urges his subordinates to prepare the final presentation a week earlier than the original deadline. Now several executives groan during the lunch break because they are now working 24/7 with a 30% decrease in **payment**. The demanding new CEO certainly makes their lives less comfortable compared with the former CEO. But during this economy, they cannot be **reckless** and hand in resignation letters. "Not just yet", according to one of the executives in the company. He said that **after the purchase of the organic farm is settled, life in the office will be back to normal**. He is hoping that all the effort will be rewarded in the year-end bonus, if there is going to be one...

公司給予執行長的蜜月期太短了，所以執行長催促他的下屬要在原先截止日期的前一週就準備好最後簡報。現在，幾位高階主管在午餐休憩時抱怨此事，因為他們現在要24小時待命的工作，但薪資又比原先少了30%。苛求的新執行長確實讓他們的日子變得更不舒適，跟先前的執行長相比。但是在這樣的景氣期間，他們不可能魯莽行事而遞交辭職信。「還沒到那個時候」，根據公司其中一位高階主管所述。他述說著在有機農場得購買談定後，在辦公司的生活就會回到正軌。他希望所有的努力會有年終獎勵，如果有的話...。

試題中譯與解析	
143. (A) dedication (B) promotion **(C) honeymoon** (D) creativity	143. (A) 奉獻、供奉、致力 (B) 升遷、促進、提倡 **(C) 蜜月假期、蜜月旅行** (D) 創意
144. (A) temperatures (B) performance (C) prediction **(D) payment**	144. (A) 溫度 (B) 表現 (C) 預測 **(D) 支付、付款、薪資**

145. (A) authoritative (B) transparent (C) replaceable **(D) reckless**	145. (A) 權威性的、可信賴的、官方的 (B) 透明的、清澈的、顯而易見的 (C) 可替換的、可置換的、可放在原處的 **(D) 不在乎的、魯莽的、不顧後果的**
146. **(A) after the purchase of the organic farm is settled, life in the office will be back to normal.** (B) a guy in the office still cannot wait until the proposal is finished, so he quits. (C) the receptionist is now forbidding to answer the call from journalists, so he hates the organic farm idea. (D) The CEO says they will be foregoing bonuses this year due to the exorbitant fee of purchasing the organic farm.	146. **(A) 在購買有機農場的事情塵埃落定後，辦公室的生活又回到往常般。** (B) 辦公室裡的一個男子無法等到提案完成，所以他遞出辭呈了。 (C) 接線員現在被禁止接新聞記者的來電，所以他恨透了有機農場的想法。 (D) 執行長述說著，他們將於今年取消獎金，由於高昂的有機農場的購買費用。

第**143**題，依句意要選honeymoon（因為蜜月期短，所以執行長才必須要在更短時間內要做出成績來，也才會有之後的催促等等的...），別誤選成promotion，故答案為**選項C**。

第**144**題，依句意要選payment，這裡指的是**薪資**，他們都要接受減薪，故答案為**選項D**。

第**145**題，依句意要選reckless，他們不能因此就**魯莽**辭掉工作，故答案為**選項D**。

第**146**題，根據上、下文和句意要選選項A，故答案為**選項A**。

Online purchase/Best retailer

Number: 000099999999 （**Premium**）
❶ Smartphone: B50+ **US 3000 dollars**
❷ Best Bag: **US 1000 dollars**
❸ Best Suitcase: **US 2000 dollars**
❹ infant outfit: **US 500 dollars**

※ Premium member of BR: **10%** discount
※ Credit card payment: **10%** discount
※ Tax: **10%**
※ Home Delivery: **US 50 dollars**/exceeding **US 5000 dollars** = free
===
Total _____?_____

verification

線上購物/倍斯特零售商

單號: 000099999999 （**優質會員**）
❶ 智慧型手機：B50+ **US 3000 元**
❷ 倍斯特手提袋：**US 1000元**
❸ 倍斯特手提箱：**US 2000元**
❹ 嬰兒全套服飾：**US 500元**

※ 倍斯特優質會員：**10%** 折扣
※ 信用卡付費：**10%** 折扣
※ 稅：**10%**
※ 家庭運送：**US 50 dollars**/消費金額超過**US 5000 dollars** = 免運
===
總計 _____?_____

確認鍵

Question 147	
147. How much is the cost of this on-line purchase by using a credit card? (A) 5200 (B) 6500 **(C) 5720** (D) 6550	147. 這次的線上購物，若以信用卡付費要支付多少錢？ (A) 5200 (B) 6500 **(C) 5720** (D) 6550

 解析

· 第**147**題，總消費金額6500元*20%折扣（**5200元**）+10%稅（**520元**）+免運（**0元**），故答案為**選項C**。

Mark 1:06 p.m. Hi, Miss Lin. Unfortunately, the ticket is not refundable, so there is nothing I can do. I am sure the clerk had told you before you made the purchase.	**馬克下午1:06** 嗨，林小姐。不幸的是，門票沒有辦法退，所以我沒有可以幫上忙的地方。我確信店員在您購票時就有告知您。
Miss Lin 1:08 p.m. Is it possible I put the photo on the website to see if someone is interested in going to the Museum for the next few days?	**林小姐下午1:08** 有可能我把照片放到網站上，看是否有人對於接下來的幾天對參訪博物館的行程有興趣嗎？
Mark 1:11 p.m. Perhaps, other travelers who are museumgoers might purchase it. You can try it by trimming down the price and with a reason that why you'd like to sell it, instead of going to the place yourself.	**馬克下午1:11** 或許其他為博物館愛好者的遊客可能會購買。你可以藉由減些零頭並附上你為什麼想要販售的原因，所以你沒辦法親自前往那個地方。

Miss Lin 1:13 p.m.	林小姐下午1:13
I have to change the schedule due to some unforeseen reasons at work... that kind of reason?	我因為一些無法預測的因素而必須要更改時程...那樣的理由嗎?
Mark 1:15 p.m.	馬克下午1:15
It wouldn't hurt to give it a try... now you have to excuse me.... customers are waiting...	試一下無妨...現在請容許我離開一下....有客戶在等...

Question 148

148. At 1:11 p.m. why does Mark mention about "trimming down the price and so on"?	148. 在下午1:11分,為什麼馬克提及「trimming down the price and so on」?
(A) The price was set too high for the museumgoers.	(A) 當初喜愛博物館者將價格設定的太高了。
(B) That way, the ticket can be sold more quickly.	**(B) 這樣的話,門票可以更快的方式銷售完。**
(C) The ticket is not refundable.	(C) 門票是無法退款的。
(D) The museum will be having the discounted price.	(D) 博物館將會有折扣。

 解析

· 第148題,建議的方式其實可以讓票更快於截止日期前銷售出,故答案為**選項B**。

Dear Mary

Now it's time that you know the truth about Bob's true identity. **(1)** On the surface, he is currently working under the title of the manager of ABC Human Resources, but indeed he works for us. **(2)** He has been feeding us with marketing strategies used by our opponent. **(3) That's why we are always one step ahead of ABC Human Resources.** Last month, he brought us client data of ABC, and I have got to say that's quite valuable to us, and our engineers have been working on that part too so that some day we can totally **dominate** the market. **(4)** When you meet Bob, just act normally. It's not a big deal that he now knows that you know, got it? You have your new role by pretending to be a coffee clerk and approach him. I feel so relieved by telling you this.
Manager of CCC HR

親愛的瑪莉

現在是你知道鮑伯真實身分的時候了。表面上，他以ABC人事經理的頭銜工作著，但是他確實是替我們工作。他已經提供給我們由我們對手所使用的行銷策略。這也是為什麼我們總是能早先ABC的人事部門一步。上個月，他帶給我們ABC的客戶資料，而我必須要說，這對我們來說真的相當有價值，而我們的工程師一直在那個部分上努力著，這樣一來有一天我們完全能夠主導這個市場。當你遇到鮑伯時，行為舉止就維持正常即可。他現在知道你知道他的身分其實沒什麼大不了的，知道嗎?你有你的新的角色，藉由偽裝成一個咖啡店員並且接近他。跟你述說這些讓我感到如釋重負。

CCC HR的經理

Questions 149-152

149. What has Mary been requested to do? (A) to be an engineer (B) to be an HR (C) to be a manager **(D) to be a barista**	149. 瑪莉被要求做什麼? (A) 成為一個工程師 (B) 成為一個人事專員 (C) 成為一個經理 **(D) 成為一個咖啡館服務生**
150. What is not mentioned about the letter? **(A) Bob is an engineer.** (B) Bob gave them information about the rival. (C) The manager has been keeping the secret for a long time. (D) Bob is a spy.	150. 關於信件的部分,沒有提及什麼? **(A) 鮑伯是個工程師。** (B) 鮑伯給他們關於對手的資訊。 (C) 經理長期保有著秘密。 (D) 鮑伯是位間諜。
151. The word "**dominate**" in the letter, line 8, line 1, is closet in meaning to (A) formulate **(B) predominate** (C) eliminate (D) translate	151. 在第一封信第八行的「支配、占優勢」,意思最接近 (A) 構想、制定 **(B) 佔主導(或支配)地位;(在數量等方面)佔優勢** (C) 排除、消除、消滅 (D) 翻譯
152. In which of the positions marked **(1)**, **(2)**, **(3)**, and **(4)** does the following sentence best belong? "**That's why we are always one step ahead of ABC Human Resources.**" (A) (1) (B) (2) **(C) (3)** (D) (4)	152. 以下這個句子最適合放在文中標記**(1)**, **(2)**, **(3)**, **(4)**的哪個位置? 「這也是為什麼我們總是能早先ABC人事部門一步。」 (A) (1) (B) (2) **(C) (3)** (D) (4)

模擬試題（一）

模擬試題（一）
模擬試題（二）
模擬試題（三）
模擬試題（四）
模擬試題（五）

解析

- **第149題**，瑪莉被要求的工作是coffee clerk 即**barista**（咖啡館服務生），故答案為**選項D**。
- **第150題**，Bob不是engineer，故答案為**選項A**。
- **第151題**，dominate = **predominate**，故答案為**選項B**。
- **第152題**，最適合放置在He has been feeding us with marketing strategies used by our opponent.後，**(3)**，故答案為**選項C**。

Best Elite Elementary School
Classification

Reading

Animal	Group	Trait
Minke whale	A	endurance
Octopus	B	versatility
Swordfish	C	speed

Math/Chemistry/Physics

Animal	Group	Trait
Raccoon	A	agileness
Octopus	B	reasoning/problem-solving
Parrot	C	mimicry
Cuckoo bird	D	cunning

Geography/History

Animal	Group	Trait
Dolphin	A	sense of direction/location
Elephant	B	memorization
Chimpanzee	C	reasoning

Note :

1. The classification is based entirely on the entrance exam taken twice

before enrolling. The reading part is solely based on student's written scores, whereas GH involves both written grades and interactions with other kids in the computerized room where students are monitored by a group of professors. Students' MCP scores depend heavily on the test conducted by the Education Bureau as a reference.

2. Whatever they are, just be happy for them. All students are required to take the test every two year, so the group to which they are belonged might change from time to time.

3. If the student has shown a striking similarity in both animals (and it's quite possible), he or she has the right to choose the group of animal they are in.

倍斯特菁英小學 分類		
閱讀		
動物	群組	特色
小鬚鯨	A	持久力
章魚	B	多才多藝
劍魚	C	速度
數學/化學/物理		
動物	群組	特色
浣熊	A	靈活度
章魚	B	理解/解決問題能力
鸚鵡	C	模仿
杜鵑鳥	D	狡詐
地裡/歷史		
動物	群組	特色
海豚	A	方向感/位置
大象	B	記憶

| 黑猩猩 | C | 理解 |

註：

1. 分類完全是根據入學之前所測驗的兩次考試。閱讀的部分僅基於學生的寫作分數，而地理和歷史牽涉到寫作分數和由一組教授在一個電腦化教室所監測的孩童間的互動。學生的數學、化學和物理分數高度仰賴由教育部所實施的考試來當作參考。

2. 不論他們被分配到哪個組別，都要替他們感到開心。所有學生每兩年都需要參與考試，所以他們所屬的組別也會因為時間可能有改變。

3. 如果學生在兩種動物中已經展現出顯著的相似性（而這是相當有可能發生的），他或她有權選擇他們所想要待的組別。

Questions 153-158	
153. How many tests do students have to take in a 6-year program in BEE School? (A) 2 (B) 3 **(C) 4** (D) 5	153. 學生們要在BEE學校的六年課程計畫中至少要參與多少次考試？ (A) 2 (B) 3 **(C) 4** (D) 5
154. What is True about the categorization? (A) Students only have to take the admission test. (B) Students can use the money to change the animal group. **(C) Students need more than paper test scores to get higher grades in GH.** (D) Students cannot have the trait of more than one animal.	154. 關於分類的部分，何者為真？ (A) 學生僅需要參加入學考試。 (B) 學生可以使用金錢來改變所屬的動物群組。 **(C) 學生需要不僅是紙本考試分數以獲取在GH科目上較高的成績。** (D) 學生們不可能有多於一種動物以上的特質。

155. What is mentioned about the dolphin? (A) It swims slower than the swordfish. (B) It has nothing to do with direction. **(C) It falls under the category of GH.** (D) Its popularity is not greater than the chimpanzee.	155. 關於海豚的部分，有提到什麼？ (A) 牠比劍魚游的慢。 (B) 牠與方向感無關。 **(C) 牠落於HG的範疇。** (D) 牠的熱門度沒有比黑猩猩高。
156. What is not stated about the categorization of the octopus? **(A) its trait irrelevant to problem-solving** (B) its trait related to reasoning (C) its trait related to versatility (D) its trait unrelated to speed	156. 關於章魚的分類，沒有提到什麼？ **(A) 牠與解決問題的能力無關。** (B) 牠的特質跟推理有關。 (C) 牠的特質與多樣性有關。 (D) 牠的特質和速度無關。
157. Which of the following creature demonstrates the charade? (A) elephant (B) octopus **(C) cuckoo bird** (D) parrot	157. 下列哪個生物展示了裝模作樣的能力？ (A) 大象 (B) 章魚 **(C) 杜鵑鳥** (D) 鸚鵡
158. Which of the following subject contains more than three categorizations? (A) History (B) Reading **(C) Chemistry** (D) Geography	158. 下列哪個科目包含了超多三項的分類？ (A) 歷史 (B) 閱讀 **(C) 化學** (D) 地理

模擬試題（一）

模擬試題（一）
模擬試題（二）
模擬試題（三）
模擬試題（四）
模擬試題（五）

解析

- **第153題**，學生要考四次，入學前兩次，以及二升三、四升五各一次，故答案為**選項C**。
- **第154題**，在GH中，學生還需要互動等項目評估，不僅僅是筆試成績，故答案為**選項C**。
- **第155題**，海豚是在GH的範疇內，故答案為**選項C**。
- **第156題**，章魚跟解決問題有關，故答案為**選項A**。
- **第157題**，charade要對應到動物特質，最有可能的是cuckoo bird的cunning，故答案為**選項C**。
- **第158題**，數學、物理、化學均有4種，故答案為**選項C**。

The basketball toss is unlike what you have seen in the night market. You have to be qualified to play the game. Our machine has been set at the yard. You have to pass the labyrinth to get here, during which a flashlight and other devices cannot be used, so you can only depend on the lighting of the fireflies. Don't feel bad if you can't find us. It's not your fault. Our place only opens after midnight. You might even have a question of why people bother to come here. It's kind of romantic to be with your loved one or close friends to embark on a new adventure here. That's the main reason why we are so popular, and we have the greatest camp and other amazing dishes here.

Tossing in a special location	
Accumulated scores	Prizes
1,000	A box of coke
5,000	A stuffed animal
80,000	The latest smartphone
500,000	A Porsche

Note:

1. Recently, we have begun to work on having other ways to play the ball, including kicking under the water, walking against the current,

and tossing a basketball ball in a desert-like environment.

籃球投擲不像你在夜市中所看到的那樣，而是你必須要具備資格才能夠玩這個遊戲。我們庭院中的機器已經架設好了。你必須要通過迷宮才能抵達這裡，在這期間，手電筒和其他裝置都不能使用，所以你僅能仰賴螢火蟲的微光。別因為你找不到我們而感到失落。這不是你的錯。我們的場地僅於午夜後才開放。你可能甚至會有疑問，那為什麼大家要勞師動眾到此呢!你若與你的摯愛或親密好友一起在此展開一趟冒險旅程的話，這樣會是相當浪漫的一件事。這也是我們會如此受歡迎的主因，而且我們有最棒的露營和其他的驚人菜餚在此。

投擲至特定的地點	
累積分數	獎項
1,000	一箱可樂
5,000	一個填充玩偶
80,000	最新型的智慧型手機
500,000	一台保時捷

註：

1. 最近，我們已經開始朝向使用其他的方法來玩籃球，包含在水下踢擊，逆流踢擊和在仿沙漠環境的籃球投擲。

Questions 159-162	
159. When can people be seen playing the basketball toss? (A) during the dinner time (B) 5 p.m. **(C) 3 a.m.** (D) during lunch hour	159. 何時可以看到人們玩籃球投擲？ (A) 在晚餐期間 (B) 下午五點鐘 **(C) 半夜三點鐘** (D) 在午餐時分

160. If an avid basketball toss player has exchanged a car, what can be inferred about the scores he has collected? (A) 90,000 (B) 80,000 (C) 5,000 **(D) 500,050**	160. 如果一位熱愛籃球投擲的玩家，已經換取了一台汽車，可以推測出他已經累積了幾分？ (A) 90,000 (B) 80,000 (C) 5,000 **(D) 500,050**
161. What can be inferred about the maze? (A) It's crowded. **(B) It's murky.** (C) It's bright. (D) It's sunny.	161. 關於迷宮的部分可以推測出什麼？ (A) 它是擁擠的。 **(B) 它是黑暗的。** (C) 它是明亮的。 (D) 它是陽光充足的。
162. What is not mentioned about "other ways" to play the game? (A) under the lake (B) in the torrents (C) under a sweltering hot weather condition **(D) under the ice**	162. 關於「其他方式」來玩這個遊戲的部分，沒有提到什麼？ (A) 在湖下面 (B) 在激流中 (C) 在悶熱的天氣情況下 **(D) 在冰下**

解析

· **第159題**，文章中有提到開放時間是午夜過後，最有可能的時間點是3 a.m.，故答案為**選項C**。

· **第160題**，a car = a Porsche，累積的點數要大於可換購的點數，故答案為**選項D**。

· **第161題**，因為一些裝置都無法使用且僅能仰賴螢火蟲的燈光，所以要選 murky，故答案為**選項B**。

· **第162題**，文章中沒有提到在冰塊下方玩，故答案為**選項D**。

Best Restaurant is planning to close in May due to the COVID-19 virus. Although we would like to thank every supporter from the past by having a feast outside the restaurant, we eventually choose not to do the celebration. **(1)** A crowd gathering might make the outbreak of the virus **rampant**, and that is the last thing that we would like to see. **(2)** In return, we would like to give free masks to those in need and send good meals to the hospitals to thank for the hard work that has been done by nurses and doctors. **(3)** If you still have the coupons that you haven't used, you get to exchange the coupon with a free meal by our delivery boy. **(4) The hot delicious meal will be sent to your doorstep.** If you still have other questions, please don't hesitate to let us know.

由於新冠肺炎病毒的因素，倍斯特餐廳正計畫於五月結束營業。儘管我們想要感謝過去的每位支持者，藉由在餐廳外頭舉辦盛宴，我們最終決定不慶祝了。群眾聚集將使病毒的爆發蔓延開來，而這也是我們最不樂見的情況。作為回報，我們想要將免費口罩贈給那些有急迫需要的人，並且贈送很棒的餐點到醫院以感謝護士和醫生們一直以來所作的付出。如果你仍有您尚未使用的優惠卷，你可以以優惠卷免費跟我們的運送員兌換一份免費的餐點。熱騰騰的美味餐點會送至你的門前。如果你仍有其他問題的話，別猶豫讓我們知道。

Questions 163-165	
163. The word "**rampant**" in line 5, is closet in meaning to (A) consistent (B) romantic **(C) uncontrollable** (D) intervened	163. 在第五行的「蔓延的、猖獗的、不能控制的」，意思最接近 (A) 一致的 (B) 浪漫的 **(C) 控制不住的、無法管束的** (D) 介入的、干預的

164. In which of the positions marked **(1)**, **(2)**, **(3)**, and **(4)** does the following sentence best belong? "**The hot delicious meal will be sent to your doorstep.**" (A) (1) (B) (2) (C) (3) **(D)(4)**	164. 以下這個句子最適合放在文中標記**(1)**, **(2)**, **(3)**, **(4)**的哪個位置？ 「熱騰騰的美味餐點會送至你的門前。」 (A) (1) (B) (2) (C) (3) **(D)(4)**
165. What is the article mainly about? (A) the vaccine for the virus (B) the celebration with a great feast **(C) the termination of the canteen** (D) the fantastic meal for nurses and doctors	165. 報導主要是關於什麼？ (A) 用於治療病毒的疫苗 (B) 以盛宴慶祝 **(C) 餐廳的結束** (D) 替護士和醫生準備的極佳餐點

解析

· 第163題，rampant = **uncontrollable**，故答案為**選項C**。
· 第164題，插入句最適合放在貼近句尾的地方，在you get to exchange the coupon with a free meal by our delivery boy.後，**(4)**，故答案為**選項D**。
· 第165題，，故答案為**選項C**。

Often people craze for a view at the Best Train Station. That makes the train earn its fame and the crowd. **(1)** But recently, local residents have begun to see the **downside** of this sightseeing business. Flowers in the surroundings are not as beautiful as usual, and they are a few weeks late to blossom. **(2) Some rare insects are missing, too.** Too many crowds gathering here means more damage to the land. Lots of people camp here and barbecue. This has created more intolerant noise during the night. **(3)** The ecological loss is **incalculable**. Ecologists have now gathered here to put a stop to this. **(4)** Local residents support the movement and protest, even if that means less cash earned by every household which relies on the sightseeing money for monthly expenditures.

通常遊客對於倍斯特火車站的景色著迷。那讓火車得其所名和贏得人潮。但是最近，當地居民已經開始目睹了觀光事業不好的一面。周遭的花朵沒有以往那麼美麗了，而且他們已經晚幾週才開花。有些罕見的昆蟲也消失蹤跡了。太多的壅擠的人潮聚集於此也意謂著對這塊土地更多的傷害。許多人在此露營和烤肉。在夜晚，這已經製造了更多令人難忍受的噪音。生態的損失更是令人難以估計。生態學家們現在已經聚集於此欲將此事終結。當地居民同意這項活動和抗議，即使這意謂著對於每月生活開支仰賴觀光收入的每戶家庭來說是將賺取更少的現金。

Questions 166-169

166. What is the article mainly about?	166. 報導主要是關於什麼？
(A) the fantastic view at the Train Station	(A) 在火車站的極佳風景
(B) flowers blossom incredibly	(B) 花朵驚人地繁茂著
(C) the disadvantages brought by the sightseeing boom	**(C) 因觀光興盛所帶來的不利處**
(D) the loss for the local residents	(D) 當地居民的損失

167. The word "**downside**" in line 3, is closet in meaning to (A) harassment (B) downsize **(C) disadvantage** (D) situation	167. 在第三行的「不利、下降趨勢」，意思最接近 (A) 騷擾 (B) 縮減開支 **(C) 不利、損失、損害** (D) 情況
168. The word "**incalculable**" in line 8, is closet in meaning to **(A) immeasurable** (B) accusatory (C) untransferable (D) estimated	168. 在第八行的「不可計算的、數不清的、（心情等）難捉摸的」，意思最接近 **(A) 不可計量的、無邊無際的、廣大的** (B) 指控的、控告的 (C) 無法轉移的 (D) 估計的
169. In which of the positions marked **(1)**, **(2)**, **(3)**, and **(4)** does the following sentence best belong? "**Some rare insects are missing, too.**" (A) (1) **(B) (2)** (C) (3) (D) (4)	169. 以下這個句子最適合放在文中標記**(1)**, **(2)**, **(3)**, **(4)**的哪個位置？ 「有些罕見的昆蟲也消失蹤跡了。」 (A) (1) **(B) (2)** (C) (3) (D) (4)

解析

・**第166題**，這題有提到很多的描述，不過主旨是the disadvantages brought by the sightseeing boom，故答案為**選項C**。

・**第167題**，downside = **disadvantage**，故答案為**選項C**。

・**第168題**，incalculable = **immeasurable**，故答案為**選項A**。

・**第169題**，最適合放在Flowers in the surroundings are not as beautiful as usual, and they are a few weeks late to blossom.後，**(2)**，故答案為**選項B**。

Dear Susan,

It's great to have that kind of ambition, but having an overt ambition can do you more harm than good. You said that you felt like you had nailed the interview and couldn't think of any reason why you didn't get picked. **(1)** After doing some thinking, I come to understand why, and most twentysomethings answer those types of questions wrong. **(2)** Just answer that you will feel satisfied with the current position and you are ready to give all you to the company. **(3)** You don't have to say something like you are aiming for a position that exceeds your current position. **(4) That can be the interviewer's job or those senior colleagues' future goals.** The point is that they don't know you, so you just have to keep that ambition to yourself. Even if you get hired, I feel a little bit concerned about your future in the company. You might encounter some hurdles that are totally **unnecessary**.

Best Column

親愛的蘇珊

有這樣的雄心壯志很好，但是有著過大的雄心可能對你弊大於利。你說你覺得你對於面試感到胸有成竹了，卻想不透你為什麼沒能雀屏中選的理由。在思考過後，我了解到原因了，而且大多數20多歲的人在回答這樣的問題時都回答錯了。僅須回答著你對於現在應徵的職位感到滿意且對於公司的事務會全力以赴。你不需要説到一些像是，你目標其實著眼於超過你現在職位的職缺。那可能是面試官的工作或是那些資深同事的未來目標。重點是他們不認識你，所以你自己知道自己的雄心就好了。即使你獲得聘用，我對於你在公司的未來感到擔憂。你可能會遭遇到有些全然不必要的阻力。
倍斯特專欄

Questions 170-172	
170. What is Not stated about the "Job Column"? **(A) The columnist does not think in Susan's shoe.** (B) Most twentysomethings answer some questions incorrectly. (C) Being too ambitious can have a bad consequence. (D) Susan didn't get the offer because of her lack of interview skills.	170. 關於「求職專欄」的部分，沒有提到什麼？ **(A) 專欄家並沒有站在蘇珊的立場想。** (B) 大多數的20幾歲人以不正確的方式回應有些問題。 (C) 太有雄心可能有著不好的影響。 (D) 蘇珊沒有獲聘因為她缺乏面試技巧。
171. The word "**unnecessary**" in the letter, line 13, is closet in meaning to (A) complimentary **(B) unessential** (C) important (D) entertain	171. 在信件中第13行的「不需要的、不必要的、多餘的」，意思最接近 (A) 恭維的、問候的、贈送的 **(B) 非本質的、不重要的** (C) 重要的 (D) 使歡樂、使娛樂
172. In which of the positions marked **(1)**, **(2)**, **(3)**, and **(4)** does the following sentence best belong? "**That can be the interviewer's job or those senior colleagues' future goals.**" (A) (1) (B) (2) (C) (3) **(D)(4)**	172. 以下這個句子最適合放在文中標記(1), (2), (3), (4)的哪個位置？ 「那可能是面試官的工作或是那些資深同事的未來目標。」 (A) (1) (B) (2) (C) (3) **(D)(4)**

- 第**170**題，columnist完全是站在蘇珊的立場，才會講到Even if you get hired, I feel a little bit concerned about your future in the company.，故答案為**選項A**。
- 第**171**題，unnecessary = **unessential**，故答案為**選項B**。
- 第**172**題，最適合放在You don't have to say something like you are aiming for a position that exceeds your current position.後，**(4)**，故答案為**選項D**。

Dear Jason,

It can take quite some time to figure out what you would like to do in the future. Unless you major in medicine and other specialized majors, it's normal that you are encountering the period of "disorientation". **(1)** And to be honest, most twentysomethings do not know that, after graduating from the university. You don't have to be so hard on yourself to hurt your inner soul. However, you have to know that sooner. You can start that by having the first few jobs. **(2)** Through trial and error, you will understand things that you don't like and get to narrow down to things that you do want to do. **(3)** You aim for a job that's better suited to your personality and other aspects. As to the reason why you have to figure out that sooner, because before 30, most interviewers can tolerate that and the job hop. **(4) You are young, still trying to figure out what you want**. And you don't know if it is what you want until you have worked in that position. But after 30, the reality sinks in. You might feel the cruelty if you are still **disoriented** in the sea of the job market and don't know where to land.

Best Column

親愛的傑森

了解你未來想要做什麼確實可能要花些時間的。除非你的主修是醫學或一些專業性的主修，碰到「迷惘」期是正常不過的事了。而且說真的，大多數的20幾歲的人在大學畢業後並不知道這點。你不必對自己如此嚴苛而傷到你內部的靈魂。然而，你必須更早去了解。可以藉由有幾份的首次工作當作開端。透過試誤學習，你了解你所不想做的事情且能夠把事情減至成你確實想要做的事情上。你把目標放在較適合你個性和其他面向的工作上。至於你該更早了解到這點的原因是，在30歲之前，大多數的面試官能夠容忍這點和跳槽。畢竟你還年輕，仍試圖了解你想要什麼。而且你不知道這是不是你想要的直到你已經在那個職位上工作了。但是過了30歲後，你漸漸了解到現實面。你可能感受到殘酷面，如果你仍迷失在就業市場的大海中，不知道你的登陸處在哪。

倍斯特專欄

Questions 173-175

173. What is Not stated about the "Job Column"?	173. 關於求職專欄的部分，沒有提及什麼？
(A) You can find the job closer to your ideal by taking a few attempts.	(A) 你可以藉由幾次的嘗試而找到近乎你理想的工作。
(B) Interviewers are lenient for someone who is not 30.	(B) 面試官對於還沒滿30歲的人是寬容的。
(C) Most twentysomethings do not know what they want.	(C) 大多數的20幾歲的人不知道他們想要什麼。
(D) The best job has already been taken by others.	**(D) 最佳的工作已經都被其他人占據了。**

174. The word "**disoriented**" in line 15, is closet in meaning to (A) certified (B) committed (C) designated **(D) directionless**	174. 在第15行的「失去方向感的」，意思最接近 (A) 被證明的、有保證的、公認的 (B) 忠誠的、堅定的 (C) 指定的、選定的 **(D) 沒有目標的、沒有方向的**
175. In which of the positions marked **(1)**, **(2)**, **(3)**, and **(4)** does the following sentence best belong? "**You are young, still trying to figure out what you want**" (A) (1) (B) (2) (C) (3) **(D) (4)**	175. 以下這個句子最適合放在文中標記**(1)**, **(2)**, **(3)**, **(4)**的哪個位置? 「你還年輕，仍試圖了解你想要什麼。」 (A) (1) (B) (2) (C) (3) **(D) (4)**

解析

・ **第173題**，文章中沒有提到這方面的資訊，故答案為**選項D**。
・ **第174題**，disoriented = **directionless**，故答案為**選項D**。
・ **第175題**，插入句最適合放在most interviewers can tolerate that and the job hop.後，**(4)**，故答案為**選項D**。

Proposal

Dear Manager,

I've drafted the proposal for the EuroStar. Participants will be required to wear a mask on the train to sell products, so they cannot rely on their appearance to **sway** the decision of the passengers. It will be more intriguing during the Halloween time, and it will be fairer to someone who is not naturally good-looking. The person who sells the most during the 2.5 hours period on the train will be the winner. What do you think of this proposal? Please let me know if there's something that needs to be modified.... Thanks.

Sincerely,
Event planner, Cindy

親愛的經理

我已經起草了歐洲之星的企劃。參加者必須要戴上面罩並於列車上銷售東西，所以他們不能靠他們的外表來動搖乘客們的決定。在萬聖節期間，這更令人感到有興致了，而且對於那些不是與生俱來就長相佼好的人來說，這會比較公平。在列車上運行的2.5個小時期間銷售最多的人將會是贏家。你認為這個企劃如何呢?讓我知道如果有些是需要修改的地方...謝謝。

活動企劃者，辛蒂 上

Dear Cindy,

(1) ABC Company did the same thing last year, and it seems that you didn't do the homework. I highly recommend that you to go to the storage room and get the copy of all our rivals' event plans from the past ten years, and study those files before you do the proposal in the future. **(2)** I will have your colleague Lucy to handle the event planning this year. **(3)** She seems well-prepared and knows what she is doing. **(4)** If you still have any questions, you can consult her and other colleagues as well. I won't be in the office for the following two weeks. I will be in Paris to have three meetings with Italian clients. That's all.

Mary Wang

親愛的辛蒂

ABC公司在去年就做過了相同的東西,似乎你並沒有做功課。我極度建議你去儲藏室裡,去拿過去十年來我們所有對手的計畫,然後在你未來提企劃之前先行研讀。我將安排你的同事露西來處理今年的活動計畫。她似乎都準備完善且知道她自己在做些什麼。我在接下來的兩週都不會進公司。我在巴黎有與義大利客戶的三個會議要開。就這樣。

瑪莉·王

Questions 176-180	
176. What is Not stated in the first letter? (A) Passengers have to sell items in less than 3 hours. (B) Passengers are asked to wear the mask. **(C) Cindy will choose the winner based on her preference.** (D) Cindy values fairness.	176. 關於第一封信,沒有提到什麼? (A) 乘客必須要在三小時內銷售物品。 (B) 乘客被要求要戴上面罩。 **(C) 辛蒂會根據她的偏好選擇獲勝者。** (D) 辛蒂重視公平性。

177. The word "**sway**" in paragraph1, line 3, is closet in meaning to (A) explain (B) organize (C) consider **(D) influence**	177. 在第一段第三行的「搖動、搖擺、歪、傾斜」，意思最接近 (A) 解釋 (B) 組織、安排 (C) 考慮 **(D) 影響**
178. In which of the positions marked **(1)**, **(2)**, **(3)**, and **(4)** does the following sentence best belong? "**ABC Company did the same thing last year, and it seems that you didn't do the homework.**" **(A) (1)** (B) (2) (C) (3) (D) (4)	178. 以下這個句子最適合放在文中標記**(1)**, **(2)**, **(3)**, **(4)**的哪個位置？ 　　「ABC公司在去年就做過了相同的東西，似乎你並沒有做功課。」 **(A) (1)** (B) (2) (C) (3) (D) (4)
179. What can be inferred about Lucy? (A) She gets the copy of the rival company (B) She has been eyeing for the event planning for months. **(C) She is the subordinate of Mary** (D) She will be in Europe for a few weeks.	179. 關於露西的部分可以推測出什麼？ (A) 她拿到對手公司的複本。 (B) 她著眼於公司的活動規劃有數個月了。 **(C) 她是瑪莉的下屬。** (D) 她將會於接下來的幾週待在歐洲。

模擬試題（一）

模擬試題（二）

模擬試題（三）

模擬試題（四）

模擬試題（五）

180. Where can Cindy get the copy of rivals' event plans? (A) in the office (B) on the desk of Mary (C) in the conference room **(D) in the storage room**	180. 辛蒂可以於何處取得對手的活動計畫? (A) 在辦公室裡 (B) 在瑪莉的辦公桌上 (C) 在會議室裡 **(D) 在儲藏室裡**

 解析

· **第176題**，Cindy並不能根據自己的偏好選勝出者，故答案為**選項C**。
· **第177題**，sway = **influence**，故答案為**選項D**。
· **第178題**，這題最適合放置在句首 **(1)**，故答案為**選項A**。
· **第179題**，Lucy是Mary的下屬，故答案為**選項C**。
· **第180題**，其實是在storage room，故答案為**選項D**。

Dear Jane,

Really sorry for the delay for the mail, but there seems to be a conflicting schedule in the photoshoot of the wedding and the event itself. Plus, according to your schedule, the photographer cannot do the photograph. He will be in Europe working with Best Magazine for the fashion shoot. And I don't know how you are going to respond to our client that their favorite photographer cannot do their wedding photograph. It's not that they are going to remarry for each other. Perhaps I should have assigned the assignment to someone more experienced. I totally overestimate your ability and let you be in charge of so many things. Therefore, I am **demoting** you to an assistant, and you now report to our new hire, Candy.

Branch manager

模擬試題（一）

模擬試題（一）

模擬試題（二）

模擬試題（三）

模擬試題（四）

模擬試題（五）

親愛的簡

對於郵件的延遲感到很抱歉，但是似乎在婚宴的拍攝上和活動本身有時程上的衝突在。再說，根據你的時程，攝影師無法進行拍攝。她會在歐洲替倍斯特雜誌進行時尚拍攝。而且，我不知道你要如何跟客戶回應說，他們最喜愛的攝影師無法替他們進行婚宴拍攝。又不是說他們會跟彼此再結一次婚。或許我早該將任務指派給更具經驗的人。我全然高估了你的能力，以及讓你控管這麼多事情。因此，我會將你降為助理，然後你現在起要向我們新聘的職員辛蒂彙報。

分公司經理

Dear manager,

I'm so sorry. I typed it wrong. **(1)** My bad. The dates of the shooting, so it will be fine. The photographer can still do the wedding photos. I'm dying to see how their wedding pics on the spot. **(2)** As for the demotion, could you please take it back... I would really appreciate it and I promise I will be more attentive and meticulous. It's just the job has been really stressful for the past few weeks. I promise it won't happen again. Totally an unrelated topic, I have contacted the principal of Best Elite Primary School. **(3) Your kids are in.** The school is more than happy to have your kids to study there. **(4)** If there is something that you would like me to do please let me know... Thanks...

Wedding editor

親愛的經理

我感到很抱歉。拍攝的日期我打錯了。這是我的錯。所以婚宴拍攝會沒有問題的。攝影師仍可以進行婚宴拍攝。我等不及想要在現場看他們的婚宴照片了。至於降職的事情，我希望你能夠收回成命...我會很感激的，而且我承諾我會更專注在工作上且行事更小心翼翼。只是過去幾週以來真的壓力太過大了。我承諾不會再發生這樣的事情了。另一個全然無關的話題，我已經跟倍斯特菁英小學聯繫上了。你的小孩錄取了。學校很樂於見到您的小孩能入學就讀。如果還有些什麼是你想要做的，請讓我知道...謝謝...。

婚宴編輯

Questions 181-185	
181. Where will the photographer be working at? **(A) Europe** (B) North America (C) South America (D) Asia	181. 攝影師將會於何處進行拍攝？ **(A) 歐洲** (B) 北美洲 (C) 南美洲 (D) 亞洲
182. What can be inferred about Candy? (A) Her ability has been overestimated. (B) She will be the assistant. (C) She will be the superior of the branch manager **(D) She is new to the company.**	182. 可以推測出辛蒂的什麼？ (A) 她的能力已經被高估。 (B) 她將會是助理。 (C) 她是分公司經理的上司。 **(D) 她是公司新進人員。**
183. The word "**demoting**" in paragraph1, line 9, is closet in meaning to **(A) degrading** (B) managing (C) promoting (D) delaying	183. 在第一段第9行的「使降級、降職」，意思最接近 **(A) 使降級、降低品格的** (B) 設法、經營 (C) 晉升、升級、促進 (D) 拖延
184. What is mentioned in the second letter? **(A) The wedding editor has the association with the principal.** (B) The job is too demanding for Candy. (C) The cameraman cannot do the photoshoot. (D) The manager doesn't want the kid in the first place.	184. 關於第二封信的部分提到了什麼？ **(A) 婚宴編輯與校長有些關係。** (B) 這份工作對於Candy來說太吃力。 (C) 攝影師無法進行拍攝。 (D) 經理起初不想要有孩子。

185. In which of the positions marked **(1)**, **(2)**, **(3)**, and **(4)** does the following sentence best belong? "**Your kids are in.**" (A) (1) (B) (2) **(C) (3)** (D) (4)	185. 以下這個句子最適合放在文中標記**(1)**, **(2)**, **(3)**, **(4)**的哪個位置？ 「你的小孩錄取了。」 (A) (1) (B) (2) **(C) (3)** (D) (4)

解析

- **第181題**，這題很明顯是歐洲，故答案為**選項A**。
- **第182題**，Candy是公司新招募的員工，故答案為**選項D**。
- **第183題**，demoting = **degrading**，故答案為**選項A**。
- **第184題**，這題可以稍微思考下，編輯能幫助主管的小孩進菁英學校，可能編輯本身跟校長有些關係，故答案為**選項A**。
- **第185題**，這題最適合放置在Totally an unrelated topic, I have contacted the principal of Best Elite Primary School.後，**(3)**，故答案為**選項C**。

Dear all,

The following is the suggested reading list for your summer vacation. Our first two weeks in the next semester, we will be discussing all mentioned books. Students enrolled in this course will be asked to write the book report for at least three books. For those who are avid readers or who do not have any plan during the summer, you can do the writing beforehand. You should write at least 1000 words for each report. Finally, for those who would like to get a higher grade for the first assignment, you are required to read through all and write no fewer than four book reports.

Dean

List of BOOKS

A *Rich Dad Poor Dad*
B *The Millionaire Next Door*
C *Millionaire Teacher*
D *The Richest Man in Babylon*
E *Millionaire Success Habits*
F *The Millionaire Fastlane*
G *Secrets of the Millionaire Mind*

給所有人

以下是你們暑假的推薦閱讀書單。在下學期的首兩週，我們會討論附檔列出的所有書籍，而所有選修這門課的學生要撰寫至少三本書的書籍報告。對於那些是閱讀狂熱的讀者或是那些在暑假期間沒有任何計畫者，你可以事先開始寫報告。對於每個報告，你至少應該要寫1000字。最後，對於那些想要在第一個功課獲得更高分數者，你必須要讀完所有書籍且撰寫不少於四本書的書評。

院長

書籍列表

A 《窮爸爸富爸爸》
B 《原來有錢人都這麼做》
C 《我用死薪水輕鬆理財賺千萬》
D 《巴比倫最富有的人》
E 《百萬成功習慣》
F 《財富快車道》
G 《有錢人跟你想的不一樣》

Writing contest

Enclosed is the English Writing Contest that is scheduled to take place after the mid-term. You can see the information on the poster yourself.

Poster

2020 English Writing Contest by Best Elite University

Requirements
4. Business majors
5. Sophomore
6. Have not received any school scholarship

Winning Prizes

Title	Money
The first place	US 5,000 dollars
Runner up	US 3,000 dollars
The third place	US 1,000 dollars

Note:
1. Students wanting to attend the contest are required to use the apps and make an on-line registration before October.

寫作比賽

檢附的是英文寫作比賽，預定於在期中後舉行。你可以看自己在海報上看到資訊。

海報

2020年英文寫作比賽 由倍斯特菁英大學舉辦

要求
1. 商學院主修
2. 大二
3. 尚未獲得任何學校的獎學金

獎項

頭銜	金額
第一名	5,000 美元
第二名	3,000美元
第三名	1,000美元

註:
1. 想要參加這項比賽的學生都必須要在10月前使用apps並線上註冊登記。

Dear all,

I'm so sorry for having emailed you guys the poster from last year. My bad. Enclosed is the update. Check out the information.

2021 English Writing Contest by Best Elite University

Requirements
4. Students in all departments
5. Junior and senior
6. Have not received any school scholarship

Winning Prizes

title	money
The first place	US 9,000 dollars
Runner up	US 6,000 dollars
The third place	US 3,000 dollars

Note:

1. Students wanting to attend the contest are required to use the apps and make an on-line registration before October.
2. Students getting the first place will participate in the National English Writing Contest, and the winner will be rewarded a signed contract with one of the top cellphone companies in the world.

給所有人

我感到很抱歉。我的錯。我寄成了去年的海報了。附檔是更新版的。你們可以自己看下。

2021 English Writing Contest by Best Elite University

要求
1. 所有系所的學生
2. 大三和大肆學生
3. 尚未得過任何學校獎學金的學生

Winning Prizes

頭銜	金額
第一名	9,000 美元
第二名	6,000 美元
第三名	3,000 美元

Note:
1. 想要參加這項比賽的學生都必須要在10月前使用apps並線上註冊登記。
2. 得到第一名的學生要參加國家英文寫作比賽,而且獲獎者會得到世界上其中一家頂尖的手機公司的簽署合約。

Questions 186-190

186. What is enclosed with the letter? **(A) the information about the recommended readings** (B) the information about students (C) the information about the money (D) the information about the contest	186. 信件附了什麼? **(A) 關於推薦書籍的資訊** (B) 關於學生的資訊 (C) 關於金錢的資訊 (D) 關於比賽的資訊

187. What does the dean want the students to do during the summer vacation? (A) fritter away the money (B) seize the time to make money **(C) seize the time to read some books** (D) fritter away the time	187. 在暑假期間，院長希望學生們做些什麼？ (A) 浪費金錢 (B) 把握時間賺錢 **(C) 把握時間閱讀一些書籍** (D) 浪費時間
188. What will the runner up of the 2020 be getting? (A) US 5,000 (B) US 3,000 (C) US 1,000 **(D) NT 90,000**	188. 2020年比賽第二名會獲得什麼？ (A) US 5,000 (B) US 3,000 (C) US 1,000 **(D) NT 90,000**
189. What will the runner up of the 2021 be getting? (A) NT 6,000 **(B) NT 180,000** (C) NT 3,000 (D) NT 90,000	189. 2021年比賽第二名會獲得什麼？ (A) NT 6,000 **(B) NT 180,000** (C) NT 3,000 (D) NT 90,000
190. What will the first place be getting in addition to the money? (A) a singing contract (B) a termination **(C) a written contract** (D) a cellphone user manual	190. 除了金錢之外，第一名會獲得什麼？ (A) 一份歌唱合約 (B) 一份中止聲明 **(C) 一份書面合同** (D) 一份手機的使用手冊

解析

· **第186題**，這題也很明顯是關於推薦書籍，故答案為**選項A**。
· **第187題**，答案很明顯是C抓緊時間閱讀，故答案為**選項C**。
· **第188題**，2020年的表格中第二名會獲得台幣九萬元，故答案為**選項D**。
· **第189題**，根據換算後是18萬元台幣，故答案為**選項B**。
· **第190題**，這題要細心些，第二名拿到的是written contract，故答案為**選項C**。

This place used to be immune from the ravage of elephants, but now with the habitat changes and many other things, elephants are the frequent visitors to the farmland. The financial loss is enormous. As we all know that local residents rely heavily on the sales of crops to live, coming up with the solution is urgent.

Enclosed is the estimated **monetary** loss for fruits and vegetables. You guys should take a look.

Fruits and vegetables	Estimated loss
Bananas	US 500,000 dollars
Mangos	US 1000,000 dollars
Watermelons	US 700,000 dollars
Durians	Zero
Cabbages	US 600,000 dollars

這個地方過去曾免於受到大象的蹂躪，但是隨著棲地的改變和許多其他事情，大象是這個農地頻繁到訪的生物。財務損失是龐大的。據我們所知，當地居民高度仰賴農作物的銷售維生，想出解決之道是迫切的。檢附的是估計的蔬果損失金額。你們應該看下。

水果和蔬菜	預估的損失
香蕉	五十萬美元
芒果	一百萬美元
西瓜	七十萬美元
榴槤	零元
高麗菜	六十萬美元

Reply

I know some of you might wonder do elephants consume watermelons? Perhaps some elephants do because watermelons contain sugary juice that can make them happy. The point is the place where they go, their powerful feet **crumble** these profitable crops. And as to those mangos, elephants are able to grab them just like they take away those bananas from your hands? I bet some of you haven't been to the camp to witness the feeding of elephants. However, local residents still have durians for sell. Perhaps their outer appearance protects them from getting harmed by a herd of elephants. Have you ever gotten hit by those durians? I bet the outer skin of elephants, even though it is strong and solid, cannot withstand those durians falling from the trees and hitting their body.

The following is the suggested methods for us to consider. Since we are just a small town, we cannot afford to spend a great deal of money on this. Even though we eventually get the fund from the city council, the money is still short for a project that is going to cost more than US 40,000 dollars.

Suggested methods	
Items	Cost
1. Erect stone walls	US 50,000,000 dollars
2. Direct elephants to wild lands	US 50,000 dollars
3. Build a circus	US 8,000,000 dollars
4. Evacuate for a while	Zero
5. Transport elephants to another continent	US 600,000 dollars

回覆

我知道你們有些人可能會想，為什麼大象要攝食西瓜呢?或許有些大象會吃，因為西瓜果汁含有糖分，這能讓牠們感到快樂。重點是他們所到之處，牠們強而有力的腳壓碎這些有利可圖的經濟作物。至於那些芒果，牠們能夠攫住芒果，就像牠們從你手中取走那些香蕉一樣。我敢打賭你們有些人未曾到露營區目睹大象餵食。然而，當地居民仍有榴槤可以用來賣售。或許榴槤的外層能保護其免於被象群所傷。你曾有過被那些榴槤擊中的經驗嗎?我敢打賭，儘管大象的外皮層很強健且碩，無法承受那些榴槤從樹而降並擊中牠們的身體。

以下是我們可供考量的建議方法。既然我們是個小鎮，我們無法在這上頭負擔起大量的金錢花費。儘管我們最終會從市議會中獲得資助，這項計畫的金錢仍舊短少，且將會需要超過4萬美元的花費。

建議方法	
項目	花費
1. 建造石牆	五千萬美元
2. 導引大象到野地	五萬美元
3. 建造一個馬戲團	八百萬美元
4. 暫時撤離	零
5. 將大象運送到另一個地方	六十萬美元

Questions 191-195

191. What is enclosed with the letter? (A) the financial loss of losing star elephants (B) the reduction in profits in several fruits and vegetables **(C) the list of crops damaged by the elephants** (D) the profits brought by the elephants	191. 信件附了什麼？ (A) 損失明星大象的財政損失 (B) 幾個水果和蔬菜的獲利下降 **(C) 被大象所損害的作物列表** (D) 由大象所帶來的利益
192. The word "**monetary**" in paragraph1, line 6, is closet in meaning to **(A) pecuniary** (B) mortgaged (C) tremendous (D) universal	192. 在第一段第6行的「金融的、財政的、貨幣的、幣制的」，意思最接近 **(A) 金錢的、錢財方面的** (B) 抵押的 (C) 巨大的、極大的、驚人的 (D) 普遍的、一般的、眾所周知的
193. The word "**crumble**" in paragraph2, line 4, is closet in meaning to (A) animate (B) standardize **(C) disintegrate** (D) transform	193. 在第2段第4行的「弄碎、摧毀、破壞」，意思最接近 (A) 賦予生命、使有生命、使活潑 (B) 使合標準、使統一 **(C) 使碎裂、使瓦解、使崩潰** (D) 使改變、使改觀、將......改成
194. What is Not stated about the reply? (A) Some elephants have a penchant for watermelons. **(B) Mangos are ignored by the elephants.** (C) Durians have the protection on the outside. (D) Elephants cannot stand those durians.	194. 關於回覆沒有提到什麼？ (A) 有些大象對於西瓜有偏好。 **(B) 芒果被大象忽略。** (C) 榴槤外頭有保護在。 (D) 大象無法忍受榴槤。

195. Which of the following suggested method costs the least money? (A) Item 1 (B) Item 2 (C) Item 3 **(D) Item 4**	195. 下列哪項建議的方法花費最少錢? (A) Item 1 (B) Item 2 (C) Item 3 **(D) Item 4**

解析

- **第191題**,這類的問法的難度都不高,看附件是什麼即可,故答案為**選項 C**。
- **第192題**,monetary = **pecuniary**,故答案為**選項A**。
- **第193題**,crumble = **disintegrate**,故答案為**選項C**。
- **第194題**,Mangos沒有被ignored,故答案為**選項B**。
- **第195題**,根據圖表花費最少的是item 4,故答案為**選項D**。

Best Acting Agency for Recruitment
We would like to hire several candidates for the Halloween shoot, and requirements are as follows.
a. Candidates should be taller than 180 cm b. With the experience of acting before c. Submit the recording of self-introduction at least 10 minutes d. Do not have the criminal record

倍斯特演藝經紀公司的招募
在萬聖節的拍攝,我們想要聘僱幾位候選人,要求如下。 a. 候選人要高於180公分 b. 先前有演戲經驗 c. 遞交至少10分鐘的自我介紹視頻 d. 未曾有犯罪紀錄

Dear recruitment team,

This is Jason Lin. I went to the interview at your agency two years ago, but didn't get chosen. This year, I'm well-prepared. I even got signed by a modeling agency right after getting turned down. I've enclosed several stunning pics of me at the English Castle, where I was asked to portray a guy in a thriller, quite scary. Hope that you guys will not be scared by these pics. Furthermore, I also had the commercial for Bestland in which I **impersonated** the ghost at a haunted house. Finally, attached please also find my recording of the self-introduction and a few recommendation letters from previous superiors. Truly hope that I have the chance to work with you in the shoot.

Jason Lin

親愛的招募團隊

我是傑森·林。兩年前，我曾到你們的機構面試過，但是並未獲得錄用。今年，我充分準備了。在被你們拒絕後，我甚至跟一間模特兒公司簽約了。我已經檢附了幾張驚豔的照片，是我在英國城堡中所拍攝的，在那裡我在驚悚片中被要求要扮演一個男子，相當可怕。希望你們沒有被這些照片驚嚇到。此外，我也有於倍斯特樂園的商業廣告拍攝，我在鬼屋中扮演一隻鬼。最後是我的自我介紹視頻和幾個我先前工作過的幾位上司的推薦信。真心希望我能有參與你們拍攝的機會。

傑森·林

Dear Jason,

We have seen your portfolio, and we love it. You seem well-prepared. Glad that you didn't quit because of the first "no", and we admire your enthusiasm and continued trying. The rejection may sting, but it is just a part of the process. Along the way, you have gradually built the brand of yours by having the commercial and other things. Since you have passed the preliminary screening with work experience, we would like you to participate in our second interview at studio 999. Make sure you bring your portfolio with you next Monday at 6 p.m. You might be asked to test your ability to perform on stage... That's all.

HR Department

親愛的傑森

我們已經看過了您的作品集，且我們很喜愛。你似乎是充分準備的。很高興你並未因第一次的拒絕就放棄了，且我們對於你的熱忱和持續的嘗試感到欽佩。拒絕可能是螯咬般的痛，但是這僅是過程中的一部分。過程中，你已經逐步地建造了你自己的品牌，藉由有了商業廣告的拍攝和其他東西。既然你已經因為有了工作經驗而通過了初步的篩選，我們想要邀請你來參加在工作室999的第二次面試。確保您攜帶你的作品集，於下個星期一下午六點鐘到此。你可能會被要求要在舞台上受測你的表演能力...就這樣囉。

人事部門

Questions 196-200	
196. From the recruitment, what is required to bring during the interview? (A) The criminal record (B) the height **(C) the recording** (D) the acting experience	196. 從招聘可以看出在面試期間要準備什麼? (A) 犯罪紀錄 (B) 高度 **(C) 錄製的視頻** (D) 表演經驗
197. What is Not indicated about Jason Lin? (A) He got the contract from a modeling agency. (B) He did an acting in a thriller. (C) He wants this opportunity badly. **(D) He rejected the offer from Bestland.**	197. 關於Jason Lin沒有提到什麼? (A) 他從模特兒經紀公司獲得合約。 (B) 他曾於驚悚片中演戲過 (C) 他非常想要此次的機會。 **(D) 他拒絕了倍斯特樂園的工作機會。**
198. The word "**impersonated**" in paragraph2, line 6, is closet in meaning to (A) animated (B) implemented **(C) portrayed** (D) transformed	198. 在第2段第6行的「履行、執行」，意思最接近 (A) 賦予生命、使有生命、使活潑 (B) 使合標準、使統一 **(C) 使碎裂、使瓦解、使崩潰** (D) 使改變、使改觀、將......改成
199. What is Not stated in the reply? (A) Jason has passed the first screening. (B) Jason is persistent. (C) Jason has to be there on time at 6 p.m. **(D) Jason have passed the second interview.**	199. 關於回覆，沒有提到什麼? (A) 傑森已經通過了首次的初選。 (B) 傑森是堅持不懈的。 (C) 傑森必須於下午六點準時到那裡。 **(D) 傑森已經通過了第二次的面試。**

| 200. What industry is Jason planning to dabble and build a career?

(A) Music
(B) Film
(C) Advertising
(D) Modeling industry | 200. 傑森正計畫要涉獵哪個產業並且以此發展職涯呢?

(A) 音樂
(B) 電影
(C) 廣告
(D) 模特兒產業 |

解析

· **第196題**,面試時需要攜帶的是**recording**,故答案為**選項C**。
· **第197題**,Jason曾於倍斯特樂園進行廣告拍攝,所以敘述不符,故答案為**選項D**。
· **第198題**,impersonated = **portrayed**,故答案為**選項C**。
· **第199題**,根據段落訊息,他僅通過初試,故答案為**選項D**。
· **第200題**,這題很明顯是電影產業,故答案為**選項B**。

Note

- 【Part 5】考生要注意一些「高階字彙」的搭配使用，有些極具鑑別度的試題，像是ｉｍａｇｅ和**authenticity**的出題都是必須要確實理解才能答對的。
- 【Part 6】考生要注意容易誤解短期工和全職聘任的部分，而這些也會連帶影響答插入句子題。另外也要注意高階副詞的搭配。
- 【Part 7】要注意細節性資訊的答題和表格題的出題，「同義轉換」的掌握也會影響答這些題目。

模擬試題（二）

READING TEST

In this section, you must demonstrate your ability to read and comprehend English. You will be given a variety of texts and asked to answer questions about these texts. This section is divided into three parts and will take 75 minutes to complete.

Do not mark the answers in your test book. Use the answer sheet that is separately.

PART 5

Directions: In each question, you will be asked to review a statement that is missing a word or phrase. Four answer choices will be provided for each statement. Select the best answer and mark the corresponding letter (A), (B), (C), or (D) on the answer sheet.

101. Because of multiple youtubers' remarks about the new product, some consumers remain -------, thinking that they have to wait until the doubt is cleared up.

(A) noticeable

(B) customizable

(C) hesitant

(D) negotiable

102. Shoppers cannot let go of the snide comments made by bloggers, so they have made up their minds to ------- a certain channel.

(A) unauthorize

(B) unsubscribe

(C) describe

(D) prescribe

103. Although the ------- of the masseur has been widely known in the neighborhood, tourists traveling here are still kept in the dark.
(A) valor
(B) fame
(C) reputation
(D) notoriety

104. Due to a lack of evidence and recordings at the scene, the ------- of the bad service made by the bank clerk cannot be verified.
(A) deviation
(B) estimation
(C) authenticity
(D) disappearance

105. Despite the fact that the CFO of the Best Consulting firm has done numerous buy-ins of the stocks before, he still cannot say for sure whether the bet can truly generate hefty -------.
(A) results
(B) fluctuations
(C) evaluations
(D) profits

106. A(n) ------- employee is like a loose cannon, and can be quite detrimental to the work setting.
    (A) inconsistent
    (B) incremental
    (C) disgruntled
    (D) marketable

107. ------- on the shelves can be a downside for anyone walking in or clients visiting the warehouse.
    (A) Disorganization
    (B) Reason
    (C) Priority
    (D) Sustainability

108. In the ------- of the 2009 financial crisis, numerous jobseekers experienced a shattered self-esteem and could not find the job for a few months.
    (A) serendipity
    (B) productivity
    (C) possibility
    (D) aftermath

109. Several start-ups can only afford a(n) ------- warehouse and have to cut expenses in other areas, such as hiring and office equipment.
    (A) biodegradable

(B) sizable

(C) undersized

(D) municipal

110. By ------- the prices, Best Cinema is finally able to outcompete other movie studios and gets the chance to work with several celebrities.

(A) refueling

(B) undercutting

(C) heightening

(D) continuing

111. ------- bonuses are needed in case the star employee wants to make a job hop and the company is not able to afford the loss.

(A) Celebration

(B) Retention

(C) Prevention

(D) Demotion

112. Situated in a secluded village where honey bees come to gather the honey near the river bank, Best Farm may be people's ------- of a stereotypical retreat.

(A) image

(B) disagreement

(C) investment

(D) appreciation

113. The winery in Germany has earned tons of ------- by tourists traveling very far from here.
(A) evaluations
(B) accolades
(C) functions
(D) descriptions

114. The ------- in the area is a sign that the land cannot be too profitable, so buyers usually have doubts and look other places.
(A) slimness
(B) dormancy
(C) productivity
(D) appropriation

115. ------- from the current circumstance, the animal doctor surmised that the wound of the koala could not be healed.
(A) To judge
(B) Judging
(C) Judged
(D) Being judged

116. Salespeople are known for their ability to sell, ------- editors are noted for their capability of editing articles.

(A) once

(B) when

(C) whereas

(D) because

117. ------- you get to know the product, the more you can say during the product launch on next Wednesday.

(A) Most

(B) More

(C) The more

(D) The most

118. Software developers are getting ------- impatient with the questioning by salespeople, so the tension is a little high.

(A) increasing

(B) increase

(C) increasingly

(D) increased

119. ------- the company cannot afford to lose the CFO at the moment, the CEO finally agrees to give him a 10% raise.

(A) Once

(B) Because

(C) If

(D) Although

120. The long-awaited promotion does not make the manager -----
-- because the responsibility is greater than before.
(A) happy
(B) more happier
(C) most happiest
(D) be happy

121. The lockdown of the city for a month has led to zero
productivity and serenity of the street ------- are not usually
seen in years.
(A) where
(B) who
(C) whom
(D) that

122. During the time of the outbreak of COVID-19 virus, bad things,
------- layoffs and plant closure have become a regular scene.
(A) like
(B) for example
(C) included
(D) such as

123. Singers and marine mammals ------- to make the wedding
more memorable and diverse, and the newlywed seems
happy.
(A) recruit

(B) are recruited

(C) recruiting

(D) recruited

124. Kitchen orders are usually enormous during the holiday, but with the invasion of the alien species, they are not as ------- as it used to be.

(A) larged

(B) largest

(C) large

(D) the largest

125. Our fruits and vegetables are under such an extensive care that they are put in an artificial setting ------- temperatures are rigorously monitored.

(A) where

(B) which

(C) when

(D) whose

126. ------- most cellphone giants, which outsource software components to other low-cost countries, Best Cellphone is doing quite the opposite.

(A) If

(B) Like

(C) Unlike

(D) Once

127. A few of the candidates we interviewed acknowledged that they ------- at least 5 job hops before finding the right one.
(A) have
(B) has had
(C) had had
(D) had

128. ------- male dates vary considerably in different occupations, your intuition and criteria for a mate can narrow candidates down to the most suitable one.
(A) Because
(B) If
(C) Once
(D) Even though

129. Best Chocolate Plant's remarkable ------- in profits has allured multiple overseas investors and sponsors.
(A) grow
(B) growth
(C) grew
(D) grown

130. ------- the productivity of Best Automobile drops 10%, the overall revenue will decrease at least 50 million dollars.

(A) Once

(B) If

(C) Although

(D) Because

PART 6

Directions: In this part, you will be asked to read four English texts. Each text is missing a word, phrase, or sentence. Select the answer choice that correctly completes the text and mark the corresponding letter (A), (B), (C), or (D) on the answer sheet.

Questions 131-134

A month has passed since the firm made the purchase of the organic farm in August. The price has been much lower than expected. The board is pleased with the first drastic measure done by the CEO, and can't wait to see **131.-------** of the farm in the future. The CEO then called an urgent meeting on Saturday, so all executives got called back during the holiday with a somewhat bad mood. They have to fire professional farmers and organic farmers for the first few months. They will be working **132.-------**. **133.-------** and handle the farm business after those part-time farmers leave the company. The HR Department will be in charge of the hiring and report only to the CEO. Organic farmers with years of experiences will be paid **134.-------**, according to the report.

131. (A) seduction

(B) recognition

(C) prosperity

(D) discovery

132. (A) temporarily

(B) inextricably

(C) incongruously

(D) continuously

133. (A) The policemen will visit the office often

(B) Only professional farmers will stay on the job

(C) The company will also hire full-time employees who can learn from those farmers

(D) Farm owners will discipline those farmers to make them qualify for the job

134. (A) consistently

(B) unilaterally

(C) handsomely

(D) artificially

Questions 135-138

Finally, the HR Department selected 10 finalists and they were going to present their already successful farm business with the CEO. The presentation **135.-------** to be held in the middle of

September was postponed due to other reasons. After the meeting in October, the CEO made the decision of hiring 5 farmers, **136.-------** different parts of the wild farm and organic farm. They are in charge, too. They were led to the conference room and signed a three-month **137.-------** . **138.-------.** The CEO has also hired 100 blue collar workers to do the heavy work and they have to obey the order given by the five farmers.

135. (A) meticulously researched
    (B) originally scheduled
    (C) legally considered
    (D) poignantly captured

136. (A) bristle with
    (B) superior to
    (C) responsible for
    (D) curious about

137. (A) contact
    (B) contract
    (C) proceedings
    (D) scenario

138. (A) Not all finalists get selected.
(B) The presentation makes some farmers too nervous to say something.

(C) The government poaches those farmers before they sign anything.

(D) They feel so honored and cannot wait for their start date.

Questions 139-142

A month has passed, and industrious workers under the **139.-------** of the professional farmers really have turned the farm into a serious business. The blueberry is **140.-------** tasty, from the account of the workers. And like those blue berries, other vegetables are **141.-------** by workers and sent to the zoo. Bears can now have baskets of fresh berries to eat and they seem satisfied. Visitors can also go to the farm and gather the berries for their favorite bears. They are not just visiting the zoo, but form the bond with these creatures. The company also has lessened the workload and reduced the manpower. It's a win-win. **142.-------** For those who have done it for a thousand times, they will be given a free ticket for a year.

139. (A) inspiration
    (B) cooperation
    (C) interpretation
    (D) guideline

140. (A) objectively
    (B) exceedingly
    (C) uncomfortably

(D) scrupulously

141. (A) impaired
    (B) transferred
    (C) orchestrated
    (D) plucked

142. (A) If the bear doesn't like the berry, the visitor will not be rewarded.
    (B) The visitor will be charged the maintenance fee in the organic farm.
    (C) The firm will also give visitors a certificate, if they hand-deliver more than a hundred baskets for the animal of their choice.
    (D) Robots are placed in the organic farm to assist children plucking fruits.

Questions 143-146

The news has become widespread, and multiple parents are eager to do this with their kids during the holiday. They can enjoy the family time in both the farm and the zoo, quite serene and pleasant. The CEO has got **143.-------** from the board, and they are planning to add something innovative, too. Visitors to the zoo can also **144.-------** corns or pluck bananas. Those can be used to feed animals, such as monkeys and elephants. They don't have to go to Thailand to do that, and it is actually a good **145.-------** for the firm. With the upload of the videos of those kids handing bananas to elephants, the zoo is more crowded than before. Videos even go **146.**------- among school children, and the zoo has decided to hold a contest.

143. (A) abdication
     (B) applause
     (C) shortcomings
     (D) slippage

144. (A) amplify
     (B) collect
     (C) rebuild
     (D) transform

145. (A) function
     (B) insurance
     (C) development
     (D) advertisement

146. (A) efficient
     (B) affectless
     (C) viral
     (D) analyzable

PART 7

Directions: In this part, you will be asked to read several texts, such as advertisements, articles, instant messages, or examples of business correspondence. Each is followed by several questions. Select the best answer and mark the corresponding letter (A), (B), (C), (D) on your answer sheet.

Question 147

Best Burger

	Sizes/types	Price	Information
French Fries	Small	US 2 dollars	
	Large	US 4 dollars	
Onion Rings	Small	US 3 dollars	
	Large	US 6 dollars	
Burgers	Chinese Mushroom	US 12 dollars	
	Bacon	US 12 dollars	
	Hawaiian	US 14 dollars	
	Double Cheese	US 16 dollars	
	Superb Beef	US 20 dollars	
Drinks	Coke	US 4 dollars	Free refill
	Wine	US 8 dollars	Adults only

※ **TAX**: 10%，taxes should be included in the overall cost.

147. What is **NOT** stated about Best Burger?

   (A) A Hawaiian Burger actually costs customers 15.4 dollars.

   (B) Large Fries indeed cost visitors 4.4 dollars.

(C) People spending 4.4 dollars on Coke get to drink more than one.

(D) Teenagers are able to buy the wine for 8.8 dollars or less.

Question 148

Mary 2:20 p.m.
Hi... Best Seafood Restaurant, thanks again for the order for giant lobsters. Those lobsters will be shipped next week, probably Wednesday...

Jennifer 2:23 p.m.
Is it possible that the shipment arrives earlier than Wednesday... there are just so many tourists during the holiday... and we just cannot use some cheap fish to replace the giant lobsters...

Mary 2:25 p.m.
Would you like to order some rare king crabs and other squids? That surely can boost your restaurant's reputation... If you are ordering those, I think our delivery guy can do the delivery on Monday...

Jennifer 2:27 p.m.
How much? I should probably consult with our boss and chefs before making a decision...

Mary 2:29 p.m.
Ok just let me know as quickly as possible...

148. At 2:25 p.m. why does Mary mention about some rare king crabs and other squids?

(A) She wants to exploit the customer.

(B) She wants the year-end bonuses.

(C) She doesn't have enough lobsters in the warehouse.

(D) Both parties can be satisfied.

Questions 149-152

Best International Balloon Festival

This year Best Transportation is doing something innovative and unprecedented. Tourists choosing the Luxury-typed are able to see the view of the Firefly Valley and **serene** Eyes of the Lake. The valley is quite a view during the night that makes our tickets already sold out. It's so romantic and a great way to propose. If you would like to propose during the air-travel, pick our Type E service. Our crew can even specifically put what you would like to say to your love one through air writing. And it's free. Furthermore, we're adding the Type F. This means 50% of the fee will be donated to the charity under your name and of course it can be deducted in your tax next year. Finally, we have the government-sponsored balloon for the elderly, people older than 65, but under one condition, you don't have any chronic illness.

	Time	Price	Descriptions
Type A (Regular)	20 minutes	US 30 dollars	assigned
Type B (Regular)	30 minutes	US 50 dollars	
Type C (Luxury)	2 hours	US 200 dollars	specifically-tailored
Type D (Luxury)	120 minutes	US 300 dollars	
Type E (Luxury)	3 hours	US 1000 dollars	
Type F (Charity)	1/4 hours	US 30 dollars	assigned

153

149. The word "**serene**" in the advertisement, line 3, is closet in meaning to

   (A) sedative

   (B) severe

   (C) tranquil

   (D) serendipitous

150. What is the perfect type for the sweethearts that favor air writing?

   (A) Type B

   (B) Type C

   (C) Type D

   (D) Type E

151. What is True about the Balloon Festival?

   (A) Type A is the cheapest.

   (B) Type C takes longer than Type D.

   (C) Type D is related to tax exemption.

   (D) A tourist who is over 70 and has a high blood pressure cannot use Type G.

152. What is the ideal type for a mother of three who has a budget of around US 150?

(A) Type A
(B) Type B
(C) Type D
(D) Type G

Questions 153-155

Dear manager,

Oh... that means he will be getting double payments from both companies... is that legal? How is he going to do the tax report? **(1)** Or are we paying him in cash, so no one will find out. **(2)** I'm completely shocked by this. So now my new role is to be a coffee clerk and I occasionally talk to him in the coffee shop during the night and get the information that's useful for us, right? **(3)** Does the coffee shop owner know about this? **(4)** But I just can't wait to try on my uniform and pretend to be the clerk... sitting in the office all day actually bores me... and I will record our conversation for further use...?

Mary, coffee clerk, starting from today

153. What is true about Bob?
    (A) He has a twofold income.
    (B) He doesn't know how to do the tax report.
    (C) He only accepts cash.
    (D) His new role is a coffee clerk.

154. What is **NOT** mentioned about the letter?

   (A) Mary doesn't know how to brew coffee.

   (B) Mary cannot stand the boredom.

   (C) Mary already gets the uniform.

   (D) Mary has to play a disguised role.

155. In which of the positions marked **(1)**, **(2)**, **(3)**, and **(4)** does the following sentence best belong?

   "**I don't know how to brew coffee and identify those beans.**"

   (A) (1)

   (B) (2)

   (C) (3)

   (D) (4)

Questions 156-159
Best Elite University

Our lab researchers have developed an incredible computer system that is quite similar to the sorting hat in the Harry Potter Series, but the difference is that it's not solely on the classification. It can even make a prediction of your accomplishment after you graduate from the university 5 years from now. The accuracy has astounded many scholars and educators, and it's true that academic success has nothing to do with the achievement outside the classroom setting.

Group	Yearly income
A	US 50,000 dollars or below
B	Around US 100,000 dollars
C	US 150,000 dollars
D	US 500,000 dollars
E	US 1,000,000 dollars
F	US 5,000,000 dollars or above

Note:

1. Most people fall directly under Group A (and that stays for the rest of their lives), and very few get the prediction in Group F.

2. The prediction of our super computer seems to coincide with the traditional Chinese forecast.

3. You have to get admitted in our school to be qualified to take the test. This requires courage and money. The fee of the test is US 50,000 dollars, and not every student can afford that plus the tuition. Furthermore, there are some people who are too timid to know the result, so they don't have the guts to face it. If you're suspicious of the test outcome, the redo fee requires US 110,000 dollars, which is more than twice the price of the initial cost.

156. What is **NOT** stated about the test?

(A) People need to have the courage to take the test.

(B) The test is not affordable for all students.

(C) Students can only take the test once in their lifetime.

(D) The test is able to make a prediction of a person's future achievement.

157. How much does it cost for the first attempt of the test?

    (A) US 50,000

    (B) US 110,000

    (C) US 150,000

    (D) US 100,000

158. Which of the following Group is what most people belong to?

    (A) B

    (B) D

    (C) F

    (D) A

159. Which of the following Group contains the least people in the population?

    (A) E

    (B) F

    (C) D

    (D) B

Questions 160-163

Best Pinball

The pinball game has been invented for centuries. In our Amusement Park, you will have a total novel experience with the game. See the huge waterslides over there and the labyrinth. You actually have to be the ball to play the game... and you will have no idea where you are going. You have to hit the red target among the fifty slides, so the chance is 1/50. The fee is US 5 for the first time player. Other fees are listed in the table. It's quite possible that people actually hit the jackpot at the first attempt. We have consolation prizes for everyone, and for those who hit the jackpot for the first time, we are giving them US 5,000 dollars. It's more like betting for money.

Number of playing	Cost
First time	5 dollars
Second	25 dollars
Third	125 dollars
Fourth	625 dollars
Fifth	3125 dollars
Sixth	15625 dollars
Seventh	78125 dollars
Eighth	390625 dollars

160. What is the probability of playing the game by using 15625 dollars?
    (A) 3/50
    (B) 1/25
    (C) 3/25
    (D) 6

161. What is the rate of winning for average players?
    (A) 8/50

(B) 1/10

(C) 2/50

(D) 1/50

162. How much does a guy have to spend in order to play the game the eighth time?

(A) 625

(B) 15,625

(C) 78,125

(D) 390,625

163. How can a person actually gain if he hits the jackpot for the first attempt?

(A) 4995

(B) 5000

(C) 5100

(D) 5005

Questions 164-166

Best Amusement Park is revising the policy of letting the customer refill the drink whether it is deliberately spilled or not. The effective date is next Monday. **(1)** That means parents should really keep a good eye on their kids. In addition, the haunted house will be adding more features. **(2)** You get to experience several real scenes in the ghost movies. It's going to be scarier than usual. **(3)** What's more, if you don't consider it horrific, you will get the refund, half the price of the ticket, but according to the staff, he says it won't, it is really scary, scary enough for you to pee your pants on the spot. **(4)** That surely is the overstatement for some people... and you have to try that to know if this is true.

164. In which of the positions marked **(1)**, **(2)**, **(3)**, and **(4)** does the following sentence best belong?

"**And he even makes a video warning people of preparing the diaper before entering the haunted house.**"

(A) (1)

(B) (2)

(C) (3)

(D) (4)

165. What is the article mainly about?

(A) watching ghost movies

(B) surveillance on children

(C) new announcements about the policy and features

(D) uploading an exaggerated video

166. What is stated about the haunted house?

(A) More features will be updated.

(B) People don't consider it scary.

(C) People urine at the scene.

(D) It uses knockoff props.

Questions 167-169

Best Cinema now wants to do the epic movie, so they are dying to find a great place to do the shoot. **(1)** Castle A is **enigmatic** and shady, but it's just weird in a way that the camera cannot get a clear shot. **(2)** Castle B really earns its name for a haunted house, but an incident at the castle the other day made the CEO question whether it is the ideal place for the movie. Castle C is not that appealing in the eyes of the editors, and the director doesn't like it. **(3)** This is about a team work, so they eventually turned down the offer given by the owner. Castle D is mysterious as well, but it needs a huge renovation. **(4)** And that will make the entire budget exceed the original estimated price. Using Castle D for the movie surely will make investors unhappy. So the search continues.

167. What is the article mainly about?
   (A) To please the executives
   (B) How an epic movie is made.
   (C) the search for an ideal castle for the shoot
   (D) the cooperation among directors and editors.

168. The word "**enigmatic**" in the paragraph, line 2, is closet in meaning to
   (A) descriptive
   (B) esoteric
   (C) inconsequential
   (D) distinctive

169. In which of the positions marked **(1)**, **(2)**, **(3)**, and **(4)** does the following sentence best belong?

★NEW

"**Executives have gone to several castles, but couldn't find a satisfied one.**"

(A) (1)

(B) (2)

(C) (3)

(D) (4)

Questions 170-172

Dear Cindy,

You just have to be aware of all trick questions. Remember the scene of the job interview in Desperate Housewives, Season 5? The heroine is smart enough to say that "if I was dumb enough to answer that, I never would've gotten into Northwestern." **(1)** Sometimes you don't have to answer all questions, and sometimes you can answer interview questions in a clever way. You don't have to be passive. **(2)** Be confident and you also have to know that you are evaluating those companies as well. That **mentality** can actually make you quite composed during an interview. **(3)** You don't have to reveal your health conditions unless your company requires you to hand in a physical check-up. **(4)** And you obviously don't have to mention that your mother is so sick that can take up much of your energy after work or during the holidays...

Best Column

170. What is **NOT** stated about the "Job Column"?
     (A) Disclosing your health conditions falls into the category of the jeopardizing.
     (B) Be confident during the interview.
     (C) Be active during the interview.
     (D) You have to answer all the questions in the interview.

171. The word "**mentality**" in the letter, line 8, is closet in meaning to
     (A) adaptation
     (B) manipulation
     (C) attitude
     (D) benevolence

172. In which of the positions marked **(1)**, **(2)**, **(3)**, and **(4)** does the following sentence best belong?
     "**Also, you have to be careful about questions that trick you into answering things that can jeopardize the hire.**"
     (A) (1)
     (B) (2)
     (C) (3)
     (D) (4)

164

Questions 173-175

As to the question for asking for a raise. Just do that whenever you think you deserve it. Life is simply too short and you do need to have the guts to say that. (even if they say no, there is no harm in asking. You are doing a better job than those who don't ask.) Of course, you don't have to piss of your boss. **(1)** Do it under the right circumstance, not during the economic downturn or the **downsizing** period. **(2)** You also have to understand your salary in the job market and your salary is based on your expertise and contribution. You don't have to mistakenly think of asking for a promotion or a raise as an embarrassment. **(3)** That means you care about your growth and you have ambitions. **(4)** That also means you are not making a job hop, and you want to contribute more. You can also ask them that, if you do expect a higher salary, how much contribution requires to do in order for that to happen...

Best Column

173. What is **NOT** stated about the "Job Column"?

(A) One has to surprise his or her boss to get the raise.

(B) One has to pick the right moment to ask for a raise.

(C) One's contribution to the job is related to the evaluation of the salary.

(D) One needs to be brave enough to ask for a raise.

174. The word "**downsizing**" in the letter, line 7, is closet in meaning to
    (A) sustaining
    (B) downside
    (C) underestimating
    (D) retrenching

175. In which of the positions marked **(1)**, **(2)**, **(3)**, and **(4)** does the following sentence best belong?

    "**Try to negotiate with the superior or the boss, you would be surprised about their reaction.**"
    (A) (1)
    (B) (2)
    (C) (3)
    (D) (4)

Questions 176-180

Dear Best Restaurant,

I went to your restaurant the other day and your clerk was **downright** rude to us for no reason. **(1)** We wore the suit and were dressed as requested, knowing that your place is a royal place for celebrities. And we did pay our meals. It was not like we didn't pay the full payment. **(2)** We deserve to be treated better. If I don't get the reasonable reply soon, I'm going to the Consumer Department and file a complaint, which will result in a frequent visit of the government officials to your place. **(3)** And I will post the entire incident to the website and ig telling people about your horrible service. **(4)** I bet a lot of people won't be visiting your restaurant, and some of my close friends are really rich, rich enough to buy your place.

Consumer Linda

Dear Linda,

Please accept my apology on behalf of the company. But I do want you to know that it was not our fault that day... well partially. I know it was not entirely, but partially. It's not that we don't admit the fault on our part. But recently, lots of guys **sneak** back to our restaurant and try to pretend to be one of our staff. Really crazy college students, who try to be us and upload the video they record to YouTube to boost the view. I've enclosed the table of guys that we caught with the help of the police, and you can go to the police station to file the lawsuit. We will give you a discount of 30% for your next visit. Anything your order. The total will be deducted in accordance with the discount.

Name	Educational Background
Jason Lin	High school
Mark Wang	College student
Neal Chen	Ph.D in philosophy

176. In which of the positions marked **(1)**, **(2)**, **(3)**, and **(4)** does the following sentence best belong?

   "**Quite a burden for you to handle.**"

   (A) (1)
   (B) (2)
   (C) (3)
   (D) (4)

177. The word "**downright**" in paragraph1, line 1, is closet in meaning to
   (A) declined
   (B) reluctant

(C) thoroughly

(D) absolute

178. What is **NOT** mentioned in both letters?

(A) The clerk didn't show the respect to the customers.

(B) The customer is planning to write a complaint.

(C) The restaurant eventually admitted the flaw and thought it was entirely responsible.

(D) The customer can file the lawsuit for what happened.

179. The word "**sneak**" in paragraph2, line 4, is closet in meaning to

(A) submit

(B) astonish

(C) creep

(D) surface

180. What is enclosed with the letter?

(A) the list of several police officers

(B) The educational background of the guys

(C) the list of guys who did the crime

(D) the list of restaurant staff

Questions 181-185

Dear Cindy

I don't think you are a whistle blower. You are just doing your job. It's great that you are telling me this. **(1)** Now I know John often **waltzes into** the conference room unprepared. I will address this in our next conference meeting. Also, I do need someone to keep a watch on several guys in the marketing department for me. **(2)** They seem ganged upon the new recruit. If anything happens, make sure I'm the first to know. **(3)** You still remain as the innocent girl who just graduated from college and glad that you have a job during a great recession. **(4)** Finally, I bought you a fashion cloth while I was having an international meeting in Germany. Hope you will like it. I am going to ask the guy from the flower shop to send it to you under the name Mark James, your secret admirer. Hope it will cause a scene in the office.

The Director

Dear Miss D,

Thanks for the gift. I do love this job by working under cover. I'm going to be so thrilled at receiving the present. And as for the other things, I happened to know the love affair between the CFO and the secretary. **(1)** Is that legal in this company? Perhaps you can use that against the CFO if he doesn't do his job well. **(2)** I'm sending you the recording as evidence, which can be used during the court. And several pics that I captured at the basement. It's turning more and more **juicy**. **(3)** I guess I will be watching them for the next few days as well. It's Thursday afternoon. Now you have to excuse me. I have to pretend to be dumb and forget to send the important emails and ask some helps from colleagues in the marketing department. **(4)**

Cindy

181. In which of the positions marked **(1)**, **(2)**, **(3)**, and **(4)** does the
 following sentence best belong? (the first letter)

   "**And you don't have to reveal your true identity.**"

   (A) (1)

   (B) (2)

   (C) (3)

   (D) (4)

模擬試題（一）

模擬試題（二）

模擬試題（三）

模擬試題（四）

模擬試題（五）

182. What is indicated about Mark James?
    (A) He has an affair with Cindy.
    (B) He is the guy who works at the flower shop
    (C) He happens to have additional flowers and wants to cause
        a scene.
    (D) He is a made-up name used by the director

183. The word "**waltzes into**" in letter 1, line 2, is closet in meaning
    to
    (A) reluctantly walks into
    (B) swaggeringly walks in
    (C) confidently dances with
    (D) persuasively talks into

184. In which of the positions marked **(1)**, **(2)**, **(3)**, and **(4)** does the
    following sentence best belong? (the second letter)
    "**A great moment to peek what they are doing ha ha...**"
    (A) (1)
    (B) (2)
    (C) (3)
    (D) (4)

185. The word "**juicy**" in letter 2, line 7, is closet in meaning to
    (A) awkward
    (B) seductive
    (C) provocative

(D) jubilant

Questions 186-190

Advertisement

Best Island was established 50 years ago. By using a **desolate** land, we have created a wonder. Lions freely roam on the land. Every year lots of people are eager to test their own courage through enrolling in our program. Some are seeking wealth by having an adventure here. Believe it or not there are plenty of gold, silver, and jewelry hidden under the sand of the island. In our castle, it's totally a new adventure. Seeking wealth involves taking a risk. Here is the place for you. Enrollees should sign the contract. According to the contract, exemption clauses are listed in a few sections. Make sure you've read through all of the clauses.

Dear Best Island,

I'm a man in his forties, and yet I still haven't accomplished anything much in life. **(1)** My friend's ancestors all went to the gold hunt during the Gold Rush period, and I don't seem a coward than any of them. **(2)** I've made up my mind to do it because life is too short. **(3)** I was wondering how to sign up for the program, and can fortune-seekers get all the gold and other things and then bring them back in the country where I'm in, or should we split the treasure with the company? **(4)** And what should I bring with me, the gear or other things. Are powerful weapons allowed to be used during the treasure hunt?
Please reply to me ASAP, thanks.

Poor Man

Dear Poor Man,

I guess you are really desperate, and I prefer not to call you a poor guy myself. It's pretty rude, and several people who self-proclaim themselves poor are actually really wealthy. It's too soon to refer you to that kind of nickname. I've listed several things for you to know more about the program. Please read it and if you have any question, please contact me 999-999-999-999.

Items	money
Payment to enroll	US 50,000 dollars

horse	US 1,000 dollars
pigeons	US 1,000 dollars
food	It depends
Meat	US 1,000 dollars
Map	US 10,000 dollars
training	US 20,000 dollars
Water/ per bottle	US 50 dollars

Best Island

186. The word "**desolate**" in paragraph1, line 1, is closet in meaning to

(A) undersized

(B) bleak

(C) undercut

(D) underestimated

187. What is being advertised?

(A) A promotional offer for the castle

(B) Recruitment for the island guard

(C) An adventurous journey to get rich

(D) A detailed explanation for the exemption clauses for free

188. In which of the positions marked **(1)**, **(2)**, **(3)**, and **(4)** does the following sentence best belong?

"Then it just hit me, why don't I give it a shot, and there is

no harm in doing that right?"

(A) (1)

(B) (2)

(C) (3)

(D) (4)

189. What is **NOT** available for an additional charge?

(A) elephant

(B) horse

(C) food

(D) water

190. How much does it cost if the Poor Man wants to enroll and purchase a map?

(A) NT 60,000

(B) NT 2,000

(C) NT 1,800,000

(D) NT 180,000

Questions 191-195

Dear Best Island,

I've received the list of items. I'm fine with the enrolled fee, but what are all other listed items for? Can I just pay the fee and start the treasure hunt myself? And why do I need pigeons... it's getting ludicrous.
Poor man

Dear Poor Man,

Normally, we don't recommend you do. A guy without an intensive training can get killed by wild animals in an instant. **(1)** Since no cellphones will be allowed to use during the treasure hunt, we kindly advise you to use pigeons. If you have any questions, you can send the pigeon to us. We can even deliver a specifically tailored food to the spot where you are located. **(2)** You won't get starved before living your dreamed life. Furthermore, meat is used to distract carnivores, so we highly recommend you to buy that kind of service. What about map? You should buy that, too. **(3)** That's pathetic. As for the training, it's entirely up to you. The training usually takes 2 months. **(4)** You can adjust yourself well in the wild, become athletic and be ready for the test in the wild. If you still have any questions, please let me know. And make sure you bring a huge bag and personal items with you because you will need those.

Best Island

Dear Best Island,

I think the pigeon thing is an **extortion**. **(1)** I definitely don't need a horse, either. It's so inhumane. **(2)** And I do have a good sense for direction, so the map is the last thing I need. **(3)** However, I do think I need the training. **(4)** By the way, is the training program intensive? I think the bank loan can cover the cost to pay the program. Please tell me how should I make the payment? Also, am I able to get the discount? I'm an enthusiastic participant, so I do think I deserve the discount.

Poor Man

191. What is Not mentioned in "the reply to the Poor Man"?

(A) Using pigeons can keep you from getting hungry.

(B) Using pigeons is suggested.

(C) the training is mandatory.

(D) the training is essential.

192. What advice is Not included in the information?

(A) It's recommended to take the training.

(B) Meat is used to divert the attention of the meat-eaters.

(C) Carry the personal belongings with you

(D) Purchase a horse to replace walking alone

193. In which of the positions marked **(1)**, **(2)**, **(3)**, and **(4)** does the following sentence best belong? (the second letter)

"**I won't condone myself seeing any customers getting lost in a vast land.**"

(A) (1)

(B) (2)

(C) (3)

(D) (4)

194. The word "**extortion**" in paragraph3, line 1, is closet in meaning to

(A) recognition

(B) discomfort

(C) blackmail

(D) extinguishment

195. In which of the positions marked **(1)**, **(2)**, **(3)**, and **(4)** does the following sentence best belong? (the third letter)

"**For a person who has a big belly, this can be a good thing.**"

(A) (1)

(B) (2)

(C) (3)

(D) (4)

Questions 196-200

Dear Poor Man,

Only people using all those services can get the discount. **(1)** It's entirely free, so don't tell other participants, ok? They will get pretty mad... you know how competitive people can get. **(2)** I guess I will see you on Monday, unless you do have other questions. Please have the money transferred to our bank account, and good luck. **(3)** You can text me while you are at the training center. **(4)** You are allowed to use your cellphone during your stay there.

Best Island

Line messages

Thanks for all the help and I'm about to embark on a new journey in life. I'm so thrilled. Thanks again. I do hope I can get rich before going back to the land.

Training center

You don't have a name here. You will be referring to by the number on your uniform. This is not some summer camps. It's about life-and-death, so be serious about it. You have to get up at five a.m. and wear your uniform. I have listed the activities on the brochure for you to read. If you don't measure up to the standard of our norm, we have the right to send you back. It goes according to the contract. That means your dream of becoming rich will be gone forever.

The activity for the first month	Time
Boxing lesson	An hour/ per day
Weight lift training	Two hours/per day
Running	2 kms/per day
Surviving skills	4 hours/per day
Cleaning the center	An hour/per day

Collecting food for the team	2 hours/per day
Collecting water	2 hours/per day

196. In which of the positions marked **(1)**, **(2)**, **(3)**, and **(4)** does the following sentence best belong?

"**But since you are an enthusiastic and vibrant man, we will give you a bow and arrows for you to defend yourself.**"

(A) (1)

(B) (2)

(C) (3)

(D) (4)

197. Which of the following premium is what the poor man will be getting?

(A) the discount

(B) weapons

(C) reduction for the transferring fee

(D) 5G smartphone service

198. What is the Poor Man hoping to get?

(A) to be physically fit after the training

(B) to defeat coaches at the Training Center

(C) to be the star at the Training Center

(D) to be wealthy

199. What is True about the Training Center?
    (A) Trainees there don't have to measure up the standard.
    (B) Trainees there can dress casually.
    (C) It's organized by having numerous activities.
    (D) It was magnificently built.

200. What is mentioned about Surviving skills?
    (A) It takes longer than Running.
    (B) It takes shorter than Weightlifting.
    (C) It takes shorter than Gathering water.
    (D) It takes longer than most activities.

模擬試題（二）

PART 5　中譯與解析

閱讀原文與中譯	
101. Because of multiple YouTubers' remarks about the new product, some consumers remain **hesitant**, thinking that they have to wait until the doubt is cleared up. (A) noticeable (B) customizable **(C) hesitant** (D) negotiable	因為許多YouTuber對該新產品的評論，有些消費者對其仍舊持著猶豫的態度，認為必須要等到疑慮消除為止。 (A) 顯著的、值得注意的 (B) 客製化的、個性化的 **(C) 遲疑的、躊躇的** (D) 可協商的、可轉讓的

答案：(C)

解析

這題是說有些消費者仍抱持著猶豫的態度，所以最適合的是**選項C**。

閱讀原文與中譯	
102. Shoppers cannot let go of the snide comments made by bloggers, so they have made up their minds to **unsubscribe** a certain channel. (A) unauthorized **(B) unsubscribe** (C) describe (D) prescribe	購物者們無法甩脫由部落客們所做的惡意評論，所以他們已經下定決心要退訂特定的頻道。 (A) 未被授權的、未經許可的 **(B) 取消訂閱** (C) 描寫、描繪、敘述 (D) 規定、指定、開（藥方）

答案：(B)

subscribe和authorize都很常見，加上否定字根的用法對有些考生可能就較不熟悉，這題是考unsubscribe的用法，故答案要選**選項B**。

閱讀原文與中譯	
103. Although the **notoriety** of the masseur has been widely known in the neighborhood, tourists traveling here are still kept in the dark. (A) valor (B) fame (C) reputation **(D) notoriety**	儘管男按摩師的惡名昭彰在整個街坊已經是廣為人知，到此地旅遊的觀光客們卻仍被蒙在鼓底。 (A) 英勇、勇氣、勇猛 (B) 聲譽、名望、名聲 (C) 名譽、名聲 **(D) 惡名昭彰、聲名狼藉**

答案：(D)

這題指的是男按摩師的惡名昭彰，故答案要選**選項D**。

閱讀原文與中譯	
104. Due to a lack of evidence and recordings at the scene, the **authenticity** of the bad service made by the bank clerk cannot be verified. (A) deviation (B) estimation **(C) authenticity** (D) disappearance	由於缺乏現場的證據和記錄，銀行行員服務差的真實性是無法辨認的。 (A) 越軌、偏向、誤差 (B) 評價、估計 **(C) 可信賴性、確實（性）** (D) 消失、失蹤、滅絕

答案：(C)

解析

這題算是考區分高階名詞的用法，由句意和後面的cannot be verified可以進一步判斷出最合適的選項是**選項C**。

閱讀原文與中譯	
105. Despite the fact that the CFO of the Best Consulting firm has done numerous buy-ins of the stocks before, he still cannot say for sure whether the bet can truly generate hefty **profits**. (A) results (B) fluctuations (C) evaluations **(D) profits**	儘管倍斯特顧問公司的財務長已經於之前從事過為數眾多的股市買進，他對於投注的賭注是否能真的產生鉅額的獲利仍無法說準。 (A) 結果、成果、效果 (B) 波動、變動、動搖 (C) 評估、估算 **(D) 利潤、盈利、收益、紅利**

答案：(D)

解析

這題的選項均為複數名詞，且有些相近的表達，但依句意和後面的搭配用profits是最合適的，故答案要選**選項D**。

閱讀原文與中譯	
106. A **disgruntled** employee is like a loose cannon, and can be quite detrimental to the work setting. (A) inconsistent (B) incremental **(C) disgruntled** (D) marketable	憤恨不平的員工就像是一枚不定時炸彈，而且可能對於工作環境是危害甚鉅的。 (A) 不一致的、不協調的、前後矛盾的 (B) 增加的、增值的 **(C) 不滿的、不高興的** (D) 可銷售的、市場的、有銷路的

答案：(C)

解析

這題儘管有好幾個高階形容詞，但是僅有C是描述其後employee最貼近的詞彙且句意符合，故答案為**選項C**。

閱讀原文與中譯	
107. **Disorganization** on the shelves can be a downside for anyone walking in or clients visiting the warehouse. **(A) disorganization** (B) reason (C) priority (D) sustainability	對於任何走進倉庫或參訪的客戶來說，架上凌亂無章是個缺點。 **(A) 組織的破壞、解體、混亂** (B) 理由、原因、動機 (C) 優先、重點、優先權 (D) 持續性、能維持性、永續性

答案：(A)

解析

這題也是一個否定字根開頭的高階名詞，表達出在架上的雜亂無章，故選項A是最符合的，故答案要選**選項A**。

閱讀原文與中譯	
108. In the **aftermath** of the 2009 financial crisis, numerous jobseekers experienced a shattered self-esteem and could not find the job for a few months. (A) serendipity (B) productivity (C) possibility **(D) aftermath**	在2009年金融危機後，許多求職者有著自尊受到粉碎的體驗，然後幾個月都無法找到工作。 (A) 意外發現的東西、奇緣 (B) 生產力、生產率、豐饒 (C) 可能性、可能的事 **(D) 後果、餘波**

答案：(D)

解析

Aftermath表示餘波、後果，用於表達於某一段時期後的介係詞片語是個固定的搭配，答案要選**選項D**。

閱讀原文與中譯	
109. Several start-ups can only afford a(n) **undersized** warehouse and have to cut expenses in other areas, such as hiring and office equipment. (A) biodegradable (B) sizable **(C) undersized** (D) municipal	幾個新創公司僅能夠負擔比普通小的倉庫，且必須要於其他項目，例如招聘和辦公室設備上刪減支出。 (A) 生物所能分解的 (B) 相當大的、大小相當的 **(C) 比普通小的、小尺寸的** (D) 市立的、地方自治的

答案：(C)

這題也是有幾個選項其實都能用於描述倉庫，但是往後看接續的表達後選項C是最符合的，故答案要選**選項C**。

閱讀原文與中譯	
110. By **undercutting** the prices, Best Cinema is finally able to outcompete other movie studios and gets the chance to work with several celebrities. (A) refueling **(B) undercutting** (C) heightening (D) continuing	藉由削價競爭，倍斯特電影公司最終能夠勝過其他間電影工作室，並且有機會與幾位名人合作。 (A)（給......）補給燃料 **(B)（比別人）廉價出售、削價競爭** (C) 加高、增高 (D) 持續

答案：(B)

解析

這題是要表達藉由削價競爭才能...，故答案要選選項B較合適，故答案為**選項B**。

模擬試題（一）

模擬試題（二）

模擬試題（三）

模擬試題（四）

模擬試題（五）

111. **Retention** bonuses are needed in case the star employee wants to make a job hop and the company is not able to afford the loss. (A) Celebration **(B) Retention** (C) Prevention (D) Demotion	留任獎金是必須的，此舉能以防表現傑出的員工想要跳槽，而公司卻無法擔負這樣的損失。 (A) 慶祝、慶祝活動、慶典 **(B) 保留、保持、記憶力** (C) 預防、防止、阻止、妨礙 (D) 降級

答案：(B)

 解析

這題是一個慣用的搭配，儘管還有幾個選項也可能是適合的，部過這題是要表達出**留任獎金**，答案為**選項B**。

112. Situated in a secluded village where honey bees come to gather the honey near the river bank, Best Farm may be people's **image** of a stereotypical retreat. **(A) image** (B) disagreement (C) investment (D) appreciation	座落於隱密的村莊，蜜蜂們都聚集在河岸邊採蜜，倍斯特農場可能是人們心中刻板印象隱密處的寫照。 **(A)（心目中的）形象、印象、寫照** (B) 意見不合、爭吵、爭論 (C) 投資、投資額 (D) 欣賞、鑑賞、賞識

答案：(A)

解析

這題較難且句式較複雜，為image較高階的表達，用以表達**「寫照」**，故答案為**選項A**。

閱讀原文與中譯	
113. The winery in Germany has earned tons of **accolades** by tourists traveling very far from here. (A) evaluations **(B) accolades** (C) functions (D) descriptions	位於德國的酒窖已經贏得了許多從遠處到訪的觀光客們的讚揚。 (A) 評估、估算 **(B) 稱讚、盛讚** (C) 功能、作用 (D) 描寫、敘述

答案：(B)

 解析

這題看到前面的earned其實就可以預期是正面的詞語，在看選項後最合適的為**選項B**。

閱讀原文與中譯	
114. The **dormancy** in the area is a sign that the land cannot be too profitable, so buyers usually have doubts and look other places. (A) slimness **(B) dormancy** (C) productivity (D) appropriation	這個地區的休耕期是這塊土地無法太有利益價值的象徵，所以買家們通常存疑而改成瀏覽其他地方。 (A) 細長、苗條 **(B) 休眠、冬眠** (C) 生產力、生產率、豐饒 (D) 撥付、撥發、撥款

答案：(B)

 解析

這題也較難，其實是dormancy用於表達**「休耕期」**的用法，故答案要選選項B。

閱讀原文與中譯	
115. **Judging** from the current circumstance, the animal doctor surmised that the wound of the koala could not be healed. (A) To judge **(B) Judging** (C) Judged (D) Being judged	從現在的情況中可以評判出，動物醫生臆測無尾熊的傷口是無法被治癒的。

答案：(B)

這題是考「**評判出...**」的用法，依語法要使用judging，故答案為**選項B**。

閱讀原文與中譯	
116. Salespeople are known for their ability to sell, **whereas** editors are noted for their capability of editing articles. (A) once (B) when **(C) whereas** (D) because	銷售人員以他們的銷售能力而聞名，而編輯們則以他們的編輯文章的能力而著名。

答案：(C)

這題可以依據兩個句子中的主詞salespeople和editors評判出句子是用以表達兩者的相異處，故很顯然要使用的連接詞是**whereas**。

閱讀原文與中譯

117. **The more** you get to know the product, the more you can say during the product launch on next Wednesday. (A) Most (B) More **(C) The more** (D) The most	你對於產品越是了解，在下週三的產品發佈期間就越有東西可以說。

答案：(C)

 解析

這題很明顯是考the more... the more的句型，故答案為**選項C**。

閱讀原文與中譯

118. Software developers are getting **increasingly** impatient with the questioning by salespeople, so the tension is a little high. (A) increasing (B) increase **(C) increasingly** (D) increased	軟體研發者對於銷售人員的質問漸漸地感到不耐煩，所以情勢是有點緊張的。

答案：(C)

 解析

這題依據語法要選**副詞**來修飾impatient故答案為**選項C**。

閱讀原文與中譯	
119. **Because** the company cannot afford to lose the CFO at the moment, the CEO finally agrees to give him a 10% raise. (A) Once **(B) Because** (C) If (D) Although	因為公司在這個當下是無法承受財務長的離開，所以執行長最終同意給予他10%的薪資增幅。

答案：(B)

 解析

這題依句意是表達因果關係，故答案要選**選項B**的because。

閱讀原文與中譯	
120. The long-awaited promotion does not make the manager **happy** because the responsibility is greater than before. **(A) happy** (B) more happier (C) most happiest (D) be happy	久盼的升遷並未使得經理感到開心，因為責任比起以往更加重了。

答案：(A)

 解析

這題根據語法要選形容詞，故答案要選happy，答案為**選項A**。

閱讀原文與中譯	
121. The lockdown of the city for a month has led to zero productivity and serenity of the street **that** are not usually seen in years. (A) where (B) who (C) whom **(D) that**	封城一個月已經導致了生產力歸零且街道的寧靜是這幾年來不尋常的景象。

答案：(D)

 解析

這題依據語法要選that，故答案為**選項D**。

閱讀原文與中譯	
122. During the time of the outbreak of COVID-19 virus, bad things, **such as** layoffs and plant closure have become a regular scene. (A) like (B) for example (C) included **(D) such as**	在新冠肺炎病毒爆發的期間，壞事，例如解雇和工廠結束營業已經成了常景了。

答案：(D)

 解析

這題依據語法要選取表達舉例的such as，故答案為**選項D**。

閱讀原文與中譯	
123. Singers and marine mammals **are recruited** to make the wedding more memorable and diverse, and the newlywed seems happy. (A) recruit **(B) are recruited** (C) recruiting (D) recruited	歌手們和海洋哺乳類動物都受僱，讓婚宴更有回憶且多樣化，而新婚夫妻對此似乎感到快樂。

答案：(B)

 解析

這題依據語法要選被動語態的**are recruited**，故答案為**選項B**。

閱讀原文與中譯	
124. Kitchen orders are usually enormous during the holiday, but with the invasion of the alien species, they are not as **large** as it used to be. (A) larged (B) largest **(C) large** (D) the largest	在假日期間，廚房的訂單通常很大筆，但是隨著外來種的入侵，訂單沒有往常那麼多了。

答案：(C)

 解析

這題根據語法要選形容詞的**large**，故答案要選**選項C**。

閱讀原文與中譯	
125. Our fruits and vegetables are under such an extensive care that they are put in an artificial setting **where** temperatures are rigorously monitored. **(A) where** (B) which (C) when (D) whose	我們的水果和蔬菜受到那樣的完善照護以致於它們被放置於溫度受到嚴密監控的人工環境裡。

答案：(A)

 解析

這題依據語法要使用**where**才符合語法，故答案為**選項A**。

閱讀原文與中譯	
126. **Unlike** most cellphone giants, which outsource software components to other low-cost countries, Best Cellphone is doing quite the opposite. (A) If (B) Like **(C) Unlike** (D) Once	不像大多數的手機大廠，將軟體組件外包到其他低成本的國家，倍斯特手機卻是反其道而行。

答案：(C)

 解析

這題依據語法和句意要使用選項C，故**答案為C**。

閱讀原文與中譯	
127. A few of the candidates we interviewed acknowledged that they **had had** at least 5 job hops before finding the right one. (A) have (B) has had **(C) had had** (D) had	我們面試過的幾位候選人承認在找到合適的工作之前，他們有至少五次的職涯跑道轉換。

答案：(C)

這題要稍微注意一下，要選「**過去完成式**」才符合語法，故答案為**選項C**。

閱讀原文與中譯	
128. **Even though** male dates vary considerably in different occupations, your intuition and criteria for a mate can narrow candidates down to the most suitable one. (A) Because (B) If (C) Once **(D) Even though**	儘管男性約會對象在不同職業中有顯著地不同，你的直覺和對男性的標準能夠將候選人窄化至最合適的那位。

答案：(D)

這題依句意要選「儘管」，故答案為**選項D**。

閱讀原文與中譯	
129. Best Chocolate Plant's remarkable **growth** in profits has allured multiple overseas investors and sponsors. (A) grow **(B) growth** (C) grew (D) grown	倍斯特巧克力廠驚人的利潤成長已經吸引了眾多的海外投資者和贊助者。

答案：(B)

這題依據語法要選「**名詞**」，故答案要選**選項B**。

閱讀原文與中譯	
130. **If** the productivity of Best Automobile drops 10%, the overall revenue will decrease at least 50 million dollars. (A) Once **(B) If** (C) Although (D) Because	如果倍斯特汽車的生產下降10%，整體收入會減少至少5千萬元。

答案：(B)

這題依據語意要選「如果」，故答案要選**選項B**。

PART 6 中譯和解析

Questions 131-134

A month has passed since the firm made the purchase of the organic farm in August. The price has been much lower than expected. The board is pleased with the first drastic measure done by the CEO, and can't wait to see **prosperity** of the farm in the future. The CEO then called an urgent meeting on Saturday, so all executives got called back during the holiday with a somewhat bad mood. They have to fire professional farmers and organic farmers for the first few months. They will be working **temporarily**. **The company will also hire full-time employees who can learn from those farmers** and handle the farm business after those part-time farmers leave the company. The HR Department will be in charge of the hiring and report only to the CEO. Organic farmers with years of experiences will be paid **handsomely**, according to the report.

自從農場於八月購得有機農場後，已經過了一個月了，購地價格比預期低。董事會對於執行長所完成的第一項急遽的措施感到滿意，等不及要在未來看到農場的盛況。於週六，執行長接著召開了緊急會議，所有高階主管都在休假時被召回，所以或多或少都帶著不悅的心情。他們必須要在起初的幾個月雇用專業的農夫和有機農夫。他們將會是短期工。公司也將雇用全職員工，其能從那些聘僱的農夫當中學習並且處理農業事務，在那些兼職農夫離開公司後。人事部門將會主掌召聘且僅向執行長彙報。根據報導，公司會支付有著幾年經驗的有機農夫可觀的薪資。

試題中譯與解析

131.	131.
(A) seduction	(A) 誘惑、魅力、吸引
(B) recognition	(B) 贊譽、認得、承認、認可、重視
(C) prosperity	**(C) 興旺、繁榮、昌盛、成功**
(D) discovery	(D) 發現

132. **(A) temporarily** (B) inextricably (C) incongruously (D) continuously	132. **(A) 暫時地** (B) 解不開地、分不開地 (C) 不一致地 (D) 持續地
133. (A) The policemen will visit the office often (B) Only professional farmers will stay on the job **(C) The company will also hire full-time employees who can learn from those farmers** (D) Farm owners will discipline those farmers to make them qualify for the job	133. (A) 警察將會更頻繁地拜訪。 (B) 僅有專業的農夫會繼續待在工作岡位。 **(C) 公司將會雇用從那些農夫身上學習的全職員工。** (D) 農場主人將鞭策那些農夫使他們都符合工作的資格。
134. (A) consistently (B) unilaterally **(C) handsomely** (D) artificially	134. (A) 一致地 (B) 單方面地 **(C) 氣派地；相當大地，可觀地** (D) 人工地

第**131**題，這題依句意要選prosperity，故答案為**選項C**。

第**132**題，這題依句意和上、下文要選temporarily，要小心這題（可以從for the first few months等關鍵字協助判答），故答案為**選項A**。

第**133**題，這題依句意要選C，才符合上、下文意，那些有經驗的農夫只是短期聘用，教授專業知識，故答案為**選項C**。

第**134**題，這題也要小心，依句意要選**handsomely**可觀的，故答案為**選項C**。

Questions 135-138

Finally, the HR Department selected 10 finalists and they were going to present their already successful farm business with the CEO. The presentation **originally scheduled** to be held in the middle of September was postponed due to other reasons. After the meeting in October, the CEO has made the decision of hiring 5 farmers, **responsible for** different parts of the wild farm and organic farm. They are in charge, too. They were led to the conference room and signed a three-month **contract**. **They feel so honored and cannot wait for their start date.** The CEO has also hired 100 blue collar workers to do the heavy work and they have to obey the order given by the five farmers.

最終，人事部門已經選擇了10位最終候選人且他們會彙報他們已經成功的農場事業給執行長。這個簡報起初時程預定在九月中旬左右，由於其他理由延期了。在10月份的會議後，執行長已經做了雇用5位農夫的決定，農夫負責不同部分的野外農場和有機農場。也有權責負責。他們被引至會議室並簽署為期三個月的合約。他們感到榮幸且對於上工日已迫不及待。執行長也雇用了100位藍領工人來從事笨重的工作，而他們必須要遵守由五位農夫所發佈的命令。

試題中譯與解析	
135. (A) meticulously researched **(B) originally scheduled** (C) legally considered (D) poignantly captured	135. (A) 小心翼翼地研究的 **(B) 起初預定地** (C) 法律考量的 (D) 慘痛地捕獲的
136. (A) bristle with (B) superior to **(C) responsible for** (D) curious about	136. (A) 充滿 (B) 優於 **(C) 對...負責** (D) 對...好奇
137. (A) contact **(B) contract** (C) proceedings (D) scenario	137. (A) 接觸、觸碰、交往；聯繫 **(B) 契約、合同** (C) 訴訟、（會議）議項、會議記錄 (D) 情節、劇本、事態、局面

138.
(A) Not all finalists get selected.
(B) The presentation makes some farmers too nervous to say something.
(C) The government poaches those farmers before they sign anything.
(D) They feel so honored and cannot wait for their start date.

138.
(A) 並非所有的決賽候選人都會雀屏中選。
(B) 簡報讓有些農夫太緊張而說不出話了。
(C) 在他們與公司簽任何東西之前，政府挖走那些農夫。
(D) 他們感覺到榮耀無比且等不及上工日的開始。

第**135**題，這題也要小心，句子中都是副詞搭形容詞的搭配，依句意要選 originally scheduled，故答案為**選項B**。
第**136**題，這題依句意要選responsible for，**負責**不同部分的野外農場和有機農場，故答案為**選項C**。
第**137**題，這題依句意要選contract（可以由前方的關鍵字sign和後面的月份協助判答），故答案為**選項B**。
第**138**題，這題依句意要選D，故答案為**選項D**。

Questions 139-142

A month has passed, and industrious workers under the **guideline** of the professional farmers really have turned the farm into a serious business. The blueberry is **exceedingly** tasty, from the account of the workers. And like those blue berries, other vegetables are **plucked** by workers and sent to the zoo. Bears can now have baskets of fresh berries to eat and they seem satisfied. Visitors can also go to the farm and gather the berries for their favorite bears. They are not just visiting the zoo, but form the bond with these creatures. The company also has lessened the workload and reduced the manpower. It's a win-win. **The firm will also give visitors a certificate, if they hand-deliver more than a hundred baskets for the animal of their choice**. For those who have done it for a thousand times, they will be given a free ticket for a year.

一個月已經過去了，勤奮的工人在專業農夫的指導方針下，真的將農場轉變成起敬的事業。藍莓嚐起來相當甜，根據工人們的說法。而那些藍莓和其他蔬菜一樣均由工人們摘起並送至動物園。熊現在有盛裝成籃的新鮮莓果可以食用，牠們因此而感到滿足。觀光客也能夠前往農場並採收莓果給他們最喜愛的熊。他們不僅僅是參觀動物園，且與那些生物都形成了情感連結。公司也能夠減輕工作量和減低人力。這是雙贏。公司將會給予參訪者證書，如果他們親手遞給他們所喜愛的動物超過一百籃的話。對於那些已經執行超過一千次的會贈予一年的免費暢遊卷。

試題中譯與解析	
139. (A) inspiration (B) cooperation (C) interpretation **(D)guideline**	139. (A) 靈感 (B) 合作 (C) 解釋、闡明、口譯 **(D)指導方針**
140. (A) objectively **(B) exceedingly** (C) uncomfortably (D) scrupulously	140. (A) 客觀地 **(B) 非常地、極度地** (C) 不舒適地、不自在地 (D) 小心翼翼地、多顧慮地
141. (A) impaired (B) transferred (C) orchestrated **(D)plucked**	141. (A) 削弱、損害、損傷 (B) 搬、轉換、調動 (C) 精心安排 **(D)採、摘、拔**

142.
(A) If the bear doesn't like the berry, the visitor will not be rewarded.
(B) The visitor will be charged the maintenance fee in the organic farm.
(C) The firm will also give the visitor a certificate, if they hand-deliver more than a hundred basket for the animal of their choice.
(D) Robots are placed in the organic farm to assist children plucking fruits.

142.
(A) 如果熊不喜歡莓果的話，觀光客就不會收到獎勵。
(B) 觀光客會被索取有機農場內的維護費用。
(C) 公司也會給觀光客證照，如果他們親自遞送超過一百籃給他們所選擇的動物。
(D) 機器人被放置在有機農場以協助小孩摘取水果。

第**139**題，這題也要小心，依句意要選guideline（under the guideline也是常見搭配），故答案為**選項D**。
第**140**題，這題依句意要選exceedingly（表程度的副詞來形容tasty），故答案為**選項B**。
第**141**題，這題依句意要選plucked，故答案為**選項D**。
第**142**題，這題依句意要選C，故答案為**選項C**。

Questions 143-146

The news has become widespread, and multiple parents are eager to do this with their kids during the holiday. They can enjoy the family time in both the farm and the zoo, quite serene and pleasant. The CEO has got **applause** from the board, and they are planning to add something innovative, too. Visitors to the zoo can also **collect** corns or pluck bananas. Those can be used to feed animals, such as monkeys and elephants. They don't have to go to Thailand to do that, and it is actually a good **advertisement** for the firm. With the upload of the videos of those kids handing bananas to elephants, the zoo is more crowded than before. Videos even go **viral** among school children, and the zoo has decided to hold a contest.

消息已經傳開了，而許多父母熱切地要與他們的小孩在假日時從事這些活動。他們可以在農場和動物園中享受家庭時光，相當寧靜且宜人。執行長受到董事會的讚許，而他們也計畫要增添一些創新想法。動物園的參觀者也能夠收集玉米或摘採香蕉。那些都能夠用於餵食動物，例如猴子和大象。他們不需要前往泰國才能做那些事情，而這確實對於公司來說也是個好廣告。隨著那些小孩遞香蕉給大象的視頻的上傳，動物園變得比起以往更為擁擠了。視頻甚至在小孩就讀的學校中爆紅，動物園也因此而決定要舉辦比賽。

試題中譯與解析	
143. (A) abdication **(B) applause** (C) shortcomings (D) slippage	143. (A) 放棄、退位、辭職 **(B) 鼓掌歡迎、喝采、稱讚、嘉許** (C) 缺點、不足 (D) 滑動、下降、跌下
144. (A) amplify **(B) collect** (C) rebuild (D) transform	144. (A) 擴大 **(B) 收集** (C) 重建、改建、重新組裝 (D) 改變、改觀、變換、轉換
145. (A) function (B) insurance (C) development **(D) advertisement**	145. (A) 功用 (B) 保險 (C) 發展 **(D) 廣告**
146. (A) efficient (B) affectless **(C) viral** (D) analyzable	146. (A) 效率高的；有能力的 (B) 無動於衷的 **(C) 病毒引起的、爆紅的** (D) 可分析的

第143題，這題依句意要選applause，執行長受到董事會的**讚許**，故答案為**選項B**。

第144題，這題依句意要選collect，故答案為**選項B**。

第145題，這題依句意要選advertisement，這對公司來說其實是很好的**廣告**，故答案為**選項D**。

第146題，這題依句意要選viral，表示**爆紅**，故答案為**選項C**。

Part 7　中譯與解析

Best Burger

	Sizes/types	Price	Information
French Fries	Small	US 2 dollars	
	Large	US 4 dollars	
Onion Rings	Small	US 3 dollars	
	Large	US 6 dollars	
Burgers	Chinese Mushroom	US 12 dollars	
	Bacon	US 12 dollars	
	Hawaiian	US 14 dollars	
	Double Cheese	US 16 dollars	
	Superb Beef	US 20 dollars	
Drinks	Coke	US 4 dollars	Free refill
	Wine	US 8 dollars	Adults only

※ **TAX**: 10%，taxes should be included in the overall cost.

Question 147

147. What is not stated about Best Burger?	147. 關於倍斯特漢堡的敘述，沒有提到什麼？
(A) A Hawaiian Burger actually costs customers 15.4 dollars.	(A) 一份夏威夷漢堡實際上花費顧客15.4元。
(B) Large Fries indeed cost visitors 4.4 dollars.	(B) 大份薯條確實花費觀光客們4.4元。
(C) People spending 4.4 dollars on Coke get to drink more than one.	(C) 花費4.4元在可樂上的消費者可以飲用不只一次。
(D) Teenagers are able to buy the wine for 8.8 dollars or less.	**(D) 青少年能夠以8.8元或更低的價格購買酒品。**

解析

· 第147題，酒的部分已經有寫adults only，故答案為**選項D**。

Mary 2:20 p.m.	瑪莉下午2:20
Hi... Best Seafood Restaurant, thanks again for the order for giant lobsters. Those lobsters will be shipped next week, probably Wednesday...	嗨...倍斯特海產餐廳，再次感謝您訂購巨型龍蝦。那些龍蝦都會於安排下週運送，很可能是下週三。
Jennifer 2:23 p.m.	**珍妮佛下午2:23**
Is it possible that the shipment arrives earlier than Wednesday... there are just so many tourists during the holiday... and we just cannot use some cheap fish to replace the giant lobsters...	有可能運送會於下週三年抵達嗎?...在假期期間，有許多觀光客們到訪...還有我們就是無法使用一些便宜的魚來取代巨型龍蝦...。
Mary 2:25 p.m.	**瑪莉下午 2:25**
Would you like to order some rare king crabs and other squids? That surely can boost your restaurant's reputation... If you are ordering those, I think our delivery guy can do the delivery on Monday...	你想要訂購一些罕見的帝王蟹和其他魷魚嗎?那樣確實會打響你餐廳的名聲...如果你訂購那些的話，我想我們的送貨員可以在週一就出貨。
Jennifer 2:27 p.m.	**珍妮佛下午 2:27**
How much? I should probably consult with our boss and chefs before making a decision...	要多少錢呢?我可能應該要先與我的老闆和廚師們商討一下，再作決定。
Mary 2:29 p.m.	**瑪莉下午2:29**
Ok just let me know as quickly as possible...	好的，請盡快讓我知道囉...。

Question 148

148. At 2:25 p.m. why does Mary mention about some rare king crabs and other squids? (A) She wants to exploit the customer. (B) She wants the year-end bonuses. (C) She doesn't have enough lobsters in the warehouse. **(D) Both parties can be satisfied.**	148. 在下午2點25分，為什麼瑪莉提及一些罕見帝王蟹和其他的魷魚？ (A) 她想要利用顧客。 (B) 她想要年終獎金。 (C) 她在倉庫中沒有足夠的龍蝦了。 **(D) 雙方都能獲得滿足。**

 解析

· **第148題**，這題需要意會一下，其實是讓雙方條件能夠達成，買方也能於期限之前取得貨物，故答案為**選項D**。

Best International Balloon Festival

This year Best Transportation is doing something innovative and unprecedented. Tourists choosing the Luxury-typed are able to see the view of the Firefly Valley and **serene** Eyes of the Lake. The valley is quite a view during the night that makes our tickets already sold out. It's so romantic and a great way to propose. If you would like to propose during the air-travel, pick our Type E service. Our crew can even specifically put what you would like to say to your love one through air writing. And it's free. Furthermore, we're adding the Type F. This means 50% of the fee will be donated to the charity under your name and of course it can be deducted in your tax next year. Finally, we have the government-sponsored balloon for the elderly, people older than 65, but under one condition, you don't have any chronic illness.

	Time	Price	Descriptions
Type A (Regular)	20 minutes	US 30 dollars	assigned
Type B (Regular)	30 minutes	US 50 dollars	

Type C (Luxury)	2 hours	US 200 dollars	specifically-tailored
Type D (Luxury)	120 minutes	US 300 dollars	
Type E (Luxury)	3 hours	US 1000 dollars	
Type F (Charity)	1/4 hours	US 30 dollars	assigned
Type G (Government-sponsored)	20 minutes	US 5 dollars	assigned

倍斯特國際氣球節

今年倍斯特運輸要做些創新和史無前例的服務。選擇豪華類別的遊客能夠目睹螢火蟲山谷的景色和寧靜的湖之眼。在夜晚的時刻，山谷的景色是相當具特色的，這也使得我們的門票銷售一空。這個地方是很浪漫且很棒的求婚場所。如果你想要在「空中旅程」中求婚的話，請選擇E類型的服務。我們的工作人員甚至會將你想對你的摯愛所表達的話透過「空中文字」的方式特別地呈現出。而且這項服務是免費的。此外，我們正新增F類型的服務。這意謂著50%的費用會以你的名義捐贈給慈善機構，當然這也能從你下個年度的報稅中扣除掉。最後，我們還有政府贊助給年長者的氣球服務，年長者歲數高於65歲者均適用，但是有個條件是，你不能有慢性病。

	時間	價格	描述
Type A （普通）	20分鐘	30美元	（指定）
Type B （普通）	30分鐘	50美元	
Type C （豪華）	2 小時	200美元	（量身訂做）
Type D （豪華）	120分鐘	300美元	
Type E （豪華）	3 小時	1000美元	
Type F （慈善用途）	1/4小時	30美元	（指定）
Type G （政府贊助）	20 分鐘	5美元	（指定）

Questions 149-152

149. The word "**serene**" in the advertisement, line 3, is closet in meaning to (A) sedative (B) severe **(C) tranquil** (D) serendipitous	149. 在廣告中第三行的「寧靜的、安詳的」，意思最接近 (A) 鎮靜的 (B) 嚴重的 **(C) 安靜的、安寧的、平穩的** (D) 意外發現的、僥倖得到的
150. What is the perfect type for the sweethearts that favor air writing? (A) Type B (B) Type C (C) Type D **(D) Type E**	150. 對於偏好空中文字的情侶，哪項是最完美的類型？ (A) Type B (B) Type C (C) Type D **(D) Type E**
151. What is True about the Balloon Festival? (A) Type A is the cheapest. (B) Type C takes longer than Type D. (C) Type D is related to tax exemption. **(D) A tourist who is over 70 and has a high blood pressure cannot use Type G.**	151. 關於氣球節的部分，何者為真？ (A) Type A是最便宜的。 (B) Type C乘坐時間比Type D長。 (C) Type D與稅的減免有關。 **(D) 超過70歲且有高血壓的觀光客無法使用Type G。**
152. What is the ideal type for a mother of three who has a budget of around US 150? **(A) Type A** (B) Type B (C) Type D (D) Type G	152. 對於一位有著三個孩子的媽媽，預算大約是150美元，最理想的類型是？ **(A) Type A** (B) Type B (C) Type D (D) Type G

解析

- 第**149**題，serene = **tranquil**，故答案為**選項C**。
- 第**150**題，Our crew can even specifically put what you would like to say to your love one through air writing.要選E類型，故答案為**選項D**。
- 第**151**題，Finally, we have the government-sponsored balloon for the elderly, people older than 65, but under one condition, you cannot have a chronic illness.和選項D敘述一致，故答案為**選項D**。
- 第**152**題，可以進行計算和看下選項中有提供的類型，故答案為**選項A**。

Questions 153-155

Dear manager,

Oh... that means he will be getting double payments from both companies... is that legal? How is he going to do the tax report? **(1)** Or are we paying him in cash, so no one will find out. **(2)** I'm completely shocked by this. So now my new role is to be a coffee clerk and I occasionally talk to him in the coffee shop during the night and get the information that's useful for us, right? **(3)** Does the coffee shop owner know about this? **(4) I don't know how to brew coffee and identify those beans.** But I just can't wait to try on my uniform and pretend to be the clerk... sitting in the office all day actually bores me... and I will record our conversation for further use...?

Mary, coffee clerk, starting from today

模擬試題（二）

模擬試題（一）

模擬試題（二）

模擬試題（三）

模擬試題（四）

模擬試題（五）

親愛的經理

噢!...那意謂著他從兩間公司中獲取兩份薪資...這樣合法嗎?這樣的話,那他要如何進行報稅呢?還是說我們是付現金給他,所以沒人可以察覺出來。得知這個真相讓我全然感到震驚。所以我現在的新角色是扮演一位咖啡店員,並且在晚上的期間,偶爾跟他講講話,然後從中獲取對於我們有用的資訊,對吧!咖啡店老闆知道關於這件事情嗎?我不知道要如何煮咖啡並且辨別那些豆子。但是我等不及要試穿我的制服且假裝成店員了...在辦公室裡坐整天確實無聊死我了...我會紀錄我們的對話以供進一步使用...?

從今日開始是咖啡店員的瑪莉

Questions 153-155

153. What is true about Bob? **(A) He has a twofold income.** (B) He doesn't know how to do the tax report. (C) He only accepts cash. (D) His new role is a coffee clerk.	153. 關於鮑伯的部分,何者為真? **(A) 他有兩份收入。** (B) 他不知道要如何做稅務報表。 (C) 他僅收取現金。 (D) 他的新角色是咖啡店店員。
154. What is not mentioned about the letter? (A) Mary doesn't know how to brew coffee. (B) Mary cannot stand the boredom. **(C) Mary already gets the uniform.** (D) Mary has to play a disguised role.	154. 關於信件的部分,沒有提到什麼? (A) 瑪莉不知道咬如何煮咖啡。 (B) 瑪莉無法忍受無聊。 **(C) 瑪莉已經拿到了制服。** (D) 瑪莉必須要扮演偽裝的角色。

| 155. In which of the positions marked **(1)**, **(2)**, **(3)**, and **(4)** does the following sentence best belong?
 "**I don't know how to brew coffee and identify those beans.**"
 (A) (1)
 (B) (2)
 (C) (3)
 (D)(4) | 155. 以下這個句子最適合放在文中標記**(1)**、**(2)**、**(3)**、**(4)**的哪個位置？
 「我不知道要如何煮咖啡並且辨別出那些豆子。」
 (A) (1)
 (B) (2)
 (C) (3)
 (D)(4) |

- 第**153**題，Bob領兩份薪水，故答案為**選項A**。
- 第**154**題，瑪莉還未取得制服，故答案為**選項C**。
- 第**155**題，最適合放在Does the coffee shop owner know about this? 後，**(4)**，故答案為**選項D**。

Best Elite University

Our lab researchers have developed an incredible computer system that is quite similar to the sorting hat in the Harry Potter Series, but the difference is that it's not solely on the classification. It can even make a prediction of your accomplishment after you graduate from the university 5 years from now. The accuracy has astounded many scholars and educators, and it's true that academic success has nothing to do with the achievement outside the classroom setting.

Group	Yearly income
A	US 50,000 dollars or below
B	Around US 100,000 dollars
C	US 150,000 dollars

D	US 500,000 dollars
E	US 1,000,000 dollars
F	US 5,000,000 dollars or above

Note:

1. Most people fall directly under Group A (and that stays for the rest of their lives), and very few get the prediction in Group F.
2. The prediction of our super computer seems to coincide with the traditional Chinese forecast.
3. You have to get admitted in our school to be qualified to take the test. This requires courage and money. The fee of the test is US 50,000 dollars, and not every student can afford that plus the tuition. Furthermore, there are some people who are too timid to know the result, so they don't have the guts to face it. If you're suspicious of the test outcome, the redo fee requires US 110,000 dollars, which is more than twice the price of the initial cost.

倍斯特菁英大學

我們的實驗室研究人員已經發展出驚人的電腦系統，相當於在哈利波特系列中出現的分類帽，但是差別在於這不僅是在於分類。這甚至可以預測出你從大學畢業五年後的成就。這項測試的準確度讓許多學者和教育專家們感到吃驚，而學術成就跟教室課堂環境外的成就是毫無相關是千真萬確的。

群組	年收入
A	五萬美元或以下
B	約十萬美元
C	十五萬美元
D	五十萬美元
E	一百萬美元
F	五百萬美元或以上

註：

1. 大多數的人都直接落於A範疇（而且他們的餘生都持續在此範疇），然後非常少的人達到所預測的F範疇裡。

2. 我們超級電腦的預測似乎和傳統中國的算命相吻合。

3. 你必須要獲得入學許可以具備能夠參加這項測試的資格。這會需要勇氣和金錢。這項測試的費用是五萬美元，而並不是每個學生都能負擔的起這個加上學費的費用。此外，有些人過於膽怯而不敢知道測試結果，所以他們沒有膽量去面對這件事。如果你對於測試的結果感到懷疑的話，重新測試的費用會需要花費您11萬美元，超過原測試費用的兩倍。

Questions 156-159	
156. What is not stated about the test? (A) People need to have the courage to take the test. (B) The test is not affordable for all students. **(C) Students can only take the test once in their lifetime.** (D) The test is able to make a prediction of a person's future achievement.	156. 關於測驗的部分，沒有提到什麼？ (A) 人們需要有勇氣參加這項測試 (B) 測驗並不是所有學生均能負擔的起的 **(C) 學生們僅能在有生之年測試一次** (D) 測驗能夠測出一個人的未來成就
157. How much does it cost for the first attempt of the test? **(A) US 50,000** (B) US 110,000 (C) US 150,000 (D) US 100,000	157. 首次嘗試這項測驗要花費多少錢呢？ **(A) US 50,000** (B) US 110,000 (C) US 150,000 (D) US 100,000

158. Which of the following Group is what most people belong to? (A) B (B) D (C) F **(D)A**	158. 大多數的人是屬於下列的哪個族群呢? (A) B (B) D (C) F **(D)A**
159. Which of the following Group contains the least people in the population? (A) E **(B) F** (C) D (D) B	159. 下列的哪個群體包含了人口中最少的占比呢? (A) E **(B) F** (C) D (D) B

解析

- 第**156**題，文中並沒有說一生只能測一次，故答案為**選項C**。
- 第**157**題，The fee of the test is US **50,000 dollars**，故答案為**選項A**。
- 第**158**題，Most people fall directly under the **Group A**，故答案為**選項 D**。
- 第**159**題，very few get the prediction in **Group F**，故答案為**選項B**。

Best Pinball

The pinball game has been invented for centuries. In our Amusement Park, you will have a total novel experience with the game. See the huge waterslides over there and the labyrinth. You actually have to be the ball to play the game... and you will have no idea where you are going. You have to hit the red target among the fifty slides, so the chance is 1/50. The fee is US 5 for the first time player. Other fees are listed in the table. It's quite possible that people actually hit the jackpot at the first attempt. We have consolation prizes for everyone, and for those who hit the jackpot for the first time, we are giving them US 5,000 dollars. It's more like betting for money.

Number of playing	Cost
First time	5 dollars
Second	25 dollars
Third	125 dollars
Fourth	625 dollars
Fifth	3125 dollars
Sixth	15625 dollars
Seventh	78125 dollars
Eighth	390625 dollars

倍斯特彈珠遊戲

彈珠遊戲的發明已經有幾個世紀了。在我們的遊樂園，你會有全新的彈珠遊戲體驗。看那裡巨型的滑水道和迷宮。你實際上要成為「彈珠球」以進行這個遊戲....你不知道你會朝哪個方向走。你必須要在50個滑水道中擊中紅色的目標，所以機會是1/50。費用是第一次5美元。其他的費用列於列表中。相當可能的是，有人在第一次嘗試就擊中了大獎。我們也有安慰獎給每個參加者，而對於那些第一次就擊中大獎者，我們會給予他們5千美元的獎金。這更像是在賭錢。

完的次數	費用
第一次	5元
第二次	25元
第三次	125元
第四次	625元
第五次	3125元
第六次	15625元
第七次	78125元
第八次	390625元

Questions 160-163

160. What is the probability of playing the game by using 15625 dollars? (A) 3/50 (B) 1/25 **(C) 3/25** (D) 6	160. 花費15625元完此項遊戲的機率是多少? (A) 3/50 (B) 1/25 **(C) 3/25** (D) 6
161. What is the rate of winning for average players? (A) 8/50 (B) 1/10 (C) 2/50 **(D) 1/50**	161. 對於一般的玩家，贏的機率是多少? (A) 8/50 (B) 1/10 (C) 2/50 **(D) 1/50**
162. How much does a guy have to spend in order to play the game the eighth time? (A) 625 (B) 15,625 (C) 78,125 **(D) 390,625**	162. 一個男子玩此項遊戲第八次將要花費多少錢? (A) 625 (B) 15,625 (C) 78,125 **(D) 390,625**
163. How can a person actually gain if he hits the jackpot for the first attempt? **(A) 4995** (B) 5000 (C) 5100 (D) 5005	163. 如果第一次就贏得頭彩的話，他實際上獲得多少錢? **(A) 4995** (B) 5000 (C) 5100 (D) 5005

解析

‧ 第**160**題，6/50 = 3/25，故答案為**選項C**。
‧ 第**161**題，1/50，故答案為**選項D**。
‧ 第**162**題，從表格中看第八次所需金額390625，故答案為**選項D**。
‧ 第**163**題，得獎金額5000要扣除花費的五元，所以是4995元，故答案為**選項A**。

Best Amusement Park is revising the policy of letting the customer refill the drink whether it is deliberately spilled or not. The effective date is next Monday. **(1)** That means parents should really keep a good eye on their kids. In addition, the haunted house will be adding more features. **(2)** You get to experience several real scenes in the ghost movies. It's going to be scarier than usual. **(3)** What's more, if you don't consider it horrific, you will get the refund, half the price of the ticket, but according to the staff, he says it won't, it is really scary, scary enough for you to pee your pants on the spot. **(4) And he even makes a video warning people of preparing the diaper before entering the haunted house.** That surely is the overstatement for some people... and you have to try that to know if this is true.

倍斯特遊樂園正著手修改讓顧客能夠免費續滿飲料的政策，不論是否飲料是故意灑出來的。生效的日期是下週一。這也意謂著父母們真的應該要看好他們的小孩。此外，鬼屋會增添更多項設施。你可以體驗幾個於鬼片中的真實場景。這比起往常來說更加可怕。更多的是，如果你認為不恐怖的話，你將會收到退款，門票的半價，但是根據員工的說法，他說不可能的，這真的很恐怖，恐怖到你會尿在現場，而他甚至製作了視頻警告遊客，在進入鬼屋之前要準備尿布。對於有些人來說，這確實是誇大其辭...但你必須要試過後才知道這是否是真的。

Questions 164-166

164. In which of the positions marked **(1)**, **(2)**, **(3)**, and **(4)** does the following sentence best belong?
"**And he even makes a video warning people of preparing the diaper before entering the haunted house.**"
(A) (1)
(B) (2)
(C) (3)
(D)(4)

164. 以下這個句子最適合放在文中標記 **(1)**、**(2)**、**(3)**、**(4)** 的哪個位置？
「而他甚至製作了視頻警告遊客，在進入鬼屋之前要準備尿布。」
(A) (1)
(B) (2)
(C) (3)
(D)(4)

165. What is the article mainly about? (A) watching ghost movies (B) surveillance on children **(C) new announcements about the policy and features** (D) uploading an exaggerated video	165. 報導主要是關於什麼? (A) 觀看鬼片 (B) 監視小孩子 **(C) 關於政策和設施的新公告** (D) 上傳誇大的視頻
166. What is stated about the haunted house? **(A) More features will be updated.** (B) People don't consider it scary. (C) People urine at the scene. (D) It uses knockoff props.	166. 關於鬼屋,提到了什麼? **(A) 更多的設施會更新** (B) 人們不認為可怕 (C) 人們在現場尿尿 (D) 其使用了仿冒品的道具

解析

- **第164題**,插入句中的敘述有誇飾,放在That surely is the overstatement for some people之前是最合適的,**(4)**,故答案為**選項D**。
- **第165題**,這題最主要的就是new announcements about the policy and features,故答案為**選項C**。
- **第166題**,其他選項均不符,故答案為**選項A**。

Best Cinema now wants to do the epic movie, so they are dying to find a great place to do the shoot. **(1) Executives have gone to several castles, but couldn't find a satisfied one.** Castle A is **enigmatic** and shady, but it's just weird in a way that the camera cannot get a clear shot. **(2)** Castle B really earns its name for a haunted house, but an incident at the castle the other day made the CEO question whether it is the ideal place for the movie. Castle C is not that appealing in the eyes of the editors, and the director doesn't like it. **(3)** This is about a team work, so they eventually turned down the offer given by the owner. Castle D is mysterious as well, but it needs a huge renovation. **(4)** And that will make the entire budget exceed the original estimated price. Using Castle D for the movie surely will make investors unhappy. So the search continues.

倍斯特電影現在想要做出壯麗的電影巨作，所以他們迫不及待地要找尋極佳的拍攝地點。高階主管已經去了幾個城堡，但是找不到一個滿意的。A城堡是神秘且陰暗的，但是某種程度上就是奇怪，相機拍不出清晰的照片。城堡B真的以其鬼屋而得其名，但是幾天前在城堡發生的一個事件讓執行長質疑，這個地方會是理想的電影拍攝場景嗎？城堡C並不如編輯們眼裡那樣引人入勝，而且導演並不喜歡它。這是關於一個團隊合作，所以他們最終拒絕了由屋主提供的提議。城堡D也是神祕的，但是它需要進行大幅度的翻修。而那將會讓整個預算超過原先所預估的價格。使用城堡D來拍攝電影確實會讓投資人感到不開心。所以找尋持續著。

Questions 167-169

167. What is the article mainly about?	167. 報導主要是關於什麼？
(A) To please the executives	(A) 討好高階主管
(B) How an epic movie is made.	(B) 史詩般的電影是如何製成的
(C) the search for an ideal castle for the shoot	**(C) 尋找理想城堡的拍攝地點**
(D) the cooperation among directors and editors	(D) 導演和編輯們之間的合作

168. The word "**enigmatic**" in the paragraph, line 2, is closet in meaning to (A) descriptive **(B) esoteric** (C) inconsequential (D) distinctive	168. 在第一段第三行的「如謎的、難以理解的」，意思最接近 (A) 描寫的、記述的 **(B) 深奧的、難理解的** (C) 不重要的、無足輕重的 (D) 有特色的、特殊的
169. In which of the positions marked **(1)**, **(2)**, **(3)**, and **(4)** does the following sentence best belong? "**Executives have gone to several castles, but couldn't find a satisfied one.**" **(A) (1)** (B) (2) (C) (3) (D) (4)	169. 以下這個句子最適合放在文中標記**(1)**, **(2)**, **(3)**, **(4)**的哪個位置？ 「高階主管已經去了幾個城堡，但是找不到一個滿意的。」 **(A) (1)** (B) (2) (C) (3) (D) (4)

解析

- 第**167**題，報導是關於the search for an ideal castle for the shoot，故答案為**選項C**。
- 第**168**題，enigmatic = **esoteric**，故答案為**選項B**。
- 第**169**題，插入句最適合放在依序介紹四個城堡之前，**(1)**，故答案為**選項A**。

Dear Cindy,

You just have to be aware of all trick questions. Remember the scene of the job interview in Desperate Housewives, Season 5? The heroine is smart enough to say that "if I was dumb enough to answer that, I never would've gotten into Northwestern." **(1)** Sometimes you don't have to answer all questions, and sometimes you can answer interview questions in a clever way. You don't have to be passive. **(2)** Be confident and you also have to know that you are evaluating those companies as well. That **mentality** can actually make you quite composed during an interview. **(3) Also, you have to be careful about questions that trick you into answering things that can jeopardize the hire.** You don't have to reveal your health conditions unless your company requires you to hand in a physical check-up. **(4)** And you obviously don't have to mention that your mother is so sick that can take up much of your energy after work or during the holidays...

Best Column

親愛的辛蒂

你就是需要意識到那些狡詐的問題。記得在慾望師奶第五季中的工作面試場景嗎?女主角聰明到回應著「如果我笨到回答這個問題的話,那麼我當初不會被西北大學錄取」。有時候你並不需要回答所有個問題,而有時候你可能要以聰明的方式去回答面試問題。你不用維持被動姿態。要有信心而你也要知道的是,你也在評估那些公司。這樣的心態確實讓你在面試期間能保有相對的沉著。而且,你對於誘答你回答那種能影響你錄取的問題回答要小心翼翼。你不必揭露你的健康情況,除非你的公司要求你要繳交健康檢查的報告。且顯而易見的是你不必提及你母親病重,所以在工作後或假日期間會耗掉你太多精力。

倍斯特專欄

Questions 170-172

170. What is Not stated about the "Job Column"? (A) Disclosing your health conditions falls into the category of the jeopardizing. (B) Be confident during the interview. (C) Be active during the interview. **(D) You have to answer all the questions in the interview.**	170. 關於「求職專欄」，沒有提到什麼？ (A) 揭露你的健康情況落入危及工作的範疇。 (B) 在面試期間要保有自信 (C) 在面試期間要保持積極 **(D) 在面試期間，你必須要回答所有的問題**
171. The word "**mentality**" in the letter, line 8, is closet in meaning to (A) adaptation (B) manipulation **(C) attitude** (D) benevolence	171. 在信件中第八行的「心態」，意思最接近 (A) 適應、適合、改編、改寫 (B) 操作、運用、操縱、控制 **(C) 態度** (D) 仁慈
172. In which of the positions marked **(1)**, **(2)**, **(3)**, and **(4)** does the following sentence best belong? "**Also, you have to be careful about questions that trick you into answering things that can jeopardize the hire.**" (A) (1) (B) (2) **(C) (3)** (D) (4)	172. 以下這個句子最適合放在文中標記**(1)**, **(2)**, **(3)**, **(4)**的哪個位置？ 「而且，你對於誘答你回答那種能影響你錄取的問題回答要小心翼翼。」 (A) (1) (B) (2) **(C) (3)** (D) (4)

- **第170題**，文中有提到不用所有的問題都回答，故答案為**選項D**。
- **第171題**，mentality = **attitude**，故答案為**選項C**。
- **第172題**，從插入句中的jeopardize the hire等可以推斷出要放在You don't have to reveal your health conditions unless your company requires you to hand in a physical check-up.之前，**(3)**，故答案為**選項C**。

As to the question for asking for a raise. Just do that whenever you think you deserve it. Life is simply too short and you do need to have the guts to say that. (even if they say no, there is no harm in asking. You are doing a better job than those who don't ask.) Of course, you don't have to piss of your boss. **(1)** Do it under the right circumstance, not during the economic downturn or the **downsizing** period. **(2)** You also have to understand your salary in the job market and your salary is based on your expertise and contribution. You don't have to mistakenly think of asking for a promotion or a raise as an embarrassment. **(3)Try to negotiate with the superior or the boss, you would be surprised about their reaction.** That means you care about your growth and you have ambitions. **(4)** That also means you are not making a job hop, and you want to contribute more. You can also ask them that, if you do expect a higher salary, how much contribution requires to do that in order for that to happen...

Best Column

模擬試題（二）

模擬試題（一）

模擬試題（二）

模擬試題（三）

模擬試題（四）

模擬試題（五）

至於要求加薪的問題的話。每當你認為你值得的時候，就提吧!人生真的太短暫，而且你確實需要有膽量去提加薪。（即使他們拒絕，也沒有什麼損失的。比起那些不敢提的已經好很多了。）當然，你不需要惹怒你的老闆。要在適當的時機下提加薪這件事，而不是在經濟蕭條時或是裁員時期提。你也要了解在就業市場中你所符的薪資，以及你薪資的核算是根據你的技能和貢獻。你也不用把要求升遷或是加薪誤會成是件令人尷尬的事情。試著與上司或者是老闆協商，對於他們的反應你會感到意外的。這也意謂著你不會跳槽，因為你想要貢獻更多。你也可以詢問他們，如果你期望有較高的薪資的話，會需要什麼樣程度的貢獻才能讓這件事情成真呢？

倍斯特專欄

Questions 173-175

173. What is Not stated about the "Job Column"? (A) **One has to surprise his or her boss to get the raise.** (B) One has to pick the right moment to ask for a raise. (C) One's contribution to the job is related to the evaluation of the salary. (D) One needs to be brave enough to ask for a raise.	173. 關於「求職專欄」，沒有提到什麼? (A) **一個人必須要使他或她的老闆吃驚以獲得加薪** (B) 一個人必須要選在對的時刻要求加薪 (C) 一個人對於工作的貢獻度與薪資評估有關係。 (D) 一個人需要有足夠的勇氣要求加薪
174. The word "**downsizing**" in the letter, line 7, is closet in meaning to (A) sustaining (B) downside (C) underestimating (D) **retrenching**	174. 在信件中第7行的「縮減人力的」，意思最接近 (A) 持續的 (B) 不利 (C) 低估的 (D) **緊縮開支的**

| 175. In which of the positions marked **(1)**, **(2)**, **(3)**, and **(4)** does the following sentence best belong? "**Try to negotiate with the superior or the boss, you would be surprised about their reaction.**" (A) (1) (B) (2) **(C) (3)** (D) (4) | 175. 以下這個句子最適合放在文中標記**(1)**, **(2)**, **(3)**, **(4)**的哪個位置? 「試著與上司或者是老闆協商,對於他們的反應你會感到意外的。」 (A) (1) (B) (2) **(C) (3)** (D) (4) |

解析

- 第**173**題,文章中有提到不要surprise,其實也要選對時機說,故答案為**選項A**。
- 第**174**題,downsizing = **retrenching**,故答案為**選項D**。
- 第**175**題,最適合放在You don't have to mistakenly think of asking a promotion or a raise as an embarrassment.後,**(3)**,故答案為**選項C**。

Dear Best Restaurant,

I went to your restaurant the other day and your clerk was **downright** rude to us for no reason. **(1)** We wore the suit and were dressed as requested, knowing that your place is a royal place for celebrities. And we did pay our meals. It was not like we didn't pay the full payment. **(2)** We deserve to be treated better. If I don't get the reasonable reply soon, I'm going to the Consumer Department and file a complaint, which will result in a frequent visit of the government officials to your place. **(3) Quite a burden for you to handle.** And I will post the entire incident to the website and ig telling people about your horrible service. **(4)** I bet a lot of people won't be visiting your restaurant, and some of my close friends are really rich, rich enough to buy your place.

Consumer Linda

親愛的倍斯特餐廳

前幾天，我到你們的餐廳用餐，然後受到你們的店員不分青紅皂白地極無禮對待。我們照著要求穿著了西裝和服飾，得知你們的地方是供給名人們用餐的皇室場所。而我們確實有付費給你們。又不是我們沒有付錢。我們值得更好的對待。如果我沒有即刻得到合理的回覆的話，我會去消費部門，然後提起抱怨的控訴，此舉會讓政府公務員更頻繁地到你們餐廳查訪。你們如要處理這類事情會是個負擔，然後我也會將整起事件發佈在網站和ig上，告訴民眾你們糟糕的服務。我相信有許多人會因此都不到你們餐廳用餐了，而我的閨密有些可是相當有錢，有錢到可以買下你的地方了。

消費者 琳達

Dear Linda,

Please accept my apology on behalf of the company. But I do want you to know that it was not our fault that day... well partially. I know it was not entirely, but partially. It's not that we don't admit the fault on our part. But recently, lots of guys **sneak** back to our restaurant and try to pretend to be one of our staff. Really crazy college students, who try to be us and upload the video they record to YouTube to boost the view. I've enclosed the table of guys we caught with the help of the police, and you can go to the police station to file the lawsuit. We will give you a discount of 30% for your next visit. Anything your order. The total will be deducted in accordance with the discount.

Name	Educational Background
Jason Lin	High school
Mark Wang	College student
Neal Chen	Ph.D in philosophy

親愛的琳達

我僅代表公司對此感到非常抱歉。但是我真的想要你知道的是，錯不在我們…嗯…僅只有部分的錯是吧。這不是要辯說，我們不承認我們的過錯。但是，最近，有許多男子溜到我們餐廳裡頭，然後試圖扮成我們的職員。真的瘋狂的大學學生，試圖要當我們的一份子並且將這些錄製成視頻放到YouTube的頻道上以提高收視率。在警方的協助下，我們逮到這些男子，我已將列表檢附在附檔，而你可以到警局並提出訴訟。我們會於你下次來用餐時，對任何你點的餐點給予你七折的折扣。總額會根據折扣進行扣除。

姓名	教育背景
傑森·林	高中
馬克·王	大學學生
尼爾·陳	哲學博士

Questions 176-180

| 176. In which of the positions marked **(1)**, **(2)**, **(3)**, and **(4)** does the following sentence best belong?
"**Quite a burden for you to handle.**"
(A) (1)
(B) (2)
(C) (3)
(D) (4) | 176. 以下這個句子最適合放在文中標記**(1)**, **(2)**, **(3)**, **(4)**的哪個位置？
「你們要處理這類事情會是個負擔」
(A) (1)
(B) (2)
(C) (3)
(D) (4) |

177. The word "**downright**" in paragraph1, line 1, is closet in meaning to (A) declined (B) reluctant **(C) thoroughly** (D) absolute	177. 在第一段第三行的「十足的、直截了當的」，意思最接近 (A) 婉拒的 (B) 不情願的、勉強的 **(C) 徹底地、認真仔細地** (D) 完全的、絕對的
178. What is Not mentioned in both letters? (A) The clerk didn't show the respect to the customers. (B) The customer is planning to write a complaint. **(C) The restaurant eventually admitted the flaw and thought it was entirely responsible.** (D) The customer can file the lawsuit for what happened.	178. 在兩封信件中沒有提到什麼？ (A) 店員沒有對顧客展現出尊重。 (B) 顧客正計畫要撰寫抱怨文。 **(C) 餐廳最終坦承疏失且認為責任全歸他們所有。** (D) 顧客可以對於所發生的事情提起訴訟。
179. The word "**sneak**" in paragraph2, line 4, is closet in meaning to (A) submit (B) astonish **(C) creep** (D) surface	179. 在第2段第4行的「偷偷地做」，意思最接近 (A) 遞交 (B) 使驚訝 **(C) 悄悄地進行** (D) 浮現
180. What is enclosed with the letter? (A) the list of several police officers (B) The educational background of the guys **(C) the list of guys who did the crime** (D) the list of restaurant staff	180. 信件中附了什麼？ (A) 幾位警官的列表 (B) 男子們的教育背景 **(C) 犯罪男子們的列表** (D) 餐廳職員的列表

- **第176題**，這題放在file a complaint, which will result in a frequent visit of the government officials to your place.後是最合適的，**(3)**，故答案為**選項C**。
- **第177題**，downright = **thoroughly**，故答案為**選項C**。
- **第178題**，餐廳並未覺得是**entirely responsible**，故答案為**選項C**。
- **第179題**，sneak = **creep**，故答案為**選項C**。
- **第180題**，附檔是犯行的男子的表格，故答案為**選項C**。

Dear Cindy

I don't think you are a whistle blower. You are just doing your job. It's great that you are telling me this. **(1)** Now I know John often **waltzes into** the conference room unprepared. I will address this in our next conference meeting. Also, I do need someone to keep a watch on several guys in the marketing department for me. **(2)** They seem ganged upon the new recruit. If anything happens, make sure I'm the first to know. **(3) And you don't have to reveal your true identity.** You still remain as the innocent girl who just graduated from college and glad that you have a job during a great recession. **(4)** Finally, I bought you a fashion cloth while I was having an international meeting in Germany. Hope you will like it. I am going to ask the guy from the flower shop to send it to you under the name Mark James, your secret admirer. Hope it will cause a scene in the office.

The Director

親愛的辛蒂

我不認為你是個吹哨者。你只是做你的工作而已。很棒的是，你告訴我這些事情。現在我知道了，約翰通常昂首闊步地走進會議室卻都毫無準備。我會在我們下次的會議室會議中提出來。而且，我確實需要你替我監視行銷部門的幾個男子。他們似乎結成一夥對付新聘人員。如果有任何事情發生的話，確保我是第一個知道的。然後你不需要揭露你的真實身分。你仍舊是那個剛從學校畢業的天真女孩，而且對於自己在景氣蕭條的情況下仍有份工作感到高興。最後，在我待在德國開國際會議的期間，我替你買了一件時尚服飾。希望你會喜歡它。我會請花店的男子以馬克·詹姆士的名義送花給你，你的祕密愛慕者。希望在辦公室裡頭會引起騷動。

總裁

Dear Miss D,

Thanks for the gift. I do love this job by working under cover. I'm going to be so thrilled at receiving the present. And as for the other things, I happened to know the love affair between the CFO and the secretary. **(1)** Is that legal in this company? Perhaps you can use that against the CFO if he doesn't do his job well. **(2)** I'm sending you the recording as evidence, which can be used during the court. And several pics that I captured at the basement. It's turning more and more **juicy. (3)** I guess I will be watching them for the next few days as well. It's Thursday afternoon. Now you have to excuse me. I have to pretend to be dumb and forget to send the important emails and ask some helps from colleagues in the marketing department. **(4) A great moment to peek what they are doing ha ha...**

Cindy

親愛的D小姐

禮物的部分謝了。我確實喜愛這份臥底的工作。對於即將要收到的禮物感到興奮異常。而至於其他事情，我碰巧得知財務長和秘書之間的戀愛。在公司中，這樣合法嗎?或許你可以用這點來制衡財務長，如果他工作做得不好的話。我正將錄影寄給妳當作證據，此能用於當作呈堂證供。然後有幾張圖片是在地下室拍攝到的。這變得越來越有可看性。我想我會在接下來的幾天也會看到他們。現在是週四下午。現在請容許我離開一下。我必須要假裝成笨拙貌的我，然後忘記寄送重要的文件，去向行銷部門的同事尋求幫助。這是個偷看他們正在幹嘛的好時機...哈哈。

辛蒂

Questions 181-185

181. In which of the positions marked **(1)**, **(2)**, **(3)**, and **(4)** does the following sentence best belong? "**And you don't have to reveal your true identity.**" (A) (1) (B) (2) **(C) (3)** (D) (4)	181. 以下這個句子最適合放在文中標記**(1)**, **(2)**, **(3)**, **(4)**的哪個位置? 「而且妳不需要揭露妳的真實身分。」 (A) (1) (B) (2) **(C) (3)** (D) (4)
182. What is indicated about Mark James? (A) He has an affair with Cindy. (B) He is the guy who works at the flower shop (C) He happens to have additional flowers and wants to cause a scene. **(D) He is a made-up name used by the director**	182. 關於Mark James提到了什麼? (A) 他與辛蒂有婚外情。 (B) 他是在花店工作的男子。 (C) 他碰巧有額外的花朵且想要引起騷動。 **(D) 他是總裁所使用的偽造名字。**

183. The word "**waltzes into**" in letter 1, line 2, is closet in meaning to (A) reluctantly walks into **(B) swaggeringly walks in** (C) confidently dances with (D) persuasively talks into	183. 在第一信第2行的「昂首闊步地走入」，意思最接近 (A) 勉強地走進 **(B) 昂首闊步地走進** (C) 自信地與...舞著 (D) 具說服力的說服
184. In which of the positions marked **(1)**, **(2)**, **(3)**, and **(4)** does the following sentence best belong? "**A great moment to peek what they are doing ha ha...**" (A) (1) (B) (2) (C) (3) **(D) (4)**	184. 以下這個句子最適合放在文中標記**(1)**, **(2)**, **(3)**, **(4)**的哪個位置? 「偷看他們正在幹嘛的好時機...哈哈。」 (A) (1) (B) (2) (C) (3) **(D) (4)**
185. The word "**juicy**" in letter 2, line 7, is closet in meaning to (A) awkward (B) seductive **(C) provocative** (D) jubilant	185. 在第二封信第7行的「生動有趣的、富刺激性的」，意思最接近 (A) 笨拙的 (B) 誘惑的、引人注意的、有魅力的 **(C) 挑撥的、刺激的** (D) 歡樂的

解析

· 第**181**題，這題的插入句放在You still remain as the innocent girl who just graduated from college and glad that you have a job during a great recession.之前是最合適的，故**(3)**，故答案為**選項C**。

· 第**182**題，Mark James是主管亂編的一個名字，用於送花的，故答案為**選項D**。

· 第**183**題，waltzes into = **swaggeringly walks in**，故答案為**選項B**。

· 第**184**題，這題的插入句放置在**(4)**最合適，故答案為**選項D**。

· 第**185**題，juicy = **provocative**，故答案為**選項C**。

Advertisement

Best Island was established 50 years ago. By using a **desolate** land, we have created a wonder. Lions freely roam on the land. Every year lots of people are eager to test their own courage through enrolling in our program. Some are seeking wealth by having an adventure here. Believe it or not there are plenty of gold, silver, and jewelry hidden under the sand of the island. In our castle, it's totally a new adventure. Seeking wealth involves taking a risk. Here is the place for you. Enrollees should sign the contract. According to the contract, exemption clauses are listed in a few sections. Make sure you've read through all of the clauses.

廣告

倍斯特島嶼創建於50年前。藉由使用荒棄的土地，我們已經創造了奇蹟。獅子能自由地在島上漫遊。每年，有許多人渴望藉由註冊我們的計畫來測試他們的勇氣。有些人則是希望藉由參與冒險而能求得財富。信不信由你，這裡有大量的金銀珠寶藏匿在島上的沙子底。在我們的城堡中，這是個全新的冒險。尋求財富牽涉到要有膽量去冒險。這裡就是你的機會之地。註冊者會需要簽署合約。根據合約，免責條款會列在幾個區塊上。請確認你已經讀過所有條則。

Dear Best Island,

I'm a man in his forties, and yet I still haven't accomplished anything much in life. **(1) Then it just hit me, why don't I give it a shot, and there is no harm in doing that right?** My friend's ancestors all went to the gold hunt during the Gold Rush period, and I don't seem a coward than any of them. **(2)** I've made up my mind to do it because life is too short. **(3)** I was wondering how to sign up for the program, and can fortune-seekers get all the gold and other things and then bring them back in the country where I'm in, or should we split the treasure with the company? **(4)** And what should I bring with me, the gear or other things. Are powerful weapons allowed to be used during the treasure hunt?
Please reply to me ASAP, thanks.

Poor Man

親愛的倍斯特島嶼

我是位40歲左右的男性，而到目前為止，我在生命中並未有任何的成就。然後，我靈光一閃，為什麼我不試試看呢，而且試試也無妨，對吧?我朋友的祖先都曾在淘金潮的時候去淘金，而且比起他們來說，我似乎也沒有比他們膽怯。我已經下定決心要參加了，因為生命太短暫了。我在想要如何能參加這項計劃呢?而抱有發財夢者都有得到所有的金子和其他東西，然後將其帶回我所待的國家嗎，或者是我們會需要跟公司分我們找到的寶藏呢?還有我該帶些什麼呢，工具還是其他東西呢?在尋寶期間，可以使用強大武器嗎?在請盡快回覆我，謝謝。

窮男人

Dear Poor Man,

I guess you are really desperate, and I prefer not to call you a poor guy myself. It's pretty rude, and several people who self-proclaim themselves poor are actually really wealthy. It's too soon to refer you to that kind of nickname. I've listed several things for you to know more about the program. Please read it and if you have any question, please contact me 999-999-999-999.
Best Island

Items	money
Payment to enroll	US 50,000 dollars
horse	US 1,000 dollars
pigeons	US 1,000 dollars
food	It depends
Meat	US 1,000 dollars
Map	US 10,000 dollars
training	US 20,000 dollars
Water/ per bottle	US 50 dollars

親愛的窮男人

我想你真的相當情急奔命，而我自己本身是不願這樣稱呼你為窮人的。這相當無禮，因為有幾個自稱他們自己窮的人，實際上卻相當相當地富有。將你與那樣的匿名有所指涉有點言之過早了。我已經列了幾項是你更需要知道關於這個計劃的事項。請閱讀它，而如果你有任何問題的話，請與我聯繫，電話是999-999-999-999。

倍斯特島嶼

項目	金錢
參加的費用	五萬美元
馬匹	一千美元
鴿子	一千美元
食物	視情況而定
肉品	一千美元
地圖	一萬美元
訓練	兩萬美元
水/每瓶	五十美元

Questions 186-190

186. The word "**desolate**" in paragraph1, line 1, is closet in meaning to
(A) undersized
(B) bleak
(C) undercut
(D) underestimated

186. 在第一段第1行的「荒蕪的、無人煙的」，意思最接近
(A) 比普通小的、小尺寸的
(B) 荒涼的、無遮蔽的
(C) 廉價出售、削價競爭
(D) 低估的

187. What is being advertised? (A) A promotional offer for the castle (B) Recruitment for the island guard **(C) An adventurous journey to get rich** (D) A detailed explanation for the exemption clauses for free	187. 廣告的項目是? (A) 城堡的促銷通知 (B) 島嶼保鑣的招聘 **(C) 致富的冒險旅程** (D) 免費對於免責條款的詳細解釋
188. In which of the positions marked **(1)**, **(2)**, **(3)**, and **(4)** does the following sentence best belong? "**Then it just hit me, why don't I give it a shot, and there is no harm in that right?**" **(A)(1)** (B) (2) (C) (3) (D) (4)	188. 以下這個句子最適合放在文中標記(1), (2), (3), (4)的哪個位置? 「然後，我靈光一閃，為什麼我不試試看呢，而且試試也無妨，對吧?」 **(A)(1)** (B) (2) (C) (3) (D) (4)
189. What is Not available for an additional charge? **(A)elephant** (B) horse (C) food (D) water	189. 什麼不是額外付費可以得到的? **(A)大象** (B) 馬匹 (C) 食物 (D) 水
190. How much does it cost if the Poor Man wants to enroll and purchase a map? (A) NT 60,000 (B) NT 2,000 **(C) NT 1,800,000** (D) NT 180,000	190. 如果窮男人想要註冊並且購買一張地圖的話，會需要花費多少錢? (A) NT 60,000 (B) NT 2,000 **(C) NT 1,800,000** (D) NT 180,000

解析

- 第186題，desolate = **bleak**，故答案為**選項B**。
- 第187題，廣告的項目其實就是**An adventurous journey to get rich**，故答案為**選項C**。
- 第188題，這題放在開頭的I'm a man in his forties, and yet I still haven't accomplished anything much in life. 後最合適，故 **(1)**，故答案為**選項A**。
- 第189題，大象不是多付款就能取得的，故答案為**選項A**。
- 第190題，enroll+map的費用是六萬塊美金，乘以30 = **1,800,000**，故答案為**選項C**。

Dear Best Island,

I've received the list of items. I'm fine with the enrolled fee, but what are all other listed items for? Can I just pay the fee and start the treasure hunt myself? And why do I need pigeons... it's getting ludicrous.

Poor Man

親愛的倍斯特島嶼

我已經收到了列表的項目了。對於註冊的費用我沒有任何問題，但是其他所有列的項目收費是要幹嘛的呢?我是否可以僅支付註冊費用然後就開始我的尋寶旅程呢?還有為什麼我會要用到鴿子呢?...這越來越荒謬了。

窮男人

Dear poor man,

Normally, we don't recommend you do. A guy without an intensive training can get killed by wild animals in an instant. **(1)** Since no cellphones will be allowed to use during the treasure hunt, we kindly advise you to use pigeons. If you have any questions, you can send the pigeon to us. We can even deliver a specifically tailored food to the spot where you are located. **(2)** You won't get starved before living your dreamed life. Furthermore, meat is used to distract carnivores, so we highly recommend you to buy that kind of service. What about map? You should buy that, too. **(3) I won't condone myself seeing any customers getting lost in a vast land.** That's pathetic. As for the training, it's entirely up to you. The training usually takes 2 months. **(4)** You can adjust yourself well in the wild, become athletic, and be ready for the test in the wild. If you still have any questions, please let me know. And make sure you bring a huge bag and personal items with you because you will need those.

Best Island

窮男人你好

通常的話，我們不建議你這樣做。沒有經過嚴密訓練的人，可能馬上就被野生動物咬死了。既然在尋寶期間，手機是不允許使用的，我們好心建議您購買鴿子。如果你有任何問題的話，你可以飛鴿傳書給我們，我們甚至可以遞送量身訂做的食物到你所待的地點喔!在實現你的夢想生活之前，你不會感到飢餓。此外，肉品是用於分散肉食動物的注意力用的，所以我們極建議您購買那項服務。那地圖呢?你也該購買地圖。我無法忍受自己目睹任何顧客在廣大的土地上迷失的樣貌。那樣很悲慘的。關於訓練的話，這全然在你。訓練通常需花費兩個月的時間。你能在野外做好自我調適且健壯體格，準備好野外的挑戰。如果你仍有任何問題的話，請讓我知道。還有確保你攜帶大型的袋子跟個人物品，因為你將會需要那些東西。

倍斯特島嶼

Dear Best Island,

I think the pigeon thing is an **extortion**. **(1)** I definitely don't need a horse, either. It's so inhumane. **(2)** And I do have a good sense for direction, so the map is the last thing I need. **(3)** However, I do think I need the training. **(4) For a person who has a big belly, this can be a good thing.** By the way, is the training program intensive? I think the bank loan can cover the cost to pay the program. Please tell me how should I make the payment? Also, am I able to get the discount? I'm an enthusiastic participant, so I do think I deserve the discount.

Poor Man

親愛的倍斯特島嶼

我認為鴿子的事真的是個敲詐。我確實也不需要一匹馬。這太不人道了。而且，我確實有很好的方向感，所以地圖是我最不需要的東西。然而，我覺得我會需要訓練。對於一個有著大肚子的我來說，訓練可能是件好事。順帶一提的是，訓練的課程很嚴密嗎？我認為我的銀行貸款能夠支付這個課程的費用。請讓我知道我要如何支付款項？然後，我能享有折扣嗎？我是個有熱忱的參與者，所以我認為我值得享有折扣。

窮男人

Questions 191-195	
191. What is Not mentioned in "the reply to the Poor Man"? (A) Using pigeons can keep you from getting hungry. (B) Using pigeons is suggested. **(C) The training is mandatory.** (D) The training is essential.	191. 關於「回覆給窮男人」沒有提到什麼？ (A) 使用鴿子可以讓你免於飢餓。 (B) 使用鴿子是建議的。 **(C) 訓練是規定性的。** (D) 訓練是必要的。

192. What advice is Not included in the information? (A) It's recommended to take the training. (B) Meat is used to divert the attention of the meat-eaters. (C) Carry the personal belongings with you **(D) Purchase a horse to replace walking alone**	192. 哪項建議沒有包含在忠告裡頭？ (A) 參加訓練是推薦的 (B) 肉品用於分散肉食動物的注意力 (C) 攜帶個人物品在身旁 **(D) 購買一匹馬以取代僅靠步行**
193. In which of the positions marked **(1)**, **(2)**, **(3)**, and **(4)** does the following sentence best belong? "**I won't condone myself seeing any customers getting lost in a vast land.**" (A) (1) (B) (2) **(C) (3)** (D) (4)	193. 以下這個句子最適合放在文中標記(1), (2), (3), (4)的哪個位置？ 「我無法忍受自己目睹任何顧客在廣大的土地上迷失的樣貌。」 (A) (1) (B) (2) **(C) (3)** (D) (4)
194. The word "**extortion**" in paragraph3, line 1, is closet in meaning to (A) recognition (B) discomfort **(C) blackmail** (D) extinguishment	194. 在第3段第1行的「敲詐、勒索、強求」，意思最接近 (A) 認出、識別、認識 (B) 不舒服、不適 **(C) 敲詐、勒索** (D) 熄滅、消滅、滅絕

| 195. In which of the positions marked **(1)**, **(2)**, **(3)**, and **(4)** does the following sentence best belong?
"**For a person who has a big belly, this can be a good thing.**"
(A) (1)
(B) (2)
(C) (3)
(D)(4) | 195. 以下這個句子最適合放在文中標記**(1)**, **(2)**, **(3)**, **(4)**的哪個位置?
「對於一個有著大肚子的我來說,訓練可能是件好事。」
(A) (1)
(B) (2)
(C) (3)
(D)(4) |

解析

- 第**191**題,文中沒有說訓練是mandatory,故答案為**選項C**。
- 第**192**題,文中沒有提到購馬以取代步行,故答案為**選項D**。
- 第**193**題,這題的插入句插在That's pathetic.前最剛好,故 **(3)**,故答案為**選項C**。
- 第**194**題,extortion = **blackmail**,故答案為**選項C**。
- 第**195**題,從a big belly等其實最適合放置的地方在However, I do think I'll be needing the training.後,故 **(4)**,故答案為**選項D**。

Dear Poor Man,

Only people using all those services can get the discount. **(1) But since you are an enthusiastic and vibrant man, we will give you a bow and arrows for you to defend yourself.** It's entirely free, so don't tell other participants, ok? They will get pretty mad... you know how competitive people can get. **(2)** I guess I will see you on Monday, unless you do have other questions. Please have the money transferred to our bank account, and good luck. **(3)** You can text me while you are at the training center. **(4)** You are allowed to use your cellphone during your stay there.

Best Island

親愛的窮男人

只有那些使用所有服務的人能夠享有折扣。但是既然你是有熱忱且具活力的男子，我們將給你一把弓和弓箭，讓你能夠用於自我防衛。這完全是免費的，所以別告訴其他參加者，知道嗎?他們將會非常生氣…人們的競爭心態就是怎樣，我想你是知道的。我想那就星期一見囉，除非你還有任何問題，然後請將錢匯款至我們的銀行帳戶，還有祝你好運。當你抵達訓練中心時，請傳個訊息給我。在你待在那裡的期間，你是允許使用手機的。

倍斯特島嶼

Line messages

Thanks for all the help and I'm about to embark on a new journey in life. I'm so thrilled. Thanks again. I do hope I can get rich before going back to the land.

Line 訊息

謝謝所有的幫助，而我生命中的一趟新的旅程即將要展開了。我感到興奮異常。再次要謝謝你。我真的希望再回到這塊土地上時，我能夠變得富有。

Training center

You don't have a name here. You will be referring to by the number on your uniform. This is not some summer camps. It's about life-and-death, so be serious about it. You have to get up at five a.m. and wear your uniform. I have listed the activities on the brochure for you to read. If you don't measure up to the standard of our norm, we have the right to send you back. It goes according to the contract. That means your dream of becoming rich will be gone forever.

The activity for the first month	Time
Boxing lesson	an hour/per day
Weight lift training	two hours/per day

Running	2 km/per day
Surviving skills	four hours/per day
Cleaning the center	an hour/per day
Collecting food for the team	2 hours/per day
Collecting water	2 hours/per day

訓練中心

在這裡你們沒有名字。我僅會根據你們制服上頭的號碼稱呼你們。這不是一些夏令營。這關乎到生死，所以請認真看待。你必須要於早上五點鐘起床且穿好你的制服。我已經將所有的活動列在手冊上供你們閱讀。如果你們沒有達到我們的標準的話，我們會將你遣返。這個規定是根據我們的合約來走。那也意謂著你們變富有的夢也永遠不可能成真了。

第一個月的活動	時間
拳擊課程	1小時/每日
重量訓練	2小時/每日
跑步	2公里/每日
生存技巧	4小時/每日
訓練中心的清潔	1小時/每日
替團隊採集食物	2小時/每日
汲取水	2小時/每日

Questions 196-200

196. In which of the positions marked **(1)**, **(2)**, **(3)**, and **(4)** does the following sentence best belong?

"**Buy since you are an enthusiastic and vibrant man, we will give you a bow and arrows for you to defend yourself.**"

(A) (1)
(B) (2)
(C) (3)
(D) (4)

196. 以下這個句子最適合放在文中標記**(1)**, **(2)**, **(3)**, **(4)**的哪個位置？
「但是既然你是有熱忱且具活力的男子，我們將給你弓箭，讓你能夠自我防衛。」
(A) (1)
(B) (2)
(C) (3)
(D) (4)

197. Which of the following premium is what the poor man will be getting?
(A) the discount
(B) weapons
(C) reduction for the transferring fee
(D) 5G smartphone service

197. 下列哪項優惠是窮男人將會獲得的？
(A) 折扣
(B) 武器
(C) 轉帳費用的削減
(D) 5G的智慧型手機服務

198. What is the Poor Man hoping to get?
(A) to be physically fit after the training
(B) to defeat coaches at the Training Center
(C) to be the star at the Training Center
(D) to be wealthy

198. 窮男人希望獲得什麼？
(A) 在訓練後，變得更體健
(B) 擊敗訓練中心的教練
(C) 成為訓練中心的明星
(D) 變富有

199. What is True about the Training Center? (A) Trainees there don't have to measure up the standard. (B) Trainees there can dress casually. **(C) It's organized by having numerous activities.** (D) It was magnificently built.	199. 關於訓練中心，何者為真？ (A) 訓練者在那裡不需要達到標準。 (B) 訓練者在那裡可以隨意地穿著。 **(C) 有許多活動所組織起來的。** (D) 是宏觀地建造的。
200. What is mentioned about Surviving skills? (A) It takes longer than Running. (B) It takes shorter than Weightlifting. (C) It takes shorter than Gathering water. **(D) It takes longer than most activities.**	200. 關於生存技巧的部分，提到了什麼？ (A) 比起跑步花費更長的時間。 (B) 比重量訓練花費較短的時間。 (C) 比起收集水源花費較短的時間。 **(D) 比起大多數活動花費較長的時間。**

 解析

· **第196題**，插入句的句子最適合放在Only people using all those services can get the discount. **(1)** 後，而因為沒有給予折扣所以才給武器，故答案為**選項A**。

· **第197題**，poor man得到的就是**weapon**（a bow and arrows），故答案為**選項B**。

· **第198題**，這題也很簡單但易錯，他就是想要變富有，故答案為**選項D**。

· **第199題**，僅有選項C的描述是正確的，故答案為**選項C**。

· **第200題**，這題掌握表格資訊即可答對，surviving skills的時間確實長於大多數的其他活動，故答案為**選項D**。

Note

- 【Part 5】的文法和單字的出題較前兩回簡易，但要注意容易錯的題目，像是given that的考點。
- 【Part 6】要注意比較不熟悉的字和陷阱題，例如 turnover, vandalize, paperwork和 aquaculture等等。
- 【Part 7】要注意易錯的題目，像是dive和drive要看清楚，以及其他的同義轉換像是diving和 snorkeling等等。另外還要注意其他的推測題，像是萬聖節火車等沒有明顯提到入場費的金額。

模擬試題（三）

READING TEST

In this section, you must demonstrate your ability to read and comprehend English. You will be given a variety of texts and asked to answer questions about these texts. This section is divided into three parts and will take 75 minutes to complete.

Do not mark the answers in your test book. Use the answer sheet that is separately.

PART 5

Directions: In each question, you will be asked to review a statement that is missing a word or phrase. Four answer choices will be provided for each statement. Select the best answer and mark the corresponding letter (A), (B), (C), or (D) on the answer sheet.

101. Restaurants and hotels are ------- from the policy of the government, and they are now predicting at least 50,000 visitors will be staying here during Christmas.
    (A) benefiting
    (B) contributing
    (C) developing
    (D) organizing

102. Of Best farm's production of strawberries, 9,000 boxes are ------- by fruit lovers from overseas, a significant boost from last year.
    (A) replenished
    (B) repaired
    (C) reserved

(D) reduced

103. Due to a(n) ------- in tourism, local residents are considering quadrupling yield of both strawberries and sugary tomatoes.
    (A) enthusiasm
    (B) purpose
    (C) surge
    (D) initiative

104. Best clothing is trying to ------- its rival from entering the Chinese market by working with other on-line giants.
    (A) detain
    (B) maintain
    (C) contain
    (D) restrain

105. With the ------- of the new equipment, Best Bakery is ultimately able to bake cakes and other items at steady temperatures.
    (A) germination
    (B) introduction
    (C) progression
    (D) infection

106. Some big companies encountered a huge obstacle during the COVID-19 virus period and came very close to make the -------

cut.

(A) pleasant

(B) painful

(C) purposeful

(D) merciful

107. Small companies are less vulnerable to the influence of the global recession, compared with large companies, which have huge ------- costs.

(A) decreased

(B) operating

(C) evaluating

(D) probation

108. Although Best Cinema is still in its ------- stages of growth, investors have a pretty good faith for the prospect of the company.

(A) perpetuated

(B) ultimate

(C) ongoing

(D) nascent

109. Best pharmaceuticals built the brand on a great deal of money, but businessowners all ------- that the cash should have spent on other aspects.

(A) refuted

(B) qualified

(C) concurred

(D) concurrent

110. During the elevator speech, the candidate tried so hard to ------- the interest of the boss, but was in vain.

(A) pique

(B) promote

(C) deliver

(D) highlight

111. The ------- of the CEO is in conflict with that of those investors, so the assistant is trying to figure out how to make another arrangement.

(A) publicity

(B) development

(C) schedule

(D) operation

112. Those ------- are told to participate in the ultimate interview in one of the famous museums in France.

(A) tycoons

(B) sponsors

(C) magnets

(D) finalists

113. Doing things unrelated to your professional field can be -------
to the career in the long run.
(A) gracious
(B) beneficial
(C) deleterious
(D) formidable

114. Candidates ------- to wear the uniforms will not be considered
by Elite Airlines because rules are rules.
(A) grateful
(B) gallant
(C) willing
(D) reluctant

115. The population of brown bears diminished to only 5,000 in
the wild, a staggering ------- from last year.
(A) decreased
(B) decreases
(C) decrease
(D) decreasing

116. ------- a significant decline of 50% in sales, the sales of pearl
milk tea ultimately made a comeback and had a loyal
customer base.
(A) Although
(B) Because

(C) Since

(D) Despite

117. An error in ------- can make a huge difference in both business activities and bank transactions.

(A) judge

(B) judged

(C) judgement

(D) judging

118. ------- the exquisite dishes on the scene, our tender sweet lamb is considered by far the most delicious food judges have ever tasted.

(A) All

(B) With

(C) Overall

(D) Of all

119. After the futile merger, the CEO is willing to do ------- needs to be done to keep the company from filing a bankruptcy.

(A) whatever

(B) what

(C) which

(D) wherever

120. According to the ruling, the criminal is sentenced to a life-

long exclusion of the United States and ------- immediately.

(A) will be deporting

(B) will be deported

(C) be deported

(D) deporting

121. If you are unaccustomed to ------- in public, you are not alone, and the performing club is here to assist you to overcome that.

(A) have performed

(B) be performed

(C) performed

(D) performing

122. ------- stinky tofu is widely acceptable in most Asian countries, its notorious smell does drive away westerners for no reason.

(A) Without

(B) While

(C) Once

(D) However

123. ------- the experienced connoisseur is able to identify fake paintings by naked eyes remains uncertain.

(A) What

(B) Whether

(C) When

(D) Whenever

124. Students enrolling in this course are eager to go to the field trip to Best Museum, a giant gallery ------- viewers can get the inspiration.
(A) which
(B) from
(C) from which
(D) whose

125. ------- Best Kitchen does not have renowned chefs to do the cooking demonstration next Friday, the CEO has come to the agreement with other executives to poach qualified candidates from other companies.
(A) Therefore
(B) Albeit
(C) As
(D) If

126. ------- the desert is sweltering hot during the day, the director eventually concedes to the protest of female models and has decided to shoot the pictures in the cellar.
(A) Unless
(B) In addition to
(C) Given that
(D) Among

127. Best dating apps have adopted the most advanced technology making it ------- to use and respond to the matched users.

(A) easiness

(B) easier

(C) more easier

(D) the most easiest

128. A Sunday spent online watching Friends won't make you more intelligent, ------- a Sunday spent learning complicated math questions just might.

(A) or

(B) yet

(C) but

(D) and

129. Finalists of Best Airline are pleased to know they are all hired and enter the job ------- fully charged batteries.

(A) at

(B) on

(C) with

(D) of

130. Job seekers can feel the ------- sense of rivalry when they are waiting outside the conference room.

(A) similarity

(B) difference

(C) same

(D) various

PART 6

Directions: In this part, you will be asked to read four English texts. Each text is missing a word, phrase, or sentence. Select the answer choice that correctly completes the text and mark the corresponding letter (A), (B), (C), or (D) on the answer sheet.

Questions 131-134

With the huge **131.-------** last month, the firm has decided to hire college students who major in arts. They can do the portrait for tourists in the zoo, and at the same time build up their portfolios. It's a great way for someone who doesn't have any work experience. This actually acts as the way to contribute to the society. Of course, the charge of doing the portrait cannot be higher than a certain amount, and since the firm doesn't **132.------- them fees for doing the portrait in the zoo. They have to do at least a free drawing for one tourist. Their actions will be strictly **133.-------** as well. They are not allowed to be rude to all tourists, and they cannot break any equipment in the zoo. They cannot **134.-------** anything in the zoo, including randomly painting something on the wall, and call it an art.

131. (A) categorization

(B) reputation

(C) turnover

(D) awareness

132. (A) charter

(B) charge

(C) cancel

(D) calculate

133. (A) monitored

(B) manipulated

(C) mismanaged

(D) prohibited

134. (A) offset

(B) accelerate

(C) exhume

(D) vandalize

Questions 135-138

In addition to the students from the Department of Arts, students majoring in design or architecture are able to use the culture center of the zoo to **135.-------** their projects for free. The time for the exhibition has to be **136.-------** three weeks in advance so that our staff can have sufficient time to make the room and process the document. The **137.-------** has to be granted by the manager of our culture department. In addition, we are also working on the souvenir self-made. It has to be specifically-tailored. The production can be low-cost and will be available to all customers. We have contacted with several deans of the Design Department to discuss further details. Tourists can **138.-------** from this gesture, and some souvenirs can be custom-made.

135. (A) conduct
     (B) liquidate
     (C) calibrate
     (D) showcase

136. (A) recorded
     (B) recoiled
     (C) reserved
     (D) relinquished

137. (A) equity
     (B) paperwork
     (C) commission
     (D) portfolio

138. (A) backfire
     (B) withdraw
     (C) benefit
     (D) backlash

Questions 139-142

Time really flies. **139.-------** We held a thank-you tea party for them in one afternoon, but the CEO was too **140.-------** with the work to attend. The firm still has a lot to do. It has begun to head towards the second phase. Instead of using frozen fish and meat to feed the marine mammals, the company has to be sustainable and **141.-------** fresh products for marine creatures. By the farm is a huge lake which can be a great asset to the company. The idea of a(n) **142.-------** can be put into use. We not only raise fish commonly known, but also several kinds of crabs and lobsters that can be used to feed marine mammals or octopuses in our aquarium.

139. (A) The CEO is about to retire because he values his family more.
   (B) Our farmers were done their missions and ready to leave.
   (C) The tea party is so luxurious that all employees don't think it's fair.
   (D) The third phase is canceled due to some unforeseen reason.

140. (A) accompanied
   (B) swamped
   (C) satisfied
   (D) provided

141. (A) support

(B) unleash

(C) impress

(D) self-generate

142. (A) miniature

(B) horticulture

(C) aquaculture

(D) agriculture

Questions 143-146

Our aquarium has only opened for three years, and it's quite new from the **143.-------** of the industry. The CEO spoken in the Wednesday conference, stating the fact that we actually had no time to waste, and the phase two had to be **144.-------**. The HR Department has since begun to interview several professionals in the industry and has been trying to find someone who is experienced enough to take care of the aquaculture in the nearby lake. The output of fish, crabs, and lobsters has to be **145.-------** enough to sustain the food supply in both Zoo kitchen and employee kitchen. **146.-------.**

143. (A) legitimacy

(B) interest

(C) authority

(D) standpoint

144. (A) harassed
    (B) hastened
    (C) heightened
    (D) hampered

145. (A) disenchanted
    (B) credible
    (C) steady
    (D) contingent

146. (A) That will take at least half a year, an expert said.
     (B) Marine creatures are too gluttonous to raise.
    (C) They are considered experienced, so the production will definitely be so successful.
    (D) The Lake is contaminated by the chemistry factory, and there is nothing they cannot do.

PART 7

Directions: In this part, you will be asked to read several texts, such as advertisements, articles, instant messages, or examples of business correspondence. Each is followed by several questions. Select the best answer and mark the corresponding letter (A), (B), (C), (D) on your answer sheet.

Question 147

According to the survey conducted by ABC Marketing team in 2019, consumers had a penchant for pink and yellow, so we have adjusted these two products in both Q1 and Q3, so you should take a look. And we only list two main features and their prices. The internal memory for Lake Blue is 1TB, quite amazing.

Best Cellphone 2025 flagship				price
Q1	Maybe Pink	Camera 108M	Battery 50W	NT 30,000
	Striking Blue	Camera 108M	Battery 50W	NT 30,000
Q2	Slightly Orange	Camera 144M	Battery 80W	NT 42,000
	Dark Brown	Camera 144M	Battery 80W	NT 42,000
Q3	Really Yellow	Camera 200M	Battery 100W	NT 60,000
Q4	Lake Blue	Camera 300M	Battery 120W	NT 90,000

147. What is not mentioned about Best Cellphone?

(A) Lake Blue costs almost US 3,000 dollars.

(B) People purchasing a Lake Blue get to buy three Maybe Pinks.

(C) The internal memory for Striking Blue is 1TB

(D) The battery for Really Yellow is 100W.

Question 148

Cindy 9:50 a.m.
Hey, I still haven't got the certificate of salvaging the brown bear cub... and I do need the certificate to apply for the college... it surely will affect the result... since I'm applying for majoring in biology with an emphasis on wild animals...

Jim 9:52 a.m.
I'm so sorry... there are just so many documents... I'm just too swamped with work... it's ok that you write down the number of the association... I will send the certificate to your current address as soon as possible...

Cindy 9:53 a.m.
Thanks...

Jim 9:58 a.m.
And by the way... do you need the recommendation from our association... the founder used to be the dean of the Biology Department... that totally can earn you some points...

Cindy 9:59 a.m.
That would be nice... thanks...

148. At 9:58 a.m. what does the Jim mean when he says "**that totally can earn you some points**..."?

(A) Because he doesn't want to hurt Cindy's feelings.

(B) Because he wants Cindy to really earn it.

(C) Because he used to be the judge.

(D) Because that will be a boost for the interview

Questions 149-152
Best Resort

We have updated all services. It really is the new adventure for you.

A. Diving for Food/Money

- Beachgoers and underwater divers will find it exhilarating since they get to dive down in the transparent water. While enjoying the scenery, they can capture marine creatures, such as giant lobsters and large crabs, and bring them back to the shore. We have accountants and chefs ready by the side. We can cook for you with additional cooking charges, or you can order multiple dishes in our restaurant. If you want to exchange for money, our accountant will do that for you by weighing the marine creature and do the calculation for you. You are actually earning money that can deduct your traveling bills.

B. Labor for Money

- You can offer your labor in exchange for money. Our resort is short of staff and in desperate need of finding someone who can move heavy bricks, mend fences, do the gardening, and so on. Of course, you can exchange the labor for a temporary stay in our luxurious hotel.

- In addition to the above-mentioned service, you can also use our water motorcycles (if you know how to drive) to get the rare seaweed for us in a remote island. It is now quite expensive in the developed countries, and its value is even greater than all seafood combined or other products.

149. Which of the following item is the most valuable?

    (A) the large crab

(B) the giant lobster

(C) the rare seaweed

(D) the seafood

150. How can the tourists get raw giant lobsters?

(A) by calculating

(B) through driving

(C) through snorkeling

(D) through cooking

151. What is not the activity that can exchange for a short stay?

(A) do the gardening

(B) drive water vehicles

(C) maintain fences

(D) move heavy bricks

152. What is **NOT** mentioned as a way to travel with less money?

(A) mend fences

(B) get the seaweed

(C) consume multiple dishes in the restaurant.

(D) dive for giant lobsters

Questions 153-155

Halloween Train

Our Halloween Train is the scariest in the world, and it has 100 railway carriages. You have to endure all the horrors on the 5-hour drive to Best Recreational Park, and I'm afraid to say that it's the only way to arrive at our place. You are under the surveillance camera to ensure your safety. People with a chronic illness are not advised to take the train. For those who do not scream or feel scared at all will be getting a coupon worth US 1,000 dollars or a free admission. You might wonder how we are going to judge that. All participants will be required to wear the specialized watch that **rigorously** monitors your temperatures, blood pressure, and brain activities. Recordings will be deleted once you are in our Park. If you pee accidentally on your pant, you will be punished by having to pay the admission fee 50% higher, US 300 dollars in total.

153. According to the advertisement, how much is the admission fee?
    (A) US 300
    (B) US 200
    (C) US 1,000
    (D) US 1,300

154. What is **NOT** mentioned about the Halloween Train?
    (A) The train is the only transportation.
    (B) There is no such a thing as a free admission fee.
    (C) A designed watch is used to monitor temperatures of customers.
    (D) Surveillance cameras are used to monitor customers.

155. The word "**rigorously**" in paragraph1, line 10, is closet in meaning to

(A) strictly

(B) productively

(C) communicatively

(D) formidably

Questions 156-158

Dear Mary,

Don't worry about the owner of the coffee shop. We have already paid him your salary beforehand. **(1)** You don't necessarily have to actually work in the coffee shop. **(2)** You are just a doll wearing the uniform of the coffee shop... What if other coworkers ask something about you? **(3)** I don't think other colleagues are going to say anything... you are thinking way too much... just do your job... ok... by the way I'm so looking forward to hearing more from him...**(4)** I've no idea what our rivals are doing and am totally clueless about the recent **publicity stunt** of their new apps. Have you used their software? I don't think it's that good... let me know what you think....

Manager

156. The phrase "**publicity stunt**" in line 9, is closet in meaning to

    (A) a technician hired by the PR department

    (B) a stunning moment that is showcased in public

    (C) a public display of affections

    (D) a ruse that can be used in advertising campaigns

157. What is **NOT** mentioned about the letter?

    (A) The owner of the shop has received the payment from the company.

    (B) Mary overthinks about the whole thing.

    (C) Mary has to wear the uniform.

    (D) Mary has to buy a doll.

158. In which of the positions marked **(1)**, **(2)**, **(3)**, and **(4)** does the following sentence best belong?

    "**I think he will probably find something to say... like you're the daughter of his relative who wants to know the industry**"

    (A) (1)

    (B) (2)

    (C) (3)

    (D) (4)

Questions 159-160
Best Elite University

Music

❶ Piano	10 points
❷ Violin	10 points
❸ Flute	10 points
❹ Organ	10 points
❺ Trumpet	10 points

Sports

❶ Basketball	10 points
❷ Baseball	10 points
❸ Soccer	10 points
❹ Badminton	10 points
❺ Freestyle	10 points

Extra Credits

❶ Cello	15 points
❷ Saxophone	20 points
❸ Harp	15 points
❹ Guzheng	25 points
❺ Parallel bars	20 points
❻ Rowing	20 points
❼ 50 M Rifle Three Positions	30 points
❽ Equestrians	35 points

Note:

1. Unlike the criteria that are used in other schools, candidates have to

be good at both music and sports to apply for our undergraduate program. (at least to be good at one item in the Music part and one item in the Sports section.) If you are good at more than one in each section, please let us know by highlighting it in the on-line application form.

2. Note : The second screening will be held in July at BEU, and the exact date is to be determined.

159. What will happen during the month of July?

(A) the announcement of the on-line application form

(B) the announcement of an admission notice

(C) the announcement of the interview date

(D) the announcement of the undergraduate program

160. What can be inferred about Best Elite University?

(A) Harp is worthy of 35 points.

(B) Cello is worthy of 25 points.

(C) It values a lot in both Music and Sports.

(D) Rowing is worthy of 30 points.

Questions 161-164

Best Balloon Darts

Cost	darts
US 5 dollars	10
US 10 dollars	20
US 15 dollars	30

US 20 dollars	40
US 30 dollars	50
Balloons	**Prize**
10 balloons	Pearl milk tea
50 balloons	Steak dinner at the restaurant
150 balloons	Luxurious buffet at the restaurant
350 balloons	Luxurious group buffet at the restaurant

Note:
1. For all your purchase of the game, 10% of the fee will be donating to the COVID-19 virus foundation to help those in need.
2. We do have an exchange program, 「**Labor for Darts**」, so you get to use your labor by filling up the balloon to earn darts. 500 balloons equate with 20 darts.
3. During the Valentine's Day, we do have the special event. Huge durable heart-shaped balloons will be made. Challengers using the mundane darts to pierce the specially-tailored balloon will get two free international flight tickets to Europe.

161. If the player spends 500 dollars on the game, how much will the foundation actually get?
    (A) 0.5
    (B) 5
    (C) 500
    (D) 50

162. How much can a person get for making 500 balloons?

(A) 5

(B) 10

(C) 15

(D) 20

163. How many balloons are needed if one wants to invite a few friends to eat at the buffet for free?

    (A) 10

    (B) 50

    (C) 150

    (D) 350

164. If the player wants to get pearl milk tea, at least he has to shoot how many balloons?

    (A) 5

    (B) 10

    (C) 15

    (D) 20

Questions 165-166

Best Surgery will be needing a candidate with strong features to do the commercial and ad campaigns for them. **(1)** If you get chosen, you will be rewarding with a 50% discount for any surgery in Best Surgery. **(2)** This shows how much they care about the commercial and ad campaigns. Right now they have the female model ready to do the shoot, yet they are still trying to find out the male candidate. **(3)** If you are interested, it won't hurt to ask or give it a try. You can also benefit from getting selected from this chance and build your modeling and acting career since. **(4)** But I do recommend you to be well-prepared. It really is a great opportunity.

165. What is the article mainly about?
    (A) the difficulty of working with the female model
    (B) the concern for hiring great cameramen
    (C) recruitment for the male model
    (D) the fund for the ad campaigns

166. In which of the positions marked **(1)**, **(2)**, **(3)**, and **(4)** does the following sentence best belong?
    "**They have hired a few great photographers from Italy to do the shoot.**"
    (A) (1)
    (B) (2)
    (C) (3)
    (D) (4)

Questions 167-169

Best Modeling Agency is about to make a new hire on Monday. **(1)** There are thousands of people waiting in line. It's really hot outside. Let's take a look at several candidates. **(2)** Candidate A has prepared a portfolio of his pics, and he has chosen the best three.

I think that's a pretty good start for the model. Candidate B is wearing a fantastic outfit. **(3)** She surely knows how to dress. Candidate C is muscularly built. I think it shows you have been working out, and it's good. But having too much can be a downside in several Modeling Agencies. Sometimes you just cannot overdo it. Candidate D is slim and confident with a pair of chic eyeglasses. **(4)** For now what I have seen is that all of them are strong candidates... I'm sure judges of the Modeling Agencies are going to have a hard time selecting the best pick.

167. In which of the positions marked **(1)**, **(2)**, **(3)**, and **(4)** does the following sentence best belong?

    "**The shoes and the jewelry are all big brands.**"
    (A) (1)
    (B) (2)
    (C) (3)
    (D) (4)

168. What is **NOT** stated about Candidate B?
    (A) the great dress
    (B) a bad taste in clothing
    (C) expensive luxuries
    (D) a penchant for famous designers

169. What is indicated about Candidate D?
    (A) the preparation for the portfolio

(B) a fantastic outfit

(C) huge muscles

(D) confidence

Questions 170-172

My advice, NO. Recharging is not the reason to leave. Most people think of this as a way for them to evade their current job. **(1)** You don't need to totally relinquish the current job to do so, and be a person who has lost the touch for the job market for a few years, only to realize that it's too late. **(2)** Your previous role has been replaced by a new rookie who can do a better job than you now, and you and your new diploma can't compete with that, and you keep wondering why spending a great deal of money and possessing a fancy diploma don't equate with having a better job opportunity. **(3)** All of a sudden you feel so lost and **disillusioned**. You find yourself on the wrong BMW, driving in a totally different direction, and it takes longer to arrive at your destination. **(4)** But time is already lost and money already spent...

Best Column

170. What is **NOT** stated about the "Job Column"?

(A) It is essential to recharge yourself with the knowledge.

(B) You have to purchase a BMW in order to drive fast.

(C) Recharging cannot be the justified excuse to escape the reality.

(D) You can have the cake and eat it too.

171. The word "**disillusioned**" in paragraph1, line 10, is closet in meaning to

(A) replenished

(B) underdeveloped

(C) disenchanted

(D) unfaithful

172. In which of the positions marked **(1)**, **(2)**, **(3)**, and **(4)** does the following sentence best belong?

"**Although replenishing yourself with the knowledge is important for your growth, you can do that during your free time.**"

(A) (1)

(B) (2)

(C) (3)

(D) (4)

Questions 173-175

Remember what's written in the bestseller? Don't use hygiene factors to determine your choice of a job. **(1)** Hygiene factors, such as a higher pay and other monetary rewards, are not the reasons that can make you truly satisfied. **(2)** Of course, you will be satisfied with having more money to spend in the very beginning. **(3)** You have the house loans, mortgages, and kid's tuition. **(4)** You have to maintain the current job to keep the life **float**. But you are so unhappy. You just have to figure out what you truly want and what actually motivates you. Finding those that can make you happy can make your life more fulfilling...

Best Column

173. What is **NOT** stated about the "Job Column"?

(A) Hygiene factors are short-term satisfactions.

(B) Hygiene factors can lead to dissatisfaction.

(C) Hygiene factors are not important.

(D) The author of the bestseller discusses the hygiene factor phenomenon.

174. The word "**float**" in line 7, is closet in meaning to

(A) immerse

(B) buoyed

(C) submerge

(D) meaningful

175. In which of the positions marked **(1)**, **(2)**, **(3)**, and **(4)** does the following sentence best belong?

"**But once you have realized that you are stuck in a position, and you cannot get out because you have accustomed to the current lifestyle.**"

(A) (1)

(B) (2)

(C) (3)

(D) (4)

Questions 176-180

Dear Mark,

The shoplifting yesterday did cost us a great fortune. Unfortunately, the insurance won't cover that, since it expired after Easter. After doing some thinking, I have decided to shut down the entire mall for the next few months. I'm not sure when the reopening date will be. I will have a few accountants to **transfer** the severance pay to all temporary workers first, and get a bank loan to pay our contract workers and full-time employees. You don't have to feel **discouraged** though. You called the police right after the shoplifting had happened. I do think we will be back on our feet a few months later.

CEO of Best Department

Dear CEO,

I'm the prosecutor of the case, and according to the evidence, we have the reason to believe that one of your employees, Mark Wang was behind this. **(1)** I do have the search warrant to search for the entire department and the police will be there Monday morning to gather evidence from all computers. **(2)** We have also detained one of your accountants. **(3)** We also found a store unit that housed all the jewelry and gold stolen from your shopping mall. **(4)** As for Mark, he is still at large. If you see him, please be calm and call the police. The police will handle this. Don't act like you already known the whole thing. Put your **veneer** on... that's all.

Mary James

176. The word "**transfer**" in the letter, line 5, is closet in meaning to
    (A) transfuse
    (B) manage
    (C) respond
    (D) shift

177. The word "**discouraged**" in the letter 1, line 7, is closet in meaning to
    (A) enlightened
    (B) empowered
    (C) depressed
    (D) unauthorized

178. What is **NOT** mentioned in both letters?
    (A) Evidence will be collected on Monday morning.
    (B) A warehouse was used to stash the valuables.
    (C) A bank loan is necessary in this incident.
    (D) The insurance won't cover the loss.

179. The word "**veneer**" in the letter 2, line 9, is closet in meaning to
    (A) facade
    (B) veneration
    (C) benediction
    (D) vehement

180. In which of the positions marked **(1)**, **(2)**, **(3)**, and **(4)** does the following sentence best belong?
    "**They will be used as evidence in court, so you just have to be patient and wait until the verdict is final.**"
    (A) (1)
    (B) (2)
    (C) (3)

(D) (4)

Questions 181-185

Dear Best News,

I saw someone slip by the swimming pool. It's a large public pool. **(1)** After dialing the number of the district police station, I went close to the crime scene only to find there was nothing I could find. **(2)** Nothing like I said. **(3)** At first, I thought I was just being paranoid, then the next morning my husband went for his usual jogging, and what he found was a corpse in the pool, and of course he called the police. **(4)** You guys have been known for your reputation of digging some dirt and gossips. I do hope you can find something and do a report on this. People don't just do the swimming in the familiar pool and you know drown himself or herself... looking forward to a great news story...

Conscientious citizen May

Best News

The doctor of the **deceased** called us a few days after the accident. The drown went to the therapy a day before the accident, asking for help because he believed someone wanted to kill him. But the doctor didn't take it too seriously and didn't prescribe any medicine for him. He asked the patient to relax for a bit by exercising. And a week later, the smartphone was found by a local resident. According to the conversation, someone **threatened** to kill him and the number was blocked. And the name remains unknown. I'm sure the police are now eager to know what actually happened that day. The weird thing is that all surveillance cameras near the public pool were removed while we were working on the report... hopefully, things will eventually come to light.

Reporter Cindy Thornes

181. In which of the positions marked **(1)**, **(2)**, **(3)**, and **(4)** does the following sentence best belong?

"**According to the police report, it ruled this as an accident, drowning, but deep down I know it's not that simple.**"

(A) (1)

(B) (2)

(C) (3)

(D) (4)

182. What is **NOT** mentioned about the first letter?

(A) May had an inspection at the swimming pool.

(B) May's husband did find the dead body.

(C) May's mental state is not stable.

(D) May eventually turned to the Best News for help.

183. What is **NOT** mentioned about the second letter?

(A) The police couldn't find the footage at the scene.

(B) The caller's number couldn't be verified.

(C) The guy did a counselling session before his death.

(D) The doctor gave the guy a prescription, but the guy ignored.

184. The word "**deceased**" in the letter 2, line 1, is closet in meaning to

(A) decreased

(B) increased

(C) departed

(D) population

185. The word "**threatened**" in the letter 2, line 6, is closet in meaning to

(A) dulled

(B) touted

(C) rotted

(D) bulldozed

Questions 186-190

Diary/Day One

I was being thankful for getting assigned to gather berries today...**(1)** it was less burdensome... and my muscle got tense while trying to **retrieve** water for the team. **(2)** We had to walk twenty kilometers to get the water from the well, and I was exhausted. **(3)** The boxing lesson went horribly as well. I got one punch by the coach, and the next thing I remembered was that I was lying on the bed, made of wood. **(4**) Perhaps I was not the guy built for the treasure hunt, and being the hero to combat wild cats. I was too tired for the day. I went to the kitchen to grab something to eat so that I could eventually have the strength to write the sort of a diary for the day. Hope tomorrow is going to be better.

Day two

The running went fine, although I was the slowest in the team. I will probably get disqualified after the two-month training, but I'm trying really hard to keep myself floating here. However, I do like the survival skills taught here, knowing the weaknesses and strengths of all wild animals, and I still have a lot to learn though. I drank plenty of milk today that helped build my muscle tremendously. I'm getting stronger. I loved the barbecue for the night. It was delicious, and I ate a lot. I did shower extensively... too bad that I couldn't get a hot bath. Can't wait for tomorrow's lesson.

Day 5

We are now required to wear heavy armors for the day whenever we go. It's too laborious and tiresome. Except the time when we go take a shower. In today's boxing lesson, I did an ok job by **withstanding** three punches from one of my teammates. I saw ostriches today, and we stole their eggs for our dinner. That was the assignment the coach gave us. Pretty heavy and there are still many eggs in the nest. It's so sustainable. Like we get to eat that everyday. Unfortunately, we heard the weird sound made by those ostriches... my instinct told me that we had to run fast... like the carnivore had been there... we eventually took the vehicle sent by the coach to safely arrive at the center.

186. The word "**retrieve**" in paragraph1, line 2, is closet in meaning to
   (A) remand
   (B) annihilate
   (C) manage
   (D) fetch

187. In which of the positions marked **(1)**, **(2)**, **(3)**, and **(4)** does the following sentence best belong?

   NEW

   "**I didn't have any energy left for the day.**"
   (A) (1)
   (B) (2)
   (C) (3)
   (D) (4)

188. What most likely is Poor Man having difficulty doing?
   (A) find something to eat in the kitchen
   (B) take the boxing lesson
   (C) get water from a well
   (D) collect the berry

189. The word "**withstanding**" in paragraph3, line 3, is closet in meaning to
   (A) enduring
   (B) streamlining
   (C) transferring

(D) generating

190. What is **NOT** indicated about Day two and Day five?
    (A) They had a meat feast on the second day.
    (B) A carnivore was used to transport them back to the center in Day Five.
    (C) Ostrich eggs can be replenished so it's good for all trainees.
    (D) They've learned the knack of dealing with wild beasts.

Questions 191-195

Bulletin board

Hey Mates... order anything you want

Food and beverage	Cost
Pearl milk tea	US 20 dollars
Hot pot/luxury	US 150 dollars
Seafood buffet	US 500 dollars
Meat of wild animals	US 2,000 dollars
Any wine/a set	US 100 dollars

We accept the credit card payments.
Use our apps to conveniently purchase whatever you want
The buffet car will come to you.
※payment exceeding 2,000 dollars will be getting 20% discounts and a bottle of pearl milk tea

Day 10

To tell the truth, I was a bit jealous because others get the **subscribed** service of "food". This means others are eating the dreamy food and drinks on the list. I just couldn't afford it. I didn't know the company even had the restaurant here. They really are the businessmen who want to dry us out completely. We haven't earned any money, and yet some of us have already spent a fortune on those things. They are good. I can even smell the aroma of wine from the person sleeping next to me... I hate my life...

Day 14

I can run **effortlessly** and don't think running 2 kms is that much. **(1)** It was a huge improvement for me, and my big belly is shrinking. I'm using the phone to record the moment. **(2)** Too bad, the phone doesn't have any signal to upload on the ig. However, something bad happened today. **(3)** We were asked to go on a lion hunt and things went horribly wrong. The assignment was to get the cub of the lion from a female lion. **(4)** The team which successfully does that will get an extra score. One of them got bitten by a lion, and bleeding badly. How awful.

191. How much does it cost if a trainee orders meat of wild animals, pearl milk tea, and a set of wine?

    (A) 1,696

    (B) 1,680

    (C) 2,120

    (D) 2,100

192. What can be inferred from the restaurant service?

    (A) the guy didn't have a dime to spend.

    (B) the guy didn't like credit card payment.

    (C) the guy couldn't resist the aroma of wine.

    (D) the guy went a splurge on the buffet car.

193. The word "**subscribed**" in paragraph2, line 1, is closet in meaning to
    (A) revered
    (B) reserved
    (C) prescribed
    (D) preserved

194. The word "**effortlessly**" in paragraph3, line 1, is closet in meaning to
    (A) facilely
    (B) typically
    (C) exceptionally
    (D) enormously

195. In which of the positions marked **(1)**, **(2)**, **(3)**, and **(4)** does the following sentence best belong?
    "**The cub should remain unharmed.**"
    (A) (1)
    (B) (2)
    (C) (3)
    (D) (4)

Questions 196-200

Day 20

It wasn't until today that I finally knew that we had to get a certain grade to pass the test... or shall I say be measured up in order to qualify for the treasure hunt. That means I have to get the score of at least 2,000 to qualify. And we didn't successfully get the lion cub... remember. I can't believe some of the guys here even have the mood to order the food through the buffet car. It's insane. The payment to enroll plus the training fee are US 70,000 dollars. How should I pay the bank loan, if I don't get qualified and get some jewelry afterwards? I am dying to know tomorrow's announcement of scores for some of the tasks.

Announcement/more to be announced

item	note	Score
Steal a lion cub	The cub should remain unharmed	50
Get the golden feather of peacock	Extremely rare	200
Get the pearl necklace from the cheetah	The cheetah should remain intact	100
Get the ivory of the elephant	It should be in a natural occurrence	250
Get rare fruits on the cliff	The fruit should be in perfect shape	200
Gather honey, a kilo	A traditional ritual is required. Water bees. The aroma of the rare fruit can attract water bees.	500
Kill a sea lion	with grasses	50
Get the liver of the whale	From carcasses	300

Day 22

After seeing the announced items, I know how hard it is to do that within two months. And only nearly a month left. I can't say it's a scam because we have learned something during the training. I guess we have to wait for an easier task to be announced later. Some of the guys here seem pretty content with the life here. What is wrong with them? The coach said we could do these tasks during our free time and we should team up to do these tasks to remain uninjured. But we have to split the credits with other teammates. You can get the help from some of the coaches here, but it's going to cost you extra. And we were told that no one before had ever succeeded in getting the water bees.

196. According to Day 20, what is **Not True**?

    (A) The requirement for the treasure hunt is at least 2,000 scores.

    (B) Trainees are at least paying the company US 70,000 dollars.

    (C) No one bought some food from the restaurant car due to the high training fee.

    (D) Trainees didn't get informed about the requirement for the treasure hunt.

197. What is the similarity among three tasks?

    (A) skills

    (B) difficulty

    (C) appearance

    (D) cooperation

198. According to the announcement, which task will get the highest score?

(A) the golden feather of the bird

(B) the pearl necklace from the carnivore

(C) water bees

(D) ivory of the herbivore

199. Which of the following task is deemed unconquerable?

(A) underwater whale livers

(B) watery sea lions

(C) water insects

(D) peacocks

200. What should trainees do to keep undamaged in the subsequent assignment?

(A) wait for the less difficult task

(B) defeat formidable water bees

(C) split the credit

(D) join forces

模擬試題（三）

 PART 5　中譯與解析

閱讀原文與中譯	
101. Restaurants and hotels are **benefiting** from the policy of the government, and they are now predicting at least 50,000 visitors will be staying here during Christmas. **(A) benefiting** (B) contributing (C) developing (D) organizing	餐廳和旅館都因為政府的政策而受益，而他們目前預測至少會有5萬名參訪者會於聖誕節期間待在此。 **(A) 得益、受惠** (B) 捐獻、捐助、貢獻 (C) 使成長、使發達、發展 (D) 組織、安排

答案：(A)

 解析

這題依據語意要選「**benefiting**」，故答案為**選項A**。

閱讀原文與中譯	
102. Of Best Farm's production of strawberries, 9,000 boxes are **reserved** by fruit lovers from overseas, a significant boost from last year. (A) replenished (B) repaired **(C) reserved** (D) reduced	在倍斯特農場的草莓生產中，9千盒被海外的水果愛好者預訂了，與去年相比有顯著的提升。 (A) 把......裝滿、補充 (B) 修理、補救、糾正 **(C) 儲備、保存、預約、預訂** (D) 減少、縮小、降低

答案：(C)

 解析

這題依據語法和語意要選「**reserved**」，故答案為**選項C**。

閱讀原文與中譯	
103. Due to a(n) **surge** in tourism, local residents are considering quadrupling yield of both strawberries and sugary tomatoes. (A) enthusiasm (B) purpose **(C) surge** (D) initiative	由於觀光產業的激增，當地居民正考慮將草莓和甜番茄的產量四倍化。 (A) 熱心、熱情、熱忱 (B) 目的、意圖、用途 **(C) 大浪、波濤、激增** (D) 主動的行動、倡議

答案：(C)

 解析

這題依據語意要選「**surge**」，故答案為**選項C**。

閱讀原文與中譯	
104. Best clothing is trying to **restrain** its rival from entering the Chinese market by working with other on-line giants. (A) detain (B) maintain (C) contain **(D) restrain**	倍斯特服飾正嘗試與其他線上大咖合作以限制其競爭對手進軍中國市場。 (A) 使耽擱、拘留、扣留 (B) 維持、保持 (C) 包含、容納、控制 **(D) 遏制、控制、限制、約束**

答案：(D)

 解析

這題依據語意要選「**restrain**」，故答案為**選項D**。

閱讀原文與中譯

105. With the **introduction** of the new equipment, Best Bakery is ultimately able to bake cakes and other items at steady temperatures.
(A) germination
(B) introduction
(C) progression
(D) infection

隨著新設備的引進，倍斯特烘焙最終能夠在穩定的溫度下烘培出蛋糕和其他品項。
(A) 萌芽、發芽、成長、發展
(B) 引進、傳入
(C) 發展、進步
(D) 傳染、侵染、傳染病

答案：(B)

這題是表達...「**隨著...的引進**」，故答案為**選項B**。

閱讀原文與中譯

106. Some big companies encountered a huge obstacle during the COVID-19 virus period and came very close to make the **painful** cut.
(A) pleasant
(B) painful
(C) purposeful
(D) merciful

有些大廠在新冠肺炎期間遭遇了巨大的障礙，情況非常接近到要做出忍痛裁員的決定。
(A) 令人愉快的、舒適的、討人喜歡的
(B) 引起痛苦的、費力的、困難的
(C) 有目的的、意味深長的、重大的
(D) 仁慈的、慈悲的、寬容的

答案：(B)

這題依據語意要選「**painful**」，故答案為**選項B**。

107. Small companies are less vulnerable to the influence of the global recession, compared with large companies, which have huge **operating** costs.
(A) decreased
(B) operating
(C) evaluating
(D) probation

比起有著高額營運開銷的大公司，小型公司較不容易受到全球不景氣的影響。
(A) 減少、減小
(B) 運作、運轉、營業、營運
(C) 評估
(D) 檢驗、鑑定、見習

答案：(B)

這題依據語意要選「**operating**」，故答案為**選項B**。

108. Although Best Cinema is still in its **nascent** stages of growth, investors have a pretty good faith for the prospect of the company.
(A) perpetuated
(B) ultimate
(C) ongoing
(D) nascent

儘管倍斯特電影仍在其成長初期，投資者對於這間公司的前景相當有信心。
(A) 永久的
(B) 最終的
(C) 進行的、不間斷的
(D) 發生中的、初期的、未成熟的

答案：(D)

這題依據語意要選「**nascent**」，故答案為**選項D**。

閱讀原文與中譯	
109. Best pharmaceuticals built the brand on a great deal of money, but businessowners all **concurred** that the cash should have spent on other aspects. (A) refuted (B) qualified **(C) concurred** (D) concurrent	倍斯特藥品商以大量的金錢創立了品牌，但是公司持有者們都認同資金早該用於其他方面。 (A) 駁斥、反駁 (B) 使具有資格、使合格 **(C) 同意、一致、同時發生** (D) 同時發生的、一致的

答案：(C)

 解析

這題依據語意要選「**concurred**」，故答案為**選項C**。

閱讀原文與中譯	
110. During the elevator speech, the candidate tried so hard to **pique** the interest of the boss, but was in vain. **(A) pique** (B) promote (C) deliver (D) highlight	在電梯簡報期間，候選人花費極大努力要引起老闆的興趣，但卻徒勞無功。 **(A) 刺激、激起（好奇心等）** (B) 促進 (C) 投遞、傳送、運送 (D) 用強光照射、照亮、強調

答案：(A)

 解析

這題依據語意要選「**pique**」，故答案為**選項A**。

| 111. The **schedule** of the CEO is in conflict with that of those investors, so the assistant is trying to figure out how to make another arrangement.

(A) publicity
(B) development
(C) schedule
(D) operation | 執行長的時程與那些投資客們的時程有衝突，所以助理正嘗試了解要如何做另一個安排。

(A)（公眾的）注意、名聲、宣傳、宣揚
(B) 發展
(C) 目錄、時間表、課程表、（火車等的）時刻表
(D) 運轉、經營、營運 |

答案：(C)

 解析

這題依據語意要選「**schedule**」，故答案為**選項C**。

| 112. Those **finalists** are told to participate in the ultimate interview in one of the famous museums in France.

(A) tycoons
(B) sponsors
(C) magnets
(D) finalists | 在法國其中一間最著名的博物館，那些候選人被告知要參加最終的面試。

(A)（企業界的）大亨、巨擘
(B) 發起者、主辦者、倡議者
(C) 磁鐵、磁石、有吸引力的人（或物）
(D) 參加決賽的人 |

答案：(D)

 解析

這題依據語意要選「**finalists**」，故答案為**選項D**。

閱讀原文與中譯	
113. Doing things unrelated to your professional field can be **beneficial** to the career in the long run. (A) gracious **(B) beneficial** (C) deleterious (D) formidable	從事與你專業領域無關的事情可能最終對於你的職涯是有所助益的。 (A) 和藹的、殷勤的、慈祥的 **(B) 有益的、有利的、有幫助的** (C) 有害的、有毒的 (D) 令人畏懼的、難以克服的

答案：(B)

（解析）

這題依據語意要選「**beneficial**」，故答案為**選項B**。

閱讀原文與中譯	
114. Candidates **reluctant** to wear the uniforms will not be considered by Elite Airlines because rules are rules. (A) grateful (B) gallant (C) willing **(D) reluctant**	菁英飛航公司不會考慮勉為其難穿上制服的候選人，因為規定就是規定。 (A) 感謝的、感激的 (B) 華麗的、豔麗的、雄偉的 (C) 願意的、樂意的 **(D) 不情願的、勉強的**

答案：(D)

（解析）

這題依據語法要選「**reluctant**」，故答案為**選項D**。

閱讀原文與中譯	
115. The population of brown bears diminished to only 5,000 in the wild, a staggering **decrease** from last year. (A) decreased (B) decreases **(C) decrease** (D) decreasing	在野外，棕熊的族群數量減至僅有5千隻，是自去年以來的驚人跌幅。

答案：(C)

這題依據語意要選「**decrease**」，故答案為**選項C**。

閱讀原文與中譯	
116. **Despite** a significant decline of 50% in sales, the sales of pearl milk tea ultimately made a comeback and had a loyal customer base. (A) Although (B) Because (C) Since **(D) Despite**	儘管在銷售上有著50%的顯著下降，珍珠奶茶最終起死回生且有著忠實的顧客群。

答案：(D)

Although後要加子句，故答案要選**despite**，所以答案為**選項D**。

閱讀原文與中譯	
117. An error in **judgement** can make a huge difference in both business activities and bank transactions. (A) judge (B) judged **(C) judgement** (D) judging	評判中的一個錯誤就能在商業活動和銀行交易中造成很顯著的差異。

答案：(C)

這題依據語法要選**「名詞」**，故答案為**選項C**。

閱讀原文與中譯	
118. **Of all** the exquisite dishes on the scene, our tender sweet lamb is considered by far the most delicious food judges have ever tasted. (A) All (B) With (C) Overall **(D) Of all**	在現場所有精緻的菜餚中，我們的柔嫩甜味羊肉被美食評審視為是目前為止所嚐過最好的。

答案：(D)

這題依據語法要選**「Of all」**，故答案為**選項D**。

閱讀原文與中譯	
119. After the futile merger, the CEO is willing to do **whatever** needs to be done to keep the company from filing a bankruptcy. **(A) whatever** (B) what (C) which (D) wherever	在無效的併購後，執行長願意極其所能的做所有能夠讓公司免於申請破產的事。

答案：(A)

這題依據語法要選「**whatever**」，故答案為**選項A**。

閱讀原文與中譯	
120. According to the ruling, the criminal is sentenced to a life-long exclusion of the United States and **will be deported** immediately. (A) will be deporting **(B) will be deported** (C) be deported (D) deporting	根據法院的判決，罪犯被判終身不得入境美國且會即刻被遣返。

答案：(B)

這題依據語法要選「**will be deported**」，故答案為**選項B**。

閱讀原文與中譯

121. If you are unaccustomed to **performing** in public, you are not alone, and the performing club is here to assist you to overcome that.
(A) have performed
(B) be performed
(C) performed
(D) performing

如果你不習慣於在大庭廣眾下表演，你一點都不孤單，而且這裡的表演社會協助你克服這些困難。

答案：(D)

 解析

這題依據語法要選「**performing**」，故答案為**選項D**。

閱讀原文與中譯

122. **While** stinky tofu is widely acceptable in most Asian countries, its notorious smell does drive away westerners for no reason.
(A) Without
(B) While
(C) Once
(D) However

雖然臭豆腐在大多數的亞洲國家是廣泛被接受的，它惡名昭彰的味道確實沒來由地讓西方人感到卻步。

答案：(B)

 解析

這題依據語法要選「**while**」，故答案為**選項B**。

123. **Whether** the experienced connoisseur is able to identify fake paintings by naked eyes remains uncertain. (A) What **(B) Whether** (C) When (D) Whenever	經驗豐富的工藝家是否能夠以肉眼辨別出繪畫贗品仍是未知的。

答案：(B)

 解析

這題依據語法要選「**Whether**」，故答案為**選項B**。

124. Students enrolling in this course are eager to go to the field trip to Best Museum, a giant gallery **from which** viewers can get the inspiration. (A) which (B) from **(C) from which** (D) whose	修習這門課的學生熱切地想要去倍斯特博物館的戶外教學，一間巨大的藝廊，觀賞人員可以從中獲得靈感。

答案：(C)

 解析

這題依據語法要選「**from which**」，故答案為**選項C**。

閱讀原文與中譯	
125. **As** Best Kitchen does not have renowned chefs to do the cooking demonstration next Friday, the CEO has come to the agreement with other executives to poach qualified candidates from other companies. (A) Therefore (B) Albeit **(C) As** (D) If	因為倍斯特廚房沒有享譽盛名的廚師於下週五來做烹飪示範，執行長已經與其他高階主管達成了協議，從其他公司獵取具資格的候選人中。

答案：(C)

這題依據語法和語意要選「**As**」，故答案為**選項C**。

閱讀原文與中譯	
126. **Given that** the desert is sweltering hot during the day, the director eventually concedes to the protest of female models and has decided to shoot the pictures in the cellar. (A) Unless (B) In addition to **(C) Given that** (D) Among	考量到沙漠在日間悶熱異常，導演最終因為女模特兒的抗議而做出讓步，並且決定了要改在地窖中拍攝相片。

答案：(C)

這題依據語法和語意要選「**Given that**」，故答案為**選項C**。

模擬試題（一）
模擬試題（二）
模擬試題（三）
模擬試題（四）
模擬試題（五）

127. Best dating apps have adopted the most advanced technology making it **easier** to use and respond to the matched users. (A) easiness **(B) easier** (C) more easier (D) the most easiest	倍斯特約會軟體已經採用最先進的技術，讓使用者在使用和回覆配對使用者時更為便利。

答案：(B)

這題依據語法要選**「easier」**，故答案為**選項B**。

128. A Sunday spent online watching Friends won't make you more intelligent, **but** a Sunday spent learning complicated math questions just might. (A) or (B) yet **(C) but** (D) and	將週日時光花在看六人行不會讓你更具智力，但是把週日時光用於學習複雜的數學問題卻是有可能的。

答案：(C)

這題依據語法和語意要選**「but」**，故答案為**選項C**。

閱讀原文與中譯

129. Finalists of Best Airline are pleased to know they are all hired and enter the job **with** fully charged batteries. (A) at (B) on **(C) with** (D) of	倍斯特航空的候選人對於得知他們都獲得聘用感到高興，帶著充滿電力的能量進入這份工作中。

答案：(C)

 解析

這題依據語法和語意要選「**with**」，故答案為**選項C**。

閱讀原文與中譯

130. Job seekers can feel the **same** sense of rivalry when they are waiting outside the conference room. (A) similarity (B) difference **(C) same** (D) various	當他們在會議室外頭等待時，求職者能夠感受到相同的競爭感。

答案：(C)

 解析

這題依據語法和語意要選「**same**」，故答案為**選項C**。

Questions 131-134

With the huge **turnover** last month, the firm has decided to hire college students who major in arts. They can do the portrait for tourists in the zoo, and at the same time build up their portfolios. It's a great way for someone who doesn't have any work experience. This actually acts as the way to contribute to the society. Of course, the charge of doing the portrait cannot be higher than a certain amount, and since the firm doesn't **charge** them fees for doing the portrait in the zoo. They have to do at least a free drawing for the tourist. Their actions will be strictly **monitored** as well. They are not allowed to be rude to all tourists, and they cannot break any equipment in the zoo. They cannot **vandalize** anything in the zoo, including randomly painting something on the wall, and call it an art.

隨著上個月鉅額的營業額，公司已經決定要雇用主修美術的大學生。在動物園，他們可以進行畫像的描繪，與此同時建立起他們的作品集。對於沒有工作經驗者來說，這是很棒的方式。這實際上可以充當成貢獻社會的一個方式。當然，收費不能高過特定的金額，而既然公司不向他們索取在動物園內繪圖的費用。他們必須要替一位觀光客免費繪製一幅畫。他們的行為也會受到嚴密監控。對於所有觀光客不禮貌也是不允許的，而且在動物園內他們不能破壞設備。他們不能蓄意破壞動物園的任何東西，包含隨意在牆上繪製一些東西，然後將其稱作是藝術。

試題中譯與解析	
131. (A) categorization (B) reputation **(C) turnover** (D) awareness	131. (A) 分類 (B) 名聲 **(C) 營業額** (D) 意識
132. (A) charter **(B) charge** (C) cancel (D) calculate	132. (A) 發執照給；給予......特權、承租 **(B) 索價；對......索費** (C) 取消 (D) 計算

133.	133.
(A) monitored	**(A) 監控、監聽、監測**
(B) manipulated	(B) 操控
(C) mismanaged	(C) 對......管理不善、對......處置失當
(D) prohibited	(D) 禁止
134.	134.
(A) offset	(A) 補償；抵銷；把......並列，襯托出
(B) accelerate	(B) 加速
(C) exhume	(C) （從墳墓處）掘出（屍體）；發掘
(D) vandalize	**(D) 任意破壞**

第**131**題，這題依句意要選turnover，因為有高額的營收才會擴編或聘用其他新人等等，故答案為**選項C**。

第**132**題，這題依句意要選charge（也可以由後面的fees for doing the portrait in the zoo等協助判答要選charge），故答案為**選項B**。

第**133**題，這題依句意要選monitored，故答案為**選項A**。

第**134**題，這題依句意要選vandalize，他們不能**蓄意破壞**動物園的任何東西，故答案為**選項D**。

Questions 135-138

In addition to the students from the Department of Arts, students majoring in design or architecture are able to use the culture center of the zoo to **showcase** their projects for free. The time for the exhibition has to be **reserved** three weeks in advance so that our staff can have sufficient time to make the room and process the document. The **paperwork** has to be granted by the manager of our culture department. In addition, we are also working on the souvenir self-made. It has to be specifically-tailored. The production can be low-cost and will be available to all customers. We have been contacting with several deans of the Design Department to discuss further details. Tourists can **benefit** from this gesture, and some souvenirs can be custom-made.

除了美術系的學生之外，主修設計或建築的學生也能夠使用動物園的文化中心來免費展示他們的作品。展覽中心的時間必須在三週前提前預訂，這樣一來我們的員工才有足夠的時間準備空間且處理那些文件。文件必須由我們文化部門的經理應允。此外，我們也朝向自製紀念品的方向走。這必須是特別量身訂做的且生產是低成本，所有顧客都能負擔得起的。我們一直都與幾個設計系的院長有聯繫以討論進一步的細節。觀光客能夠從這些舉動中受惠，還有這些紀念品能夠是客製化的。

試題中譯與解析	
135. (A) conduct (B) liquidate (C) calibrate **(D) showcase**	135. (A) 帶領；實施；處理 (B) 償付；清算 (C) 校準 **(D) 陳列、使展現、使亮相**
136. (A) recorded (B) recoiled **(C) reserved** (D) relinquished	136. (A) 記載，記錄、進行錄音（或錄影） (B) 退卻、畏縮、退縮 **(C) 儲備、保存、預約、預訂** (D) 放棄、撤出、棄絕
137. (A) equity **(B) paperwork** (C) commission (D) portfolio	137. (A) 公平、公正 **(B) 日常文書工作、規劃工作、書面作業** (C) 佣金、委任、委託 (D) 代表作品
138. (A) backfire (B) withdraw **(C) benefit** (D) backlash	138. (A) 產生和預期情況完全相反的結果、事與願違 (B) 收回、取回、提取 **(C) 利益、好處、優勢** (D) 強烈反應、強烈反對

模擬試題（三）

模擬試題（一）

模擬試題（二）

模擬試題（三）

模擬試題（四）

模擬試題（五）

第**135**題，這題依句意要選showcase（showcase搭project剛好），故答案為**選項D**。

第**136**題，這題依句意要選reserved（可以由後面的three weeks in advance等協助判答），故答案為**選項C**。

第**137**題，這題依句意要選paperwork（可以由前面的process the document. 和後面的 has to be granted等協助判答），故答案為**選項B**。

第**138**題，這題依句意要選benefit（benefit搭配from），故答案為**選項C**。

Questions 139-142

Time really flies. **Our farmers were done their missions and ready to leave.** We held a thank-you tea party for them in one afternoon, and the CEO was too **swamped** with the work to attend. The firm still has a lot to do. It has begun to head towards the second phase. Instead of using frozen fish and meat to feed the marine mammals, the company has to be sustainable and **self-generate** fresh products for marine creatures. By the farm is a huge lake which can be a great asset to the company. The idea of an **aquaculture** can be put into use. We not only raise fish commonly known, but also several kinds of crabs and lobsters that can be used to feed marine mammals or octopuses in our aquarium.

時光真的飛逝。我們的農夫已經完成了他們的任務且準備要離開了。我們在下午會舉辦感謝下午茶會，而執行長卻忙到無法參加。公司仍有許多事情要做。這已經朝向了第二階段了。並非使用冷凍魚和肉品來餵食海洋哺乳類動物，公司必須要永續發展且能自產自給的提供海洋生物新鮮食材。在農地旁，有一個巨型湖泊對於公司來說是個很大的資產。水耕養殖的想法可以付諸實行了。我們不僅可以養殖廣為人知的魚類，也養殖幾種螃蟹和龍蝦用於餵食海洋哺乳類動物或章魚。

139. (A) The CEO is about to retire because he values his family more. **(B) Our farmers have done their missions and ready to leave.** (C) The tea party is so luxurious that all employees don't think it's fair. (D) The third phase is canceled due to some unforeseen reason.	139. (A) 執行長正要退休了，因為他更為重視家庭了。 **(B) 我們的農夫已經完成他們的任務且準備要離開了。** (C) 下午茶派對是如此的奢華以致於所有的員工都覺得不公平。 (D) 第三階段已經取消了，因為有些不可預知的原因。
140. (A) accompanied **(B) swamped** (C) satisfied (D) provided	140. (A) 陪同、伴隨 **(B) 沉浸在** (C) 滿足 (D) 提供
141. (A) supports (B) unleashes (C) impresses **(D) self-generates**	141. (A) 支持 (B) 釋放；宣洩（感情） (C) 給......極深的印象、使感動 **(D) 自我生產**
142. (A) miniature (B) horticulture **(C) aquaculture** (D) agriculture	142. (A) 縮圖、小型物、微型畫、小畫像 (B) 園藝、園藝術 **(C) 水產養殖** (D) 農業、農耕、農藝、農學

第139題，這題依句意要選B，那些農夫的任務完成了，所以下句才有公司替他們辦的感恩茶會，故答案為**選項B**。

第140題，這題依句意要選swamped，故答案為**選項B**。

第141題，這題依句意要選self-generate，他們必須要自給自足，故答案為**選項D**。

第142題，這題包含了四個culture結尾的字的出題，依句意要選aquaculture，故答案為**選項C**。

Questions 143-146

Our aquarium has only opened for three years, and it's quite new from the **standpoint** of the industry. The CEO spoken in the Wednesday conference, stating the fact that we actually had no time to waste, and the phase two had to be **hastened**. The HR Department has since begun to interview several professionals in the industry and has been trying to find someone who is experienced enough to take care of the aquaculture in the nearby lake. The output of fish, crabs, and lobsters has to be **steady** enough to sustain the food supply in both Zoo kitchen and employee kitchen. **That will take at least half a year, an expert said.**

我們的水族館僅營業為期三年，以這個產業的觀點來說還算是相當新。執行長在週三的會議中述說到，我們實際上沒有時間可以浪費了，而二階段的計畫必須要加速進行。從那刻起，人事部門已經開始著手面試幾位業界的專業人士，並且試圖找尋一位經驗豐富並足以照顧鄰近湖泊的水耕養殖的人才。魚、螃蟹和龍蝦的產量必須要穩定到足以維持動物園廚房和員工廚房的食物供應。根據專家所述，那至少要花費至少一年的時間。

試題中譯與解析	
143. (A) legitimacy (B) interest (C) authority **(D) standpoint**	143. (A) 合法（性）；正統（性）；合理 (B) 興趣 (C) 權、權力 **(D) 立場、觀點、看法**
144. (A) harassed **(B) hastened** (C) heightened (D) hampered	144. (A) 使煩惱、煩擾、不斷騷擾 **(B) 催促、加速** (C) 加高、增高、增加 (D) 妨礙、阻礙、牽制、束縛
145. (A) disenchanted (B) credible **(C) steady** (D) contingent	145. (A) 不抱幻想的；不再著迷的 (B) 可信的、可靠的 **(C) 平穩的、穩定的、不變的** (D) 附帶的、可能的、難以預料的

146.	146.
(A) That takes at least half a year, an expert said.	**(A)** 那至少要花一年的時間，專家說道。
(B) Marine creatures are too gluttonous to raise.	(B) 海洋生物都太嗜吃而無法難養育。
(C) They are considered experienced, so the production will definitely be so successful.	(C) 他們被認為是具經驗的，所以生產將確定會是很成功的。
(D) The Lake is contaminated by the chemistry factory, and there is nothing they cannot do.	(D) 湖泊受到化學工廠的汙染，而且他們也無可奈何。

第**143**題，這題依句意要選standpoint（從quite new等字的訊息可以排除像是authority等字），故答案為**選項D**。

第**144**題，這題依句意要選hastened（可以由前面的had no time to waste協助判答），故答案為**選項B**。

第**145**題，這題依句意要選steady（不只是有output而已，還包含穩定度，是否能持續的供應），故答案為**選項C**。

第**146**題，其實這些東西都才新開始，也沒這麼快就能完成，這題依句意要選A，故答案為**選項A**。

Part 7 中譯與解析

According to the survey conducted by ABC Marketing team in 2019, consumers had a penchant for pink and yellow, so we have adjusted these two products in both Q1 and Q3, so you should take a look. And we only list two main features and their prices. The internal memory for Lake Blue is 1TB, quite amazing.

Best Cellphone 2025 flagship			price
Q1	**Maybe Pink**	Camera 108M	Battery 50W	NT 30,000
	Striking Blue	Camera 108M	Battery 50W	NT 30,000
Q2	**Slightly Orange**	Camera 144M	Battery 80W	NT 42,000
	Dark Brown	Camera 144M	Battery 80W	NT 42,000
Q3	**Really Yellow**	Camera 200M	Battery 100W	NT 60,000
Q4	**Lake Blue**	Camera 300M	Battery 120W	NT 90,000

根據由ABC行銷團隊於2019年所進行的調查，消費者偏愛粉紅色和黃色，我們已經於第一季和第三季有作了調整，所以你應該要看下。而我們僅列出兩個主要特色和手機的價格。湖泊藍的內建記憶體是1TB相當驚人。

2025年倍斯特旗艦手機			價格
Q1	有點粉紅	相機 108M	電池 50W	台幣 30,000元
	耀眼藍	相機 108M	電池 50W	台幣30,000元
Q2	有點橙	相機 144M	電池 80W	台幣42,000元
	暗棕色	相機 144M	電池 80W	台幣42,000元
Q3	真正黃	相機 200M	電池 100W	台幣60,000元
Q4	湖泊藍	相機 300M	電池 120W	台幣90,000元

模擬試題（一）

模擬試題（二）

模擬試題（三）

模擬試題（四）

模擬試題（五）

Question 147

147. What is not mentioned about Best Cellphone? (A) Lake Blue costs almost US 3,000 dollars. (B) People purchasing a Lake Blue get to buy three Maybe Pinks. **(C) The internal memory for Striking Blue is 1TB** (D) The battery for Really Yellow is 100W.	147. 關於倍斯特手機沒有提到什麼? (A) 湖泊藍一支花費幾乎三千美元。 (B) 購買湖泊藍的人可以賣三支有點粉。 **(C) 耀眼藍的內建記憶體是1TB。** (D) 真的黃的電池是100W。

- 第**147**題,The internal memory for Lake Blue is 1TB,Lake Blue才是,故答案為**選項C**。

Cindy 9:50 a.m. Hey, I still haven't got the certificate of salvaging the brown bear cub... and I do need the certificate to apply for the college... it surely will affect the result... since I'm applying for majoring in biology with an emphasis on wild animals...	辛蒂上午9:50 嗨,我仍未收到拯救棕熊寶寶的證書...而我確實需要這個證照以用於申請大學...這確實會影響結果...既然我欲申請生物學主修,專攻野生動物...。
Jim 9:52 a.m. I'm so sorry... there are just so many documents... I'm just too swamped with work... it's ok that you write down the number of the association... I will send the certificate to your current address as soon as possible...	吉姆上午9:52 對此我感到很抱歉...這裡還有許多文件...我都因為工作忙碌不過來了...你寫下那些機構的電話號碼是可行的...我會盡快把證照送至你現在的居住地址。

Cindy 9:53 a.m. Thanks...	辛蒂上午 9:53 謝謝...。
Jim 9:58 a.m. And by the way... do you need the recommendation from our association... the founder used to be the dean of the Biology Department... that totally can earn you some points...	吉姆上午9:58 而附帶一提的是...你會需要我們機構的推薦嗎?...機構的創辦人過去曾是生物學系的院長...這全然可以替你增分不少...。
Cindy 9:59 a.m. That would be nice... thanks...	辛蒂上午9:59 那就太好了...謝謝...。

Question 148

| 148. At 9:58 a.m. what does the Jim mean when he says "**that totally can earn you some points...**"?
(A) Because he doesn't want to hurt Cindy's feelings.
(B) Because he wants Cindy to really earn it.
(C) Because he used to be the judge.
(D)Because that will be a boost for the interview | 148. 在上午9:58，當他說「**that totally can earn you some points...**」吉姆指的是什麼?
(A) 因為他不想要傷害辛蒂的感受
(B) 因為他想要辛蒂真的憑實力獲得它
(C) 因為他過去是評審
(D)因為那對於面試有幫助 |

 解析

· 第**148**題，因為那對於面試是加分的，故答案為**選項D**。

Best Resort

We have updated all services. It really is the new adventure for you.

C. Diving for Food/Money
- Beachgoers and underwater divers will find it exhilarating since they get to dive down in the transparent water. While enjoying the scenery, they can capture marine creatures, such as giant lobsters and large crabs, and bring them back to the shore. We have accountants and chefs ready on the beach. We can cook for you with additional cooking charges, or you can order multiple dishes in our restaurant. If you want to exchange for money, our accountant will do that for you by weighing the marine creature and do the calculation for you. You are actually earning money that can deduct your traveling bills.

D. Labor for Money
- You can offer your labor in exchange for money. Our resort is short of staff and in desperate need of finding someone who can move heavy bricks, mend fences, do the gardening, and so on. Of course, you can exchange the labor for a temporary stay in our luxurious hotel.
- In addition to the above-mentioned service, you can also use our water motorcycles (if you know how to drive) to get the rare seaweed for us in a remote island. It is now quite expensive in the developed countries, and its value is even greater than all seafood combined or other products.

倍斯特名勝

我們已經新增添了所有服務。這確實是你的一趟新的冒險旅程。

A. 潛水換取食物/金錢
- 海灘愛好者和水中的潛水客會覺得這是振奮人心的，因為他們要潛到清澈的水裡。在享受景色之餘，他們可以捕捉海洋生物，例如巨型蝦子和大型的螃蟹到岸上。我們在海岸邊備有會計師和廚師們。我們可以替你烹飪並收取額外的烹煮費用，或是你可以點我們餐廳的多樣化菜餚。如果你想要換成現金的話，我們的會計師也會替你安排，藉由秤量海洋生物的體重並且替你計算。你實際上賺取的費用可以扣掉你的旅行費用。

B. 勞力換取現金
- 你也可以提供你的勞力以換取現金。我們的渡假勝地目前人力短缺，迫切需要有人能夠搬運沉重的磚頭、修護圍籬、做園藝和等等的。當然，你可以以勞力換取短暫待在我們豪華旅館的住宿。

- 除了上述的服務之外，你也可以使用我們的水上摩托車（如果你懂得如何駕駛的話）替我們前往一個遙遠的島嶼上採集罕見的海藻。現在這些海藻在已開發國家中相當昂貴，其甚至比起所有海味的結合或其他產品更具價值。

Questions 149-152

149. Which of the following item is the most valuable? (A) the large crab (B) the giant lobster **(C) the rare seaweed** (D) the seafood	149. 下列哪個項目最有價值？ (A) 大型螃蟹 (B) 巨型龍蝦 **(C) 罕見藻類** (D) 海產
150. How can the tourists get raw giant lobsters? (A) by calculating (B) through driving **(C) through snorkeling** (D) through cooking	150. 觀光客要如何獲取生的巨型龍蝦？ (A) 藉由計算 (B) 透過駕駛 **(C) 透過潛水** (D) 透過烹飪
151. What is not the activity that can exchange for a short stay? (A) do the gardening **(B) drive water vehicles** (C) maintain fences (D) move heavy bricks	151. 哪個活動能夠用於兌換短暫住宿？ (A) 做園藝 **(B) 駕駛水上交通工具** (C) 維護圍籬 (D) 移動沉重的磚頭
152. What is not mentioned as a way to travel with less money? (A) mend fences (B) get the seaweed **(C) consume multiple dishes in the restaurant.** (D) dive for giant lobsters	152. 以較少的金錢旅行的方式中，哪個沒有被提到？ (A) 修護圍籬 (B) 獲取水藻 **(C) 在餐廳中，攝食多樣的佳餚** (D) 潛水換取巨型龍蝦

315

Halloween Train

Our Halloween Train is the scariest in the world, and it has 100 railway carriages. You have to endure all the horrors on the 5-hour drive to Best Recreational Park, and I'm afraid to say that it's the only way to arrive at our place. You are under the surveillance camera to ensure your safety. People with a chronic illness are not advised to take the train. For those who do not scream or feel scared at all will be getting a coupon worth US 1,000 dollars or a free admission. You might wonder how we are going to judge that. All participants will be required to wear the specialized watch that **rigorously** monitors your temperatures, blood pressure, and brain activities. Recordings will be deleted once you are in our Park. If you pee accidentally on your pant, you will be punished by having to pay the admission fee 50% higher, US 300 dollars in total.

萬聖節火車

我們的萬聖節火車是世界上最可怕的，而且其有100節火車車廂。你必須要在前往倍斯特遊樂園的五個小時途中能夠忍受所有恐怖戲碼，而恐怕這是唯一到達我們主題樂園的唯一方式。你會受到監視器的監視以確保你的安全。有慢性病史的人是不建議搭乘火車的。對於那些不大叫或一點也不覺得害怕者會得到一千美元的優惠卷或是可以免費的入場。你可能會想我們會是如何評估的呢?所有的參加者都會被要求要穿戴特製的手錶以嚴密監控你的體溫、血壓以及腦部活動。一旦你抵達我們的主題樂園，紀錄將會移除。如果你不經意地尿在你的褲子上頭，你會因此而受懲罰而必須要支付高於入場費50%的費用也就是300美元。

Questions 153-155	
153. According to the advertisement, how much is the admission fee? (A) US 300 **(B) US 200** (C) US 1,000 (D) US 1,300	153. 根據廣告，入學費用是多少錢？ (A) US 300 **(B) US 200** (C) US 1,000 (D) US 1,300
154. What is Not mentioned about the Halloween Train? (A) The train is the only transportation. **(B) There is no such a thing as a free admission fee.** (C) A designed watch is used to monitor temperatures of customers. (D) Surveillance cameras are used to monitor customers.	154. 關於萬聖節火車什麼沒有提及？ (A) 火車是唯一的交通工具。 **(B) 沒有所謂的免費的入場費。** (C) 特製的手錶會用於監控顧客的體溫。 (D) 監視器會用於監控顧客。
155. The word "**rigorously**" in paragraph1, line 10, is closet in meaning to **(A) strictly** (B) productively (C) communicatively (D) formidably	155. 在第一段第10行的「嚴厲地、殘酷地」，意思最接近 **(A) 嚴厲地、嚴格地** (B) 有結果地、有成果地 (C) 溝通地 (D) 可怕地、難以對付地

- 第**153**題，文章中唯一有出現數字的地方是在段落結尾If you pee accidentally on your pant, you will be punished by having to pay the admission fee 50% higher, US 300 dollars.，回推後可以得知金額是200元，故答案為**選項B**。
- 第**154**題，文中有提到a free admission跟B選項敘述不一致，故答案為**選項B**。
- 第**155**題，rigorously = **strictly**，故答案為**選項A**。

Dear Mary,

Don't worry about the owner of the coffee shop. We have already paid him your salary beforehand. **(1)** You don't necessarily have to actually work in the coffee shop. **(2)** You are just a doll wearing the uniform of the coffee shop... What if other coworkers ask something about you? **(3) I think he will probably find something to say... like you're the daughter of his relative who wants to know the industry**... I don't think other colleagues are going to say anything... you are thinking way too much... just do your job... ok... by the way I'm so looking forward to hearing more from him...**(4)** I've no idea what our rivals are doing and am totally clueless about the recent **publicity stunt** of their new apps. Have you used their software? I don't think it's that good... let me know what you think....

Manager

親愛的瑪莉

別擔心咖啡店雇主的事情。我們已經事先支付了他你的薪資。實際上，你並不需要做咖啡店裡頭的工作。你僅需要像個娃娃穿著制服出現在咖啡店裡頭。...如果其他同事們詢問關於你的事怎麼辦呢?我認為他可能會有些說法...像是你是他親戚的女兒，想要多了解下這個產業...我不認為其他同事會說任何事情...你想太多了...就做好你現在的工作就好...好嘛...順帶一提的是，我很期待能聽到關於他的事情...對於我們競爭對手目前正在做些什麼我沒有任何想法，且關於他們新的apps的宣傳噱頭毫無頭緒。你有使用過他們的軟體嗎?我不認為他們的軟體有這麼好...讓我知道你對此的想法是什麼...。

經理

Questions 156-158

156. The phrase "**publicity stunt**" in line 9, is closet in meaning to (A) a technician hired by the PR department (B) a stunning moment that is showcased in public (C) a public display of affections **(D)a ruse that can be used in advertising campaigns**	156. 在第9行的「宣傳噱頭」，意思最接近 (A) 由公關部門所聘用的技術工 (B) 一個令人震驚的時刻展示於公眾場合 (C) 公眾之下展示愛情 **(D)能用於廣告活動宣傳的花招**
157. What is not mentioned about the letter? (A) The owner of the shop has received the payment from the company. (B) Mary overthinks about the whole thing. (C) Mary has to wear the uniform. **(D)Mary has to buy a doll.**	157. 關於信件沒有提到什麼? (A) 店的雇主已經收到了公司的款項 (B) 瑪莉對於整件事情過度思考了。 (C) 瑪莉必須要穿著制服。 **(D)瑪莉必須要購買洋娃娃。**

| 158. In which of the positions marked **(1)**, **(2)**, **(3)**, and **(4)** does the following sentence best belong?
"**I think he will probably find something to say... like you're the daughter of his relative who wants to know the industry**"
(A) (1)
(B) (2)
(C) (3)
(D) (4) | 158. 以下這個句子最適合放在文中標記**(1)**、**(2)**、**(3)**、**(4)**的哪個位置?
「我認為他可能有些說法...像是你是他親戚的女兒,想要多了解下這個產業...」
(A) (1)
(B) (2)
(C) (3)
(D) (4) |

解析

· 第**156**題,這題比一般的同義字考點難,**stunt = ruse**,publicity stunt = a ruse that can be used in advertising campaigns,故答案為**選項D**。

· 第**157**題,文中沒有提到購買娃娃,只有提到她要假裝成,故答案為**選項D**。

· 第**158**題,這題剛好接續在I don't think other colleagues are going to say anything之前,**(3)**,故答案為**選項C**。

Best Elite University

Music	
❶ Piano	10 points
❷ Violin	10 points
❸ Flute	10 points
❹ Organ	10 points
❺ Trumpet	10 points
Sports	
❶ Basketball	10 points

❷ Baseball	10 points
❸ Soccer	10 points
❹ Badminton	10 points
❺ Freestyle	10 points
Extra Credits	
❶ Cello	15 points
❷ Saxophone	20 points
❸ Harp	15 points
❹ Guzheng	25 points
❺ Parallel bars	20 points
❻ Rowing	20 points
❼ 50 M Rifle Three Positions	30 points
❽ Equestrians	35 points

Note:

1. Unlike the criteria that are used in other schools, candidates have to be good at both music and sports to apply for our undergraduate program. (at least to be good at one item in the Music part and one item in the Sports section.) If you are good at more than one in each section, please let us know by highlighting it in the on-line application form.

2. The second screening will be held in July at BEU, and the exact date is to be determined.

Best Elite University

Music	
❶ 鋼琴	10分
❷ 小提琴	10分

❸ 長笛	10分
❹ 風琴	10分
❺ 喇叭	10分
Sports	
❶ 籃球	10分
❷ 棒球	10分
❸ 足球	10分
❹ 羽球	10分
❺ 自由式	10分
Extra Credits	
❶ 大提琴	15分
❷ 薩克斯風	20分
❸ 豎琴	15分
❹ 古箏	25分
❺ 雙槓	20分
❻ 划船	20分
❼ 50米步槍三種姿勢	30分
❽ 馬術	35分

Note:

1. 不同於其他學校所使用的標準，候選人必須要都擅長音樂和運動以申請我們的大學課程。（至少於音樂和運動項目各擅長其中一項）如果你在各自項目中擅長的不只一項的話，請在線上申請表格上強調以讓我們知道。
2. 第二次的篩選將於七月舉行，確切的日期未定。

Questions 159-160

159. What will happen during the month of July? (A) the announcement of the on-line application form (B) the announcement of an admission notice **(C) the announcement of the interview date** (D) the announcement of the undergraduate program	159. 在七月份期間會發生什麼事情？ (A) 線上申請表格的公告 (B) 入學通知的公告 **(C) 面試日期的公告** (D) 大學課程的公告
160. What can be inferred about Best Elite University? (A) Harp is worthy of 35 points. (B) Cello is worthy of 25 points. **(C) It values a lot in both Music and Sports.** (D) Rowing is worthy of 30 points.	160. 關於倍斯特菁英大學可以推測出什麼？ (A) 豎琴值35分。 (B) 大提琴值25分。 **(C) 學校重視音樂和體育表現。** (D) 划船值30分。

解析

- 第**159**題，7月份會宣布的是面試日期，故答案為**選項C**。
- 第**160**題，此間大學著重於音樂和體育，故答案為**選項C**。

Best Balloon Darts	
Cost	**darts**
US 5 dollars	10
US 10 dollars	20
US 15 dollars	30
US 20 dollars	40
US 30 dollars	50

Balloons	Prize
10 balloons	Pearl milk tea
50 balloons	Steak dinner at the restaurant
150 balloons	Luxurious buffet at the restaurant
350 balloons	Luxurious group buffet at the restaurant

Note:

1. For all your purchase of the game, 10% of the fee will be donating to the COVID-19 virus foundation to help those in need.

2. We do have an exchange program, 「**Labor for Darts**」, so you get to use your labor by filling up the balloon to earn darts. 500 balloons equate with 20 darts.

3. During the Valentine's Day, we do have the special event. Huge durable heart-shaped balloons will be made. Challengers using the mundane darts to pierce the specially-tailored balloon will get two free international flight tickets to Europe.

倍斯特射飛鏢	
費用	飛鏢數
5 美元	10
10美元	20
15美元	30
20美元	40
30美元	50
氣球	獎品
10顆氣球	珍珠奶茶
50顆氣球	牛排（餐廳裡）
150顆氣球	豪華自助餐（餐廳裡）
350顆氣球	豪華群眾自助餐（餐廳裡）

註：

1. 關於你所有的飛鏢體驗，10%的遊戲費用將會捐贈給新冠肺炎協會幫助那些需要幫助的人。

2. 我們確實有交換計畫**「勞力換取飛鏢」**，所以你可以使用你的勞力填充氣球，每500顆氣球等值20個飛鏢。

3. 在情人節期間，我們會有特別活動，巨大耐用的心型氣球會製作好。挑戰者使用普通的飛鏢，然後刺穿特別製作好的氣球將會得到兩張免費到歐洲的國際機票。

模擬試題（一）
模擬試題（二）
模擬試題（三）
模擬試題（四）
模擬試題（五）

Questions 161-164

161. If the player spends 500 dollars on the game, how much will the foundation actually get? (A) 0.5 (B) 5 (C) 500 **(D) 50**	161. 如果玩家花費500員在這項遊戲上，基金會實際上會獲得多少錢？ (A) 0.5 (B) 5 (C) 500 **(D) 50**
162. How much can a person get for making 500 balloons? (A) 5 **(B) 10** (C) 15 (D) 20	162. 製作500顆氣球能獲得多少錢？ (A) 5 **(B) 10** (C) 15 (D) 20
163. How many balloons are needed if one wants to invite a few friends to eat at the buffet for free? (A) 10 (B) 50 (C) 150 **(D) 350**	163. 如果一個人想要邀請幾位朋友享用免費的自助大餐，將會需要多少顆氣球？ (A) 10 (B) 50 (C) 150 **(D) 350**

164. If the player wants to get pearl milk tea, at least he has to shoot how many balloons? (A) 5 **(B) 10** (C) 15 (D) 20	164. 如果玩家想要獲得珍珠奶茶的話，他至少要射擊幾個氣球？ (A) 5 **(B) 10** (C) 15 (D) 20

解析

- 第**161**題，定位到10% of the fee will be donating，所以花費500元的話有50元是捐贈給foundation的，故答案為**選項D**。
- 第**162**題，定位到500 balloons equate with 20 darts.，20 darts = 10 dollars，故答案為**選項B**。
- 第**163**題，由表格資訊可以對應到需要350顆氣球，故答案為**選項D**。
- 第**164**題，也是由表格中看出會需要10顆，故答案為**選項B**。

Best Surgery will be needing a candidate with strong features to do the commercial and ad campaigns for them. **(1)** If you get chosen, you will be rewarding with a 50% discount for any surgery in Best Surgery. **(2) They have hired a few great photographers from Italy to do the shoot.** This shows how much they care about the commercial and ad campaigns. Right now they have the female model ready to do the shoot, yet they are still trying to find out the male candidate. **(3)** If you are interested, it won't hurt to ask or give it a try. You can also benefit from getting selected from this chance and build your modeling and acting career since. **(4)** But I do recommend you to be well-prepared. It really is a great opportunity.

倍斯特外科將需要一位有優秀特質的候選人來替他們做商業廣告和廣告活動。如果你雀屏中選的話，你會享有倍斯特外科任何手術的五折折扣。他們已經雇用了幾位來自義大利很棒的攝影師來拍攝。這顯示出他們有多麼在乎這個商業廣告和廣告活動。現在他們備有女性模特兒來做拍攝，但是他們仍在找尋男性候選人。如果你有興趣的話，詢問一下或試試看都無妨。你也可以從這個機會中的獲選而受益，並且自此建立起你的模特兒和表演職涯。但是我實在地建議你要做充分準備。因為這真的是個很棒的機會。

Questions 165-166

165. What is the article mainly about? (A) the difficulty of working with the female model (B) the concern for hiring great cameramen **(C) recruitment for the male model** (D) the fund for the ad campaigns	165. 報導主要是關於什麼？ (A) 與女性模特兒工作的困難度 (B) 聘用優秀攝影師的考量 **(C) 男性模特兒的招聘** (D) 廣告活動的資金
166. In which of the positions marked **(1)**, **(2)**, **(3)**, and **(4)** does the following sentence best belong? "**They have hired a few great photographers from Italy to do the shoot.**" (A) (1) **(B) (2)** (C) (3) (D) (4)	166. 以下這個句子最適合放在文中標記**(1)**, **(2)**, **(3)**, **(4)**的哪個位置？ 「他們已經雇用了幾位來自義大利很棒的攝影師來拍攝。」 (A) (1) **(B) (2)** (C) (3) (D) (4)

 解析

· **第165題**，主要是關於**recruitment** for the male model，故答案為**選項C**。

· **第166題**，插入句最適合放在This shows they how much they care about the commercial and ad campaigns.之前，**(2)**，故答案為**選項B**。

Best Modeling Agency is about to make a new hire on Monday. **(1)** There are thousands of people waiting in line. It's really hot outside. Let's take a look at several candidates. **(2)** Candidate A has prepared a portfolio of his pics, and he has chosen the best three. I think that's a pretty good start for the model. Candidate B is wearing a fantastic outfit. **(3) The shoes and the jewelry are all big brands.** She surely knows how to dress. Candidate C is muscularly built. I think it shows you have been working out, and it's good. But having too much can be a downside in several Modeling Agencies. Sometimes you just cannot overdo it. Candidate D is slim and confident with a pair of chic eyeglasses. **(4)** For now what I have seen is that all of them are strong candidates... I'm sure judges of the Modeling Agencies are going to have a hard time selecting the best pick.

倍斯特模特兒經紀公司正於週一要聘用一位新雇員。有數千人排隊等著。外頭確實是相當炎熱。讓我們看下幾位候選人吧!候選人A已經準備了他的作品集,而且他已經選了最佳的三張照片。我認為這對於模特兒來說是個相當好的開始。候選人B穿著極佳的套裝。鞋子和珠寶都是大廠牌製的。她真的知道如何穿扮。候選人C肌肉健碩。我認為這顯示出你一直都有在健身,而這是件相當好的事情。但是過多的話在幾間模特兒經紀公司來看會是個缺失。有時候你就是不能太過頭了。候選人D是苗條的且戴著時髦的太陽眼鏡展現出自信。就目前所看到的,都是強勁的候選人...我確信模特兒經紀公司的評審們將會很難抉擇出最佳人選。

Questions 167-169

167. In which of the positions marked **(1)**, **(2)**, **(3)**, and **(4)** does the following sentence best belong?
"**The shoe and the jewelry are all big brands.**"
(A) (1)
(B) (2)
(C) (3)
(D) (4)

167. 以下這個句子最適合放在文中標記**(1)**、**(2)**、**(3)**、**(4)**的哪個位置?
「鞋子和珠寶都是大廠牌製的。」
(A) (1)
(B) (2)
(C) (3)
(D) (4)

168. What is Not stated about Candidate B? (A) the great dress **(B) a bad taste in clothing** (C) expensive luxuries (D) a penchant for famous designers	168. 關於候選人B沒有提到什麼？ (A) 很棒的服飾 **(B) 對服飾的糟糕品味** (C) 昂貴的奢侈品 (D) 對於名設計師的偏好
169. What is indicated about Candidate D? (A) the preparation for the portfolio (B) a fantastic outfit (C) huge muscles **(D) confidence**	169. 關於候選人D提到什麼？ (A) 準備作品集 (B) 很棒的套裝 (C) 巨肌 **(D) 自信**

 解析

· **第167題**，最適合放置在She surely knows how to dress.之前，**(3)**，故答案為**選項C**。
· **第168題**，最不可能是a bad taste，故答案為**選項B**。
· **第169題**，關於D有提到的是自信，故答案為**選項D**。

My advice, NO. Recharging is not the reason to leave. Most people think of this as a way for them to evade their current job. **(1) Although replenishing yourself with the knowledge is important for your growth, you can do that during your free time.** You don't need to totally relinquish the current job to do so, and be a person who has lost the touch for the job market for a few years, only to realize that it's too late. **(2)** Your previous role has been replaced by a new rookie who can do a better job than you now, and you and your new diploma can't compete with that, and you keep wondering why spending a great deal of money and possessing a fancy diploma don't equate with having a better job opportunity. **(3)** All of a sudden you feel so lost and **disillusioned**. You find yourself on the wrong BMW, driving in a totally different direction, and it takes longer to arrive at your destination. **(4)** But time is already lost and money already spent…

Best Column

我的建議是「否」。大多數的人把這個思考成是他們逃避現在工作的一種方式。儘管將自己充電再裝滿知識對於你的成長來說是重要的，你可以在你閒暇的時間在去做這件事情。你不需要全然放棄「現職」去做這件事，而成了一個有幾年都與就業市場失去接觸的人，然後意識到一切都太遲了。你先前的工作已經被新的菜鳥所頂替了，他也可能比你現在做的更好，你和你的新學歷無法與之相比，而你不斷地想著為什麼花費了大量的金錢和有著亮眼的學歷卻無法跟有較好的工作機會劃上等號呢?突然之間，你感到迷失且幻想破滅。你發現自己在錯的BMW車上駛向截然不同的方向，卻花了更長的時間抵達你的目的地。但是時間已經消逝掉了且錢也花掉了。

倍斯特專欄

模擬試題（一）

模擬試題（二）

模擬試題（三）

模擬試題（四）

模擬試題（五）

Questions 170-172

170. What is Not stated about the "Job Column"? (A) It is essential to recharge yourself with the knowledge. **(B) You have to purchase a BMW in order to drive fast.** (C) Recharging cannot be the justified excuse to escape the reality. (D) You can have the cake and eat it too.	170. 關於求職專欄的部分，沒有提到什麼？ (A) 充電新的知識對於你個人來說是重要的。 **(B) 你必須要購買一台BMW以開得更快。** (C) 充電不是逃避現實的合理藉口。 (D) 你可以魚和熊掌均得。
171. The word "**disillusioned**" in paragraph1, line 10, is closet in meaning to (A) replenished (B) underdeveloped **(C) disenchanted** (D) unfaithful	171. 在第一段第10行的「不抱幻想的、幻想破滅的」，意思最接近 (A) 充滿的 (B) 發展不完全的、發育不良的 **(C) 不抱幻想的、不再著迷的** (D) 不忠誠的
172. In which of the positions marked **(1)**, **(2)**, **(3)**, and **(4)** does the following sentence best belong? "**Although replenishing yourself with the knowledge is important for your growth, you can do that during your free time.**" **(A) (1)** (B) (2) (C) (3) (D) (4)	172. 以下這個句子最適合放在文中標記(1)、(2)、(3)、(4)的哪個位置？ 「儘管將自己再裝滿知識對於你的成長來說是重要的，你可以在你閒暇的時間在去做這件事情。」 **(A) (1)** (B) (2) (C) (3) (D) (4)

Remember what's written in the bestseller? Don't use hygiene factors to determine your choice of a job. **(1)** Hygiene factors, such as a higher pay and other monetary rewards, are not the reasons that can make you truly satisfied. **(2)** Of course, you will be satisfied with having more money to spend in the very beginning. **(3) But once you have realized that you are stuck in a position, and you cannot get out because you have accustomed to the current lifestyle.** You have the house loans, mortgages, and kid's tuition. **(4)** You have to maintain the current job to keep the life **float**. But you are so unhappy. You just have to figure out what you truly want and what actually motivates you. Finding those that can make you happy can make your life more fulfilling...

Best Column

記得在暢銷書中所寫的嗎?別用保健因素做選擇工作的決定。保健因素，例如較高的薪資和其他金錢性的報酬都不是能讓你真正感到滿意的原因。當然，在起初時，你會對於能有更多的金錢來揮霍感到滿意。但是，一旦你開始意識到你困在某個職位，而你卻無法甩脫，因為你已經習慣了現有的生活方式。你有家庭貸款、抵押貸款以及小孩的學費。你必須要維持現有的工作來讓生活無慮。但是你卻很不快樂。你就是必須要了解你真正想要的是什麼，以及什麼是能夠激勵你的部分。找到那些能夠讓妳快樂的因素使你的生活更滿足...。

倍斯特專欄

Questions 173-175

173. What is Not stated about the "Job Column"? (A) Hygiene factors are short-term satisfactions. (B) Hygiene factors can lead to dissatisfaction. **(C) Hygiene factors are not important.** (D) The author of the bestseller discusses the hygiene factor phenomenon.	173. 關於求職專欄，沒有提到什麼？ (A) 保健因素是短期的滿足。 (B) 保健因素可能導致不滿足。 **(C) 保健因素不重要。** (D) 暢銷書作者討論了保健因素的現象。
174. The word "**float**" in line 7, is closet in meaning to (A) immerse **(B) buoyed** (C) submerge (D) meaningful	174. 在第7行的「浮、使浮起」，意思最接近 (A) 浸泡 **(B) 浮著的** (C) 把……浸入水中、淹沒 (D) 有意義的
175. In which of the positions marked **(1)**, **(2)**, **(3)**, and **(4)** does the following sentence best belong? "**But once you have realized that you are stuck in a position, and you cannot get out because you have accustomed to the current lifestyle.**" (A) (1) (B) (2) **(C) (3)** (D) (4)	175. 以下這個句子最適合放在文中標記**(1)**, **(2)**, **(3)**, **(4)**的哪個位置？ 「但是，一旦你開始意識到你困在某個職位，而你卻無法甩脫，因為你已經習慣了現有的生活方式。」 (A) (1) (B) (2) **(C) (3)** (D) (4)

- 第173題，這題有些難度，所以要多注意，且文章中未提到這是不重要的，故答案為**選項C**。
- 第174題，float = buoyed，故答案為**選項B**。
- 第175題，從插入句中的訊息像是stuck in the position等可以推斷最佳放置位置在You have the house loans, mortgages, and kid's tuition fees.前，**(3)**，故答案為**選項C**。

Dear Mark,

The shoplifting yesterday did cost us a great fortune. Unfortunately, the insurance won't cover that, since it expired after Easter. After doing some thinking, I have decided to shut down the entire mall for the next few months. I'm not sure when the reopening date will be. I will have a few accountants to **transfer** the severance pay to all temporary workers first, and get a bank loan to pay our contract workers and full-time employees. You don't have to feel **discouraged** though. You called the police right after the shoplifting had happened. I do think we will be back on our feet a few months later.

CEO of Best Department

親愛的馬克

昨天發生的商店行竊確實造成我們很大的財務損失，而不幸的是，保險並未擔保該損失，因為在復活節後保險即失效了。在經過一些思考後，我已經決定要於接下來的幾個月關閉整個購物商場。我不確定商場重新開張的時間會是甚麼時候。我會請幾位會計師先將遣散費匯給所有的短期工作者，以及向銀行貸款用以支付我們合約工作者和全職的員工。你不用覺得灰心喪氣。在商店行竊發生後你就打電話報警了。我認為我們在幾個月後就能回到正軌了。

倍斯特百貨公司的執行長

Dear CEO,

I'm the prosecutor of the case, and according to the evidence, we have the reason to believe that one of your employees, Mark Wang was behind this. **(1)** I do have the search warrant to search for the entire department and the police will be there Monday morning to gather evidence from all computers. **(2)** We have also detained one of your accountants. **(3)** We also found a store unit that housed all the jewelry and gold stolen from your shopping mall. **(4) They will be used as evidence in court, so you just have to be patient and wait until the verdict is final.** As for Mark, he is still at large. If you see him, please be calm and call the police. The police will handle this. Don't act like you have already known the whole thing. Put your **veneer** on... that's all.

Mary James

親愛的執行長

我是這起案件的檢控官，而根據我們現有的證據，我們有理由相信你們其中一位員工，馬克·王是幕後的主使。我持有整個部門的搜查令，而警方會於週一早上從所有電腦那裡匯整好所有證據。我們也已經拘留了你們其中一位會計師。我們也發現一個儲藏室存有所有在購物商場中失竊的珠寶和黃金。他們將會被用作呈堂證據，所以你必須要有耐心些，並等到最後的法庭宣判。至於馬克，他仍在逃。如果你有看到他，請保持鎮定並報警。警方會處理的。別裝作你已經知道整起事件的來龍去脈了。把你的偽裝戴上吧...就這樣。

瑪莉·詹姆士

Questions 176-180

176. The word "**transfer**" in the letter, line 5, is closet in meaning to (A) transfuse (B) manage (C) respond **(D) shift**	176. 在信件中第五行的「轉換、調動」，意思最接近 (A) 輸（血）、注射、灌輸 (B) 管理、經營、處理、控制 (C) 回應 **(D) 轉移、移動、替換、更換**

177. The word "**discouraged**" in the letter 1, line 7, is closet in meaning to (A) enlightened (B) empowered **(C) depressed** (D) unauthorized	177. 在第1封信第7行的「灰心的、沮喪的、氣餒的」，意思最接近 (A) 開明的、有知識的 (B) 經過授權的 **(C) 沮喪的、消沉的、憂鬱的** (D) 未被授權的、未被批准的
178. What is not mentioned in both letters? (A) Evidence will be collected on Monday morning. (B) A warehouse was used to stash the valuables. **(C) A bank loan is necessary in this incident.** (D) The insurance won't cover the loss.	178. 在兩封信中，沒有提到什麼？ (A) 證據會於週一早晨收集。 (B) 一間倉庫用於儲藏有價值的物品。 **(C) 在這起事件中，銀行貸款是必須的。** (D) 保險不會支付損失。
179. The word "**veneer**" in the letter 2, line 9, is closet in meaning to **(A) facade** (B) veneration (C) benediction (D) vehement	179. 在第2封信第9行的「外表鑲飾」，意思最接近 **(A) 表面、外觀** (B) 尊敬 (C) 祝福、祝願 (D) 感情激烈的、熱烈的

180. In which of the positions marked **(1)**, **(2)**, **(3)**, and **(4)** does the following sentence best belong?

"**They will be used as evidence in court, so you just have to be patient and wait until the verdict is final.**"

(A) (1)
(B) (2)
(C) (3)
(D)(4)

180. 以下這個句子最適合放在文中標記**(1)**, **(2)**, **(3)**, **(4)**的哪個位置？
「他們將會被用作呈堂證據，所以你必須要有耐心些，並等到最後的法庭宣判。」

(A) (1)
(B) (2)
(C) (3)
(D)(4)

解析

- 第**176**題，transfer = **shift**，故答案為**選項D**。
- 第**177**題，discouraged = **depressed**，故答案為**選項C**。
- 第**178**題，第一封信中確實有提到bank loan，但是在第二封信中遺失的物品均找回來了，所以其實不需要bank loan的，敘述卻描述成a bank loan 是necessary的，故答案為**選項C**。
- 第**179**題，veneer = **facade**，故答案為**選項A**。
- 第**180**題，根據上、下文等最適合放置的地方在 **(4)**，，store unit後的那句，故答案為**選項D**。

Dear Best News,

I saw someone slip by the swimming pool. It's a large public pool. **(1)** After dialing the number of the district police station, I went close to the crime scene only to find there was nothing I could find. **(2)** Nothing like I said. **(3)** At first, I thought I was just being paranoid, then the next morning my husband went for his usual jogging, and what he found was a corpse in the pool, and of course he called the police. **(4)** **According to the police report, it ruled this as an accident, drowning, but deep down I know it's not that simple.** You guys have been known for your reputation of digging some dirt and gossips. I do hope you can find something and do a report on this. People don't just do the swimming in the familiar pool and you know drown himself or herself... looking forward to a great news story...

Conscientious citizen May

親愛的倍斯特新聞

我目睹有人在游泳池旁滑倒。這是個大型的公眾泳池。在撥打電話給地區警局後，我實際到了犯罪現場卻一無所獲。就像我所說的沒有東西。起初，我也認為只是我太偏執狂，緊接著次日早晨我的丈夫像往常一樣的去慢跑，而在泳池旁他發現了一個屍體，而想當然的他報警。根據警方的報告，其判定這是個意外，是溺水事件，但是我打從心底覺得這不是這麼簡單的一件事。你們一直以你們挖醜聞和八卦而聞名。我真心希望你們能找到些什麼並以此做個報導。人們不會在自己熟悉的泳池游泳做這樣的事情，然後你知道的，溺死自己...期待看到很棒的新聞故事...。

認真的市民瑪莉

Best News

The doctor of the **deceased** called us a few days after the accident. The drown went to the therapy a day before the accident, asking for help because he believed someone wanted to kill him. But the doctor didn't take it too seriously and didn't prescribe any medicine for him. He asked the patient to relax for a bit by exercising. And a week later, the smartphone was found by a local resident. According to the conversation, someone **threatened** to kill him and the number was blocked. And the name remains unknown. I'm sure the police are now eager to know what actually happened that day. The weird thing is that all surveillance cameras near the public pool were removed while we were working on the report... hopefully, things will eventually come to light.

Reporter Cindy Thornes

倍斯特新聞

死者的醫生在意外發生後的幾天致電給我們。死者在事發的前一天曾去諮商，尋求幫助，因為有人想要殺他。但是並沒有人把這當一回事，而且醫生並未開處方給他任何藥品。只是希望他能藉由運動而放鬆一些。而一週後，有一位當地居民發現了其智慧型手機。根據對話，有個人威脅要將他殺死且電話號碼是鎖住的。而且對方姓名是匿名。我確信警方現在迫切地想知道在當日到底發生了什麼事情。最奇怪的是，當我們在做這則新聞報導時，在接近公眾泳池附近的監視器都被移除了…希望事情最終會有曙光。

記者 辛蒂·索恩

181. In which of the positions marked **(1)**, **(2)**, **(3)**, and **(4)** does the following sentence best belong? "**According to the police report, it ruled this as an accident, drowning, but deep down I know it's not that simple.**" (A) (1) (B) (2) (C) (3) **(D) (4)**	181. 以下這個句子最適合放在文中標記**(1)**, **(2)**, **(3)**, **(4)**的哪個位置? 「根據警方的報告,其判定這是個意外,是溺水,但是我打從心底覺得這不是這麼簡單的一件事。」 (A) (1) (B) (2) (C) (3) **(D) (4)**
182. What is Not mentioned about the first letter? (A) May had an inspection at the swimming pool. (B) May's husband did find the dead body. **(C) May's mental state is not stable.** (D) May eventually turned to the Best News for help.	182. 關於第一封信,沒有提到什麼? (A) 瑪莉在游泳池曾進行檢查。 (B) 瑪莉的丈夫找到了死者屍體。 **(C) 瑪莉的心智狀態不穩定。** (D) 瑪莉最終向倍斯特新聞求助。
183. What is Not mentioned about the second letter? (A) The police couldn't find the footage at the scene. (B) The caller's number couldn't be verified. (C) The guy did a counselling session before his death. **(D) The doctor gave the guy a prescription, but the guy ignored.**	183. 關於第二封信,沒有提到什麼? (A) 警方並未於現場中找到視頻。 (B) 來電電話沒辦法被證明。 (C) 在他死之前,男子做了諮商。 **(D) 醫生開給男子處方,但被男子所忽視。**

184. The word "**deceased**" in the letter 2, line 1, is closet in meaning to (A) decreased (B) increased **(C) departed** (D) population	184. 在第二封信第一行的「死者」，意思最接近 (A) 減少 (B) 增加 **(C) 過去的、往昔的** (D) 人口
185. The word "**threatened**" in the letter 2, line 6, is closet in meaning to (A) dulled (B) touted (C) rotted **(D) bulldozed**	185. 在第二封信第6行的「威脅、恐嚇」，意思最接近 (A) 變得遲鈍、減輕 (B) 招徠顧客、兜售 (C) 腐爛、腐壞、腐朽 **(D) 恫嚇、欺凌**

解析

・**第181題**，最適合的地方是放在called the police後，**(4)**，故答案為**選項 D**。

・**第182題**，第一封信並未提到May的mental state等，故答案為**選項C**。

・**第183題**，醫生並未給予prescription等，故答案為**選項D**。

・**第184題**，要注意deceased指的是人，在此等同於**departed**，故答案為**選項C**。

・**第185題**，threatened = **bulldozed**，故答案為**選項D**。

Diary/Day One

I was being thankful for getting assigned to gather berries today...**(1)** it was less burdensome... and my muscle got tense while trying to **retrieve** water for the team. **(2)** We had to walk twenty kilometers to get the water from the well, and I was exhausted. **(3) I didn't have any energy left for the day.** The boxing lesson went horribly as well. I got one punch by the coach, and the next thing I remembered was that I was lying on the bed, made of wood. **(4)** Perhaps I was not the guy built for the treasure hunt, and being the hero to combat wild cats. I was too tired for the day. I went to the kitchen to grab something to eat so that I could eventually have the strength to write the sort of a diary for the day. Hope tomorrow is going to be better.

日記/第一天

對於今天被指派採集莓果任務感到感恩...這個任務負擔較不重...但是當我在替團隊汲取水的時候，我的肌肉變得緊繃。我們必須要走20公里的路去井裡取水，而我感到筋疲力竭。整天的精力都點滴不剩了。拳擊課程也可怕地進行著。我被教練擊到一拳，接下來，我只記得我躺在由木頭製的床上。或許我體格並非打造成能參加寶藏狩獵和戰勝野外大貓的英雄。這天我過於疲累，然後我到廚房找尋些食物來吃，最終有些力氣來寫下像是每日日記的東西。希望明天能變得更好。

Day two

The running went fine, although I was the slowest in the team. I will probably get disqualified after the two-month training, but I'm trying really hard to keep myself floating here. However, I do like the survival skills taught here, knowing the weaknesses and strengths of all wild animals, and I still have a lot to learn though. I drank plenty of milk today that helped build my muscle tremendously. I'm getting stronger. I loved the barbecue for the night. It was delicious, and I ate a lot. I did shower extensively... too bad that I couldn't get a hot bath. Can't wait for tomorrow's lesson.

第二天

跑步進行的還可以，儘管我是隊上跑的最慢的一位。可能最終會在兩個月的訓練之後失去資格，但是在這裡我試圖非常認真地讓自己跟上進度。然而，我確實喜歡這裡所授的生存技能課程，知道所有野生動物的優缺點，當然我仍有許多事情是需要學習的。我今天喝下大量的牛奶，這對於我的肌肉建造有很大的幫助。我變得更強健了。我喜愛今晚的烤肉。很美味，我因此吃了很多。我大量地淋浴...不巧地是，我不能有個熱水澡。等不及要上明天的課程了。

Day 5

We are now required to wear heavy armors for the day whenever we go. It's too laborious and tiresome. Except the time when we go take a shower. In today's boxing lesson, I did an ok job by **withstanding** three punches from one of my teammates. I saw ostriches today, and we stole their eggs for our dinner. That was the assignment the coach gave us. Pretty heavy and there are still many eggs in the nest. It's so sustainable. Like we get to eat that everyday. Unfortunately, we heard the weird sound made by those ostriches... my instinct told me that we had to run fast... like the carnivore had been there... we eventually took the vehicle sent by the coach to safely arrive at the center.

第五天

我們現在被要求不論走到哪裡都要穿戴厚重的裝甲。這太費力且累人了。除了我們淋浴的時間之外。今天的拳擊課程我表現得還可以，能抵禦我其中一位隊友三擊拳擊。我今天看見鴕鳥了，然後我們偷取了牠們的蛋當作我們的晚餐。那是教練給我的任務。鴕鳥蛋相當沉重，當然在巢穴中，仍有許多鴕鳥蛋在裡頭。這真的相當永續。像是我們能於每天都能吃到般。不幸的是，我聽見由那些鴕鳥所發出的奇怪聲音...我的本能告訴我，我必須要跑得快些...這就像是有肉食動物在那裡...我們最終乘坐由教練所送至的交通工具安全抵達訓練中心。

186. The word "**retrieve**" in paragraph1, line 2, is closet in meaning to (A) remand (B) annihilate (C) manage **(D) fetch**	186. 在第一段第2行的「重新得到、收回、汲取」，意思最接近 (A) 遣回、送還 (B) 殲滅、消滅、徹底擊潰 (C) 管理、經營、處理 **(D)（去）拿來**
187. In which of the positions marked **(1)**, **(2)**, **(3)**, and **(4)** does the following sentence best belong? "**I didn't have any energy left for the day.**" (A) (1) (B) (2) **(C) (3)** (D) (4)	187. 以下這個句子最適合放在文中標記**(1)**, **(2)**, **(3)**, **(4)**的哪個位置？ 「整天的精力都點滴不剩了。」 (A) (1) (B) (2) **(C) (3)** (D) (4)
188. What most likely is Poor Man having difficulty doing? (A) find something to eat in the kitchen **(B) take the boxing lesson** (C) get water from a well (D) collect the berry	188. 什麼最可能是窮男人有困難做的事情？ (A) 在廚房裡找些東西吃 **(B) 修拳擊課程** (C) 從井中獲取水 (D) 採集莓果
189. The word "**withstanding**" in paragraph3, line 3, is closet in meaning to **(A) enduring** (B) streamlining (C) transferring (D) generating	189. 在第3段第三行的「抵擋、反抗、禁得起」，意思最接近 **(A) 忍耐、忍受** (B) 使簡化、使有效率 (C) 搬、轉換、調動 (D) 產生、造成

190. What is Not indicated about Day two and Day five?	190. 關於第二天和第五天沒有提到什麼？
(A) They had a meat feast on the second day.	(A) 在第二天他們有肉食盛宴。
(B) A carnivore was used to transport them back to the center in Day Five.	**(B) 在第五天時，肉食動物被用於運送他們回到中心。**
(C) Ostrich eggs can be replenished so it's good for all trainees.	(C) 鴕鳥蛋可以是不斷補充的，所以對於所有訓練人員來說是件好事。
(D) They've learned the knack of dealing with wild beasts.	(D) 他們已經學習到應付野獸的訣竅。

解析

- 第**186**題，retrieve = **fetch**，故答案為**選項D**。
- 第**187**題，從exhausted和後面訊息可以推知，最合適的插入點是 **(3)**，故答案為**選項C**。
- 第**188**題，從敘述可以得知是拳擊課程，他連一擊都承受不住，故答案為**選項B**。
- 第**189**題，withstanding = **enduring**，故答案為**選項A**。
- 第**190**題，有些選項均有同義改寫，但運送他們回中心的是vehicle而非carnivore，故答案為**選項B**。

Bulletin board

Hey Mates... order anything you want

Food and beverage	Cost
Pearl milk tea	US 20 dollars
Hot pot/luxury	US 150 dollars
Seafood buffet	US 500 dollars
Meat of wild animals	US 2,000 dollars
Any wine/a set	US 100 dollars

We accept credit card payments.
Use our apps to conveniently purchase whatever you want
The buffet car will come to you.
※payment exceeding 2,000 dollars will be getting 20% discounts and a
   bottle of pearl milk tea

佈告欄

嗨!夥伴…點任何你所想要的東西吧!

食物和飲料	費用
珍珠奶茶	20美元
火鍋（豪華版）	150美元
海產自助餐	500美元
野生動物的肉	2,000美元
任何酒品/一組	100美元

我們接受信用卡付款
使用我們的軟體，便利點你所想要購買的物品
自助餐車會自己上門
※消費超過兩千美元會獲得八折折扣。

Day 10

To tell the truth, I was a bit jealous because others get the **subscribed** service of "food". This means others are eating the dreamy food and drinks on the list. I just couldn't afford it. I didn't know the company even had the restaurant here. They really are the businessmen who want to dry us out completely. We haven't earned any money, and yet some of us have already spent a fortune on those things. They are good. I can even smell the aroma of wine from the person sleeping next to me... I hate my life...

第10天

坦白説，我有點忌妒，因為我的同袍都訂購了餐點服務。這意謂著，其他人都能享用清單上夢幻的食物和飲料。我卻負擔不起那些。我不知道公司在這裡竟有餐廳。他們真的是商人，想要把我們完全榨乾。我們都尚未賺取任何金錢，而我們之中有些人卻已經在那些東西上頭花費不貲。他們真的很厲害。我甚至可以聞到睡在我身旁的同袍的所有酒味...我好恨我的生命。

Day 14

I can run **effortlessly** and don't think running 2 kms is that much. **(1)** It was a huge improvement for me, and my big belly is shrinking. I'm using the phone to record the moment. **(2)** Too bad, the phone doesn't have any signal to upload on the ig. However, something bad happened today. **(3)** We were asked to go on a lion hunt and things went horribly wrong. The assignment was to get the cub of the lion from a female lion. **(4) The cub should remain unharmed.** The team which successfully does that will get an extra score. One of them got bitten by a lion, and bleeding badly. How awful.

第14天

我能不費吹灰之力地跑步了且不覺得跑兩公里是個大負擔。對我來説，這是個很大的進步，而我的大肚子正在消退中。我正使用手機紀錄這個時刻。不巧的是，手機沒有任何訊號能將這些上傳到ig上頭。然而，今天發生了件壞事。我們被要求要去獵捕獅子，而事情進行的糟透了。指派的任務是從雌性母獅身上取得獅子幼獸。可是幼獸要維持毫髮無傷。成功獲取的團隊將會得到額外的分數。他們其中一人被獅子咬到，血流的很嚴重。好可怕。

Questions 191-195

191. How much does it cost if a trainee orders meat of wild animals, pearl milk tea, and a set of wine? **(A) 1,696** (B) 1,680 (C) 2,120 (D) 2,100	191. 如果訓練者訂購野生動物的肉、珍珠奶茶和一組酒，要花費多少錢？ **(A) 1,696** (B) 1,680 (C) 2,120 (D) 2,100
192. What can be inferred from the restaurant service? **(A) The guy didn't have a dime to spend.** (B) The guy didn't like credit card payment. (C) The guy couldn't resist the aroma of wine. (D) The guy went a splurge on the buffet car.	192. 可以從餐廳服務推測出什麼？ **(A) 男子沒有花一分錢。** (B) 男子不喜歡信用卡付費。 (C) 男子無法抵抗酒的氣味。 (D) 男子在餐車上揮霍了一筆。
193. The word "**subscribed**" in paragraph2, line 1, is closet in meaning to (A) revered **(B) reserved** (C) prescribed (D) preserved	193. 在第2段第三行的「訂購、訂閱」，意思最接近 (A) 尊敬、崇敬、敬畏 **(B) 保存、保留、預約、預訂** (C) 規定、指定、開（藥方） (D) 保存、保藏、防腐
194. The word "**effortlessly**" in paragraph3, line 1, is closet in meaning to **(A) facilely** (B) typically (C) exceptionally (D) enormously	194. 在第3段第1行的「不費吹灰之力的」，意思最接近 **(A) 容易地、輕快地** (B) 代表性地、作為特色地、典型地 (C) 例外地、異常地、特殊地 (D) 巨大地、龐大地

| 195. In which of the positions marked **(1)**, **(2)**, **(3)**, and **(4)** does the following sentence best belong?
"**The cub should remain unharmed.**"
(A) (1)
(B) (2)
(C) (3)
(D) (4) | 195. 以下這個句子最適合放在文中標記**(1)**, **(2)**, **(3)**, **(4)**的哪個位置？
「幼獸要維持毫髮無傷。」
(A) (1)
(B) (2)
(C) (3)
(D) (4) |

解析

- **第191題**，總共金額是2120元，然後超過兩千元有八折折扣，故答案為**選項A**。
- **第192題**，他沒有多餘的錢可以花在餐點上，故答案為**選項A**。
- **第193題**，subscribed = **reserved**，故答案為**選項B**。
- **第194題**，effortlessly = **facilely**，故答案為**選項A**。
- **第195題**，由插入句中的the cub定位回去，可以定位到The assignment was to get the cub of the lion from a female lion.，故最合適的插入點在 **(4)**，故答案為**選項D**。

Day 20

It wasn't until today that I finally knew that we had to get a certain grade to pass the test... or shall I say be measured up in order to qualify for the treasure hunt. That means I have to get the score of at least 2,000 to qualify. And we didn't successfully get the lion cub... remember. I can't believe some of the guys here even have the mood to order the food through the buffet car. It's insane. The payment to enroll plus the training fee are US 70,000 dollars. How should I pay the bank loan, if I don't get qualified and get some jewelry afterwards? I am dying to know tomorrow's announcement of scores for some of the tasks.

第20日

直到今天我才最終知道我們必須要拿到特定的分數才能通過考試...或者是我該說成，是要達標才能夠進行寶藏狩獵。那意謂著，我必須要獲得至少2000分的分數才能有資格。而我們無法成功地取得獅子幼獸...記得嘛。我不敢相信這裡的有些人還有心情透過自助餐車點餐。這太瘋狂了。我們所註冊的款項加上訓練費用是7萬美元。我應該要如何支付銀行貸款，如果我無法獲取資格且於之後找到一些珠寶呢?我迫切地想要知道明日對於有些任務分數的公告。

Announcement/more to be announced		
Item	Note	Score
Steal a lion cub	The cub should remain unharmed	50
Get the golden feather of peacock	Extremely rare	200
Get the pearl necklace from the cheetah	The cheetah should remain intact	100
Get the ivory of the elephant	It should be in a natural occurrence	250
Get rare fruits on the cliff	The fruit should be in perfect shape	200
Gather honey, a kilo	A traditional ritual is required. Water bees. The aroma of the rare fruit can attract water bees.	500
Kill a sea lion	with grasses	50
Get the liver of the whale	From carcasses	300

公告/更多待工告		
項目	筆記	分數
竊取獅子幼獸	幼獸要維持毫髮無傷	50
獲取孔雀的金羽毛	極難尋獲	200

從獵豹身上取得珍珠項鍊	獵豹要維持完整	100
獲取象牙	這必須是自然現象。	250
在峭壁摘取罕見水果	水果必須要是完美的型態	200
採集一斤的蜂蜜	一個傳統儀式是必須的。水蜂。罕見水果的香氣能吸引水蜂。	500
殺死海獅	用草	50
獲取鯨魚的肝臟	從鯨魚屍體中汲取	300

Day 22

After seeing the announced items, I know how hard it is to do that within two months. And only nearly a month left. I can't say it's a scam because we have learned something during the training. I guess we have to wait for an easier task to be announced later. Some of the guys here seem pretty content with the life here. What is wrong with them? The coach said we could do these tasks during our free time and we should team up to do these tasks to remain uninjured. But we have to split the credits with other teammates. You can get the help from some of the coaches here, but it's going to cost you extra. And we were told that no one before had ever succeeded in getting the water bees.

第22天

在觀看公告的項目後，我知道要在兩個月內達成這些有多困難了。還有僅約剩下一個月的時間了。我不能說這是場詐騙，因為我們確實在訓練期間學到了些東西。我想，我必須要等到稍後所宣布的更輕鬆些的任務。有些同袍似乎很滿意在這的生活。他們到底有沒有問題啊？教練說，在我們的閒暇時間，我們可以去執行這些任務，而我們必須要團隊去做這些任務且維持毫髮無傷。但是我們必須要跟我們的團隊成員均分這些分數。你可以從這裡的有些教練獲得幫助，但是你這樣會花費額外的費用。且我們被告知目前為止沒有人成功取得水蜂過。

Questions 196-200

196. According to Day 20, what is Not True? (A) The requirement for the treasure hunt is at least 2,000 scores. (B) Trainees are at least paying the company US 70,000 dollars. **(C) No one bought some food from the restaurant car due to the high training fee.** (D) Trainees didn't get informed about the requirement for the treasure hunt.	196. 關於第20日，下列何者為非？ (A) 對於獵寶的要求要至少2000分。 (B) 訓練者至少要支付公司7萬美元的金額。 **(C) 由於高昂的訓練費用，沒有人從餐車上購買一些食物。** (D) 訓練者沒有被告知獵寶的需求。
197. What is the similarity among three tasks? (A) skills (B) difficulty **(C) appearance** (D) cooperation	197. 其中三項任務有著什麼樣的相似性存在？ (A) 技巧 (B) 困難度 **(C) 外觀** (D) 合作
198. According to the announcement, which task will get the highest score? (A) the golden feather of the bird (B) the pearl necklace from the carnivore **(C) water bees** (D) ivory of the herbivore	198. 根據公告，哪項任務會獲取最高的分數？ (A) 鳥類的金色羽毛 (B) 肉食動物那取得的珍珠項鍊 **(C) 水蜂** (D) 草食動物的象牙
199. Which of the following task is deemed unconquerable? (A) underwater whale livers (B) watery sea lions **(C) water insects** (D) peacocks	199. 下列哪項任務被認為是無法克服的？ (A) 水下的鯨魚肝 (B) 水域裡的海獅 **(C) 水昆蟲** (D) 孔雀

| 200. What should trainees do to keep undamaged in the subsequent assignment?
(A) wait for the less difficult task
(B) defeat formidable water bees
(C) split the credit
(D) join forces | 200. 訓練者要如何在後續的任務中免於受到傷害？
(A) 等待困難度較低的任務
(B) 擊敗令人敬畏的水蜜蜂
(C) 分獲得的分數
(D) 結合力量 |

解析

- **第196題**，文中有提到儘管有高昂的訓練費等，還是有學員叫了餐車，故答案為**選項C**。
- **第197題**，其中有三項任務都是要取得完整的物件，故答案為**選項C**。
- **第198題**，從表格中可以很快看出是**water bees**，故答案為**選項C**。
- **第199題**，這題要看到段落訊息中的最後一句And we were told no one before had ever succeeded in getting the water bees.= **is deemed unconquerable**，然後bees換成了選項中的**insects**，故答案為**選項C**。
- **第200題**，這題有些難，但是訊息中也有提到他們是要team up，其實就是join forces的意思，故答案為**選項D**。

- 【Part 5】要注意foregoing, injunction, locale等的出題。文法題則要特別注意代名詞指代和脫節修飾語的出題。

- 【Part 6】要注意skyscraper, recruitment, handpick, concurred等較不易答的題目。。

- 【Part 7】要注意計算題、表格題、細節性資訊和插入句的答題，這些連續答下來其實也頗耗腦力。

模擬試題（四）

In this section, you must demonstrate your ability to read and comprehend English. You will be given a variety of texts and asked to answer questions about these texts. This section is divided into three parts and will take 75 minutes to complete.

Do not mark the answers in your test book. Use the answer sheet that is separately.

PART 5

Directions: In each question, you will be asked to review a statement that is missing a word or phrase. Four answer choices will be provided for each statement. Select the best answer and mark the corresponding letter (A), (B), (C), or (D) on the answer sheet.

101. Landing an international flight safely is not as easy as it seems because there are other ------- factors during the landing.
    (A) operative
    (B) manipulative
    (C) uncontrollable
    (D) manageable

102. To drive ------- in the sweltering hot desert, one needs to take years of practice and patience to eventually do that.
    (A) effortlessly
    (B) remarkably
    (C) difficultly
    (D) emotionally

103. The CEO really wants to know whether the candidate is able to do the work well under pressure, especially in the face of ------- challenges.
   (A) uncorrelated
   (B) laudable
   (C) tough
   (D) credulous

104. The judge ruled in favor for the defendant, issuing an ------- shutting down the website.
   (A) application
   (B) continuation
   (C) installation
   (D) injunction

105. The ------- of the smartphone is shorter than that of the refrigerator, according to the software report.
   (A) appearance
   (B) experimentation
   (C) warranty
   (D) installation

106. To our amazement, the once profitable software company is ------- bonuses for the entire sales department this year.
   (A) showcasing
   (B) sustaining

(C) foregoing

(D) integrating

107. Weak ties can be the luck for someone who is looking for the job because they know someone outside your ------- friend circles.

(A) meticulous

(B) mutual

(C) knowledgeable

(D) unilateral

108. The ------- for the film is harder to find, so the director and investors have agreed to postpone the day of shooting.

(A) investment

(B) expenditure

(C) landscape

(D) locale

109. It is advisable for newly recruits to ------- the good relationships with their coworkers and superiors.

(A) allocate

(B) defray

(C) nurture

(D) diffuse

110. For each unit marketed, game salespeople will get a fantastic

------- from the boss, a quite rare opportunity in this economy.

(A) resiliency

(B) bonus

(C) profitability

(D) congratulation

111. Researchers at Best Chemistry Lab are now worrying that the released date of the latest merchandise will be postponed because of ------- detected by the Health Bureau.

(A) solutions

(B) rewards

(C) rebates

(D) residues

112. Despite the fact that Ann has a stunning look and fantastic portfolios shot by renowned photographers, her ------- movement at the go-see costs her a place in the competition.

(A) uncoordinated

(B) coincided

(C) gracious

(D) effortless

113. A glowing ------- is what most recent graduates need, but they still have to differentiate themselves from other competitors.

(A) subsidy

(B) forgiveness

(C) baby

(D) recommendation

114. According to an author of the bestsellers, "------- are just lists and lists are not compelling", so you still need to work on your personality and others.

(A) superstars

(B) resumes

(C) economies

(D) valuations

115. ------- 2% of people in the village have the access to drinkable water, according to the report.

(A) Few

(B) Fewer

(C) Less

(D) Fewer than

116. The privacy is ------- valued here at Best Cinema, so the retention rate is extremely high.

(A) exacerbation

(B) especiality

(C) especial

(D) especially

117. By ------- the workforce, the cash flow of Best Music is able to

sustain the operating costs for the following year.

(A) reducing

(B) reduce

(C) reduced

(D) being reduced

118. ------- the CEO is gracious enough to forgive the employee, the police still handcuff him to the station for a statement.

(A) Because

(B) However

(C) Notwithstanding

(D) Although

119. Bears are now incapable ------- finding wild crabs hidden under the rock due to the pollution.

(A) in

(B) with

(C) on

(D) of

120. The warehouse is ------- a labyrinth, so only store workers are able to find the items in a quick manner.

(A) such as

(B) for instance

(C) including

(D) like

121. The population of raccoons abated ------- due to illegal hunting activities and habit changes.
    (A) remarkable
    (B) remarkably
    (C) remark
    (D) remake

122. The CEO of Best Cinema found the cost of repairing the lobby -------, compared with that of the divorce fee.
    (A) trivial
    (B) triviality
    (C) trivialize
    (D) trivialization

123. ------- the economy in tatters, employees have to cut their recreational expenses to save more money.
    (A) During
    (B) Both
    (C) With
    (D) Among

124. The underlying asset ------- 30/70 between my client and her husband.
    (A) shall be distributing
    (B) should distribute
    (C) is distributed

(D) shall be distributed

125. The price of the A-list coffee machine is more expensive than ------- of the copier.
    (A) that
    (B) those
    (C) its
    (D) them

126. The prosecutor is threatening to have the defendant's wife ------- to where she is from to make him concede in the criminal court tomorrow.
    (A) deported
    (B) be deported
    (C) deporting
    (D) to be deported

127. ------- money you earn, the salary that is deposited in your bank account will be deducted by numerous taxes.
    (A) Whenever
    (B) Whichever
    (C) Whatever
    (D) However

128. To differentiate ------- from other competitors, this candidate finds a way of putting his resume on the desk of the HR

manager.

(A) it

(B) itself

(C) himself

(D) themselves

129. Instead of letting the customer -------, the beverage owner has come up with a more efficient system to make the drink.

(A) wait

(B) waited

(C) waiting

(D) to wait

130. After ------- to the Best Animal Shelter, the injured raccoon received extensive care and experienced a speedy recovery.

(A) taking

(B) taken

(C) it takes

(D) been taken

PART 6

Directions: In this part, you will be asked to read four English texts. Each text is missing a word, phrase, or sentence. Select the answer choice that correctly completes the text and mark the corresponding letter (A), (B), (C), or (D) on the answer sheet.

Questions 131-134

The search for the fishermen continues, and the company has started to work on building an organic farm in an artificial setting for safety concerns and risk management. "A tornado or typhoon can **131.-------** destroy what we have built so far", said a manager in last week's meeting. The CEO plans to buy a(n) **132.-------** to do the farm business vertically, and the **133.-------** for lab researchers and farmers has already begun. You can see the advertisement of the job hunt in every subway station. Lab researchers are required to wear goggles and masks while they are in the room. Expensive equipment will be **134.-------** to rigorously monitor the temperature of all fruits and vegetables. But that's not enough, and the CEO is unsatisfied with the current work done by the team.

131. (A) perpetually
     (B) confidentially
     (C) instantly
     (D) intentionally

132. (A) robot
     (B) insecticide
     (C) fertilizer
     (D) skyscraper

133. (A) document

(B) recruitment

(C) crisis

(D) advertisement

134. (A) celebrated

(B) augmented

(C) pursued

(D) purchased

Questions 135-138

All executives are required to go to the Popular Organic Building to make an observation. **135.-------** are designed on each roll to accurately monitor the temperature. Lab workers or researchers can see the data through computers outside the growing room. The data will be **136.-------** in the main computer and will be analyzed by the so-called data scientists every month. As you can see mushrooms and vegetables there are as fresh as you can imagine. Hot pot owners are here to **137.-------** them for the restaurant so that customers get to taste the genuine and healthy food. According to one owner, customers can feel that too, and it does help to build his brand reputation because food tastes healthy. **138.-------** He told us in last week's news report.

135. (A) Benefits

(B) Decisions

(C) Apparatuses

(D) Outcomes

136. (A) widely distributed
     (B) safely stored
     (C) regrettably constrained
     (D) confidentially duplicated

137. (A) compensate
     (B) weaken
     (C) handpick
     (D) improve

138. (A) You just have to look for the long-term, and not the short
         term.
     (B) They have to take MBA lessons to learn more about brand
         management.
     (C) It takes years to build, so Organic Building won't be ready
         until 5 years later.
     (D) The previous report took the data that is confidential to
         the company.

Questions 139-142

That's not it. Executives went to the restaurant on the first floor of
the Popular Organic Building, and ordered several dishes, including
fried mushrooms and chicken soup. They were **139.-------** by the
taste. It felt like the natural sweetness and elevated flavors

combined together. They had the soup like people addicted to the Coke, the carbonated soft drink that makes people **140.-------**. When they were back to the office, they were **141.-------** by what they saw and how they felt it. They can also make the company huge by gradually expanding their organic business and then think of some ways to innovate the company. Ultimately, the company will have a more competitive edge and can replace the company like the Popular Organic Building, **142.-------** He goes for a big idea and wants to buyout the Popular Organic.

139. (A) astonished
    (B) flummoxed
    (C) reminisced
    (D) stalled

140. (A) convinced
    (B) hooked
    (C) educated
    (D) inspired

141. (A) blindsided
    (B) sidetracked
    (C) energized
    (D) contradicted

142. (A) The CEO wants to cultivate the crops individually.

(B) The CEO doesn't want others to steal his credit of find the Popular Building.

(C) The CEO thinks their own company is competitive enough.

(D) but the CEO seems to have a different idea.

Questions 143-146

At the shareholder meeting, he said to a group of investors that it was the fastest way to do, and they don't have to find the place and start the business from scratch. Almost all shareholders **143.------** with the idea. He then made the phone call with the CEO of the PO to discuss the **144.-------** of buying their company. The CEO of the PO seemed intrigued, but just couldn't make a decision. The CEO of Best Zoo talked to the CFO and financial experts to **145.------** the value of the PO. **146.-------**, including their performance after they go public and their financial reports as well. Three days later, he got a phone call from the CEO of the PO who would be free next Monday to discuss the deal with them. Then they had a chat in a VIP room at the five-star hotel.

143. (A) concurred
    (B) conducted
    (C) cooperated
    (D) salvaged

144. (A) burden

    (B) acknowledgement

    (C) relationship

    (D) possibility

145. (A) stipulate

    (B) underestimate

    (C) evaluate

    (D) overrule

146. (A) The CFO already has the copy of confidential documents of the PO

    (B) They had to look at several aspects of the PO

    (C) The PO is known notoriously hard to get to

    (D) Financial experts proclaim that they don't have enough experience to go through these reports.

PART 7

Directions: In this part, you will be asked to read several texts, such as advertisements, articles, instant messages, or examples of business correspondence. Each is followed by several questions. Select the best answer and mark the corresponding letter (A), (B), (C), (D) on your answer sheet.

Questions 147-148

Best Clothing and Shoe

Item for sales	price	Discounts
Dark hoodie	US 200	20% off
Silver jacket	US 250	20% off
Eye glasses	US 450	30% off
Jean	US 300	30% off
High heels	US 600	**50% off**

Opening（**DEC**）

MON	TUE	WED	THUR	FRI	SAT
20 10 AM -8 PM	**21** 10 AM -8 PM	**22** 11 AM -9 PM	**23** 11 AM -11 PM	**24** 10 AM -9 PM	**25** 1 PM -11 PM

※ **TAX**: 10%，taxes should be included in the overall cost.

147. What can be inferred about the festival?

(A) It's Christmas

(B) It's Labor Day Weekend

(C) It's Thanksgiving

(D) It's Easter

148. How much does it cost if a personal buys 3 pairs of high heels and two silver jackets?

(A) 2300

(B) 2530

(C) 1300

(D) 1430

Question 149

Jack 4:01 p.m.
I'm so sorry. Your order will be delayed...

Cindy 4:05 p.m.
What? it's Valentine's Day... it's our busiest time... what are we gonna sell?

Jack 4:08 p.m.
There's been a terrible accident on the super highway... the truck is on fire... the monetary loss is uncalculated...

Cindy 4:10 p.m.
Oh my god... is the truck driver ok?

Jack 4:13 p.m.
He is still in the hospital... and we will compensate you by delivering some fresh flowers in the next few days... **by the helicopter... if it's ok**

Cindy 4:15 p.m.
Thanks...

---

149. At 4:13 p.m. what does Jack mean when he says "**by the** **helicopter... if it's ok**"?

    (A) He is gonna drive the helicopter himself.

    (B) He is afraid that the vehicle might be too unexpecting.

    (C) He knows Cindy is a huge fan of the helicopter.

    (D) Because it's their busiest time.

Questions 150-152

Dear Manager,

The uniform suits me perfectly... thanks... it's still a little bit weird

模擬試題（四）

模擬試題（一）

模擬試題（二）

模擬試題（三）

模擬試題（四）

模擬試題（五）

that I'm the only one here that doesn't have to do the work...**(1)** and I'm having a tuna sandwich with a hot cappuccino in the employee's room. **(2)** We're not allowed to eat or drink in public... kind of like working in the Disneyland where employees have to eat in the employee restaurant... not in front of the customer...**(3)** Bob says that it's the only time that he will be available... and he is going to tell us something big...**(4)** I can't contact him too often by using LINE... It's just too weird... and he says he will disguise himself by putting on eyeglasses and a wig... that makes it even funnier...

Mary

150. What is Mary responsible for at the coffee shop?
    (A) Do nothing.
    (B) Clean the employee restaurant.
    (C) Make a fantastic tuna sandwich
    (D) Make a decent cappuccino

151. In which of the positions marked **(1)**, **(2)**, **(3)**, and **(4)** does the following sentence best belong?
    "**I'm counting down the time till Thursday night**"
    (A) (1)
    (B) (2)
    (C) (3)
    (D) (4)

152. What is **NOT** mentioned about the letter?

    (A) Mary has an odd feeling of not having to actually work.

    (B) Mary loves her outfit at the coffee shop.

    (C) Mary is currently working at the Disneyland.

    (D) Bob is planning to say the big news to them.

Questions 153-157

Best Technology Center 2050

Now it's 2050. Best Technology has developed a list of magic potions for people to choose from. For some people, it's like a dream come true. However, we do caution people that there are side effects for each potion, so you have to take it more seriously, and do not overuse it. As for the youth potion, you have to use at least 50 bottles to have a remarkable change, and with it, lots of women don't have to use cosmetic products anymore. Furthermore, school students are forbidden to use both wisdom and memory potions, so they are for adults only. And adults taking the National Exam are also not allowed to use them, and before entering the test room, everyone is required to take the pill to remove the effect. We have been working on developing potion with lasting effects for people, and we do have the concern about the rich get richer phenomenon, because richer people might actually get younger.

Magic portions			
items	effects	duration	costs
Fly	Flying ability	a day	US 1,000
Wisdom	super smart	a day	US 5,000
Memory	excellent memory	a day	US 5,000
Power	Incredible strength	temporary	US 3,000
Youth	10 days younger	lasting	US 3,000
Muscle-building	Can reach an instant American Captain-like build	eternal	US 10,000

153. Which of the following has to be taken repeatedly to have a noticeable effect?
    (A) Youth
    (B) Wisdom
    (C) Memory
    (D) Power

154. Which of the following falls into the category of transient effects?
    (A) Youth
    (B) Muscle-building
    (C) Fly
    (D) Power

155. What can be inferred about the magic potions?
    (A) They all have fleeting effects.

(B) They all look equally the same.

(C) They all have side effects.

(D) They all have lasting effects.

156. What can be inferred about the person who has taken "Memory" before the NE test?

(A) His score is bound to have a significant boost.

(B) His score will be experiencing a slight increase.

(C) His score will be experiencing a moderate decrease.

(D) His score will not have anything to do with the Memory

157. What can be inferred about the future trend of the cosmetics?

(A) increasingly expensive

(B) gloomy

(C) productive

(D) prosperous

Questions 158-162

The game of the goldfish scoop has been known for a few years. By far, ours is the largest in the city. We have 50 pools that can **accommodate** for at least 200 people to play. There are five types of nets that you can choose from or I shall say, choose from wisely. Selecting a right type of nets will definitely influence your chances of catching the goldfish, although most of the time it depends on the skills.

Type	composition	Cost
Type A	Thin paper	US 3 dollars
Type B	Hard paper	US 6 dollars
Type C	Durable paper	US 9 dollars
Type D	Leaf	US 15 dollars
Type E	specially-made 7-colored paper	US 50 dollars

Note:

1. Type E is used to lure the rarest goldfish that houses beneath the castle of the props. Sometimes it won't come out for a few days. The person who catches it will be rewarded with a smartphone.
2. The person who has gathered a hundred goldfish will get a huge teddy bear or a stuffed animal.

158. What is **NOT** stated about the game?

(A) Luck is more important than the skills.

(B) The prize includes a teddy bear.

(C) The rarest goldfish is concealed.

(D) It contains 50 pools.

159. Which of the following costs the least money?

(A) Type B

(B) Type C

(C) Type D

(D) Type E

160. Which of the following is used to earn a popular gadget?

　　(A) Type B

　　(B) Type C

　　(C) Type D

　　(D) Type E

161. Which of the following looks splendid?

　　(A) Type B

　　(B) Type C

　　(C) Type D

　　(D) Type E

162. The word "**accommodate**" in paragraph1, line 1, is closet in meaning to

　　(A) collaborate

　　(B) supply

　　(C) assimilate

　　(D) resume

Questions 163-166

Have you experienced losing a loved one and you cannot let go? If you fit into the category, then you definitely have to come to the Best Remedy Center. **(1)** Scientists and engineers here can create an identical robot for you, and they can even instill the emotion of your loved one into the robot for you. **(2)** From these descriptions, you know the cost cannot be too cheap. It's like **implanting** a soul into the robot. **(3)** Just hearing the voice gives me the creep... that's my mother. They have several models for you to choose from. **(4)** Even I myself want to buy a new one. The major difference is that they won't age for a bit, but we humans do. So if you request a 30 year old husband robot, he is going to remain the specific age. You are going to look older than he is and have unwanted wrinkles on your forehead while he laughs at you...

163. What is the article mainly about?
    (A) a novel experience for a reporter
    (B) how to stay youthful
    (C) an advanced technology that brings possibility and hopes
    (D) finding the cure for unwanted wrinkles

164. In which of the positions marked **(1)**, **(2)**, **(3)**, and **(4)** does the following sentence best belong?
    "**It mimics the actions and emotions of your loved one.**"
    (A) (1)
    (B) (2)
    (C) (3)
    (D) (4)

165. What is **NOT** stated about the Best Remedy Center?
    (A) The treatment cannot be low-priced.
    (B) the imitation of actions and emotions of a person
    (C) the use of a robot to replace a real person

(D) The soul will be removed from the robot.

166. The word "**implanting**" in the advertisement, line 7, is closet in meaning to
    (A) inserting
    (B) reducing
    (C) exterminating
    (D) extracting

Questions 167-170

Best Zoo is seeking an AI specialist who can tackle the problem for customers. What's more, they are adding the interactive features for the customer. **(1)** And it's randomly assigned by the computer. **(2)** What if you are the animal that you don't like? The effect has to last for at least three hours and the cost of playing is US $ 900. **(3)** Still you can see the crowd waiting in line and dying to try it out. Perhaps after the experience, you can really cherish the life of animals more. **(4)** And according to the policy of the company, I have to play at least once and write a report on that. I think I'm getting very nervous about experiencing... candidates do remain inanimate on the machine they are sitting... but it's free... and now I have to "press" the button.

167. What is the article mainly about?
    (A) getting the discount for the game
    (B) the new interactive features that bring the prosperity for

the zoo

(C) a revision of the company policy

(D) how to stay animate when playing the game

168. In which of the positions marked **(1)**, **(2)**, **(3)**, and **(4)** does the following sentence best belong?

"**Once you press the button of this so-called "Exchange Life", you are on a journey of becoming an animal**"

(A) (1)

(B) (2)

(C) (3)

(D) (4)

169. What is **NOT** stated about Best Zoo?

(A) People will show no sign of life on the machine after playing.

(B) The new interactive game has attracted lots of crowds.

(C) The effect of transforming into an animal lasts longer than 2 hours.

(D) Nervousness can cause several side effects when playing.

170. How much does it cost if the father of the four can only afford two kids to have this interactive experience?

(A) US 900

(B) US 1,800

(C) US 2,700

(D) US 3,600

Questions 171-172

I've got to say, if it is your first job, then do it for at least two years. Unfortunately, that's the kind of the rule that was passed down from generation to generation. **(1)** To be stricter, then 3 years. You can hardly say that you have already known your current position, if you haven't been working in that industry for three years. **(2)** And trust me, when you are job hopping, that's the criteria that all interviewers are looking for. **(3)** Three also means a thorough experience in that job and can do the job independently. You will find yourself doing your job a lot more smoothly than someone with less than three years of working experience. **(4)** Even if you don't make a job hop, you will be shouldering more job responsibility from the boss or superiors... so try to do your current job for at least two years before making the transition...

Best Column

171. What is **NOT** stated about the "Job Column"?
　　(A) The rigorous standard for a job is to work for three years.
　　(B) Interviewers value someone with lots of job hop experiences.
　　(C) One will be given more responsibility after years of experience at the job.
　　(D) It takes three years to accumulate a complete job

experience.

172. In which of the positions marked **(1)**, **(2)**, **(3)**, and **(4)** does the
following sentence best belong?

   "**And that also demonstrates stability, and that's very important.**"
   (A) (1)
   (B) (2)
   (C) (3)
   (D) (4)

Questions 173-175

Be as early as possible, preferably during four years of your undergraduate study. Study intensively, and at the same time try to participate as many activities as possible. **(1)** You might find something that you don't think you love, but deep down you do. **(2)** In addition, don't pretend to be someone that you are not. Don't go after something that is against your inner voice. **(3)** I understand it's a time that you rely heavily on how your classmates think of you, but it's your life that we are talking about. **(4)** It might be so cool and get the most attention, but it's kind of the **regrettable** decision for many college students. So seize the moment and explore your broadest self...

Best Column

173. What is Not stated about the "Job Column"?
  (A) College students always make the right decision.
  (B) College students care about how their fellows perceive of them.
  (C) Pursue things that are consistent with your inner voice.
  (D) College students should participate in multiple activities.

174. The word "**regrettable**" in the letter, line 10, is closet in meaning to
  (A) notable
  (B) advisable
  (C) categorical
  (D) remorseful

175. In which of the positions marked **(1)**, **(2)**, **(3)**, and **(4)** does the following sentence best belong?
  "**The popular trend or the golden internship will ultimately be a waste of time, if that's not something you truly want.**"
  (A) (1)
  (B) (2)
  (C) (3)
  (D) (4)

Questions 176-180

Dear Manager at the headquarter,

This morning I went to the basement, a place where we usually stock our chocolate packages for international shipment, but I couldn't find one. Should I call the police? Or could it be mistaken? But I saw it with my own eyes. Or should I believe that "to see is not to believe."? I think I will be waiting for your reply to determine how to respond to this particular incident. I guess I will just prepare some documents for later use and wait in my cubicle.

Cindy Lin

Dear Manager at the headquarter,

Sorry, my bad... I went to the wrong basement... they all look equally the same... I'm so sorry. **(1)** I guess in my twenties my amnesia already gets to me, and that's probably not the reason that you hired me. **(2)** The company has a secret code for hiring only twentysomethings. **(3)** And I do have other things I do need to report to you, and it's really serious. All packages were opened. A thousand of them. I guess we do have unwanted companies. The raccoons. **(4)** However, I do take a few shots of those raccoons to test whether my latest smartphone is worth the money. It's the camera with 1.08 M pixels. I don't think it's a loss... although that's just from my stupid viewpoint... but I do think we can record videos and sell them to a few major news centers to compensate for our loss. They are going to pay us according to the number of viewers. And several photos can be used as the ad campaign pics "Look, they are just being naughty" at the company building. It's not entirely a loss... and I am sure some of the smart guys in the office can think of something brilliant than this...

Cindy Lin

176. What would Cindy be doing after the incident?

   (A) compose files

   (B) reexamine the chocolate packages

   (C) find out the felon

   (D) flee the country

177. In which of the positions marked **(1)**, **(2)**, **(3)**, and **(4)** does the following sentence best belong?

"**I don't even know how to get rid of them, and they are still eating.**"

(A) (1)

(B) (2)

(C) (3)

(D) (4)

178. What is **NOT** stated in the second letter?

(A) Cindy has been diagnosed with amnesia.

(B) The company has a preference for younger workers.

(C) Her smartphone has incredible pixels.

(D) All packages were opened.

179. What can be the possible solution for the package?

(A) invite some unwanted companies

(B) use the video to their advantage

(C) punish those miscreants

(D) purchase a phone with 1.08 pixels

180. Who can possibly buy the recorded video?

(A) A new startup

(B) International Shipping company

(C) News Center

(D) Advertising company

Questions 181-185

Dear Boss

Recently, we have begun to work on the AI experience with game lovers. To make it more authentic, we have added several elements into it, and I'm afraid that now is still not the time to tell you guys. And we do fear that people cannot **withdraw** themselves from the artificial settings. That's our sole consideration. One of our engineers got infatuated with one of the new designs because he recently lost a loved one. It would be too painful to cut him off from using the AI experience. In reality, without these designs, we do have other ways to counter the pain of losing our loved one. We do some counseling with doctors and eventually move on with our life. So the creation of our AI products does have several drawbacks that need to improve though...

Engineer Director

Dear Jason,

It's ok. Everything has its advantage and disadvantage. I would like to see those products next Monday. **(1)** I heard from a team member of yours that the game experience is incredible. **(2)** You can even feel it. That means you don't necessarily have to be rich or handsome to date your ideal lover. **(3)** Is it possible that we create a system that can make people never feel bored... you know how things go... especially a relationship... after you know the novelty wears off... I just cannot wait to try that myself...**(4)** I will invite several CEOs to visit the room. Be prepared. That's all.

Neal

181. The word "**withdraw**" in paragraph1, line 4, is closet in meaning to
(A) repair
(B) confide
(C) extract
(D) embrace

182. What is **NOT** stated about the first letter?
    (A) The AI software still has some glitches.
    (B) The addiction of the company's employee for the software.
    (C) The painful cut for the engineer
    (D) The company has made the experience more real.

183. What can be the new expectation by the CEO?
    (A) A design that gets rid of boredom
    (B) A design that removes the novelty
    (C) A design that earns more profits
    (D) A design that makes people good-looking

184. In which of the positions marked **(1)**, **(2)**, **(3)**, and **(4)** does the following sentence best belong?

    "**The design can compensate that, as long as you have the product.**"
    (A) (1)
    (B) (2)
    (C) (3)
    (D) (4)

185. What will happen next Monday?
    (A) The CEO is going to ship the product himself.
    (B) The CEO is going to pay a visit.
    (C) The CEO is going to dress handsomely.

(D) The CEO wants to see something novel.

Questions 186-190

Day 30

I have changed amazingly from a chubby person to an almost fit guy. The feeling is so great. And I have teamed up with several guys here. We have specific goals to work as a team to achieve the following tasks. It's a pretty good start. I have pretty good faith in myself and my teammate. By the way, we bought a jeep from the company... US 50,000 dollars... so that we can do the task faster... and hopefully gather enough scores before the deadline.

Day 31

We were all well-prepared and ready for the trip. We aimed to get plenty of rare fruits today. **(1)** Unfortunately, we **circled** the same area for the first few hours and couldn't seem to find one. Finally, we arrived at the valley and saw the cliff. We made the wood ladder trying hard to get the rare fruit we saw... **(2)** It is really rare. However, by the time we had climbed to the certain altitude, trying to grab the fruit... an eagle flew by... it was not like his nest was close by... Due to the disturbance of the eagle... it was highly unlikely that we got the fruit successfully... **(3)** I eventually yelled no... no... please... my teammate already grabbed the fruit from the branch.... **(4)** Our hope just shattered and I turned my anger into shooting the eagle...

Day 36

For the next few days, we kept searching for the rare fruit and things came to light. We eventually got five rare fruit, but like I said earlier, we had to spilt the credit, so we **respectively** got 200 scores... still way short of the amount needed for graduation... which is 2,000 in total... back to the training center... we heard that other teams went for other tasks, such as getting the golden feather and so on. I guess we have to exchange the valuable information to **maximize** the scores in the shortest time. And they still couldn't find the peacock with golden feathers... if so... can we dye the feathers of the peacock instead?

186. In which of the positions marked **(1)**, **(2)**, **(3)**, and **(4)** does the ⭐ following sentence best belong?

"Then all of a sudden it dropped to the ground"

(A) (1)

(B) (2)

(C) (3)

(D) (4)

187. What is **NOT** indicated about the rare fruit?

    (A) The location of the rare fruit was hard to find.

    (B) The total score for the gathered rare fruits is 1,000.

    (C) The rare fruit dropped to the ground, but unexpectedly remained intact.

    (D) The nuisance of the eagle made it difficult to get.

188. The word "**circled**" in paragraph2, line 2, is closet in meaning to

    (A) stayed

    (B) encircled

    (C) regulated

    (D) returned

189. The word "**respectively**" in paragraph3, line 3, is closet in meaning to

    (A) artificially

    (B) respectfully

    (C) automatically

    (D) individually

190. The word "**maximize**" in paragraph3, line 6, is closet in meaning to

(A) duplicate

(B) execute

(C) optimize

(D) document

Questions 191-195

Day 40

We were instructed to do the basic training for a month before continuing on our challenge. It was mainly due to the injury of one of our fellow members the other day. Luckily, they have extended the time frame from getting the score in two months to three months. We have more time to do that and more skills to complete assignments. Unfortunately, things are back to usual. After running and the boxing lesson, some guys would call the cafeteria car and order some food. For the first time, I kind of pampered myself by ordering the first pearl milk tea. It was great. The sugar kept me **heightened** even during the water gathering assignment in the afternoon.

Day 50

I have become almost athletically built... and can be mistakenly thought of as a gym coach or something. I'm more than ready to finish the assignment and get all the scores I desperately need. I heard from the coach that more assignments will be announced tomorrow... just can't wait to know. One of the teams even wanted to hire the coach to do the task with them so that this can give them a leg up. I was kind of surprised that even the coach didn't have the map. The map is going to cost you extra, remember? Everything is all about money... that's ludicrous.

Announcement/more to be announced

item	note	Score
Golden eggs of a peacock	Per egg, has something related to history	100
Golden eggs of an ostrich	Per egg, has something related to geography	50
Silver feather of the eagle	Extremely rare, electrified stones	100
Gather a 7-colored stone	Can get yourself wet, monkeys	100
Consume raw snails for 50	Can generate **infestation**	10
Take down a giant spider	Fortune is associated	500
Get rare seaweed	A box, a **submerged** castle	50
Take down a giant snake	with wooden swords, diamonds	600

191. The word "**heightened**" in paragraph1, line 8, is closet in meaning to
   (A) composed
   (B) reduced
   (C) enhanced
   (D) complicated

192. What is mentioned as the recent change for the guy?
   (A) He was unfortunately injured when performing a difficult task.
   (B) He quit ordering drinks from the restaurant car to be healthy.
   (C) He bought the map and tried to get acquainted with it.
   (D) He is physically ready to do the assignment.

193. The word "**infestation**" in the announcement, is closet in meaning to
    (A) production
    (B) invasion
    (C) visibility
    (D) allocation

194. What can be inferred from the announcement?
    (A) The silver feather of the eagle is easy to find.
    (B) Wealth may be around the corner in a particular new task.
    (C) Four items have the same score.
    (D) Nine new items are being added into the list.

195. The word "**submerged**" in the announcement, is closet in meaning to
    (A) serendipitous
    (B) subsequent
    (C) underwater
    (D) underdeveloped

Day 70

We all have received the intensive training for an additional month and all cannot wait to start our journey. **(1)** Something happened today. Mysteriously, we got an urn near the dorm. All hundreds of us gathered here and opened it. **(2)** Then, we all wondered where this place is, and were dying to find this place. **(3)** Like I said our team bought a jeep, so after getting prepared, we all sat on the car ready to find the waterfall. **(4)** After driving for two hours, we found a small trail and we pulled over... headed in there. The view was beyond anything... and there were monkeys making noises. At last, we discovered a waterfall... what is hidden beneath?

Day 71

The water pressure was quite powerful. The torrents were strong, so we managed to tie several ropes around the trees... in case something happened. While we were trying to get to the middle of water... we couldn't withstand the torrents. Two of us, while still grabbing the rope, almost got washed away. We were in the abysmal water and we didn't have any life vests on. After a while, I kind of vaguely saw the seven colored stones... They were down at the bottom of the waterfall. When we were all safely back to the ground, I told other teammates about the stones. We tried to think of a way to get them. It's a good sign, even though we have to split the credit and we didn't know how many were down there. And why did the company know these stones? Who sent the urn to the dorm?

Day 72

We set a tent here and dried all our clothes. While making the fried fish for dinner, we figured out a way to get the stones. We swam down there to get them. Of course, we had to hold our breath long enough to get them. That required a piece of equipment. Luckily, one of our teammates was a great swimmer. He made a few attempts and couldn't get one. While we were about to give up, the monkey pointed to something in the place where we camped. It said "press". Out of curiosity, I pressed the button. Then the huge wall gradually rose up and the water became less violent. It was actually the good time for us to gather all of the stones. We eventually got 10 stones, which boosted our morale.

196. In which of the positions marked **(1)**, **(2)**, **(3)**, and **(4)** does the following sentence best belong?

    "**It had a short letter stating that more is to be revealed in the waterfall.**"

    (A) (1)

    (B) (2)

    (C) (3)

    (D) (4)

197. What is **NOT** mentioned about the water?

    (A) Its pressure was really strong.

    (B) It couldn't stop the team because they had a good swimmer.

    (C) It was still too powerful even with the help of the rope.

    (D) It became less violent due to the apparatus.

198. What is **Not True** about the 7 colored stone?

    (A) They had to wait until the tide dwindled at dawn.

    (B) The team will get the credit by getting it.

    (C) It was situated in the bottom of the waterfall.

    (D) They ultimately got these stones in a less turbulent water condition.

199. What can be inferred about the monkey?

    (A) It placed the urn in front of the dorm.

    (B) It swam down to assist the team.

(C) It gave the hint to the team.

(D) It turned the torrent into less tempestuous one.

200. What is not used during the journey of collecting the 7 colored stone?

(A) a jeep

(B) an instrument

(C) life vests

(D) a rope

模擬試題（四）

PART 5 　中譯與解析

閱讀原文與中譯	
101. Landing an international flight safely is not as easy as it seems because there are other **uncontrollable** factors during the landing. (A) operative (B) manipulative **(C) uncontrollable** (D) manageable	國際班機的安全降落並不如看起來的那樣容易，因為在降落期間有其他無法控制的因素存在著。 (A) 操作的、運行著的、從事生產勞動的 (B) 操控的、用手控制的、巧妙處理的 **(C) 控制不住的、無法管束的** (D) 易辦的；可管理的；可控制的

答案：(C)

 解析

這題依據語法和語意要選「**uncontrollable**」，故答案為**選項C**。

閱讀原文與中譯	
102. To drive **effortlessly** in the sweltering hot desert, one needs to take years of practice and patience to eventually do that. **(A) effortlessly** (B) remarkably (C) difficultly (D) emotionally	在悶熱異常的沙漠中要不費吹灰之力的駕駛，需要花費數年的練習和耐力最終才能達成這項目標。 **(A) 輕鬆地、毫不費勁地** (B) 引人注目地、明顯地 (C) 困難地 (D) 情緒上、衝動地

答案：(A)

這題依據語法和語意要選「**effortlessly**」，故答案為**選項A**。

閱讀原文與中譯	
103. The CEO really wants to know whether the candidate is able to do the work well under pressure, especially in the face of **tough** challenges. (A) uncorrelated (B) laudable **(C) tough** (D) credulous	執行長真的想要知道候選人是否能夠在壓力下執行工作，尤其是在面對艱困的挑戰時。 (A) 毫無關聯的 (B) 值得讚賞的 **(C) 堅韌的、牢固的** (D) 輕信的、易受騙的

答案：(C)

 解析

這題依據語法和語意要選「**tough**」，故答案為**選項C**。

閱讀原文與中譯	
104. The Judge ruled in favor for the defendant, issuing an **injunction** shutting down the website. (A) application (B) continuation (C) installation **(D)injunction**	法官判定被告勝訴，並頒布一道禁制令將網站關閉。 (A) 應用、適用、運用、申請 (B) 繼續不斷、延續 (C) 就任、就職、安裝、設置 **(D)（法院的）禁止令；強制令**

答案：(D)

解析

這題依據語法和語意要選「**injunction**」，故答案為**選項D**。

閱讀原文與中譯

105. The **warranty** of the smartphone is shorter than that of the refrigerator, according to the software report. (A) appearance (B) experimentation **(C) warranty** (D) installation	智慧型手機的保證書比起冰箱的保證期更短，根據軟體報導。 (A) 出現、顯露、外表 (B) 實驗 **(C) 保證書、保單、擔保** (D) 就任、就職、安裝、設置

答案：(C)

 解析

這題依據語意要選「**warranty**」，故答案為**選項C**。

閱讀原文與中譯

106. To our amazement, the once profitable software company is **foregoing** bonuses for the entire sales department this year. (A) showcasing (B) sustaining **(C) foregoing** (D) integrating	出乎我們意料之外，曾經獲利的軟體公司於今年取消了整個銷售部門的獎金。 (A) 陳列、使展現、使亮相 (B) 承擔、維持、供養 **(C) 放棄、取消** (D) 使成一體、使完整

答案：(C)

 解析

這題依據語意要選「**foregoing**」，故答案為**選項C**。

| 107. Weak ties can be the luck for someone who is looking for the job because they know someone outside your **mutual** friend circles.

(A) meticulous
(B) mutual
(C) knowledgeable
(D) unilateral | 對於一個正在找工作的人來説，弱連結可能就是幸運點，因為他們認識妳共同朋友圈之外的人。
(A) 過分精細的、小心翼翼的
(B) 相互的、彼此的、共有的
(C) 有知識的、博學的、有見識的
(D) 一方的、單邊的、單方面的 |

答案：(B)

這題依據語法和語意要選「**mutual**」，故答案為**選項B**。

| 108. The **locale** for the film is harder to find, so the director and investors have agreed to postpone the day of shooting.

(A) investment
(B) expenditure
(C) landscape
(D)locale | 電影的拍攝場所較難尋獲，所以導演和投資者都已經同意要將拍攝的日期延期。
(A) 投資、投入
(B) 消費、支出、用光
(C) （陸上的）風景、景色
(D)（事情發生的）現場、場所 |

答案：(D)

這題依據語法和語意要選「**locale**」，故答案為**選項D**。

閱讀原文與中譯

109. It is advisable for newly recruits to **nurture** the good relationships with their coworkers and superiors. (A) allocate (B) defray **(C) nurture** (D) diffuse	對於新聘雇員來說，與他們的同事和上司培養出良好關係是明智的。 (A) 分派、分配 (B) 支付、支付......的費用 **(C) 養育、培育、教養** (D) 擴散、滲出、傳播

答案：(C)

 解析

這題依據語法和語意要選「**nurture**」，故答案為**選項C**。

閱讀原文與中譯

110. For each unit marketed, game salespeople will get a fantastic **bonus** from the boss, a quite rare opportunity in this economy. (A) resiliency **(B) bonus** (C) profitability (D) congratulation	對於銷售出每台遊戲機，遊戲銷售人員將從老闆那裡獲得很棒的獎金，在這樣的經濟環境下是相當罕見的。 (A) 彈性、恢復力 **(B) 獎金；額外津貼；特別補助** (C) 有利、有益 (D) 祝賀、慶賀

答案：(B)

 解析

這題依據語法和語意要選「**bonus**」，故答案為**選項B**。

閱讀原文與中譯	
111. Researchers at Best Chemistry Lab are now worrying that the released date of the latest merchandise will be postponed because of **residues** detected by the Health Bureau. (A) solutions (B) rewards (C) rebates **(D) residues**	倍斯特化學實驗室的研究人員正擔心最新商品的發佈日期將會延期，因為健保局檢驗出了殘留物。 (A) 解答、解決（辦法）、解釋 (B) 獎賞、報應、酬金、賞金、獎品 (C) 折扣、貼現 **(D) 殘餘、剩餘、渣滓**

答案：(D)

解析

這題依據語法和語意要選「**residues**」，故答案為**選項D**。

閱讀原文與中譯	
112. Despite the fact that Ann has a stunning look and fantastic portfolios shot by renowned photographers, her **uncoordinated** movement at the go-see costs her a place in the competition. **(A) uncoordinated** (B) coincided (C) gracious (D) effortless	儘管安有著驚人的外貌和由知名攝影師拍攝的極佳作品集，她在面試時不協調的動作讓她在比賽中失去資格。 **(A) 不協調的、不同等的、不對等的** (B) 一致的 (C) 優雅的、仁慈的 (D) 不費力的

答案：(A)

解析

這題依據語法和語意要選「**uncoordinated**」，故答案為**選項A**。

閱讀原文與中譯

113. A glowing **recommendation** is what most recent graduates need, but they still have to differentiate themselves from other competitors. (A) subsidy (B) forgiveness (C) baby **(D) recommendation**	耀眼的推薦函是大多數剛畢業的大學生所需要的，但是他們仍必須要將自己和其他競爭對手區隔出來。 (A) 津貼、補貼、補助金 (B) 原諒 (C) 嬰兒 **(D) 推薦**

答案：(D)

 解析

A glowing recommendation是一個慣用搭配，故答案要選**選項D**。

閱讀原文與中譯

114. According to an author of the bestsellers, "**resumes** are just lists and lists are not compelling", so you still need to work on your personality and others. (A) superstars **(B) resumes** (C) economies (D) valuations	根據暢銷書作家，「履歷僅是清單，而清單並不引人入勝」，所以你仍必須要在你的個性和其他方面上作努力。 (A) 超級明星 **(B) 履歷** (C) 經濟 (D) 估價、評估

答案：(B)

 解析

這題依據語法和語意要選「**resumes**」，故答案為**選項B**。

115. **Fewer than** 2% of people in the village have the access to drinkable water, according to the report. (A) Few (B) Fewer (C) Less **(D) Fewer than**	在村莊裡頭，少於2%的人能夠汲取到飲用水，根據報導。

答案：(D)

 解析

這題依據語法和語意要選「**Fewer than**」，故答案為**選項D**。

116. The privacy is **especially** valued here at Best Cinema, so the retention rate is extremely high. (A) exacerbation (B) especiality (C) especial **(D) especially**	隱私在倍斯特電影公司是特別受到珍視的，所以留任率是相當高的。

答案：(D)

 解析

這題依據語法和語意要選「**especially**」，故答案為**選項D**。

閱讀原文與中譯

117. By **reducing** the workforce, the cash flow of Best Music is able to sustain the operating costs for the following year. **(A) reducing** (B) reduce (C) reduced (D) being reduced	藉由減少人力，倍斯特音樂的現金流能夠維持於接下來年度的營運成本。

答案：(A)

 解析

這題依據語法和語意要選「**reducing**」，故答案為**選項A**。

閱讀原文與中譯

118. **Although** the CEO is gracious enough to forgive the employee, the police still handcuff him to the station for a statement. (A) Because (B) However (C) Notwithstanding **(D) Although**	儘管執行長大方到足以原諒員工，警方仍舊將他上銬並帶到警局作筆錄。

答案：(D)

 解析

這題依據語法和語意要選「**Although**」，故答案為**選項D**。

閱讀原文與中譯	
119. Bears are now incapable **of** finding wild crabs hidden under the rock due to the pollution. (A) in (B) with (C) on **(D) of**	由於汙染，熊現在不能夠找到藏匿在岩石下方的野生螃蟹。

答案：(D)

這題依據語法和語意要選「**of**」，故答案為**選項D**。

閱讀原文與中譯	
120. The warehouse is **like** a labyrinth, so only store workers are able to find the items in a quick manner. (A) such as (B) for instance (C) including **(D) like**	這間倉庫像是迷宮一般，所以僅有店裡的工人能夠以快速的方式找到品項。

答案：(D)

這題依據語法和語意要選「**like**」，故答案為**選項D**。

閱讀原文與中譯	
121. The population of raccoons abated **remarkably** due to illegal hunting activities and habit changes. (A) remarkable **(B) remarkably** (C) remark (D) remake	由於非法的獵捕活動和習慣改變，浣熊的族群數量有著顯著的減少。

答案：(B)

 解析

這題依據語法和語意要選「**remarkable**」，故答案為**選項B**。

閱讀原文與中譯	
122. The CEO of Best Cinema found the cost of repairing the lobby **trivial**, compared with that of the divorce fee. **(A) trivial** (B) triviality (C) trivialize (D) trivialization	比起離婚費用的花費，倍斯特電影的執行長發覺修復大廳的花費是不重要的。

答案：(A)

 解析

這題依據語法和語意要選「**trivial**」，故答案為**選項A**。

閱讀原文與中譯	
123. **With** the economy in tatters, employees have to cut their recreational expenses to save more money. (A) During (B) Both **(C) With** (D) Among	隨著經濟受重挫，員工必須要刪減娛樂支出以儲蓄更多的金錢。

答案：(C)

 解析

這題依據語法和語意要選「**With**」，故答案為**選項C**。

閱讀原文與中譯	
124. The underlying asset **shall be distributed** 30/70 between my client and her husband. (A) shall be distributing (B) should distribute (C) is distributed **(D) shall be distributed**	潛在的資產應該以30/70的比例分配給我的客戶和她的丈夫。

答案：(D)

 解析

這題依據語法和語意要選「**shall be distributed**」，故答案為**選項D**。

閱讀原文與中譯	
125. The price of the A-list coffee machine is more expensive than **that** of the copier. **(A) that** (B) those (C) its (D) them	一流咖啡機的價格比起印表機的價格更為昂貴。

答案：(A)

 解析

這題依據語法和語意要選「**that**」，that代替price，故答案為**選項A**。

閱讀原文與中譯	
126. The prosecutor is threatening to have the defendant's wife **deported** to where she is from to make him concede in the criminal court tomorrow. **(A) deported** (B) be deported (C) deporting (D) to be deported	檢控官正威脅要將被告的妻子遣返到她原居住地，藉此要讓被告於明日的犯罪庭上讓步。

答案：(A)

 解析

這題依據語法和語意要選「**deported**」，故答案為**選項A**。

127. **However** money you earn, the salary that is deposited in your bank account will be deducted by numerous taxes. (A) whenever (B) whichever (C) whatever **(D) however**	不論你如何賺取金錢，存入你銀行帳戶的薪資都會先扣除多條目的稅。

答案：(D)

 解析

這題依據語法和語意要選「**however**」，故答案為**選項D**。

128. To differentiate **itself** from other competitors, this candidate finds a way of putting his resume on the desk of the HR manager. (A) it (B) itself **(C) himself** (D) themselves	為了與其他競爭者作出區隔化，這位候選人發現了一個方法，把自己的履歷直接放到人事經理的桌上。

答案：(C)

 解析

這題依據語法和語意要選「**himself**」，故答案為**選項C**。

閱讀原文與中譯

129. Instead of letting the customer **wait**, the beverage owner has come up with a more efficient system to make the drink.
(A) **wait**
(B) waited
(C) waiting
(D) to wait

為了不讓顧客等待，飲品持有者已經想出了更有效率的系統來製作飲料。

答案：(A)

 解析

這題依據語法和語意要選「**wait**」，故答案為**選項A**。

閱讀原文與中譯

130. After **taken** to the Best Animal Shelter, the injured raccoon received extensive care and experienced a speedy recovery.
(A) taking
(B) **taken**
(C) it takes
(D) been taken

在被送往倍斯特動物庇護所後，受傷的浣熊接受了完善的照護，並且有著快速康復的經歷。

答案：(B)

 解析

這題依據語法和語意要選「**taken**」，因為是被送往，別誤選成taking，故答案為**選項B**。

Questions 131-134

The search for the fishermen continues, and the company has started to work on building an organic farm in an artificial setting for safety concerns and risk management. "A tornado or typhoon can **instantly** destroy what we have built so far", said a manager in last week's meeting. The CEO plans to buy a(n) **skyscraper** to do the farm business vertically, and the **recruitment** for lab researchers and farmers has already begun. You can see the advertisement of the job hunt in every subway station. Lab researchers are required to wear goggles and masks while they are in the room. Expensive equipment will be **purchased** to rigorously monitor the temperature of all fruits and vegetables. But that's not enough, and the CEO is unsatisfied with the current work done by the team.

公司持續在找尋漁夫，而基於安全性考量和風險管理，公司已經開始要在人工環境中建造有機農場。颶風或颱風會對我們目前所建造的造成即刻性的損害，一位經理於上週的會議中述說著。執行長計畫要購買摩天大樓來垂直地進行有機農場，而招募實驗室的研究人員和農夫都已經開始了。在每個地鐵站，你可以看到獵人才的廣告。實驗室的研究人員必須要帶上護目鏡和面罩，當他們在房間裡頭時。將會購買昂貴的設備以嚴密監控所有蔬菜和水果的溫度。但這都還不夠，而執行長對於團隊目前所完成的工作仍感到不滿意。

試題中譯與解析

131.	131.
(A) perpetually	(A) 永恆地、終身地
(B) confidentially	(B) 祕密地、親密地、十分信任地
(C) instantly	**(C) 立即地**
(D) intentionally	(D) 故意地
132.	132.
(A) robot	(A) 機器人
(B) insecticide	(B) 殺蟲劑
(C) fertilizer	(C) 肥料、促進發展者
(D) skyscraper	**(D) 摩天樓**

133. (A) document **(B) recruitment** (C) crisis (D) advertisement	133. (A) 用文件證明；為......提供文件（或證據等） **(B) 招聘** (C) 危機 (D) 廣告
134. (A) celebrated (B) augmented (C) pursued **(D) purchased**	134. (A) 慶祝 (B) 擴大；增加；加強；提高 (C) 追求 **(D) 買、購買、獲得**

第131題，這題依句意要選instantly（這題很容易誤選，因為perpetually or intentionally好像也對，但是從we've built so far可以推知是颱風依襲擊的話很可能是即刻毀掉一切），故答案為**選項C**。

第132題，這題依句意要選skyscraper，要運用前後出現的關鍵字，vertically就是一個很好的線索（摩天大樓看似無關，但卻是正確答案），有了摩天大樓就能進行**垂直**耕種且更省面積，水平耕種太耗地，故答案為**選項D**。

第133題，這題依句意要選recruitment（雖然也很容易誤選），故答案為**選項B**。

第134題，這題依句意要選purchased（equipment被purchased），故答案為**選項D**。

Questions 135-138

All executives are required to go to the Popular Organic Building to make an observation. **Apparatuses** are designed on each roll to accurately monitor the temperature. Lab workers or researchers can see the data through computers outside the growing room. The data will be **safely stored** in the main computer and will be analyzed by the so-called data scientists every month. As you can see mushrooms and vegetables there are as fresh as you can imagine. Hot pot owners are here to **handpick** them for the restaurant so that customers get to taste the genuine and healthy food. According to owner, customers can feel that too, and it does help to build his brand reputation because food tastes healthy. **You just have to look for the long-term, and not the short term**. He told us in last week's news report.

所有高階主管都必須要到流行有機大樓去做觀察。儀器設計在每排架上用以精確地監控溫度。實驗室工人或研究人員可以透過繁殖室外的電腦上看到數據。數據將會被安全地儲存在主要的電腦上且將被所謂的數據科學家於每個月進行分析。你可以看到那裡的蘑菇和蔬菜，就如同你想像般的新鮮。這裡的火鍋店店主親自摘取至餐廳，這樣一來顧客能夠品嚐到真實且健康的食物。根據雇主，顧客也能夠感受到，而這確實幫助建立品牌名聲，因為食物嚐起來是很健康的。你就是必須要看長期，而不是短期。他於上週的新聞報導中告訴我們。

試題中譯與解析	
135. (A) Benefits (B) Decisions **(C) Apparatuses** (D) Outcomes	135. (A) 利益、好處、優勢 (B) 決定 **(C) 儀器、設備、裝置** (D) 結果、結局、後果
136. (A) widely distributed **(B) safely stored** (C) regrettably constrained (D) confidentially duplicated	136. (A) 廣泛分布地 **(B) 安全地儲藏著** (C) 悔恨地受限制 (D) 機密地複製

137.	137.
(A) compensate	(A) 補償、賠償、酬報
(B) weaken	(B) 削弱、減弱、減少
(C) handpick	**(C) 用手採摘、精選、親自挑選**
(D) improve	(D) 改進、改善、增進、提高
138.	138.
(A) You just have to look for the long-term, and not the short term.	**(A) 你就是必須要看長遠，而不是短期。**
(B) They have to take MBA lessons to learn more about brand management.	(B) 他們必須要修MBA 課程以更了解品牌經營。
(C) It takes years to build, so Organic Building won't be ready until 5 years later.	(C) 品牌要花費數年建立，所以流行有機大樓要直到五年後才能完備。
(D) The previous report took the data that is confidential to the company.	(D) 稍早的報導所採的資料對公司來說是機密的。

第135題，這題依句意要選apparatuses（儀器用以精確地監控溫度），故答案為**選項C**。

第136題，這題依句意要選safely stored（安全地儲藏在主電腦上，D選項也也是乍看下很順的一個選項，但最符合的還是B），故答案為**選項B**。

第137題，這題依句意要選handpick（親自挑選），故答案為**選項C**。

第138題，這題依句意要選A，從上、下文可以得知，名牌的建立不易，所以要看長期而非短期的，故答案為**選項A**。

Questions 139-142

That's not it. Executives went to the restaurant on the first floor of the Popular Organic Building, and ordered several dishes, including fried mushrooms and chicken soup. They were **astonished** by the taste. It felt like the natural sweetness and elevated flavors combined together. They had the soup like people addicted to the Coke, the carbonated soft drink that makes people **hooked**. When they were back to the office, they were **energized** by what they saw and how they felt it. They can also make the company huge by gradually expanding their organic business and then think of some ways to innovate the company. Ultimately, the company will have a more competitive edge and can replace the company like the Popular Organic Building, **but the CEO seems to have a different idea**. He goes for a big idea and wants to buyout the Popular Organic.

這還不是全部。高階主管們都前往流行有機大樓位於一樓的餐廳,且點了幾項菜餚,包含了炸蘑菇和雞湯。他們都因為這個味道感到震驚。這感覺像是天然的甜味和提升的口感綜合在一起的感覺。他們喝湯就像是人們對可樂的上癮一樣。輕碳酸飲料讓人們上癮。當他們回到辦公室後,他們因為所見和所感受的部分而感到充滿活力。藉由逐漸地擴大他們的有機事業這能夠讓公司壯大,然後思考一些方式來創新公司。最終,這是有競爭優勢的,且可以取代像是流行有機大樓這樣的公司,但是執行長似乎有著不同的想法。他的想法更為大膽並想要收購流行有機。

試題中譯與解析

139.	139.
(A) astonished	**(A) 使吃驚、使驚訝**
(B) flummoxed	(B) 使困惑、使慌亂
(C) reminisced	(C) 追憶、回想
(D) stalled	(D) 把......關入畜舍、使陷入泥潭、使動彈不得

140. (A) convinced **(B) hooked** (C) educated (D) inspired	140. (A) 使確信、使信服、說服 **(B) 引（人）上鉤、欺騙** (C) 教育、培養、訓練 (D) 鼓舞、激勵、驅使
141. (A) blindsided (B) sidetracked **(C) energized** (D) contradicted	141. (A) 出其不意 (B) 使...轉移話題 **(C) 供給......能量、激勵、使精力充沛** (D) 否定、反駁
142. (A) The CEO wants to cultivate the crops individually. (B) The CEO doesn't want others to steal his credit of finding the Popular Building. (C) The CEO thinks their own company is competitive enough. **(D) but the CEO seems to have a different idea**.	142. (A) 執行長想要獨自地培植作物。 (B) 執行長不想要其他人竊取他找到流行有機大樓的功勞。 (C) 執行長認為他們的公司已經很有競爭力了。The CEO thinks their own company is competitive enough. **(D) 但是執行長似乎有著不同的想法。**

第**139**題，這題依句意要選astonished（可以由combined together等判別），故答案為**選項A**。

第**140**題，這題依句意要選hooked（可以由前方的可樂的比喻和addicted等協助判斷），故答案為**選項B**。

第**141**題，這題依句意要選energized（因為所見所聞激起他們的...），故答案為**選項C**。

第**142**題，這題依句意要選D（可以由後面的那句話He goes for a big idea and wants to buyout the Popular Organic.協助判答），故答案為**選項D**。

Questions 143-146

At the shareholder meeting, he said to a group of investors that it was the fastest way to do, and they don't have to find the place and start the business from scratch. Almost all shareholders **concurred** with the idea. He then made the phone call with the CEO of the PO to discuss the **possibility** of buying their company. The CEO of the PO seemed intrigued, but just couldn't make a decision. The CEO of Best Zoo talked to the CFO and financial experts to **evaluate** the value of the PO. **They had to look at several aspects of the PO**, including their performance after they go public and their financial reports as well. Three days later, he got a phone call with the CEO of PO who would be free next Monday to discuss the deal with them. Then they had a chat in a VIP room at the five-star hotel.

在股東大會上，他對一群投資客述說著，這是最快的方式了，且他們不需要找地點和從頭開始。幾乎所有的股東都贊同這個想法。接著，他致電給流行有機的執行長並討論關於購買他們公司的可能性。流行有機的執行長對此似乎感到有興趣，但是他無法做決定。倍斯特動物園的執行長與公司的財務長和財務專家談話並要他們評估流行有機的價值。他們必須要看流行有機大樓的幾個面向，包含他們在上市後的表現，還有他們的財務報表。三天後他們接到一通來自流行有機執行長的電話，說他下週一有空且願意與他們談論交易。然後他們在五星級酒店的貴賓室進行談話。

試題中譯與解析	
143. **(A) concurred** (B) conducted (C) cooperated (D) salvaged	143. **(A) 同意、一致、贊成** (B) 帶領、實施、處理、經營 (C) 合作 (D) 救助、營救、搶救、挽救
144. (A) burden (B) acknowledgement (C) relationship **(D) possibility**	144. (A) 重負、重擔 (B) 承認、致謝 (C) 關係、關聯 **(D) 可能性**

模擬試題（一）
模擬試題（二）
模擬試題（三）
模擬試題（四）
模擬試題（五）

145. (A) stipulate (B) underestimate **(C) evaluate** (D) overrule	145. (A) 規定、約定 (B) 低估 **(C) 評價、給...估值、評判** (D) 否決、駁回、拒絕
146. (A) The CFO already has the copy of confidential documents of the PO. **(B) They have to look at several aspects of the PO.** (C) The PO is known notoriously hard to get to. (D) Financial experts proclaim that they don't have enough experience to go through these reports.	146. (A) 財務長已經有了流行有機公司機密文件的副本。 **(B) 他們必須要檢視流行有機公司的某幾個部分。** (C) 流行有機公司是出了名的難取得的。 (D) 財務專家宣稱他們不需要有足夠的經驗來查看那些報告。

第143題，這題依句意要選concurred（可以由後面的致電討論等，得知股東們對於此計畫是贊同的），故答案為**選項A**。

第144題，這題依句意要選possibility（致電後依句意，最有可能的是洽談**可能性**...），故答案為**選項D**。

第145題，這題依句意要選evaluate（要對欲進行收購的...進行**評估**），故答案為**選項C**。

第146題，從前面的評估等線索和後面including等列舉中得知，這題要選B，故答案為**選項B**。

PART 7   中譯與解析

Best Clothing and Shoe

Item for sales	price	Discounts
Dark hoodie	US 200	20% off
Silver jacket	US 250	20% off
Eye glasses	US 450	30% off
Jean	US 300	30% off
High heels	US 600	**50% off**

Opening（DEC）

MON	TUE	WED	THUR	FRI	SAT
20 10 AM -8 PM	**21** 10 AM -8 PM	**22** 11 AM -9 PM	**23** 11 AM -11 PM	**24** 10 AM -9 PM	**25** 1 PM -11 PM

※**TAX**: 10%，taxes should be included in the overall cost.

倍斯特服飾和鞋子

銷售項目	價格	折扣
暗黑帽T	US 200	8折
銀光夾克	US 250	8折
眼鏡	US 450	7折
牛仔褲	US 300	7折
高跟鞋	US 600	**5折**

開放時間（12月）

MON	TUE	WED	THUR	FRI	SAT
20 10 AM -8 PM	**21** 10 AM -8 PM	**22** 11 AM -9 PM	**23** 11 AM -11 PM	**24** 10 AM -9 PM	**25** 1 PM -11 PM

※**稅**: 10%，稅應該要涵蓋在整體花費裡頭。

Questions 147-148	
147. What can be inferred about the festival? **(A) It's Christmas** (B) It's Labor Day Weekend (C) It's Thanksgiving (D) It's Easter	147. 可以推測出這是關於什麼節慶？ **(A) 聖誕節** (B) 勞工日週 (C) 感恩節 (D) 復活節
148. How much does it cost if a personal buys 3 pairs of high heels and two silver jackets? (A) 2300 (B) 2530 **(C) 1300** (D) 1430	148. 如果要買三雙高跟鞋和兩件銀夾克要花費多少錢？ (A) 2300 (B) 2530 **(C) 1300** (D) 1430

解析

· 第**147**題，從表格中的日期和月份很明顯可以推測出是聖誕節假期，故答案為**選項A**。

· 第**148**題，項目分別折扣完的和是**1300**元，故答案為**選項C**。

Jack 4:01 p.m. I'm so sorry. Your order will be delayed...	傑克下午4:01 我感到抱歉。你的訂單會延遲。
Cindy 4:05 p.m. What? it's Valentine's Day... it's our busiest time... what are we gonna sell?	辛蒂下午4:05 什麼?在情人節的時候....這是我們最忙碌的時候...我們要販售什麼呢？

Jack 4:08 p.m. There's been a terrible accident on the super highway... the truck is on fire... the monetary loss is uncalculated...	**傑克下午 4:08** 在高速公路上發生了一場可怕的意外事件...卡車著火了...金錢的損失是無法估計的...。
Cindy 4:10 p.m. Oh my god...is the truck driver ok?	**辛蒂下午 4:10** 我的天啊!...卡車司機還好嗎?
Jack 4:13 p.m. He is still in the hospital... and we will compensate you by delivering some fresh flowers in the next few days... **by the helicopter...if it's ok**	**傑克下午4:13** 他目前仍在醫院裡頭...而我們會補償你,所以於接下來的幾天會把一些花送至...以直升機的方式...如果這樣是可以的話...。
Cindy 4:15 p.m. Thanks...	**辛蒂下午 4:15** 謝謝...。

Question 149	
149. At 4:13 p.m. what does Jack mean when he says "**by the helicopter... if it's ok**"? (A) He is gonna drive the helicopter himself. **(B) He is afraid that the vehicle might be too unexpecting.** (C) He knows Cindy is a huge fan of the helicopter. (D) Because it's their busiest time	149. 在下午4:13分,當他説「**by the helicopter... if it's ok**」傑克指的是什麼? (A) 他要自己駕乘直升機。 **(B) 他怕運輸工具太出乎意料之外。** (C) 他知道辛蒂是直升機迷。 (D) 因為這是他們最忙碌的時段

· **第149題**,他是擔心會有點太出其不意,因為是用直升機送,故答案為**選項 B**。

Questions 150-152

Dear Manager,

The uniform suits me perfectly... thanks... it's still a little bit weird that I'm the only one here that doesn't have to do the work...**(1)** and I'm having a tuna sandwich with a hot cappuccino in the employee's room. **(2)** We're not allowed to eat or drink in public... kind of like working in the Disneyland where employees have to eat in the employee restaurant... not in front of the customer... **(3) I'm counting down the time till Thursday night**. Bob says that it's the only time that he will be available... and he is going to tell us something big...**(4)** I can't contact him too often by using LINE... It's just too weird... and he says he will disguise himself by putting on eyeglasses and a wig... that makes it even funnier...

Mary

親愛的經理

這件制服跟我很相襯...謝謝...仍然感到有些奇怪，我是這裡唯一一位不需要工作的員工...而且我正在員工室裡頭享用鮪魚三明治配熱卡布奇諾。在公眾場合下，我們不被允許飲食...有點像是在迪士尼工作，員工必須在員工餐廳裡頭吃飯...而不是在顧客面前...週四晚間來臨之前...我在數時間了。鮑伯説，這僅是他唯一有空的時間...他即將告訴我們一件大事...我無法很頻繁的跟他用line聯繫...這樣會太奇怪...而且他説道，他會穿戴眼鏡和假髮以偽裝自己...這讓事情變得更有趣了...。

瑪莉

| 150. What is Mary responsible for at the coffee shop?
(A) Do nothing.
(B) Clean the employee restaurant.
(C) Make a fantastic tuna sandwich
(D) Make a decent cappuccino | 150. 瑪莉在咖啡店負責什麼？
(A) 什麼都不用做
(B) 清潔員工餐廳
(C) 製作極佳的鮪魚三明治
(D) 製作合宜的卡布奇諾 |

151. In which of the positions marked **(1)**, **(2)**, **(3)**, and **(4)** does the following sentence best belong? "**I'm counting down the time till Thursday night**" (A) (1) (B) (2) **(C) (3)** (D) (4)	151. 以下這個句子最適合放在文中標記**(1)**、**(2)**、**(3)**、**(4)**的哪個位置？ 「週四晚間來臨之前…我在數時間了。」 (A) (1) (B) (2) **(C) (3)** (D) (4)
152. What is not mentioned about the letter? (A) Mary has an odd feeling of not having to actually work. (B) Mary loves her outfit at the coffee shop. **(C) Mary is currently working at the Disneyland.** (D) Bob is planning to say the big news to them.	152. 關於信件沒有提到什麼？ (A) 對於真的不用工作，瑪莉有種奇怪的感覺。 (B) 瑪莉喜愛她在咖啡店的服飾。 **(C) 瑪莉正於迪士尼樂園工作。** (D) 鮑伯正計畫要跟他們說個驚人的消息

解析

· **第150題**，瑪莉在咖啡廳中是不需要做任何事的，故答案為**選項A**。

· **第151題**，從Bob says that it's the only **time** that he is available，time 對應到插入句中的時間點Thursday night，**(3)**是最合適的，故答案為**選項C**。

· **第152題**，文中有提到迪士尼樂園，但沒有提到瑪莉正在那裡工作，故答案為**選項C**。

Best Technology Center 2050

Now it's 2050. Best Technology has developed a list of magic potions for people to choose from. For some people, it's like a dream come true. However, we do caution people that there are side effects for each potion, so you have to take it more seriously, and do not overuse it. As for the youth potion, you have to use at least 50 bottles to have a remarkable change, and with it, lots of women don't have to use cosmetic products anymore. Furthermore, school students are forbidden to use both wisdom and memory potions, so they are for adults only. And adults taking the National Exam are also not allowed to use them, and before entering the test room, everyone is required to take the pill to remove the effect. We have been working on developing potion with lasting effects for people, and we do have the concern about the rich get richer phenomenon, because richer people might actually get younger.

Magic potion			
items	effects	duration	costs
Fly	Flying ability	a day	US 1,000
Wisdom	super smart	a day	US 5,000
Memory	excellent memory	a day	US 5,000
Power	Incredible strength	temporary	US 3,000
Youth	10 days younger	lasting	US 3,000
Muscle-building	Can reach an instant American Captain-like build	eternal	US 10,000

2050年，倍斯特科技中心

現在是西元2050年。倍斯特科技公司已經研發出一系列的魔法藥水可供人們選擇。對於有些人來說，這就像是夢想成真一般。然而，我們要告誡使用者，每個藥水都有其副作用，所以你必須要更認真地看待且別過度使用。關於青春藥水你必須要使用50瓶才會有顯著的改變，而隨著使用青春藥水，許多女性不用再使用化妝用品了。此外，學校學生禁止使用智慧和記憶藥水，所以僅成年人可以使用。成年人有參與國家考試者也不允許使用，在進入試場時，每個人都必須要吃藥以除去藥水的效果。我們一直努力研發永久性效果的藥水提供給使用者，而我們確實也有富者越富的考量在，因為越富有者可能實際上更年輕了。

魔法藥水			
項目	效果	持續期間	費用
飛行	飛行能力	一天	1,000美元
智慧	超級聰明	一天	5,000美元
記憶	卓越的記憶力	一天	5,000美元
力量	驚人的力量	暫時	3,000美元
青春	年輕10日	永久	3,000美元
肌肉建造	能即刻具備像美國隊長般的體格	永久	10,000美元

Questions 153-157

153. Which of the following has to be taken repeatedly to have a noticeable effect?
(A) Youth
(B) Wisdom
(C) Memory
(D) Power

153. 下列哪項藥水是需要重複性地服用才能有顯著效果?
(A) 青春
(B) 智慧
(C) 記憶
(D) 力量

154. Which of the following falls into the category of transient effects?
(A) Youth
(B) Muscle-building
(C) Fly
(D) Power

154. 下列哪項藥水落入短暫效果的範疇?
(A) 青春
(B) 肌肉建造
(C) 飛行
(D) 力量

155. What can be inferred about the magic potions?
(A) They all have fleeting effects.
(B) They all look equally the same.
(C) They all have side effects.
(D) They all have lasting effects.

155. 關於魔法藥水的部分可以推測出什麼?
(A) 他們都有短暫的效果。
(B) 他們都看起來相同。
(C) 他們都有副作用。
(D) 他們均有持久效果。

156. What can be inferred about the person who has taken "Memory" before the NE test? (A) His score is bound to have a significant boost. (B) His score will be experiencing a slight increase. (C) His score will be experiencing a moderate decrease. **(D) His score will not have anything to do with the Memory**	156. 一位考生於NE考試前服用記憶藥水，可以推測出什麼？ (A) 他的分數必定會有顯著的升高。 (B) 他的分數將會經歷些微的上升。 (C) 他的分數將有著微幅的降低。 **(D) 他的分數與記憶藥水沒有關聯。**
157. What can be inferred about the future trend of the cosmetics? (A) increasingly expensive **(B) gloomy** (C) productive (D) prosperous	157. 可以推測出未來的化妝品趨勢為？ (A) 日益昂貴的 **(B) 悲觀的** (C) 多產的 (D) 繁榮的

解析

· **第153題**，從段落As for the youth portion, you have to use at least 50 bottles to have a **remarkable** change...對應到試題，故答案為**選項A**。
· **第154題**，題目中transient可以對應到temporary，所以是power，故答案為**選項D**。
· **第155題**，從前面段落的敘述中可以得知，都是有副作用的，故答案為**選項C**。
· **第156題**，要選D因為在考試前，藥水效果會被消除掉，故答案為**選項D**。
· **第157題**，因為有青春藥水的發明，所以其實對於化妝品未來的前景要選gloomy，因為大家不需要化妝品了，直接使用青春藥水，故答案為**選項B**。

The game of the goldfish scoop has been known for a few years. By far, ours is the largest in the city. We have 50 pools that can **accommodate** for at least 200 people to play. There are five types of nets that you can choose from or I shall say, choose from wisely. Selecting a right type of nets will definitely influence your chances of catching the goldfish, although most of the time it depends on the skills.

Type	composition	Cost
Type A	Thin paper	US 3 dollars
Type B	Hard paper	US 6 dollars
Type C	Durable paper	US 9 dollars
Type D	Leaf	US 15 dollars
Type E	specially-made 7-colored paper	US 50 dollars

Note:

1. Type E is used to lure the rarest goldfish that houses beneath the castle of the props. Sometimes it won't come out for a few days. The person who catches it will be rewarded with a smartphone.
2. The person who has gathered a hundred goldfish will get a huge teddy bear or a stuffed animal.

撈金魚的遊戲在這幾年一直是廣為人知的。到目前為止,我們的撈金魚遊戲是市區中最大型的。我們有50個泳池可以容納至少兩百人參與玩撈金魚。有五種不同的網,你可以從中挑選或是我應該說要有智慧地挑選。選擇對的類型的網確實會影響到你捕獲金魚的機會,儘管大多數的時候還是要看你的技巧。

類型	組成	費用
Type A	薄紙	3美元
Type B	硬紙	6美元
Type C	耐用紙張	9美元
Type D	葉子	15美元

| Type E | 特製的七彩紙 | 50美元 |

註：

1. Type E用於捕獲最罕見的金魚，其位於道具城堡的下方。有時候牠甚至幾天都不會探頭出來。抓到罕見金魚者會得到一隻智慧型手機當作報償。

2. 已經收集到100隻金魚者會獲得一個巨型的泰迪熊玩偶或是一個填充娃娃。

Questions 158-161

158. What is not stated about the game? **(A) Luck is more important than the skills.** (B) The prize includes a teddy bear. (C) The rarest goldfish is concealed. (D) It contains 50 pools.	158. 關於這項遊戲，沒有提到什麼？ **(A) 幸運比起技巧來說更重要。** (B) 獎項包含泰迪熊。 (C) 罕見金魚是隱匿起來的。 (D) 它包含50個泳池。
159. Which of the following costs the least money? **(A) Type B** (B) Type C (C) Type D (D) Type E	159. 下列哪個類別花費最少錢？ **(A) Type B** (B) Type C (C) Type D (D) Type E
160. Which of the following is used to earn a popular gadget? (A) Type B (B) Type C (C) Type D **(D) Type E**	160. 下列哪個類別用於獲得流行裝置？ (A) Type B (B) Type C (C) Type D **(D) Type E**
161. Which of the following looks splendid? (A) Type B (B) Type C (C) Type D **(D) Type E**	161. 下列哪個類別看起來華麗？ (A) Type B (B) Type C (C) Type D **(D) Type E**

162. The word "**accommodate**" in paragraph1, line 1, is closet in meaning to (A) collaborate **(B) supply** (C) assimilate (D) resume	162. 在第一段第三行的「能容納、能提供......膳宿」，意思最接近 (A) 合作 **(B) 供給、供應、提供** (C) 消化吸收（食物）、吸收（知識等）、理解 (D) 繼續、恢復、重返

解析

- 第**158**題，訊息中未出現luck和skills間的比較，故答案為**選項A**。
- 第**159**題，這題很明顯花費最少的是B，故答案為**選項A**。
- 第**160**題，Type E = will be rewarded with a smartphone，a smartphone = **a popular gadget**，故答案為**選項D**。
- 第**161**題，Type E是Specialized 7-colored paper也等同於**splendid**，故答案為**選項D**。
- 第**162**題，accommodate = **supply**，故答案為**選項B**。

Have you experienced losing a loved one and you cannot let go? If you fit into the category, then you definitely have to come to the Best Remedy Center. **(1)** Scientists and engineers here can create an identical robot for you, and they can even instill the emotion of your loved one into the robot for you. **(2)** From these descriptions, you know the cost cannot be too cheap. It's like **implanting** a soul into the robot. **(3) It mimics the actions and emotions of your loved one.** Just hearing the voice gives me the creep... that's my mother. They have several models for you to choose from. **(4)** Even I myself want to buy a new one. The major difference is that they won't age for a bit, but we humans do. So if you request a 30 year old husband robot, he is going to remain the specific age. You are going to look older than he is and have unwanted wrinkles on your forehead while he laughs at you...

你有經歷過失去摯愛過而且你無法放手嗎?如果你符合這個範疇的話，那麼你確實需要來趙倍斯特修復中心。這裡的科學家和工程師們能替你創造出相似的機器人。從這些描述來看，你知道花費肯定不便宜。這就像是靈魂植入了機器人中一般。它模仿了你摯愛的行為和情緒。僅聽到聲音就讓我感到毛骨悚然了...那是我母親。他們有幾個你可以選的模式。甚至我都想要買一個新的。最主要的差異在於他們不會有絲毫歲月的痕跡在，但是我們卻會隨時間而衰老。所以如果你要求一個30歲的機器人丈夫的話，他會一直維持在特定的年紀。你將會看起來比他老，到時候你額頭上有著不想要的皺紋，而他對著你嘲笑...。

Questions 163-166

163. What is the article mainly about? (A) a novel experience for a reporter (B) how to stay youthful **(C) an advanced technology that brings possibility and hopes** (D) finding the cure for unwanted wrinkles	163. 報導主要是關於什麼? (A) 對於記者來說是個新奇的體驗 (B) 如何維持青春 **(C) 先進科技帶來可能性和希望** (D) 找到討厭的皺紋的治療法門
164. In which of the positions marked **(1)**, **(2)**, **(3)**, and **(4)** does the following sentence best belong? "**It mimics the actions and emotions of your loved one.**" (A) (1) (B) (2) **(C) (3)** (D) (4)	164. 以下這個句子最適合放在文中標記**(1)**, **(2)**, **(3)**, **(4)**的哪個位置? 「它模仿了你摯愛的行為和情緒。」 (A) (1) (B) (2) **(C) (3)** (D) (4)

165. What is Not stated about the Best Remedy Center? (A) The treatment cannot be low-priced. (B) the imitation of actions and emotions of a person (C) the use of a robot to replace a real person **(D) The soul will be removed from the robot.**	165. 關於倍斯特治療中心，沒有提到什麼？ (A) 治療不可能是低價的 (B) 一個人的行為和情緒的模仿 (C) 使用機器人可以取代一個真實的人。 **(D) 靈魂會從機器人中移除。**
166. The word "**implanting**" in the advertisement, line 7, is closet in meaning to **(A) inserting** (B) reducing (C) exterminating (D) extracting	166. 在廣告中第7行的「植入、灌輸」，意思最接近 **(A) 插入** (B) 減少 (C) 根除、滅絕、消滅 (D) 抽出、採掘、提取、提煉

解析

- 第**163**題，最符合的是an advanced technology that brings possibility and hopes，故答案為**選項C**。
- 第**164**題，找到implanting a soul那句，插入句最適合放置於此，**(3)**，故答案為**選項C**。
- 第**165**題，文中未提及the soul will be removed from the robot.，故答案為**選項D**。
- 第**166**題，implanting = **inserting**，故答案為**選項A**。

模擬試題（四）

模擬試題（一）

模擬試題（二）

模擬試題（三）

模擬試題（四）

模擬試題（五）

Best Zoo is seeking an AI specialist who can tackle the problem for customers. What's more, they are adding the interactive features for the customer. **(1) Once you press the button of this so-called "Exchange Life", you are on a journey of becoming an animal**. And it's randomly assigned by the computer. **(2)** What if you are the animal that you don't like? The effect has to last for at least three hours and the cost of playing is US $ 900. **(3)** Still you can see the crowd waiting in line and dying to try it out. Perhaps after the experience, you can really cherish the life of animals more. **(4)** And according to the policy of the company, I have to play at least once and write a report on that. I think I'm getting very nervous about experiencing... candidates do remain inanimate on the machine they are sitting... but it's free... and now I have to "press" the button.

倍斯特動物園正尋找一位能夠替顧客處理問題的AI專家。此外，他們替顧客增添了互動性的特色商品。一旦你按下這個所謂的「生命互換鍵」，你會進行一趟成為動物的旅程，而這是由電腦隨意指定的。如果你成了你不喜歡的動物怎麼辦呢？這個效果會持續至少三個小時，並且此項玩樂的花費是900美元。你仍然可以看到群眾排隊等著，然後躍躍欲試。而根據公司這項政策，我必須要玩至少一次且寫份關於那個的報導。我認為我對於那樣的體驗感到相當緊張…參加者會維持坐姿的姿態無生命的待在機器上…但是這次體驗是免費的…然後現在我必須要按按鈕了。

Questions 167-170

167. What is the article mainly about?
(A) getting the discount for the game
(B) **the new interactive features that bring the prosperity for the zoo**
(C) a revision of the company policy
(D) how to stay animate when playing the game

167. 報導主要是關於什麼？
(A) 獲取遊戲的折扣
(B) **新的互動特色替動物園帶來繁榮**
(C) 公司政策的修改
(D) 當進行遊戲時，如何維持活力

168. In which of the positions marked **(1)**, **(2)**, **(3)**, and **(4)** does the following sentence best belong? "**Once you press the button of this so-called "Exchange Life", you are on a journey of becoming an animal**" **(A) (1)** (B) (2) (C) (3) (D) (4)	168. 以下這個句子最適合放在文中標記**(1)**, **(2)**, **(3)**, **(4)**的哪個位置? 「一旦你按下這個所謂的「生命互換鍵」,你會進行一趟成為動物的旅程。」 **(A) (1)** (B) (2) (C) (3) (D) (4)
169. What is Not stated about Best Zoo? (A) People will show no sign of life on the machine after playing. (B) The new interactive game has attracted lots of crowds. (C) The effect of transforming into an animal lasts longer than 2 hours. **(D) Nervousness can cause several side effects when playing.**	169. 關於倍斯特動物園沒有提到什麼? (A) 在遊戲後,機器上的人沒有顯示生命跡象。 (B) 新的互動遊戲已經吸引了許多群眾。 (C) 轉變成動物的效果持續長於2小時。 **(D) 當進行遊戲時,緊張可能引起幾項副作用。**
170. How much does it cost if the father of the four can only afford two kids to have this interactive experience? (A) US 900 **(B) US 1,800** (C) US 2,700 (D) US 3,600	170. 如果一位有四個孩子的父親僅能負擔得起兩位小孩進行這項互動性體驗,要花費多少錢? (A) US 900 **(B) US 1,800** (C) US 2,700 (D) US 3,600

解析

- **第167題**，主要是談論這些新的體驗帶動人潮，進而增加了動物園的獲利，故答案為**選項B**。
- **第168題**，可以從it's randomly assigned協助判答，所以最可能插入句是在其之前，故答案為**選項A**。
- **第169題**，全文沒有提及所引起的副作用，故答案為**選項D**。
- **第170題**，將費用乘以2，故答案為**選項B**。

I've got to say, if it is your first job, then do it for at least two years. Unfortunately, that's the kind of the rule that was passed down from generation to generation. **(1)** To be stricter, then 3 years. You can hardly say that you have already known your current position, if you haven't been working in that industry for three years. **(2)** And trust me, when you are job hopping, that's the criteria that all interviewers are looking for. **(3)** Three also means a thorough experience in that job and can do the job independently. You will find yourself doing your job a lot more smoothly than someone with less than three years of working experience. **(4) And that also demonstrates stability, and that's very important.** Even if you don't make a job hop, you will be shouldering more job responsibility from the boss or superiors... so try to do your current job for at least two years before making the transition...

Best column

我必須要説。如果這是第一份工作的話，那麼請至少做滿兩年。不幸的是，這是世代間流傳下來的那樣的規則。更嚴格的要求的話，就是三年。你很難表明你已經了解你的現職，如果你沒有在這個產業工作三年的時間。而且相信我，當你要跳槽時，這是所有面試官都在尋求的標準。「三」也意謂著在這份工作上一個完整的經驗，而且能夠在這份工作上獨當一面。你將發現你會比起工作經驗少於三年的人更順利。而這也顯示著穩定性，這是非常重要的。即使你不想要跳槽，你將發現老闆或上司也會讓你承擔著更多的工作責任...所以試著在你的現任工作上做至少兩年在做跑到轉換...

倍斯特專欄

Questions 171-172	
171. What is Not stated about the "Job Column"? (A) The rigorous standard for a job is to work for three years. **(B) Interviewers value someone with lots of job hop experiences.** (C) One will be given more responsibility after years of experience at the job. (D) It takes three years to accumulate a complete job experience.	171. 關於「求職專欄」的敘述，沒有提到什麼？ (A) 工作的嚴格標準是要工作三年。 **(B) 面試官重視有許多跳槽經驗的工作者。** (C) 在該份工作上有幾年經驗後，將會被賦予更多責任。 (D) 一份完整的工作經驗要花三年的時間累積。
172. In which of the positions marked **(1)**, **(2)**, **(3)**, and **(4)** does the following sentence best belong? "**And that also demonstrates stability, and that's very important.**" (A) (1) (B) (2) (C) (3) **(D) (4)**	172. 以下這個句子最適合放在文中標記**(1)**, **(2)**, **(3)**, **(4)**的哪個位置？ 「而且這也顯示著穩定性，而這是非常重要的。」 (A) (1) (B) (2) (C) (3) **(D) (4)**

解析

· **第171題**，面試官重視的是具年資且具穩定性的工作者，故答案為**選項B**。
· **第172題**，可以由三年工作經驗協助判答，這點跟stability有關連，故答案為**選項D**。

Be as early as possible, preferably during four years of your undergraduate study. Study intensively, and at the same time try to participate as many activities as possible. **(1)** You might find something that you don't think you love, but deep down you do. **(2)** In addition, don't pretend to be someone that you are not. Don't go after something that is against your inner voice. **(3) The popular trend or the golden internship will ultimately be a waste of time, if that's not something you truly want.** I understand it's a time that you rely heavily on how your classmates think of you, but it's your life that we are talking about. **(4)** It might be so cool and get the most attention, but it's kind of the **regrettable** decision for many college students. So seize the moment and explore your broadest self...

Best Column

盡可能越早越好，偏好在你大學四年研讀的期間。密集地研讀，而且與之同時盡可能試圖參加越多活動越好。你可能發現一些你不認為你愛的，但在你心底深處你其實喜愛的事情。此外，別假裝成不符合你本身特質。別追求一些與你內心聲音相違抗的事情。流行的趨勢和黃金的實習機會最終都只會是浪費時間，如果那些事情不是你真心想要的。我了解到這是個你高度仰賴你的同學們如何評價你的時期，但是我們在談論的是你的人生啊?這可能會是相當酷的事情且得到最多的關注，但是這對於許多大學生來說是令人感到遺憾的決定。所以抓緊時機然後探索最廣闊的自我...。

倍斯特專欄

Questions 173-175	
173. What is Not stated about the "Job Column"? **(A) College students always make the right decision.** (B) College students care about how their fellows perceive of them. (C) Pursue things that are consistent with your inner voice. (D) College students should participate in multiple activities.	173. 關於求職專欄的部分，沒有提及什麼？ **(A) 大學生總是做出對的決定。** (B) 大學學生在乎他們的同袍怎麼評價他們。 (C) 追求與你內在聲音一致的事物。 (D) 大學生們應該要參加多樣的活動。
174. The word "**regrettable**" in the letter, line 10, is closet in meaning to (A) notable (B) advisable (C) categorical **(D) remorseful**	174. 在信件中第10行的「使人悔恨的、令人遺憾的」，意思最接近 (A) 值得注意的、顯著的 (B) 可取的、適當的、明智的 (C) 絕對的、明白的 **(D) 極為後悔的**
175. In which of the positions marked **(1)**, **(2)**, **(3)**, and **(4)** does the following sentence best belong? "**The popular trend or the golden internship will ultimately be a waste of time, if that's not something you truly want.**" (A) (1) (B) (2) **(C) (3)** (D) (4)	175. 以下這個句子最適合放在文中標記**(1)**, **(2)**, **(3)**, **(4)**的哪個位置？ 　「流行的趨勢和黃金的實習機會最終都只會是浪費時間，如果那些事情不是你真心想要的。」 (A) (1) (B) (2) **(C) (3)** (D) (4)

解析

- **第173題**，用always等過於絕對，且文中沒有提到此點，故答案為**選項A**。
- **第174題**，regrettable其實就是remorseful的意思，故答案為**選項D**。
- **第175題**，可以由Don't go after something that is against your inner voice.協助判答，最有可能是插入在其之後，故答案為**選項C**。

Dear Manager at the headquarter,

This morning I went to the basement, a place where we usually stock our chocolate packages for international shipment, but I couldn't find one. Should I call the police? Or could it be mistaken? But I saw it with my own eyes. Or should I believe that "to see is not to believe."? I think I will be waiting for your reply to determine how to respond to this particular incident. I guess I will just prepare some documents for later use and wait in my cubicle.

Cindy Lin

親愛的總部經理

今天早晨我到了地下室，我們通常儲備用於國際運輸的巧克力包裹的地下室，但是我卻找不到任何包裹。我應該報警嗎?還是可能是我搞錯了呢?但是這是我親眼目睹的。還是我該相信「不該信你所親眼見到的事情」。我想我會等你的回覆後以決定要如何回應這起特別的事件。我想我會準備一些文件以供稍後使用且在辦公桌候著。

辛蒂·林

Dear Manager at the headquarter,

Sorry, my bad... I went to the wrong basement... they all look equally the same... I'm so sorry. **(1)** I guess in my twenties my amnesia already gets to me, and that's probably not the reason that you hired me. **(2)** The company has a secret code for hiring only twentysomethings. **(3)** And I do have other things I do need to report to you, and it's really serious. All packages were opened. A thousand of them. I guess we do have unwanted companies. The raccoons. **(4) I don't even know how to get rid of them, and they are still eating.** However, I do take a few shots of those raccoons to test whether my latest smartphone is worth the money. It's the camera with 1.08 M pixels. I don't think it's a loss... although that's just from my stupid viewpoint... but I do think we can record videos and sell them to a few major news centers to compensate for our loss. They are going to pay us according to the number of viewers. And several photos can be used as the ad campaign pics "Look, they are just being naughty" at the company building. It's not entirely a loss... and I am sure some of the smart guys in the office can think of something brilliant than this...

Cindy Lin

親愛的總部經理

抱歉,是我的錯...我去錯間地下室了...地下室看起來都一模一樣...我感到很抱歉。我想在我20幾歲期間,失憶症就已經找上門了,而那不太可能是當初你雇用我的原因。這間公司的秘密規則是僅雇用20幾歲的人。然後我還有其他事情需要向您稟報,這是相當嚴重的事情。所有的包裹都被打開了。一千個包裹。我想我們有些不速之客。浣熊。我甚至不知道要如何趕走牠們,牠們仍在吃東西。然而,我拍了幾張浣熊的照片檢視我最新的相機是否值那個價錢。是個1.08億畫素的相機。我不認為這是個損失...儘管這僅是從我的拙見...但是我認為我們可以錄製視頻,將視頻售給幾間主要的新聞中心以補償我們的損失。他們會根據瀏覽人數來支付費用。而且幾張照片可以用於廣告活動的宣傳照「瞧,他們只是頑皮了些」在我們的公司建築物上頭。這起事件不全然是個損失...我相信公司有些聰明的員工對這起事件可以想出比這個更棒的點子...

辛蒂·林

Questions 176-180

176. What would Cindy be doing after the incident? **(A) compose files** (B) reexamine the chocolate packages (C) find out the felon (D) flee the country	176. 在事件發生後，辛蒂在做什麼？ **(A) 整理檔案** (B) 重新檢查巧克力包裹 (C) 找尋罪犯 (D) 逃離國家
177. In which of the positions marked **(1)**, **(2)**, **(3)**, and **(4)** does the following sentence best belong? **"I don't even know how to get rid of them, and they are still eating."** (A) (1) (B) (2) (C) (3) **(D) (4)**	177. 以下這個句子最適合放在文中標記**(1)**, **(2)**, **(3)**, **(4)**的哪個位置？ 「我甚至不知道要如何趕走牠們，而牠們仍在吃東西。」 (A) (1) (B) (2) (C) (3) **(D) (4)**
178. What is Not stated in the second letter? **(A) Cindy has been diagnosed with amnesia.** (B) The company has a preference for younger workers. (C) Her smartphone has incredible pixels. (D) All packages were opened.	178. 關於第二封信沒有提到什麼？ **(A) 辛蒂被診斷出有失憶症。** (B) 公司對於年輕的工作者有偏好。 (C) 她的智慧型手機有驚人的像素。 (D) 所有的包裹都被打開了。

179. What can be the possible solution for the package? (A) invite some unwanted companies **(B) use the video to their advantage** (C) punish those miscreants (D) purchase a phone with 1.08 pixels	179. 關於包裹的可能解決之道為? (A) 邀請一些不速的公司 **(B) 把視頻用於對他們有利的部分** (C) 懲罰那些罪犯 (D) 購買一隻1.08億畫素的手機
180. Who can possibly buy the recorded video? (A) A new startup (B) International Shipping company **(C) News Center** (D) Advertising company	180. 誰可能購買錄製的視頻? (A) 一間新創公司 (B) 國際運輸公司 **(C) 新聞中心** (D) 廣告公司

- 第**176**題，Cindy接下來會整理文件等等，故答案為**選項A**。
- 第**177**題，插入句前是the raccoons和後面的插入句訊息they are still eating等，可以推斷出最合適的插入地方是**(4)**，故答案為**選項D**。
- 第**178**題，文中只是比喻，但是沒有提到他確診的部分，故答案為**選項A**。
- 第**179**題，其實女職員的靈活表現，就是選項B的體現，故答案為**選項B**。
- 第**180**題，選項中有出現一些干擾訊息，但明確提到sell them to a few major news centers，故答案為**選項C**。

模擬試題（四）

模擬試題（一）

模擬試題（二）

模擬試題（三）

模擬試題（四）

模擬試題（五）

Dear Boss

Recently, we have begun to work on the AI experience with game lovers. To make it more authentic, we have added several elements into it, and I'm afraid that now is still not the time to tell you guys. And we do fear that people cannot **withdraw** themselves from the artificial settings. That's our sole consideration. One of our engineers got infatuated with one of the new designs because he recently lost a loved one. It would be too painful to cut him off from using the AI experience. In reality, without these designs, we do have other ways to counter the pain of losing our loved one. We do some counseling with doctors and eventually move on with our life. So the creation of our AI products does have several drawbacks that need to improve though...

Engineer Director

親愛的老闆

最近，我們已經開始著手遊戲愛好者的AI體驗。為了讓此體驗更真實，我們已新增幾項元素在其中，而恐怕現在仍不是告訴你們的時機。而我確實恐懼人們無法從人工環境中將自己抽離出來。那也是我們唯一的考量。我們其中的一位工程師也成癮在我們的其中一項設計中，因為他最近失去了摯愛。要他切斷與AI的體驗是很不忍的。在現實生活中，沒有這些設計的話，我們確實有其他的方式以應對，當我們的摯愛死亡後，面臨失去的問題。我們確實需要與醫生進行諮商，並且最終在生活中能繼續前進。所以我們AI產品的創造確實仍有幾項缺點是需要改進的說...

工程師總負責

Dear Jason,

It's ok. Everything has its advantage and disadvantage. I would like to see those products next Monday. **(1)** I heard from a team member of yours that the game experience is incredible. **(2)** You can even feel it. That means you don't necessarily have to be rich or handsome to date your ideal lover. **(3) The design can compensate that, as long as you have the product.** Is it possible that we create a system that can make people never feel bored... you know how things go... especially a relationship... after you know the novelty wears off... I just cannot wait to try that myself...**(4)** I will invite several CEOs to visit the room. Be prepared. That's all.

Neal

親愛的傑森

沒關係。每件事情都有其優缺點在。我想要於下週一看下那些產品。我從一位你們的團隊成員那裡聽說這個遊戲體驗是驚人的。你甚至可以深切感受到。那也意謂著，你不需要有錢或英俊以跟你的理想情人約會。此項設計可以補足這點，只要你擁有這項產品。我們有可能創造一個系統讓人們不要感到無聊嗎?...你知道的，事情的走向是如何的...特別是戀情...在新奇感消失後...我已經等不及要親自嘗試了...我會邀請幾位執行長去參觀那間房。做好準備。就這樣囉。

尼爾

Questions 181-185

| 181. The word "**withdraw**" in paragraph1, line 4, is closet in meaning to
(A) repair
(B) confide
(C) extract
(D) embrace | 181. 在第一段第4行的「取回、提取」，意思最接近
(A) 維修
(B) 透露、吐露
(C) 抽出、採掘、提取
(D) 擁抱 |

182. What is Not stated about the first letter?
(A) The AI software still has some glitches.
(B) The addiction of the company's employee for the software.
(C) The painful cut for the engineer
(D) The company has made the experience more real.

182. 關於第一封信沒有提到什麼？
(A) AI軟體仍有些小毛病在
(B) 公司員工對於這個軟體的成癮
(C) 慘痛地裁掉工程師
(D) 公司已經讓這個體驗更為真實。

183. What can be the new expectation by the CEO?
(A) A design that gets rid of boredom
(B) A design that removes the novelty
(C) A design that earns more profits
(D) A design that makes people good-looking

183. 什麼會是執行長的新期望？
(A) 免除無聊的設計
(B) 移除新奇感的設計
(C) 賺取更多利潤的設計
(D) 讓人們看起來姣好的設計

184. In which of the positions marked **(1)**, **(2)**, **(3)**, and **(4)** does the following sentence best belong?
"**The design can compensate that, as long as you have the product.**"
(A) (1)
(B) (2)
(C) (3)
(D) (4)

184. 以下這個句子最適合放在文中標記**(1)**, **(2)**, **(3)**, **(4)**的哪個位置？
「此項設計可以補足這點，只要你擁有這項產品。」
(A) (1)
(B) (2)
(C) (3)
(D) (4)

185. What will happen next Monday? (A) The CEO is going to ship the product himself. **(B) The CEO is going to pay a visit.** (C) The CEO is going to dress handsomely. (D) The CEO wants to see something novel.	185. 下週一會發生什麼事情？ (A) 執行長會自行運送產品。 **(B) 執行長會拜訪。** (C) 執行長會盛裝打扮。 (D) 執行長像要看些新奇的東西。

 解析

- 第**181**題，withdraw = **extract**，故答案為**選項C**。
- 第**182**題，原文中有提到It's too painful to cut him off from using...跟 painful cut無關，故答案為**選項C**。
- 第**183**題，we create a system that can make people never feel bored 對應到選項A的敘述，故答案為**選項A**。
- 第**184**題，從That means you don't necessarily have to be rich or handsome to date your ideal lover.到下面的can compensate that可以 推斷出最適合的插入地方是 **(3)**，故答案為**選項C**。
- 第**185**題，這題很明顯出現在段落訊息中，執行長的拜訪，故答案為**選項 B**。

Day 30

I have changed amazingly from a chubby person to an almost fit guy. The feeling is so great. And I have teamed up with several guys here. We have specific goals to work as a team to achieve the following tasks. It's a pretty good start. I have pretty good faith in myself and my teammate. By the way, we bought a jeep from the company... US 50,000 dollars... so that we can do the task faster... and hopefully gather enough scores before the deadline.

模擬試題（四）

模擬試題（一）

模擬試題（二）

模擬試題（三）

模擬試題（四）

模擬試題（五）

第30天

我已經由一位體態圓滾滾的男子變成幾乎是精實態了。這種的感覺很棒。還有我已經與這裡的幾位同袍合作。我們集結成一個團隊，有著特定的目標，來達成接下來的任務。這是個相當好的開端。我對於我自己和我的隊員有相當大的信念。附帶一提的是，我們跟公司買了一台吉普車...5萬美元...這樣一來，我們就能更快完成任務了...而且希望能夠在截止日期之前集到足夠的分數。

Day 31

We were all well-prepared and ready for the trip. We aimed to get plenty of rare fruits today. **(1)** Unfortunately, we **circled** the same area for the first few hours and couldn't seem to find one. Finally, we arrived at the valley and saw the cliff. We made the wood ladder trying hard to get the rare fruit we saw... **(2)** It is really rare. However, by the time we had climbed to the certain altitude, trying to grab the fruit... an eagle flew by... it was not like his nest was close by... Due to the disturbance of the eagle... it was highly unlikely that we got the fruit successfully... **(3)** I eventually yelled no... no... please... my teammate already grabbed the fruit from the branch.... **(4) Then all of a sudden it dropped to the ground**. Our hope just shattered and I turned my anger into shooting the eagle...

第31日

我們都已經充分準備好了，並且準備要開啟旅程了。我們今天的目標是罕見水果。不幸的是，我們在起初的幾個小時繞了一陣子，且似乎無法找到水果的所在處。最後，我們抵達山谷且看到了峭壁。我們製作了木製的階梯，試圖要摘取我們視野所及的罕見水果...這真的相當罕見。然而，到我們爬至特定高度，試圖摘取水果時，一隻老鷹飛過...根本不是地巢穴在附近...在老鷹的干擾之下...有很大的可能是，我們無法獲取水果...我最後大喊著...不...不...請別這樣...我的隊友從樹枝上摘到了水果...然後突然之間，水果掉到地面上。我們的希望都瞬間破碎，然後我將我的怒氣轉至射獵老鷹...。

Day 36

For the next few days, we kept searching for the rare fruit and things came to light. We eventually got five rare fruit, but like I said earlier, we had to spilt the credit, so we **respectively** got 200 scores... still way short of the amount needed for graduation... which is 2,000 in total... back to the training center... we heard that other teams went for other tasks, such as getting the golden feather and so on. I guess we have to exchange the valuable information to **maximize** the scores in the shortest time. And they still couldn't find the peacock with golden feathers... if so... can we dye the feathers of the peacock instead?

第36天

在接下來的幾天，我們持續找尋罕見水果，而事情露出了曙光。我們最終摘到了五個罕見水果，但是就像是我先前所述，我們要均分分數，所以我們分別得到200分...對於離我們的畢業分數...也就是總計2000分的分數...仍短少超多分...回到訓練中心...我們聽到其他的隊伍去執行其他的任務，例如取得金色羽毛等等的。我想我們必須要互換資訊以在最短的時間內將分數最大化。還有，我們仍舊找不到有金色羽毛的孔雀...如果是這樣的話...取而代之的是，我們可以替孔雀染色嘛？

Questions 186-190

186. In which of the positions marked **(1)**, **(2)**, **(3)**, and **(4)** does the following sentence best belong? "**Then all of a sudden it dropped to the ground**" (A) (1) (B) (2) (C) (3) **(D) (4)**	186. 以下這個句子最適合放在文中標記**(1)**, **(2)**, **(3)**, **(4)**的哪個位置？ 「然後突然之間，水果掉到地面上。」 (A) (1) (B) (2) (C) (3) **(D) (4)**

187. What is Not indicated about the rare fruit? (A) The location of the rare fruit was hard to find. (B) The total score for the gathered rare fruits is 1,000. **(C) The rare fruit dropped to the ground, but unexpectedly remained intact.** (D) The nuisance of the eagle made it difficult to get.	187. 關於罕見水果，沒有提及什麼？ (A) 罕見水果的地點很難找到。 (B) 獲取罕見水果的總分數是1000分。 **(C) 罕見水果掉至地面，但出乎意料之外地保持完好無缺。** (D) 討人厭的老鷹讓其很難取得
188. The word "**circled**" in paragraph2, line 2, is closet in meaning to (A) stayed **(B) encircled** (C) regulated (D) returned	188. 在第2段第2行的「盤旋、旋轉、環行」，意思最接近 (A) 維持 **(B) 環繞、包圍、繞行** (C) 管制 (D) 回、返回
189. The word "**respectively**" in paragraph3, line 3, is closet in meaning to (A) artificially (B) respectfully (C) automatically **(D) individually**	189. 在第3段第三行的「分別地、各自地」，意思最接近 (A) 人工地、人為地、不自然地 (B) 恭敬地 (C) 自動地、無意識地、不自覺地 **(D) 單獨地、逐個地、分別地**
190. The word "**maximize**" in paragraph3, line 6, is closet in meaning to (A) duplicate (B) execute **(C) optimize** (D) document	190. 在第3段第3行的「使增加至最大限度、對……極為重視」，意思最接近 (A) 複製 (B) 執行 **(C) 最有效地進行、使完美、最佳化** (D) 紀錄

解析

- 第186題，從dropped to the ground和後面的希望破碎都可以推斷出最合適的插入地方是 **(4)**，故答案為**選項D**。
- 第187題，罕見水果落地後並未保持完整無缺，故答案為**選項C**。
- 第188題，circled = **encircled**，故答案為**選項B**。
- 第189題，respectively = **individually**，故答案為**選項D**。
- 第190題，maximize = **optimize**，故答案為**選項C**。

Day 40

We were instructed to do the basic training for a month before continuing on our challenge. It was mainly due to the injury of one of our fellow members the other day. Luckily, they have extended the time frame from getting the score in two months to three months. We have more time and more skills to complete assignments. Unfortunately, things are back to usual. After running and the boxing lesson, some guys would call the cafeteria car and order some food. For the first time, I kind of pampered myself by ordering the first pearl milk tea. It was great. The sugar kept me **heightened** even during the water gathering assignment in the afternoon.

第40天

我們被指示繼續我們的任務挑戰之前要再接受一個月的基礎訓練。主要是由於我們其中一位成員在前幾天受傷了。幸運的是，他們將在兩個月內要達到分數延長至三個月的時間點。我們有更多的時間和具備更多技巧去執行那些任務。不幸的是，事情回到往常般。在跑步和拳擊課程後，有些同袍會叫自助餐車且點些食物。這是第一次我有點寵自己而點了第一杯珍珠奶茶。感覺很棒。糖分讓我興奮度增高，甚至持續到在下午執行取水任務時。

模擬試題（四）

模擬試題（一）
模擬試題（二）
模擬試題（三）
模擬試題（四）
模擬試題（五）

Day 50

I have become almost athletically built... and can be mistakenly thought of as a gym coach or something. I'm more than ready to finish the assignment and get all the scores I desperately need. I heard from the coach that more assignments will be announced tomorrow... just can't wait to know. One of the teams even wanted to hire the coach to do the task with them so that this can give them a leg up. I was kind of surprised that even the coach didn't have the map. The map is going to cost you extra, remember? Everything is all about money... that's ludicrous.

第50天

我已經變得近乎是體格健碩了...而且可能會被誤成是健身教練之類的了。我比起以往準備的更為充足了，更能完成任務和達到我迫切需要的分數。我從教練那裡聽說明日會宣布更多的任務...等不及要看所宣布的任務了。其中一位團員甚至想要雇用教練一起去從事任務挑戰，所以這樣就有人可以助他們一臂之力。我對於甚至是教練都沒有地圖的這件事情感到震驚。記得嘛，地圖是要額外花你一筆錢的。每件事都跟錢有關...這太荒謬了。

Announcement/more to be announced		
Item	Note	Score
Golden eggs of a peacock	Per egg, has something related to history	100
Golden eggs of an ostrich	Per egg, has something related to geography	50
Silver feather of the eagle	Extremely rare, electrified stones	100
Gather a 7-colored stone	Can get yourself wet, monkeys	100
Consume raw snails for 50	Can generate **infestation**	10
Take down a giant spider	Fortune is associated	500
Get rare seaweed	A box, a **submerged** castle	50

Take down a giant snake	with wooden swords, diamonds	600

公告/更多待公告		
項目	筆記	分數
孔雀的金蛋	每個蛋，與歷史相關聯	100
鴕鳥的金蛋	每個蛋，與地理相關聯	50
老鷹的銀翼	極為罕見，電力石	100
收集七彩石頭	會讓你全身都溼透，猴群	100
攝食50隻生蝸牛	會產生寄生蟲感染	10
擊倒巨型蜘蛛	與財富相關聯	500
取得罕見水藻	一盒，水下城堡	50
擊倒巨蛇	須以木劍擊倒，鑽石	600

Questions 191-195

191. The word "**heightened**" in paragraph1, line 8, is closet in meaning to (A) composed (B) reduced (C) **enhanced** (D) complicated	191. 在第一段第8行的「增高的」，意思最接近 (A) 鎮靜的、沉著的 (B) 減少的 (C) **增加的** (D) 複雜的

192. What is mentioned as the recent change for the guy? (A) He was unfortunately injured when performing a difficult task. (B) He quit ordering drinks from the restaurant car to be healthy. (C) He bought the map and tried to get acquainted with it. **(D) He is physically ready to do the assignment.**	192. 關於男子近期的改變提到了什麼？ (A) 他在執行困難的任務時，不幸地受到傷害。 (B) 他戒除了餐車上的飲料以維持健康。 (C) 他購買了地圖且嘗試熟悉它。 **(D) 他體態上已經準備好要執行這項任務了。**
193. The word "**infestation**" in the announcement, is closet in meaning to (A) production **(B) invasion** (C) visibility (D) allocation	193. 在公告中的「侵擾、騷擾、（動、植物的）寄生蟲侵擾」，意思最接近 (A) 生產、製作 **(B) 入侵、侵略** (C) 能見度、明顯性 (D) 分派、分配
194. What can be inferred from the announcement? (A) The silver feather of the eagle is easy to find. **(B) Wealth may be around the corner in a particular new task.** (C) Four items have the same score. (D) Nine new items are being added into the list.	194. 關於公告，推測出什麼？ (A) 老鷹的銀色羽毛很容易尋獲。 **(B) 在特定的新任務中，財富可能近在咫尺** (C) 四個項目有著相同的分數 (D) 九個新項目新增到清單中

195. The word "**submerged**" in the announcement, is closet in meaning to (A) serendipitous (B) subsequent **(C) underwater** (D) underdeveloped	195. 在公告中的「在水中的、淹沒的」，意思最接近 (A) 意外發現的、僥倖得到的 (B) 其後的、隨後的 **(C) 水中的、水面下的** (D) 發展不完全的、發育不良的

解析

· 第191題，heightened = **enhanced**，故答案為**選項C**。
· 第192題，這題根據段落敘述很明顯是選項D，故答案為**選項D**。
· 第193題，infestation = **invasion**，故答案為**選項B**。
· 第194題，這題有些難，不過可以根據表格訊息來評判這四項敘述，選項的敘述Wealth may be around the corner in a particular new task.等同於表格中的**fortune is associated**，故答案為**選項B**。
· 第195題，submerged = **underwater**，故答案為**選項C**。

Day 70

We all have received the intensive training for an additional month and all cannot wait to start our journey. **(1)** Something happened today. Mysteriously, we got an urn near the dorm. All hundreds of us gathered here and opened it. **(2) It had a short letter, stating that more is to be revealed in the waterfall.** Then, we all wondered where this place is, and were dying to find this place. **(3)** Like I said our team bought a jeep, so after getting prepared, we all sat on the car ready to find the waterfall. **(4)** After driving for two hours, we found a small trail and we pulled over... headed in there. The view was beyond anything... and there were monkeys making noises. At last, we discovered a waterfall... what is hidden beneath?

第70天

我們都已經接受了為期一個月的額外嚴密訓練，也都迫不及待地要展開我們的旅程了。今天發生了一些事情。我們在靠近宿舍處神秘地獲取了一個甕。我們一百位團員聚集於此並將其打開。裡頭有封短信陳述著，在瀑布那裡有更多的事情會揭露。然後，我們都在想這個地方在哪裡呢？且迫切要去找尋這個地方。就像我先前所述，我們購買了一部吉普車，所以在備妥後，我們都坐上車且準備要找尋瀑布。在行駛兩個小時後，我們發現了一個小徑，然後我們停靠在旁...朝裡頭前進。景色無與倫比...還有這裡有猴群在製造噪音。最後，我們發現了瀑布...到底有什麼藏匿其中呢？

Day 71

The water pressure was quite powerful. The torrents were strong, so we managed to tie several ropes around the trees... in case something happened. While we were trying to get to the middle of water... we couldn't withstand the torrents. Two of us, while still grabbing the rope, almost got washed away. We were in the abysmal water and we didn't have any life vests on. After a while, I kind of vaguely saw the seven colored stones... They were down at the bottom of the waterfall. When we were all safely back to the ground, I told other teammates about the stones. We tried to think of a way to get them. It's a good sign, even though we have to split the credit and we didn't know how many were down there. And why did the company know these stones? Who sent the urn to the dorm?

第71日

這裡的水壓相當的強勁。激流很猛烈，所以我們設法要使用幾條繩子綁在樹上...以防有什麼事情發生。當我們試圖要走到水中央時...我們無法承受激流衝擊。我們其中的兩個成員，儘管攬住了繩子，幾乎要被水沖走了。我們身處深不見底的水裡，而我們卻沒有身穿任何的救生背心。在過了一會兒後，我有點模糊地看見了七彩石頭...就在瀑布的底部。當我們都回到陸地上時，我告訴其他成員這件事情。我們試圖要想出取得那些石頭的辦法。這是個好的徵兆，儘管我們必須要平分這些分數，還有我們並不知道到底底部有多少石頭？而為什麼公司知道有這些七彩石頭呢？又是誰將甕送來宿舍的呢？

Day 72

We set a tent here and dried all our clothes. While making the fried fish for dinner, we figured out a way to get the stones. We swam down there to get them. Of course, we had to hold our breath long enough to get them. That required a piece of equipment. Luckily, one of our teammates was a great swimmer. He made a few attempts and couldn't get one. While we were about to give up, the monkey pointed to something in the place where we camped. It said "press". Out of curiosity, I pressed the button. Then the huge wall gradually rose up and the water became less violent. It was actually the good time for us to gather all of the stones. We eventually got 10 stones, which boosted our morale.

第72天

我們搭建了一個帳篷且將我們的衣服都烘乾。當我們在烤魚當晚餐時,我們得知了獲取石頭的方式。我們游到底部然後拿取石頭。當然,我們必須要屏住呼吸,憋氣長到足以拿到那些石頭。那需要一件設備。幸運的是,我們其中一位成員是個游泳健將。他做了幾次嘗試但卻是徒勞無功。當我們正打算放棄時,有隻猴子指向我們露營處的一個地方。上頭寫著「按」。出於好奇心,我按下按鍵。然後,巨大的牆逐漸地上升,而水流變得較不猛烈了。這確實是我們收集所有石頭的良好時機。我們最終拿到了10枚石頭,這增添了我們的士氣。

Questions 196-200

196. In which of the positions marked **(1)**, **(2)**, **(3)**, and **(4)** does the following sentence best belong?
"It had a short letter stating that more is to be revealed in the waterfall."
(A) (1)
(B) (2)
(C) (3)
(D) (4)

196. 以下這個句子最適合放在文中標記**(1)**, **(2)**, **(3)**, **(4)**的哪個位置?
「裡頭有封短信陳述著,在瀑布那裡有更多的事情會揭露。」
(A) (1)
(B) (2)
(C) (3)
(D) (4)

197. What is Not mentioned about the water? (A) Its pressure was really strong. **(B) It couldn't stop the team because they had a good swimmer.** (C) It was still too powerful even with the help of the rope. (D) It became less violent due to the apparatus.	197. 關於水，沒有提到什麼？ (A) 它的壓力相當強勁。 **(B) 它無法阻擋團隊，因為他們有位游泳健將。** (C) 即使有著繩索的幫助，它仍舊強大。 (D) 由於儀器的關係，它變得較不猛烈。
198. What is Not True about the 7 colored stone? **(A) They had to wait until the tide dwindled at dawn.** (B) The team will get the credit by getting it. (C) It was situated in the bottom of the waterfall. (D) They ultimately got these stones in a less turbulent water condition.	198. 關於七彩石的敘述，何者為非？ **(A) 他們要等到黃昏時潮汐降低。** (B) 團隊會因獲取石頭而得到分數。 (C) 七彩石位於瀑布的底部。 (D) 在較不猛烈的水流情況下，他們最終獲得這些石頭。
199. What can be inferred about the monkey? (A) It placed the urn in front of the dorm. (B) It swam down to assist the team. **(C) It gave the hint to the team.** (D) It turned the torrent into less tempestuous one.	199. 關於猴子可以推測出什麼？ (A) 牠將甕放置到宿舍前方。 (B) 牠游到瀑布底以協助團隊。 **(C) 牠給予團隊暗示。** (D) 牠讓激流變得較不狂暴。

200. What is not used during the journey of collecting the 7 colored stone? (A) a jeep (B) an instrument **(C) life vests** (D) a rope	200. 在收集7彩石的期間，沒有用到什麼？ (A) 一部吉普車 (B) 一台儀器 **(C) 救生衣** (D) 一條繩子

解析

- 第196題，根據上、下文最適合的插入點在 **(2)**，故答案為**選項B**。
- 第197題，文中有提到Luckily, one of our teammates was a great swimmer. He made a few attempts and couldn't get one.，所以在水流下連游泳健將也無法抵禦，故答案為**選項B**。
- 第198題，文章中沒有出現They had to wait until the tide dwindled at dawn.，故答案為**選項A**。
- 第199題，猴子有給他們暗示，他們才能取得七彩石，故答案為**選項C**。
- 第200題，這題要注意提過的物件，文中有明確提到他們沒有穿救生背心，故答案為**選項C**。

Note

- 【Part 5】要注意forgery, automatically, unwillingly, loopholes等的單字題。文法題的部分要注意has been experimenting, once和被動語態的出題。
- 【Part 6】要注意groom, thwarted, paralyzed, detained, tampered等高階動詞的考點，這些對大部分考生來說較難。
- 【Part 7】同樣要注意插入句子題，可能會耗掉考生較多的答題時間。另外也要多注意表格題的問法。思考較靈活的考生比較容易答這類題目。

模擬試題（五）

In this section, you must demonstrate your ability to read and comprehend English. You will be given a variety of texts and asked to answer questions about these texts. This section is divided into three parts and will take 75 minutes to complete.

Do not mark the answers in your test book. Use the answer sheet that is separately.

PART 5

Directions: In each question, you will be asked to review a statement that is missing a word or phrase. Four answer choices will be provided for each statement. Select the best answer and mark the corresponding letter (A), (B), (C), or (D) on the answer sheet.

101. To ------- the facility, the principal in Best Elite School discreetly accepted the bribe from those parents last fall without feeling any guilt.

    (A) overestimate

    (B) upgrade

    (C) downgrade

    (D) downplay

102. Unable to get a decent grade on the standardized test, the student threatened the examiner of test reports to make a ------- yesterday.

    (A) note

    (B) signature

    (C) forgery

(D) transaction

103. Best Software has made an unprecedented growth by inventing the robot that can fix customer issues -------.
(A) automatically
(B) paradoxically
(C) surreptitiously
(D) artificially

104. After the performance at the luxurious hotel, Best Cinema made the decision of not ------- the contract of multiple actors in the press conference.
(A) proposing
(B) renewing
(C) retaining
(D) reproducing

105. The company's morale has suffered due to a series of lawsuits by the rival, and employees have to attend the court ------- to be the witnesses.
(A) effectively
(B) individually
(C) voluntarily
(D) unwillingly

106. ------- by the scandal of the actor (just signed a month ago)

the warehouse of Best Music is now full of unsold music albums.

(A) Accompanied

(B) Considered

(C) Distinguished

(D) Exacerbated

107. Since Cindy lost her 401k and could not get the ------- pay from her employer, she moved back home to live with her parents for the time being.

(A) severance

(B) profit

(C) bonus

(D) benefit

108. ------- costs resulting from improper use of the electronic equipment are tremendous, and sometimes they can be close to buying a new one.

(A) Permission

(B) Delegation

(C) Procedure

(D) Repair

109. According to the new property tax, multiple items are now considered ------- expenses, a phenomenon that taxpayers are willing to see.

(A) important
(B) deductible
(C) expensive
(D) luxurious

110. With various lucrative benefits and monthly fees, credit cards of Best Bank are widely ------- among students and businessmen.
(A) extensive
(B) acceptable
(C) expensive
(D) unfavorable

111. Best Cellphone is now considering to launch several products that are ------- to college students and the lower middle class.
(A) accessible
(B) competitive
(C) eligible
(D) unavailable

112. The unexpected ------- of the CFO shocked the boss and his parrot last Friday, and it was turned down in an open letter.
(A) investigation
(B) confirmation
(C) resignation
(D) registration

113. Moving the money under the watch of federal agents was not easy, so Mark took a private jet to a remote island to discuss further details with other government -------.
(A) underperformers
(B) superintendents
(C) correspondents
(D) officials

114. Before filing the divorce paper, Cindy has already hired an attorney to find the potential ------- and hide the assets so that her husband will get less than he deserves.
(A) risks
(B) problems
(C) documents
(D) loopholes

115. For the past 10 years, Best Technology ------- a product whose innovation transcends current inventions.
(A) has experimented
(B) has been experimented
(C) has been experimenting
(D) had experimented

116. Best Technology invented a powerful vaccine which ------- doctors to instantly prevent patients' internal organs from getting attacked by the virus.

(A) enables

(B) enabled

(C) is enabled

(D) enabling

117. The ingredient of the smartphone ------- by a local resident who thought it could withstand the heat a little longer than other elements.

(A) unearths

(B) unearthed

(C) unearthing

(D) was unearthed

118. The unprecedented business model was invented when the rookie accidentally discovered the ------- document in the basement.

(A) confide

(B) confidence

(C) confidential

(D) confidentiality

119. ------- employees are able to get year-end bonuses and free international travels at the luxurious hotels.

(A) Hire

(B) Hiring

(C) Hired

(D) To hire

120. Luck does play a role in people's successes, but it sometimes remains ------- in places that cannot be found.
(A) hide
(B) hidden
(C) been hidden
(D) hid

121. Rookies on the Best Basketball more or less have fears of ------- by senior players.
(A) judged
(B) judging
(C) been judged
(D) being judged

122. In our research, ------- by numerous famous scholars, we have found evidence that weakens the health of the blood vessels.
(A) pioneer
(B) pioneered
(C) pioneering
(D) being pioneered

123. In 2010, researchers at Best Chemistry were told that they ------- to disinfect themselves in the shower room before leaving the lab.

(A) have

(B) had

(C) had had

(D) have had

124. In 2010, researchers at Best Chemistry were ------- than investigators at Elite Lab, according to the report.

(A) more happier

(B) happy

(C) less happier

(D) happier

125. The name of the mayor is ------- familiar than that of the president, according to the poll, conducted in 2018.

(A) more

(B) much

(C) the most

(D) less

126. Students ------- score higher than teachers in the math section and the biology test will be rewarded with the 7-11 coupons.

(A) which

(B) who

(C) whose

(D) whom

127. People ------- high levels of confidence tend to perform well in difficult tasks than those who do not have any.
(A) in
(B) for
(C) at
(D) with

128. ------- the screening process is complete, HR managers can begin the next step and select candidates for the second interview.
(A) Although
(B) While
(C) However
(D) Once

129. Most of the time, interviewers from the HR department start the interview process by asking ------- questions.
(A) stress
(B) stressed
(C) less stressful
(D) more stressful

130. Best Museum always provides visitors ------- longer viewing time and discounts, so it is considered to be the friendliest museum.
(A) for

(B) with

(C) during

(D) against

PART 6

Directions: In this part, you will be asked to read four English texts. Each text is missing a word, phrase, or sentence. Select the answer choice that correctly completes the text and mark the corresponding letter (A), (B), (C), or (D) on the answer sheet.

Questions 131-134

After the buyout, the stock of Best Zoo(BZ) **131.-------** 19.8 point to the new high, and outside investors were happy to see the result. One of the executives then got promoted to the new CEO of the PO and will report only to the CEO of Best Zoo. **132.-------** has run especially high among executives, who deem the promotion not totally fair. The CEO of BZ advanced the executive to **133.-------** his influence in the company. The decision was **134.-------** by outside investors in the board meeting on Friday, saying that the executive was not experienced and competent enough to run the PO. Things progressed to a surprise ending that the executive still got promoted, but under the scrutiny of all investors. He will have a three-month honeymoon period. If he is not qualified, other executives will have the chance to compete for the position.

131. (A) confirmed

(B) deferred

    (C) boosted

    (D) discerned

132. (A) Satisfaction

    (B) Sympathy

    (C) Jealousy

    (D) Compatibility

133. (A) terminate

    (B) groom

    (C) subvert

    (D) loom

134. (A) thwarted

    (B) reconciled

    (C) annihilated

    (D) determined

Questions 135-138

The promotion dinner was set on the next Wednesday night, and around 50 people in the company were invited to attend the party. Safeguards had been doing the routine **135.-------** so that nothing estranged would happen. Other executives all came to the table to **136.-------** him on the promotion. The promoted executive even received a thick red envelope from the CEO of BZ. The **137.-------** was really jubilant and contagious. The king lobsters were sent to every table as the first course. Then the frozen sugary golden apple was scheduled to make its **138.-------**. All cameras had been ready to take the shot of the seldom-made dessert in the restaurant. The night went well until the final dish arrived and everyone was too full to eat.

135. (A) manipulation
     (B) examination
     (C) collection
     (D) cooperation

136. (A) depend
     (B) capitalize
     (C) communicate
     (D) congratulate

137. (A) motivation
     (B) consumption
     (C) atmosphere
     (D) contamination

138. (A) development
     (B) succession
     (C) interaction
     (D) appearance

Everything seemed to go very well and it's about time to call it a night. Suddenly, the new CEO of the PO vomited **139.-------**, gastric juices along with various worms were found clearly on the scene. The CEO was listless and then felt **140.-------**. Several guests were astonished by the worms and then screamed for a few seconds. The restaurant owner called the ambulance and swore that their food was totally healthy, claiming that they had nothing to do with this. Then the police arrived a few moments later at the scene and **141.-------** several chefs for a further statement. Then a guest murmured something "Oh my god he's been poisoned." But by whom? **142.-------**.

139. (A) voluntarily
    (B) insufficiently
    (C) possibly
    (D) incessantly

140. (A) relieved
    (B) paralyzed
    (C) routinized
    (D) neutralized

141. (A) detained
    (B) mitigated
    (C) manipulated

(D) underplayed

142. (A) The restaurant owner is guilty of committing the crime.

(B) The doctor is accusing the owner of adding too many ingredients that can be harmful to the body.
(C) Everyone was a suspect.
(D) The CEO is pronounced dead on the scene, quite tragic.

Questions 143-146

After a week's queries to all attendants and the search on the scene, the police found the evidence and knew who did it. The CEO of the PO was still in the hospital right now, and eager to know the truth. It was the chef, who didn't know him. So the question remained why did the chef have to go some extraordinary lengths to cause him harm? He then explained to the police that he was **143.-------** by someone and he didn't know his real **144.-------**. He had a gambling problem so he was desperately in need of 10,000 dollars. He got an unknown letter on the front lawn of his home. He then did the thing he was not proud of. He just wanted to pay off the debts. The prosecutor was not **145.-------** by his account, saying that it's just his way of saying and he wouldn't **146.-------** to find out who was behind this.

143. (A) annoyed
    (B) incentivized
    (C) tantalized

(D) tampered

144. (A) buzzword
   (B) agenda
   (C) identity
   (D) aficionado

145. (A) fully convinced
   (B) purely financial
   (C) routinely checked
   (D) adequately learned

146. (A) revolutionize
   (B) horrify
   (C) tolerate
   (D) hesitate

PART 7
Directions: In this part, you will be asked to read several texts, such as advertisements, articles, instant messages, or examples of business correspondence. Each is followed by several questions. Select the best answer and mark the corresponding letter (A), (B), (C), (D) on your answer sheet.

Question 147

Receptionist 2:20 p.m.
I'm so sorry... I know Mother's Day is just around the corner... your designed cake won't be ready until next week... we totally overestimate our ability... and your cake actually requires two days of work... so we cannot seem to make it in time...

Receptionist 2:21 p.m.
But I already paid the payment through the credit card... is it possible that I get all the money back...

Receptionist 2:23 p.m.
If you have decided to cancel, we will transfer the money to you after Mother's Day... however, there is a deducted fee of 5% of the order...

Customer 2:25 p.m.
Ok... I just want my money back...

Receptionist 2:26 p.m.
Let me check it for you... so you are gonna get 950 dollars... on 5/17

147. At 2:26 p.m. what can be inferred about the price of the cake?

(A) 998

(B) 950

(C) 955

(D) 1000

Questions 148-151

Best Forest

Open: July to September/ 5 a.m to 1 p.m

(For the rest of the month, the forest is closed for maintenance and renovation.)

Fees: adults/US 500, children/US 200, researchers/US 100, chefs/ US 50, local villagers/free

Features:
- You get to taste the most delicious food that is naturally made in the forest.
- You will be interacting with local villagers and learn the dance move and music that nourish your mental soul and make you peaceful.
- You can go to our orchard to either cultivate or pluck all vegetables and fruits for the meal.
- You get to interact with wild animals in a close distance. Of course, under the guidance of our professionals.
- You will get the certificate, if you complete at least 100 hours of service in the forest. The certificate is quite valuable in that you can get extra credits during the interview in several National Parks.

148. Which of the following is the time that the Forest is under construction?
    (A) September
    (B) August
    (C) January
    (D) July

149. Which of the following do not have to pay for the stay in Best Forest?
    (A) adults
    (B) residents
    (C) kids
    (D) chefs

150. What is **NOT** mentioned as a feature in Best Forest?
    (A) the certificate for free service
    (B) the consumption of great foods
    (C) the marriage with local villagers
    (D) interaction with wild animals

151. According to the advertisement, who will value the significance of the certificate?
    (A) local residents
    (B) animal specialists
    (C) interviewers
    (D) social workers

Questions 152-154

Dear Manger,

I do love Bob's wig... it's red... Bob handed me lots of documents and told me to hide them for the further use. **(1)** I will do as instructed and I put them in the warehouse A, the one you had rent it. It was in the storage unit on the second floor, Room B. **(2)** He told me he almost got caught by the copyboy, but he gave him another assignment that should be done immediately. The guy went directly downstairs and that gave him enough room to print the files. **(3)** Those documents are sealed, so I don't even know what's in there. **(4)** It's kind of late and the coffee shop is about to close... I still haven't finished the steak and some fried chicken. I was too busy listening to what Bob had to say... talk to you tomorrow... and be careful while you are on your way to the warehouse.

Mary

152. What is **NOT** mentioned about the letter?
　　(A) Bob was smart enough to distract the copyboy.
　　(B) Mary already finished some fired chicken.
　　(C) Papers were put in the warehouse A.
　　(D) Mary has no idea what's written on those documents.

153. In which of the positions marked **(1)**, **(2)**, **(3)**, and **(4)** does the following sentence best belong?
　　"**He told me he almost got caught by the copyboy, but he gave him another assignment that should have been done immediately.**"
　　(A) (1)
　　(B) (2)

(C) (3)

(D) (4)

154. Where can the manager get the confidential documents?

(A) in room B

(B) in the restaurant kitchen warehouse

(C) in the coffee shop storage unit

(D) in the copy room

Questions 155-159
Best Technology Center 2070

It's been twenty years since we launched the magic potions. We have some great news. That is, we have successfully developed love, cancer-free, and longer youth products. Still the effects of the flying potions remain temporary, so you have to retake it. Also, both memory and wisdom portions are more expensive than before, since they are now eternal. However, we do have suggested numbers of taking those potions. After a certain point (IQ 180), they won't boost your intelligence and memory. Because of the research development, school tests rarely examine students' ability solely on memorization and recitation. Lastly, the love potion is especially helpful for someone who wants to find a faithful life partner or someone who loves someone one-sided. It's great news for marriage partners who both take the love potion. They will love each other till death, so the divorce rate will be significantly reduced.

Magic portions

items	effects	duration	costs
Fly	Flying ability	a day	US 1,000
Wisdom	super smart	perpetual	US 50,000
Memory	excellent memory	eternal	US 50,000
Power	Incredible strength	temporary	US 3,000
Youth	10 days younger	lasting	US 1,000
Youth	A year younger	lasting	US 99,999
Muscle-building	reach American Captain-like built instantly	eternal	US 10,000
Cancer-free	Immunity	perpetual	US 99,999
love	love	eternal	US 20,000

155. What can be inferred about the number of gym users?
(A) tripling
(B) decreasing
(C) enhancing
(D) quadrupling

156. What can be inferred about the trend of the single parent?
(A) inconclusive
(B) increasing
(C) declining
(D) pending

157. What can be inferred about the doctor with expertise in treating pancreatic cancer?
    (A) His value boosts
    (B) His value won't change.
    (C) His value increases
    (D) His value dwindles

158. Which of the following is film-related?
    (A) Fly
    (B) Wisdom
    (C) Muscle-building
    (D) Love

159. What is not stated about wisdom potions?
    (A) They are more expensive.
    (B) They don't have any limit.
    (C) They are now eternal
    (D) They can be used to increase your intelligence

Questions 160-162

Best Museum will be closing for the following three months for the renovation. **(1)** The typhoon hit especially hard at the huge glass window and several major buildings. **(2)** Although moisture has influenced some ancient manuscripts, the museum owner is planning to erect a room that can keep them from getting affected. **(3)** After the renovation, the museum is scheduled to open in July for a major auction. Countless rich people are going to be here for great treasures and paintings. According to the norm, the auction is held for the charity, but from a reliable source, the rich are using this as a way to deduct increasing taxes. **(4)** Finally, the fee of the maintenance is predicted at US $5 million dollars, and even the revenue of the museum cannot cover the cost.

160. What is the article mainly about?

   (A) Moisture in the room was caused by the typhoon damage.

   (B) the importance of preserving all paintings

   (C) the closure of the Museum for the better

   (D) the financial predicament of the Museum

161. What is **NOT** stated about Best Museum?

   (A) The timetable for the new opening is July

   (B) Auctioned items cannot be exempted from the tax.

   (C) The typhoon caused quite a lot damage.

   (D) A special room will be established.

162. In which of the positions marked **(1)**, **(2)**, **(3)**, and **(4)** does the following sentence best belong?

   NEW

   "**According to the staff member, who prefers to remain anonymous, all paintings stay intact.**"

   (A) (1)

   (B) (2)

(C) (3)

(D) (4)

Questions 163-166

According to the morning news, four bank robberies happened at the exact same timeframe, which piqued the interest of criminal psychologists. **(1)** So far, the police still have no clue about the whereabouts of criminals. This means they are still at large. **(2)** From the statement of the bank clerk at the first bank, three criminals walked in with guns. He handed them two bags of fake money, and they just left, but where is the guard? **(3)** This meant they were serious about this, and they went in, demanding all clerks knee down. **(4)** They took away the real cash, and the amount was tremendous. The third robbery was about two women who went in the bank with knives and electric guns. They aimed directly at two guards, who suffered serious injury. The odd thing was that they didn't take the money. The fourth bank got robbed of a thousand dollars. We are still waiting for the police officer to make the statement at the News Center.

163. What is the article mainly about?

    (A) attribution of the responsibility to the police department

    (B) an analysis done by several criminal psychologists

    (C) four major crimes occurring at banks

    (D) injuries caused by the felons

164. In which of the positions marked **(1)**, **(2)**, **(3)**, and **(4)** does the following sentence best belong?

NEW

"**As to the second bank, four criminals shot the citizen.**"

(A) (1)

(B) (2)

(C) (3)

(D) (4)

165. What can be inferred about the location of the larcener?

(A) certain

(B) inconclusive

(C) predictable

(D) reachable

166. Which of the following bank suffered from both the most monetary loss and personal loss?

(A) The first

(B) The second

(C) The third

(D) The fourth

Questions 167-168

According to the golden rule, he who first mentions the salary loses. Of course, during the job search, we are going to encounter different types of companies. Some large companies have a specific and fixed salary for every position, so you don't have much room for discussion. **(1)** And that's not within the range of our discussion. As for other companies, you don't have to mention the salary first, if they are really interested in you, it's highly likely that they are going to mention it or make a phone call and ask you about that. **(2)** You can totally escape the expected salary question by saying that you would like to know more about the role and job content to figure it out. **(3)** It's best that you write a range, instead of an exact figure, so that you have the room for further negotiation. **(4)** You also need to do your homework about the salary for the current position in different companies... and good luck...

Best Column

167. What is **NOT** stated about the "Job Column"?
    (A) Mentioning the salary first can hurt you in some ways.
    (B) It's likely that you are asked to write down about your expected salary.
    (C) Writing a range is better than writing a fixed number.
    (D) You have to be persistent in negotiating the salary with the larger company.

168. In which of the positions marked **(1)**, **(2)**, **(3)**, and **(4)** does the following sentence best belong?
    "**Also, you are bound to encounter a situation that you have to write down your expected salary.**"

(A) (1)
(B) (2)
(C) (3)
(D) (4)

Questions 169-171

To be honest, you don't have to say something that will be used against you during the job interview. **(1)** You have to craft your ability to talk, too. **(2)** There are times that you will be asking about your personal information, and it does matter. Everything you have said can be a consideration. Don't give them any doubts and instead clear the doubt. Sometimes you can sense that. **(3)** For example, if you are sensing that the interviewer has a concern about the expected salary you wrote earlier, you can instantly respond by saying you are willing to trim it down a little. **(4)** And you obviously don't have to reveal your plan to study abroad or other plans so you can only work in the company **temporarily**... be smarter than that...

Best Column

169. What is **NOT** stated about the "Job Column"?
    (A) One needs a fantastic resume to have a chance.
    (B) Personal information can be a deciding factor.
    (C) Be careful about the word that comes out of your mouth.
    (D) It's ok to disclose your future goals.

170. The word "**temporarily**" in line 11, is closet in meaning to
    (A) permanently
    (B) fleetingly
    (C) increasingly
    (D) potentially

171. In which of the positions marked **(1)**, **(2)**, **(3)**, and **(4)** does the following sentence best belong?

    "**Of course, you will need a great resume and a convincing autobiography to be invited to a job interview.**"
    (A) (1)
    (B) (2)
    (C) (3)
    (D) (4)

Questions 172-175

The game of the ring toss has been intriguing for people of all ages, so it never fades. Recently, we have begun to include more incentives to lure more customers, and we have different geographical locations for adventurous people. For example, three gifts have been set in front of the huge waterfall. It's slippery in the place where you initiate a toss. The prize is actually money in a **translucent** bottle. You have no idea the amount until you toss the ring. Of course, nowadays people get to use the smartphone with 108M pixels to take a peek to decide whether they are going to play, and there are other geographical locations, too.

Setting	Number of tosses erected
Lake	5
Waterfall	3
River bank	8
High cliff	6
Volcano	9
Tunnel	10
Moving train	19

Note:

1. It's kind of hard to play ring toss game in a moving train, so the prize is going to be higher. Unlike other settings, it's a folded check in the bottle, so you can't take a peek at the amount written on it.

172. What is **NOT** mentioned about the game?

    (A) Different locations are used to attract adventurous people.
    (B) Three gifts have been set in front of the huge waterfall.
    (C) The tunnel has the most tosses established.
    (D) The checks will be put into the bottle in the moving train location.

173. The word "**translucent**" in paragraph1, line 7, is closet in meaning to

    (A) semitransparent
    (B) opaque

(C) transparent

(D) sparingly

174. Which of the following is related to players' resistance to heat?

(A) Waterfall

(B) Lake

(C) High cliff

(D) Volcano

175. Which of the following prize has been kept invisible?

(A) Waterfall

(B) Moving train

(C) Tunnel

(D) High cliff

Questions 176-180

Dear CEO

Thanks I'm finally getting the bonus and the raise. I was **passed over** when the company cannot afford to lose Cindy Lin as a CMO. The second time, it was the new recruit who had the information that could be used against the rival company. He did not want the money. He just wanted the title. The scandal between the CFO and the advertising manager cost a place for my promotion. The fourth time it was because of the economic downturn, and we were in a difficult time. We had a hiring freeze, let alone having a promotion thing. Luckily, after a **circuitous** route, if it's yours then it's yours. I eventually got the position. I'm going to the HR department to change the new ID badge. It's quite worth the wait.

Jack

Dear Jack,

Again thanks for having great faith in the company. We have been working so hard since the start of the company... that means working here for 20 years. You have shown your loyalty, and you are quite admired by coworkers and subordinates, and that's kind of the rare quality that we are looking for as a leader. You didn't make a job hop. Not once. That surprised me. It's great that you didn't accept the offer from ABC Cosmetics. The Marketing Director had a plane accident last July. It was **hijacked** by some mobs who were unsatisfied with the government... to cut to the chase... good luck with everything...

CEO

176. The word "**passed over**" in paragraph1, line 1, is closet in meaning to
    (A) disconnected by
    (B) dialed down
    (C) penalized by
    (D) left aside

177. What is **NOT** stated about the letter written by Jack?
    (A) He finally gets the perks.
    (B) The new recruit had confidential documents.
    (C) The company went through the hiring freeze phase.
    (D) The HR Department refused to renew the ID badge.

178. The word "**circuitous**" in the letter 1, line 8, is closet in meaning to
    (A) circled
    (B) meandering
    (C) relinquishing

(D) conflicting

179. What would have happened to Jack, if he had taken the MD position?

(A) have the desired title

(B) get killed

(C) get the perks

(D) earn a great fortune

180. The word "**hijacked**" in letter 2, line 7, is closet in meaning to

(A) unimportantly menaced

(B) proudly imprisoned

(C) unlawfully seized

(D) influentially captured

Questions 181-185

Statement from the company

To be clear, our company does not **condone** sexual scandals. Therefore, we have to make the painful cut for our employee, who was accused of the sexual harassment and possession of recordings of several minors a month ago. We are a company that has built our name on our integrity and honesty. We have to caution all employees working in the company to remain vigilant and be responsible for their actions, and we don't accept any **misconduct** that may damage the reputation of the company. From now on, the hiring process will be lengthier and involve the scrutiny of me and other CEOs.

2022 0504

Recruitment of the CFO

Experience: at least working in the car industry for 5 years
Degree: university or above
Recommendation: from the previous boss
Talent: great with numbers and accounting
Self-introduction: 500 words in English
Languages: Spanish or German, and English

Note: Candidates must use the on-line application form and fill out all the necessary details on the website. Send the document to the HR department before 2020 July 1. Selected candidates will participate in the first and second interviews in Europe. Finalists will be attending the great exhibition of our car in Japan. We will make the final decision in our headquarter, California. The new CFO will start their new journey in our branch office (South America) to get familiar with every part of our business.

181. The word "**condone**" in paragraph1, line 1, is closet in meaning to

    (A) tolerate

    (B) concede

    (C) conclude

    (D) conduct

182. Who most likely can be the person that got the accusation?

    (A) CMO

    (B) CEO

    (C) CFO

    (D) The boss

183. The word "**misconduct**" in paragraph1, line 6, is closet in meaning to
    (A) decorum
    (B) misbehavior
    (C) misunderstanding
    (D) miscommunication

184. What is **NOT** stated about the qualification?
    (A) Chinese
    (B) familiarity with the industry
    (C) diploma
    (D) autobiography

185. Where will the new CFO be working at, if hired?
    (A) Europe
    (B) North America
    (C) South America
    (D) California

Questions 186-190

Day 73

We've decided to celebrate for a day and called the food truck to order some food and drinks. After some wine, I began to feel dizzy and tried to get some water by the river. I got two buckets of water. When I got back to the tent, some of our teammates yelled "They are still in the box", right? That scared the hell out of me. It turned out those pebbles weren't stolen. Imagine my relief. I opened the box and it hit me out of nowhere that I wanted to clean the surface of the pebbles to make it striking and stainless. After a moment, I regretted the action that I had done. The color on these pebbles **obliterated**. I couldn't believe it and thought I probably got drunk and mistakenly.... until my teammates all verified that. All gone. We've got nothing. And the person who wrote the letter played us... and big... but who did that?

Day 74

We were completely **blindsided** by that, and couldn't think of what to do next...**(1)** Should we trust what's written on the letter? **(2)** But since we didn't know what to do next... we followed the instruction given and went to the other side of the bank. A tall bush and then a forest. We were all wet. **(3)** Fortunately, things in our package didn't. We set up a tent and was ready to rest. **(4)** My instinct told me that something strange was going to happen. Then I woke up some guys, fearing that a wild beast was lurking in there. We walked several miles and there was a cave... I was like no... a giant spider? We could all get killed.

Day 75

A guy in our team would like to quit, and of course I said no... there is no quitting... and we have to find who's behind this. **(1)** Then all of a sudden, another team arrived at the scene as well, which increased our confidence to check if there actually was a giant spider in there, and of course we have to evenly split the credits with them... but fine... some of us were ready to ambush and some of us were ready to strike with the weapon. **(2)** We stayed **motionless** for a moment and decided to toss a coin to decide which team went in the cave first. Our team members lighted the torch and went in there. A giant spider horrifically stood there and we yelled loudly. So ten of us v.s the giant spider. **(3)** We threw several knifes and it remained undamaged. Then I threw the torch out of my hands for no reason... perhaps because I was too nervous... so the fight ended... the spider was a fake... and we found boxes of heavy stuff in the cave... **(4)** ...we are going to get rich...

186. The word "**obliterated**" in paragraph1, line 8, is closet in meaning to
    (A) strengthened
    (B) emerged
    (C) disappeared
    (D) surged

187. The word "**blindsided**" in paragraph2, line 1, is closet in meaning to
    (A) do something in blindfold
    (B) do something in an unexpected way
    (C) disturbed
    (D) enraged

188. In which of the positions marked **(1)**, **(2)**, **(3)**, and **(4)** does the following sentence best belong? (the second letter)
    "**Then one of the monkeys handed a box to us that included a letter as well.**"
    (A) (1)
    (B) (2)
    (C) (3)
    (D) (4)

189. The word "**motionless**" in paragraph3, line 7, is closet in meaning to
    (A) molested

(B) counterproductive

(C) flexible

(D) stationary

190. In which of the positions marked **(1)**, **(2)**, **(3)**, and **(4)** does the following sentence best belong? (the third letter)

"**Oh my god it was gold**"

(A) (1)

(B) (2)

(C) (3)

(D) (4)

Questions 191-195

Day 76

It was as authentic as it could be... because I even bit the gold.... it was real...**(1)** Since day one... I couldn't say I hadn't had the slightest doubt about the program thing. **(2)** Now without finishing all goals here and went on to find the real treasure on the island. We hit the lottery by finding it first. We were so happy and were so angry at the same time. **(3)** The fake spider was **inflamed** due to the torch I threw at it a moment before... we had to move boxes of gold outside before the fire was too big. The smoke was so unbearable. **(4)** We could have died here by inhaling too much deleterious gas. We had to retreat and find something to extinguish the fire.

Day 77

Miraculously, the fire was put out. And we all knew that boxes of gold had to be equally split between 10 people. Still it was a great fortune, enough for any of us to use for the rest of our lives. Of course, I didn't want any confrontations with others. I gathered everyone here and told them that each of us would get 1/10 share of what we found. All of them agreed. We moved all of the boxes outside the cave and decided to **calculate** the amount of gold in those boxes. A real giant spider approached. Some of the guys said run... hurry... ran away... what a coward? Without a weapon, I had to run, too.

Day 78

We decided to regroup and launch an attack. By the time we got back to the original place, the giant spider was gone. So were boxes of gold. Who did that? The spider couldn't do that right? The ten of us went back to where we camped and were too exhausted. The wealth was just within reach, and now it was all gone. We had to start somewhere. We weren't in the mood to call the restaurant car. Then we saw several ostriches chasing by the cheetah and we grasped the chance to take a closer look at the nest. No golden ostrich eggs could be found, but there was something else. We moved several ostrich eggs to our jeep and then we found that it was like a floorboard thing. It's a gateway to the basement. Another new finding... good for us...

191. The word "**inflamed**" in paragraph1, line 6, is closet in meaning to

    (A) terrified

    (B) lit up

    (C) led to

    (D) unaware of

192. In which of the positions marked **(1)**, **(2)**, **(3)**, and **(4)** does the following sentence best belong?

    "**The fake spider must have been made by a harmful substance.**"

    (A) (1)

    (B) (2)

    (C) (3)

    (D) (4)

193. The word "**calculate**" in paragraph2, line 6, is closet in meaning to
    (A) profuse
    (B) capitalize
    (C) compute
    (D) calibrate

194. What is **NOT** Mentioned about discovered gold?
    (A) The gold was authentic
    (B) They eventually knew who took the gold that they miraculously discovered.
    (C) The gold had to be evenly distributed to all attendances.
    (D) It was stashed in different containers.

195. What is **NOT** indicated about the team during and after "the spider incident"?
    (A) They were now professionally trained, so they were gallant enough to tackle the real spider.
    (B) They couldn't stand the gas generated by the burning of the counterfeit spider.
    (C) Their hope shattered because the gold unexpectedly disappeared.
    (D) The appearance of ostriches led them to another new adventure.

Questions 196-200

Day 79

We lit several torches and found several paintings on the basement wall. A guy on our team boldly removed one of the paintings on the wall. **(1)** What was hidden behind... golden ostriches' eggs. Miraculously, we got these. **(2)** Let us out... who did that? I assumed it was the person from the beginning. **(3)** The person on the ground ignored our crying for help. Fine, then we destroyed all the paintings. We removed all paintings and found something intriguing. We assembled all the paintings on the ground, and surprisingly discovered that it was the map of this island. We got the map without costing a cent. Remember the company tried to sell the map to each of us. **(4)** That gave our team a leg up. Then I heard the voice of people on the ground. Were they coaches? That's...

Day 80

I took out the pen and drew exactly the same map on the paper. While I was drawing the map, other guys either broke all golden ostrich eggs or tried to find the exit. There was a tunnel that could lead us somewhere. Great. And we grabbed all the keys on the ground. They came from the breaking of these golden ostrich eggs. It could be useful in the future... great... no I kind of like this adventure... hopefully, we would all be safe and back to the training center. In the very end of the tunnel, we found some light. That was great. Based on the map, we would be arriving at the peacock valley... I was sure more amazing things were to be revealed...(to be continued)

School Newspaper

"During 80 adventures" is actually a **shortened** version of what we found in our school library. There are three theories accounting for the story. The first one was backed by an archaeologist. It actually happened 50 years ago... about an adventure and the author wrote the diary to record all the information. The second theory indicated that this was an AI game created by a game company... and it was so believable that during the trial time... the government shut it down, fearing that it could be detrimental to our health, and once you were in the game, there was no turning back. Even if they unplugged the electricity, the game player's body might have suffered severe injuries. The third theory revolved around a promising young college student who wrote the story in cursive writings on the old paper hoping it could eventually get published... and he wrote it on and off. Only 80-day diary remains.

196. In which of the positions marked **(1)**, **(2)**, **(3)**, and **(4)** does the following sentence best belong?

   "**When we were about to move these eggs back to our jeep, the gateway closed.**"

   (A) (1)

   (B) (2)

   (C) (3)

   (D) (4)

197. What is **NOT** mentioned about the map?

   (A) The map can give the team an upper hand.

   (B) Because they were locked under the basement, they had no choice but to purchase the map from the company.

   (C) They extracted all the paintings from the wall.

   (D) The guy imitated the map to sketch an identical one.

198. What is **Not True** about golden ostriches' eggs?

   (A) They were concealed behind these paintings

   (B) Keys were in these eggs.

   (C) They were shattered by the guy's teammate.

   (D) They were carried back to the jeep successfully.

199. The word "**shortened**" in paragraph3, line 1, is closet in meaning to

   (A) summary

   (B) adaptation

(C) descriptive

(D) abbreviated

200. What is **NOT** indicated about three theories?

(A) The first theory stated a story entirely based on the diary of the writer.

(B) The third theory was about a story that never got printed.

(C) The first one is more believable than the other two since it was backed up by a scholar.

(D) The second theory revolved around an incredible experience in an AI setting.

模擬試題（五）

 PART 5　中譯和解析

閱讀原文與中譯	
101. To **upgrade** the facility, the principal in Best Elite School discreetly accepted the bribe from those parents last fall without feeling any guilt. (A) overestimate **(B) upgrade** (C) downgrade (D) downplay	為了將設備升級，倍斯特菁英學校的校長於去年秋季謹慎地收了那些父母的賄賂而從未感到任何愧疚感。 (A) 對......評價過高；對......估計過高 **(B) 使升級、提高、提升** (C) 使降級、降低、貶低、小看 (D) 將......輕描淡寫、貶低、低估
答案：(B)	

這題依據語意要選「**upgrade**」，故答案為**選項B**。

閱讀原文與中譯	
102. Unable to get a decent grade on the standardized test, the student threatened the examiner of test reports to make a **forgery** yesterday. (A) note (B) signature **(C) forgery** (D) transaction	無法在標準化測驗上獲取合宜的分數，這位學生於昨日威脅考試報告的檢測官幫其偽造文書。 (A) 筆記、記錄、註、註釋 (B) 簽名 **(C)（文件、藝術品等的）偽造、偽造物、贗品** (D) 辦理、處置、執行、交易
答案：(C)	

這題依據語法和語意要選「**forgery**」，故答案為**選項C**。

閱讀原文與中譯	
103. Best Software has made an unprecedented growth by inventing the robot that can fix customer issues **automatically**. **(A) automatically** (B) paradoxically (C) surreptitiously (D) artificially	藉由發明能夠自動地修復顧客問題的機器人，倍斯特軟體公司的來客數有著史無前例的成長。 **(A) 自動地** (B) 似非而是地、悖理地、反常地 (C) 祕密地、暗中地、不正當地 (D) 人工地

答案：(A)

這題依據語法和語意要選「**automatically**」，故答案為**選項A**。

閱讀原文與中譯	
104. After the performance at the luxurious hotel, Best Cinema made the decision of not **renewing** the contract of multiple actors in the press conference. (A) proposing **(B) renewing** (C) retaining (D) reproducing	在豪華旅館的表演後，倍斯特電影在新聞發佈會上做了不與眾多演員續簽合約的決定。 (A) 提議、建議、推薦 **(B) 使更新、使復原、使恢復** (C) 保留、保持、留住 (D) 繁殖、生殖、複製、翻拍、複寫

答案：(B)

解析

這題依據語法和語意要選「**renewing**」，故答案為**選項B**。

閱讀原文與中譯

105. The company's morale has suffered due to a series of lawsuits by the rival, and employees have to attend the court **unwillingly** to be the witnesses. (A) effectively (B) individually (C) voluntarily **(D) unwillingly**	由於一系列由競爭對手所發起的法律訴訟，公司的士氣已經受到影響，而員工必須不情願地出席法庭並充當證人。 (A) 有效地、生效地、實際上 (B) 單獨地、逐個地、分別地 (C) 自動地、自發地 **(D) 不情願地、勉強地**

答案：(D)

 解析

這題依據語法和語意要選「**unwillingly**」，故答案為**選項D**。

閱讀原文與中譯

106. **Exacerbated** by the scandal of the actor (just signed a month ago) the warehouse of Best Music is now full of unsold music albums. (A) Accompanied (B) Considered (C) Distinguished **(D) Exacerbated**	於一個月前才剛續簽合同，銷售卻因這位演員的醜聞而惡化，現在倍斯特音樂的倉庫放滿了未售出的音樂專輯。 (A) 伴隨而來 (B) 考量到 (C) 卓越的、著名的、高貴的 **(D) 使惡化、使加重**

答案：(D)

 解析

這題依據語法和語意要選「**exacerbated**」，故答案為**選項D**。

閱讀原文與中譯

107. Since Cindy lost her 401k and could not get the **severance** pay from her employer, she moved back home to live with her parents for the time being. **(A) severance** (B) profit (C) bonus (D) benefit	因為辛蒂失去了她的401k而且無法從她的雇主那裡拿到遣散費，她暫時搬回家與她的父母同住。 **(A) 隔離、分離、分開、資遣** (B) 利潤、盈利、收益、紅利 (C) 獎金、額外津貼、特別補助 (D) 利益、好處、優勢、津貼、救濟金

答案：(A)

 解析

這題依據語法和語意要選「**severance**」，故答案為**選項A**。

閱讀原文與中譯

108. **Repair** costs resulting from improper use of the electronic equipment are tremendous, and sometimes they can be close to buying a new one. (A) Permission (B) Delegation (C) Procedure **(D) Repair**	導因於電器用品的不當使用而衍伸的維修費用是巨大的，而且有時候費用可能接近於要購買一台新的了。 (A) 允許、許可、同意 (B) 代表的委派、委任、授權 (C) 程序、手續、步驟 **(D) 修理、維修**

答案：(D)

 解析

這題依據語法和語意要選「**Repair**」，故答案為**選項D**。

| 109. According to the new income tax, multiple items are now considered **deductible** expenses, a phenomenon that taxpayers are willing to see.

(A) important
(B) deductible
(C) expensive
(D) luxurious | 根據新的所得稅，眾多品項都被視成是可以扣除的支出，這是一個所有繳稅者都樂見的現象。

(A) 重要的
(B) 可扣除的、可減免的
(C) 高價的、昂貴的、花錢的
(D) 驕奢淫逸的、豪華的 |

答案：(B)

這題依據語法和語意要選「**deductible**」，故答案為**選項B**。

| 110. With various lucrative benefits and monthly fees, credit cards of Best Bank are widely **acceptable** among students and businessmen.

(A) extensive
(B) acceptable
(C) expensive
(D) unfavorable | 隨著不同有利可圖的利益和月費，倍斯特銀行的信用卡在學生們和商人之間受到廣泛使用。

(A) 廣闊的、廣泛的、大規模的
(B) 可接受的
(C) 昂貴的
(D) 不利的、不適宜的、不順利的 |

答案：(B)

這題依據語法和語意要選「**acceptable**」，故答案為**選項B**。

閱讀原文與中譯

111. Best Cellphone is now considering to launch several products that are **accessible** to college students and the lower middle class. **(A) accessible** (B) competitive (C) eligible (D) unavailable	倍斯特手機現在正考慮發佈幾項大學生和下層中產階級都能購得的產品。 **(A) 可（或易）得到的、可（或易）使用的** (B) 競爭性的、好競爭的 (C) 有資格當選的、法律上合格的 (D) 無法利用的、達不到的、沒有效果的

答案：(A)

 解析

這題依據語法和語意要選「**accessible**」，故答案為**選項A**。

閱讀原文與中譯

112. The unexpected **resignation** of the CFO shocked the boss and his parrot last Friday, and it was turned down in an open letter. (A) investigation (B) confirmation **(C) resignation** (D) registration	上週五，財務長突如其來的辭職讓老闆和他的鸚鵡感到震驚，而在一封公開信中辭職受到拒絕。 (A) 研究、調查 (B) 確定、確證、批准 **(C) 辭職、放棄、辭呈** (D) 登記、註冊

答案：(C)

 解析

這題依據語法和語意要選「**resignation**」，故答案為**選項C**。

閱讀原文與中譯

113. Moving the money under the watch of federal agents was not easy, so Mark took a private jet to a remote island to discuss further details with other government **officials**. (A) underperformers (B) superintendents (C) correspondents **(D) officials**	在聯邦探員的監視下移動資金並不容易，所以馬克搭乘了私人噴射機到遙遠的島嶼中與其它政府官員討論進一步的細節。 (A) 表現不佳者 (B) 監管者、（機關，企業等的）主管、負責人 (C) 對應物、通訊記者、特派員 **(D) 官員、公務員**

答案：(D)

 解析

這題依據語法和語意要選「**officials**」，故答案為**選項D**。

閱讀原文與中譯

114. Before filing the divorce paper, Cindy has already hired an attorney to find the potential **loopholes** and hide the assets so that her husband will get less than he deserves. (A) risks (B) problems (C) documents **(D) loopholes**	在提出離婚書申請前，辛蒂已經雇用了一位律師去找潛在的漏洞並藏匿資產，這樣她的丈夫就會拿到比本該獲得的金額更少。 (A) 風險 (B) 問題 (C) 文件 **(D) 小孔、（法律等的）漏洞**

答案：(D)

 解析

這題依據語法和語意要選「**loopholes**」，故答案為**選項D**。

閱讀原文與中譯	
115. For the past 10 years, Best Technology **has been experimenting** a product whose innovation transcends current inventions. (A) has experimented (B) has been experimented **(C) has been experimenting** (D) had experimented	過去十年期間，倍斯特科技公司一直都在試驗一個產品，其創新度超越現在的發明。

答案：(C)

 解析

這題依據語法和語意要選「**has been experimenting**」，故答案為**選項C**。

閱讀原文與中譯	
116. Best Technology invented a powerful vaccine which **enabled** doctors to instantly prevent patients' internal organs from getting attacked by the virus. (A) enables **(B) enabled** (C) is enabled (D) enabling	倍斯特科技公司發明了一項強而有力的疫苗，讓醫生能夠立即阻止病人內部的器官免於受到病毒的攻擊。

答案：(B)

 解析

這題依據語法和語意要選「**enabled**」，故答案為**選項B**。

117. The ingredient of the smartphone **was unearthed** by a local resident who thought it could withstand the heat a little longer than other elements.

(A) unearths
(B) unearthed
(C) unearthing
(D) was unearthed

當地居民挖掘出智慧型手機的組成物，認為其比起其它元素能更為耐熱。

答案：(D)

 解析

這題依據語法和語意要選「**was unearthed**」，故答案為**選項D**。

118. The unprecedented business model was invented when the rookie accidentally discovered the **confidential** document in the basement.

(A) confide
(B) confidence
(C) confidential
(D) confidentiality

當菜鳥無意間發現在地下室的機密文件，史無前例的商業模式就應運而生了。

答案：(C)

 解析

這題依據語法和語意要選「**confidential**」，故答案為**選項C**。

模擬試題（五）

閱讀原文與中譯	
119. **Hired** employees are able to get year-end bonuses and free international travels at the luxurious hotels. (A) Hire (B) Hiring **(C) Hired** (D) To hire	受雇的員工能夠獲得年終獎金且享有在豪華旅館中的免費國際旅遊。

答案：(C)

 解析

這題依據語法和語意要選「**hired**」，故答案為**選項C**。

閱讀原文與中譯	
120. Luck does play a role in people's successes, but it sometimes remains **hidden** in places that cannot be found. (A) hide **(B) hidden** (C) been hidden (D) hid	幸運確實在人們的成功上扮演著一定的角色，但是有時候它卻藏匿在找不到的地方上。

答案：(B)

 解析

這題依據語法和語意要選「**hidden**」，故答案為**選項B**。

模擬試題（一）模擬試題（二）模擬試題（三）模擬試題（四）模擬試題（五）

閱讀原文與中譯

121. Rookies on the Best Basketball more or less have fears of **being judged** by senior players. (A) judged (B) judging (C) been judged **(D) being judged**	倍斯特籃球的菜鳥或多或少都存在著被資深球員評判的恐懼。

答案：(D)

 解析

這題依據語法和語意要選「**being judged**」，故答案為**選項D**。

閱讀原文與中譯

122. In our research, **pioneered** by numerous famous scholars, we have found evidence that weakens the health of the blood vessels. (A) pioneer **(B) pioneered** (C) pioneering (D) being pioneered	在由許多有名的學者所倡導的研究中，我們發現了弱化血管健康的證據。

答案：(B)

 解析

這題依據語法和語意要選「**pioneered**」，故答案為**選項B**。

閱讀原文與中譯	
123. In 2010, researchers at Best Chemistry were told that they **had** to disinfect themselves in the shower room before leaving the lab. (A) have **(B) had** (C) had had (D) have had	在2010年，倍斯特化學廠的研究人員被告知，在離開實驗室前，要在淋浴間消毒。

答案：(B)

 解析

這題依據語法和語意要選「**had**」，故答案為**選項B**。

閱讀原文與中譯	
124. In 2010, researchers at Best Chemistry were **happier** than investigators at Elite Lab, according to the report. (A) more happier (B) happy (C) less happier **(D) happier**	在2010年，倍斯特化學廠的研究人員比精英實驗室的調查人員更快樂，根據一則報導。

答案：(D)

 解析

這題依據語法和語意要選「**happier**」，故答案為**選項D**。

閱讀原文與中譯	
125. The name of the mayor is **less** familiar than that of the president, according to the poll, conducted in 2018. (A) more (B) much (C) the most **(D)less**	比起總統的名字，市長的名字對大眾來說較為陌生，根據一項於2018年所做的民調。

答案：(D)

 解析

這題依據語法和語意要選「**less**」，故答案為**選項D**。

閱讀原文與中譯	
126. Students **who** score higher than teachers in the math section and the biology test will be rewarded with the 7-11 coupons. (A) which **(B) who** (C) whose (D) whom	在數學部分與生物學測驗中獲得比老師高分的學生將會得到7-11優惠卷的獎勵。

答案：(B)

 解析

這題依據語法和語意要選「**who**」，故答案為**選項B**。

閱讀原文與中譯

127. People **with** high levels of confidence tend to perform well in difficult tasks than those who do not have any.
(A) in
(B) for
(C) at
(D) with

| 具備高度信心的人比起那些不具任何信心的人在具難度的任務上傾向表現的更好。 |

答案：(D)

 解析

這題依據語法和語意要選「**with**」，故答案為**選項D**。

閱讀原文與中譯

128. **Once** the screening process is complete, HR managers can begin the next step and select candidates for the second interview.
(A) although
(B) while
(C) however
(D) once

| 一旦篩選過程完成後，人事經理能夠開始下個步驟並且選出參加第二次面試的候選人。 |

答案：(D)

 解析

這題依據語法和語意要選「**once**」，故答案為**選項D**。

閱讀原文與中譯	
129. Most of the time, interviewers from the HR department start the interview process by asking **less stressful** questions. (A) stress (B) stressed **(C) less stressful** (D) more stressful	大多數的時候，人事部門的面試官會藉由詢問較不具壓力的問題當作面試過程的開頭。
答案：(C)	

這題依據語法和語意要選「**less stressful**」，故答案為**選項C**。

閱讀原文與中譯	
130. Best Museum always provides visitors **with** longer viewing time and discounts, so it is considered to be the friendliest museum. (A) for **(B) with** (C) during (D) against	倍斯特博物館總是提供觀光客較長的瀏覽時間和折扣，所以它被視為是最友善的博物館。
答案：(B)	

這題依據語法和語意要選「**with**」，故答案為**選項B**。

模擬試題（五）

模擬試題（一）

模擬試題（二）

模擬試題（三）

模擬試題（四）

模擬試題（五）

PART 6 中譯和解析

Questions 131-134

After the buyout, the stock of Best Zoo (BZ) **boosted** 19.8 point to the new high, and outside investors were happy to see the result. One of the executives then got promoted to the new CEO of the PO and will report only to CEO of the Best Zoo. **Jealousy** has run especially high among executives, who deem the promotion not totally fair. The CEO of BZ advances the guy to **groom** his influence in the company. The decision was **thwarted** by outside investors in the board meeting on Friday, saying that the executive was not experienced and competent enough to run the PO. Things progressed to a surprise ending that the executive still got promoted, but under the scrutiny of all investors. He will have a three-month honeymoon period. If he is not qualified, other executives will have the chance to compete for the position.

在收購後，倍斯特動物園的股價增加19.8來到新高，而外部投資客們都很開心看到這個結果。其中一位高階主管接著晉升成流行有機的執行長，且僅要向倍斯特動物園的執行長彙報。在這些高階主管之中，忌妒感特別高昂，認為這個升遷不全然是公平的。倍斯特動物園的執行長提升此人以培育自己在公司的影響力。在週五的董事會時，這項決定受到了外部投資客們的阻饒，認為這位主管的經驗不足，無法勝任經營流行有機公司一職。事情發展到了出乎意料之外的結果，這位高階主管仍會受到晉升，但是要受到所有投資客的檢視。他將有三個月的蜜月期，如果他不適任的話，其他高階主管就有機會能夠角逐這個職位。

試題中譯與解析	
131. (A) confirmed (B) deferred **(C) boosted** (D) discerned	131. (A) 證實、確定 (B) 推遲、延期 **(C) 推動、幫助、促進 、提高** (D) 識別、看出、察覺
132. (A) Satisfaction (B) Sympathy **(C) Jealousy** (D) Compatibility	132. (A) 滿意、滿足、稱心 (B) 同情、同情心 **(C) 妒忌、猜忌、戒備** (D) 適合性、一致、協調

133.	133.
(A) terminate	(A) 結束、終止
(B) groom	**(B) 準備、推薦、培育**
(C) subvert	(C) 推翻、破壞
(D) loom	(D) 隱約地出現、陰森地逼近
134.	134.
(A) thwarted	**(A) 阻撓、使受挫折、挫敗**
(B) reconciled	(B) 使和解、使和好
(C) annihilated	(C) 徹底擊潰、毀滅、廢止、使無效
(D) determined	(D) 決定、使決定

第**131**題，這題依句意要選boosted（增加或升至），故答案為**選項C**。

第**132**題，這題依句意要選Jealousy（可以由後句的not fair等判斷出最有可能是忌妒），故答案為**選項C**。

第**133**題，這題依句意要選groom（groom搭配influence剛好且符合句意），故答案為**選項B**。

第**134**題，這題依句意要選thwarted（可以由後面的saying that等協助判斷出outside visitor其實不滿意這個人事決定...進而**阻撓**），故答案為**選項A**。

Questions 135-138

The promotion dinner was set on the next Wednesday night, and around 50 people in the company were invited to attend the party. Safeguards had been doing the routine **examination** so that nothing estranged would happen. Other executives all came to the table to **congratulate** him on the promotion. The promoted executive received a thick red envelope from the CEO of BZ. The **atmosphere** was really jubilant and contagious. The king lobsters were sent to every table as the first course. Then the frozen sugary golden apple was scheduled to make its **appearance**. All cameras had been ready to take the shot of the seldom-made dessert in the restaurant. The night went well until the final dish arrived and everyone was too full to eat.

升遷的晚宴定於隔週三晚上，而大約50位公司的人員會受邀參加這個派對。保全人員執行著例行的檢測，如此一來不會有脫序的事情發生。其他高階主管都來到桌旁慶祝他的升遷。這位主管甚至收到了倍斯特動物園執行長的豐碩紅包。氣氛是真的喜氣洋洋且具感染性的。帝王龍蝦被送至每個餐桌充當第一道菜餚。然後凍糖霜蘋果預定接著亮相。所有相機都備緒要拍攝這道在這餐廳中很少製作的甜點。晚宴進行的很好直到最後一道菜餚上菜後，而每個人都吃得太飽了。

試題中譯與解析	
135. (A) manipulation **(B) examination** (C) collection (D) cooperation	135. (A) 操縱 **(B) 檢查、調查、考試** (C) 收集、採集、收取 (D) 合作、協力
136. (A) depend (B) capitalize (C) communicate **(D) congratulate**	136. (A) 相信、信賴、依靠、依賴 (B) 利用 (C) 傳達、傳遞、傳播 **(D) 祝賀、恭禧**
137. (A) motivation (B) consumption **(C) atmosphere** (D) contamination	137. (A) 動機、推動；積極性；幹勁 (B) 消耗、用盡、消耗量 **(C) 大氣、氣氛** (D) 汙染、弄髒、玷汙
138. (A) development (B) succession (C) interaction **(D) appearance**	138. (A) 生長、進化、發展 (B) 連續、接續 (C) 互相影響、互動 **(D) 出現、顯露、外表**

第135題，這題依句意要選examination（routine搭配examination剛好），故答案為**選項B**。

第136題，這題依句意要選congratulate（congratulate搭配on，且其後是祝賀promotion符合句意），故答案為**選項D**。

第137題，這題依句意要選atmosphere（可以由jubilant and contagious判斷出要選「**氣氛**」），故答案為**選項C**。

第138題，這題依句意要選appearance（這裡指的是**亮相**，所以要選appearance），故答案為**選項D**。

Questions 139-142

Everything seemed to go very well and it's about time to call it a night. Suddenly, the new CEO of the PO vomited **incessantly**, gastric juices along with various worms were found clearly on the scene. The CEO was listless and then felt **paralyzed**. Several guests were astonished by the worms and then scream for a few seconds. The restaurant owner called the ambulance and swore that their food was totally healthy, claiming that they had nothing to do with this. Then the police arrived a few moments later at the scene and **detained** several chefs for a further statement. Then a guest murmured something that "Oh my god! he's been poisoned." But by whom**? Everyone was a suspect**.

每件事都進行的恰如其分，也是時候要結束了。突然之間，流行有機的新執行長不斷地嘔吐，現場中可以看到嘔吐出的胃液和各類的蟲子。執行長無精打采的且感到癱瘓。幾個賓客被蟲子嚇到，然後大叫了幾秒。餐廳持有者打電話叫救護車且發誓他們的食物絕對是健康的，宣稱他們跟這起事件無關。然後警方於稍後到場並且拘留了幾個廚師進行進一步的詢問。然後一個賓客耳語一些事，我的天啊!他被下毒了。但是會是誰呢? 現場的每個人都有可疑。

試題中譯與解析	
139. (A) voluntarily (B) insufficiently (C) possibly **(D) incessantly**	139. (A) 志願地、自動地 (B) 不夠充分地 (C) 也許、可能 **(D) 不斷地、不停地**

140. (A) relieved **(B) paralyzed** (C) routinized (D) neutralized	140. (A) 緩和、減輕、解除 **(B) 使癱瘓、使全面停頓、使無力** (C) 使程序化、常規化 (D) 使無效、抵銷、使中立化
141. **(A) detained** (B) mitigated (C) manipulated (D) underplayed	141. **(A) 留住、使耽擱、拘留** (B) 使緩和、減輕 (C) 操作、運用、巧妙地處理、操縱 (D) 對......輕描淡寫、貶低......的重要性
142. (A) The restaurant owner is guilty of committing the crime. (B) The doctor is accusing the owner of adding too many ingredients that can be harmful to the body. **(C) Everyone was a suspect.** (D) The CEO is pronounced dead on the scene, quite tragic.	143. (A) 餐廳老闆對犯罪感到愧疚。 (B) 醫生正控訴餐廳老闆添加許多對人體有害的許多成分。 **(C) 每個人都有嫌疑犯下此罪。** (D) 執行長在當場就宣告不治，相當的悲劇性。

第**139**題，這題依句意要選incessantly（**不斷地**嘔吐），故答案為**選項D**。
第**140**題，這題依句意要選paralyzed（依句意推斷最有可能是癱軟），故答案為**選項B**。
第**141**題，這題依句意要選detain（由後面的for a further statement最有可能要選拘留），故答案為**選項A**。
第**142**題，這題依句意要選C，故答案為**選項C**。

Questions 143-146

After a week's queries to all attendants and the search on the scene, the police found the evidence and knew who did it. The CEO of the PO was still in the hospital right now, and eager to know the truth. It was the chef, who didn't know him. So the question remained why did he have to go some extraordinary lengths to cause him harm? He then explained to the police that he was **tampered** by someone and he didn't know his real **identity**. He had a gambling problem so he was desperately in need of 10,000 dollars. He got an unknown letter on the front lawn of his home. He then did the thing he was not proud of. He just wanted to pay off the debts. The prosecutor was not **fully convinced** by his account, saying that it's just his way of saying and wouldn't **hesitate** to find out who was behind this.

在幾週的詢問所有參加者和在當場收尋後，警方發現證據並且知道嫌犯是誰。流行有機的執行長現在仍在醫院，他迫切想知道事情真相。下毒的是一位廚師，但是執行長不認識他。所以問題仍舊存在著，為什麼他必須要大費周章地傷害他呢？然後，他向警方解釋道他受賄做這起勾當，但是他不知道對方的真實身分。他有賭博的習慣，所以他急迫地需要1萬美元。他在他家前方草坪收到一封匿名信。於是，他接著做了他自己也感到不光采的事情。他只是想要償還賭債。檢控官對於他的說法不全然相信，述說這僅他的說法且對於要找出真兇不會有任何遲疑。

試題中譯與解析	
143. (A) annoyed (B) incentivized (C) tantalized **(D) tampered**	143. (A) 惹惱、使生氣、困擾 (B) 激勵 (C) 逗惹、逗弄、吊人胃口、折磨 **(D) 損害、削弱、竄改、賄賂**
144. (A) buzzword (B) agenda **(C) identity** (D) aficionado	144. (A) 行話 (B) 議程、日常工作事項 **(C) 身分、本身、本體** (D) 狂、迷

145.	145.
(A) fully convinced	**(A) 完全信服地**
(B) purely financial	(B) 純粹財務地
(C) routinely checked	(C) 定期地檢視
(D) adequately learned	(D) 適宜地學習
146.	146.
(A) revolutionize	(A) 使革命化
(B) horrify	(B) 使恐懼、使驚懼
(C) tolerate	(C) 忍受、容忍、寬恕
(D) hesitate	**(D) 躊躇、猶豫**

第**143**題，這題依句意要選tampered，故答案為**選項D**。
第**144**題，這題依句意要選identity（他並不了解對方的真實**身分**），故答案為**選項C**。
第**145**題，這題依句意要選fully convinced（檢控官對於他的說法不全然相信），故答案為**選項A**。
第**146**題，這題依句意要選hesitate（**won't hesitate**），故答案為**選項D**。

PART 7 中譯和解析

Receptionist 2:20 p.m.	**接線生下午2:20**
I'm so sorry... I know Mother's Day is just around the corner... your designed cake won't be ready until next week... we totally overestimate our ability... and your cake actually requires two days of work... so we cannot seem to make it in time...	對此我感到很抱歉...我知道母親節迫近...你要的特製蛋糕要到下週才能製作完成...我們全然低估了我們的能力了...而你的蛋糕實際上會需要兩天的工作日來製作...所以我們似乎沒辦法及時製作完成...。

Receptionist 2:21 p.m. But I already paid the payment through the credit card... is it possible that I get all the money back...	**接線生下午2:21** 但是，我已經透過信用卡付費了...有可能我可以拿回所有金額嗎？
Receptionist 2:23 p.m. If you have decided to cancel, we will transfer the money to you after Mother's Day... however, there is a deducted fee of 5% of the order...	**接線生下午2:23** 如果你已經決定要取消，我們會於母親節後把款項匯給你...然而，我們會收取該筆訂單5%的費用...。
Customer 2:25 p.m. Ok... I just want my money back...	**顧客下午2:25** 好的...我只是想要把錢拿回來...。
Receptionist 2:26 p.m. Let me check it for you... so you are gonna get 950 dollars... on 5/17	**接線生下午 2:26** 讓我替你檢查一下...所以你會於5月17日收到款項950元...。

Question 147	
147. At 2:26 p.m. what can be inferred about the price of the cake? (A) 998 (B) 950 (C) 955 **(D) 1000**	147. 在下午2:26分，可以推測出蛋糕的價格為？ (A) 998 (B) 950 (C) 955 **(D) 1000**

 解析

- **第147題**，由對話中段的a deducted fee of 5% of the order和結尾的you are gonna get 950 dollars可以計算出蛋糕的價格是1,000元，故答案為**選項D**。

模擬試題（五）

模擬試題（一）

模擬試題（二）

模擬試題（三）

模擬試題（四）

模擬試題（五）

Best Forest

Open: July to September/ 5 a.m to 1 p.m
(For the rest of the month, the forest is closed for maintenance and renovation.)
Fees: adults/US 500, children/US 200, researchers/US 100, chefs/US 50, local villagers/free

Features:
- You get to taste the most delicious food that is naturally made in the forest.
- You will be interacting with local villagers and learn the dance move and music that nourish your mental soul and make you peaceful.
- You can go to our orchard to either cultivate or pluck all vegetables and fruits for the meal.
- You get to interact with wild animals in a close distance. Of course, under the guidance of our professionals.
- You will get the certificate, if you complete at least 100 hours of service in the forest. The certificate is quite valuable in that you can get extra credits during the interview in several National Parks.

倍斯特森林

開放時間： 七月至九月/ 上午五點至下午一點
（至於其餘的月份，森林會關閉以進行維護和修繕）
費用： 成人/500美元，小孩/200美元，研究人員/100美元，廚師/50美元，當地村民/免費

特色：
- 你可以品嚐到森林中天然製作的美食。
- 你將與當地村民們互動並且從他們身上學習舞步和音樂，此能滋養你內在靈魂且讓你感到平靜。
- 你可以去我們的果園，耕種或摘所有蔬菜和水果來當作餐點。
- 你可以近距離與野生動物互動。當然會是在我們專業人員的指導下。
- 也會授予你證書，如果你在森林中至少完成100小時的免費服務。證書是非

常有價值的，因為你可以在幾個國家公園中的面試中獲取額外的分數。

Questions 148-151	
148. Which of the following is the time that the Forest is under construction? (A) September (B) August **(C) January** (D) July	148. 下列何時是森林在整修的時候？ (A) 九月 (B) 八月 **(C) 一月** (D) 七月
149. Which of the following do not have to pay for the stay in Best Forest? (A) adults **(B) residents** (C) kids (D) chefs	149 下列哪一類別待在倍斯特森林不需要支付費用？ (A) 成人 **(B) 居民** (C) 小孩 (D) 廚師
150. What is not mentioned as a feature in Best Forest? (A) the certificate for free service (B) the consumption of great foods **(C) the marriage with local villagers** (D) interaction with wild animals	150. 關於倍斯特森林的特色，沒有提到？ (A) 免費服務的證書 (B) 很棒食物的攝取 **(C) 與當地村民的婚姻** (D) 與野生動物的互動
151. According to the advertisement, who will value the significance of the certificate? (A) local residents (B) animal specialists **(C) interviewers** (D) social workers	151. 根據廣告，誰將重視這個證書的重要性？ (A) 當地居民 (B) 動物專家們 **(C) 面試官** (D) 社工

解析

- **第148題**，可以從July to September得知扣除這幾個月份之外的都是在整修中的月份，故答案為**選項C**。
- **第149題**，從訊息中可以得知villagers不用，villagers即residents，故答案為**選項B**。
- **第150題**，features中沒有提到marriage，故答案為**選項C**。
- **第151題**，這題需要稍微思考下，但僅有可能是**interviewers**，故答案為**選項C**。

Dear Manger,

I do love Bob's wig... it's red... Bob handed me lots of documents and told me to hide them for the further use. **(1)** I will do as instructed and I put them in the warehouse A, the one you had rent it. It was in the storage unit on the second floor, Room B. **(2) He told me he almost got caught by the copyboy, but he gave him another assignment that should have been done immediately.** The guy went directly downstairs and that gave him enough room to print the files. **(3)** Those documents are sealed, so I don't even know what's in there. **(4)** It's kind of late and the coffee shop is about to close... I still haven't finished the steak and some fried chicken. I was too busy listening to what Bob had to say... talk to you tomorrow... and be careful while you are on your way to the warehouse.

Mary

親愛的經理

我確實喜愛鮑伯的假髮...是紅色的...鮑伯遞給我許多文件且告訴我文件要藏起來留作進一步使用。我會照指示去做，而且我會將文件放置在A倉庫裡頭，你先前承租的倉庫。會放置在位於二樓，B室的儲藏室裡頭。他告訴我他幾乎快要因為影印室的影印男孩而露出馬腳，但是鮑伯給他另一項他必須要立即完成的工作。男子直接下樓，而這給他足夠的時間去印所有的檔案。那些文件都是密封的，所以我也不知道裡頭寫的會是什麼。有點晚了而咖啡店也快要關門了...我仍舊還沒吃完點好的牛排餐和炸雞。我忙於聽鮑伯想說什麼...明天在跟你說了...然後你在前往倉庫的途中要小心點喔...。

瑪莉

Questions 152-154

152. What is not mentioned about the letter?	152. 關於信件沒有提到什麼？
(A) Bob was smart enough to distract the copyboy.	(A) 鮑伯聰明到能夠分散影印男孩的注意力。
(B) Mary already finished some fired chicken.	**(B) 瑪莉已經吃完一些炸雞了。**
(C) Papers were put in the warehouse A.	(C) 資料被放置在A倉庫。
(D) Mary has no idea what's written on those documents.	(D) 瑪莉不知道那些文件上頭寫些什麼。

| 153. In which of the positions marked **(1)**, **(2)**, **(3)**, and **(4)** does the following sentence best belong?

"**He told me he almost got caught by the copyboy, but he gave him another assignment that should be done immediately.**"
(A) (1)
(B) (2)
(C) (3)
(D) (4) | 153. 以下這個句子最適合放在文中標記**(1)**, **(2)**, **(3)**, **(4)**的哪個位置？
「他告訴我他幾乎快要因為影印室的影印男孩而露出馬腳，但是鮑伯給他另一項他必須要立即完成的工作。」
(A) (1)
(B) (2)
(C) (3)
(D) (4) |
| 154. Where can the manager get the confidential documents?
(A) in Room B
(B) in the restaurant kitchen warehouse
(C) in the coffee shop storage unit
(D) in the copy room | 154. 經理能從何處獲取機密文件呢？
(A) 在B室
(B) 在餐廳廚房的倉庫
(C) 在咖啡店的儲藏室
(D) 在影印室 |

 解析

· 第**152**題，信件中沒有提到Mary already finished some fried chicken，故答案為**選項B**。
· 第**153**題，從空格後句The guy went directly downstairs and that gave him enough room to print the files.和其他線索可以推斷出，最適合放置的位置是這句話之前 **(2)**，故答案為**選項B**。
· 第**154**題，這題很明顯答案是**room B**，故答案為**選項A**。

Best Technology Center 2070

It's been twenty years since we launched the magic potions. We have some great news. That is, we have successfully developed love, cancer-free, and longer youth products. Still the effects of the flying potions remain temporary, so you have to retake it. Also, both memory and wisdom potions are more expensive than before, since they are now eternal. However, we do have suggested numbers of taking those potions. After a certain point (IQ 180), they won't boost your intelligence and memory. Because of the research development, school tests rarely examine students' ability solely on memorization and recitation. Lastly, the love portion is especially helpful for someone who wants to find a faithful life partner or someone who loves someone one-sided. It's great news for marriage partners who both take the love portion. They will love each other till death, so the divorce rate will be significantly reduced.

Magic portions			
items	effects	duration	costs
Fly	Flying ability	a day	US 1,000
Wisdom	super smart	perpetual	US 50,000
Memory	excellent memory	eternal	US 50,000
Power	Incredible strength	temporary	US 3,000
Youth	10 days younger	lasting	US 1,000
Youth	A year younger	lasting	US 99,999
Muscle-building	reach American Captain-like built instantly	eternal	US 10,000
Cancer-free	Immunity	perpetual	US 99,999
love	love	eternal	US 20,000

2070年，倍斯特科技中心

自從我們推出魔法藥水後，20年的時光過去了。我們有些好消息。就是，我們成功地研發了愛情、癌症豁免和較長的年輕藥水產品。飛行藥水仍舊是維持短暫的時效，所以你必須要重新服用。而且，記憶和智慧藥水都比往常更昂貴，因為它們現在的效果是永久的。然而，對於那些藥水，我們確實有建議量。在達到特定點（智商180）後，你的智力和記憶力不會再提升了。因為這些研發，學校考試幾乎很少檢測學生要純仰賴記憶和背誦的部分。最後，愛情藥水對於想要找尋一個忠實人生伴侶或是單戀者特別有幫助。婚姻伴侶彼此都服用愛情藥水是很棒的消息。他們會終生愛著對方至死，所以離婚率會大幅減低。

Magic portions			
項目	效果	持續期間	花費
飛行	飛行能力	一天	1,000美元
智慧	超級聰明	永久	50,000美元
記憶	卓越的記憶力	永久	50,000美元
力量	驚人的力量	暫時	3,000美元
青春	年輕10日	永久	1,000美元
青春	年輕一年時光	永久	99,999美元
肌肉建造	能即刻達到像美國隊長般的體格	永久	10,000美元
癌症豁免	免疫力	永久	99,999美元
愛情	愛情	永久	20,000美元

Questions 155-159

155. What can be inferred about the number of gym users?
(A) tripling
(B) decreasing
(C) enhancing
(D) quadrupling

155. 關於健身中心的使用者數量，可以推測出什麼？
(A) 三倍增加的
(B) 降低的
(C) 增加的
(D) 四倍增加的

156. What can be inferred about the trend of the single parent?
(A) inconclusive
(B) increasing
(C) declining
(D) pending

156. 關於單親父母的趨勢，可以推測出什麼？
(A) 無法下定論的
(B) 增加的
(C) 下降的
(D) 懸而不決的

157. What can be inferred about the doctor with expertise in treating pancreatic cancer? (A) His value boosts (B) His value won't change. (C) His value increases **(D) His value dwindles**	157. 關於有著治療胰臟癌專業的醫生，可以推測出什麼？ (A) 他的價值提升 (B) 他的價值不會改變 (C) 他的價值提升 **(D) 他的價值降低**
158. Which of the following is film-related? (A) Fly (B) Wisdom **(C) Muscle-building** (D) Love	158. 下列哪一項是與電影相關的？ (A) 飛行 (B) 智慧 **(C) 肌肉建造** (D) 愛情
159. What is not stated about wisdom potions? (A) They are more expensive. **(B) They don't have any limit.** (C) They are now eternal. (D) They can be used to increase your intelligence.	159. 關於智慧藥水的敘述，沒有提到什麼？ (A) 它們更昂貴了。 **(B) 它們沒有任何限制。** (C) 它們現在效果是永久的。 (D) 它們能用於增進你的智力。

解析

- **第155題**，答案是decreasing，因為有了永久的muscle-building藥水了，故答案為**選項B**。
- **第156題**，答案是declining，因為有了永久的戀愛藥水，不可能變心了(till death)，故答案為**選項C**。
- **第157題**，這題要做出更多的綜合推論，而因為有了cancer-free的藥水了，所以癌症醫生的價值會減低，故答案為**選項D**。
- **第158題**，這題的film-related可以很快對應到美國隊長，所以是muscle-building，故答案為**選項C**。
- **第159題**，智慧藥水仍是有侷限的，故答案為**選項B**。

Best Museum will be closing for the following three months for the renovation. **(1)** The typhoon hit especially hard at the huge glass window and several major buildings. **(2) According to the staff member, who prefers to remain anonymous, all paintings stay intact.** Although moisture has influenced some ancient manuscripts, the museum owner is planning to erect a room that can keep them from getting affected. **(3)** After the renovation, the museum is scheduled to open in July for a major auction. Countless rich people are going to be here for great treasures and paintings. According to the norm, the auction is held for the charity, but from a reliable source, the rich are using this as a way to deduct increasing taxes. **(4)** Finally, the fee of the maintenance is predicted at US $5 million dollars, and even the revenue of the museum cannot cover the cost.

倍斯特博物館將於接下來的三個月關閉進行翻修。颱風對於巨型玻璃窗和幾個主要建築物擊的特別重。根據一位偏好維持匿名的職員所述，所有的畫作都維持完整。儘管濕氣已經影響有些古代的手稿，博物館持有人正計畫要建造一間能夠保持所有東西免於受影響的房間。在翻修之後，博物館預定於7月份的時程開放並且舉行一場主要的拍賣會。無數的有錢人都為了巨大的寶藏和畫作聚於此。根據標準，拍賣會是替慈善會舉辦的，但是從一則可靠的消息來源，富人正使用此方式來扣抵日漸增加的稅。最後，維修的費用預估是在5百萬美元，而甚至博物館的收益都無法蓋過這項支出。

Questions 160-162

160. What is the article mainly about?
(A) moisture in the room was caused by the typhoon damage
(B) the importance of preserving all paintings
(C) the closure of the Museum for the better
(D) the financial predicament of the Museum

160. 報導主要是關於什麼？
(A) 房間裡的溼氣是受到颱風損害的引起
(B) 保存所有畫作的重要性
(C) 博物館的關閉以待更佳的呈現
(D) 博物館的財政困境

161. What is not stated about Best Museum? (A) The timetable for the new opening is July **(B) Auctioned items cannot be exempted from the tax.** (C) The typhoon caused quite a lot damage. (D) A special room will be established.	161. 關於倍斯特博物館的敘述，沒有提到什麼？ (A) 新開幕的時程表是在七月。 **(B) 拍賣的項目不能用於稅額的扣除。** (C) 颱風會造成相當大的損害。 (D) 會設立特別的房間。
162. In which of the positions marked **(1)**, **(2)**, **(3)**, and **(4)** does the following sentence best belong? "**According to the staff, who prefers to remain anonymous, all paintings stay intact.**" (A) (1) **(B) (2)** (C) (3) (D) (4)	162. 以下這個句子最適合放在文中標記**(1)**, **(2)**, **(3)**, **(4)**的哪個位置？ 「根據一位偏好維持匿名的職員所述，所有個畫作都維持完整。」 (A) (1) **(B) (2)** (C) (3) (D) (4)

解析

· 第160題，這題最符合的是the closure of the Museum for the better其他都有點太片段了，故答案為**選項C**。

· 第161題，文章中有提到the rich are using this as a way to deduct increasing taxes，跟B選項敘述不一致，故答案為**選項B**。

· 第162題，這題的插入句放在颱風襲擊後最適合，**(2)**，故答案為**選項B**。

According to the morning news, four bank robberies happened at the exact same timeframe, which piqued the interest of criminal psychologists. **(1)** So far, the police still have no clue about the whereabouts of criminals. This means they are still at large. **(2)** From the statement of the bank clerk at the first bank, three criminals walked in with guns. He handed them two bags of fake money, and they just left, but where was the guard? **(3) As to the second bank, four criminals shot a citizen.** This meant they were serious about this, and they went in, demanding all clerks knee down. **(4)** They took away the real cash, and the amount was tremendous. The third robbery was about two women who went in the bank with knives and electric guns. They aimed directly at two guards, who suffered serious injury. The odd thing was that they didn't take the money. The fourth bank got robbed of a thousand dollars. We are still waiting for the police officer to make the statement at the News Center.

根據晨間新聞，四間銀行搶案發生在相同的時間點內，這也引起了犯罪心理學家們的興趣。到目前為止，警方對於罪犯的蹤跡仍舊毫無線索。這也意謂著罪犯們仍在逃。從第一間銀行職員的證詞，三位搶匪都有槍。他將裝有偽鈔的兩個袋子遞交給他們，然後搶匪們就走了，但是保全去哪了呢？至於第二間銀行，四位嫌犯槍擊一位市民。這意謂著他們是來真的，而他們走進內部，要求所有的銀行行員跪下。他們拿走了真鈔，金額是龐大的。第三起搶案是關於兩個女子攜著刀和電擊槍走進銀行。他們直接瞄準兩位保安人員，將兩人重傷。奇怪的是，他們並未拿走任何的金錢。第四間銀行被搶走一千元。我們仍等著警官於新聞中心做的陳述。

Questions 163-166

163. What is the article mainly about?
(A) attribution of the responsibility to the police department
(B) an analysis done by several criminal psychologists
(C) four major crimes occurring at banks
(D) injuries caused by the felons

163. 報導主要是關於什麼？
(A) 將責任歸咎給警方
(B) 幾個犯罪心理學家所做的分析
(C) 銀行發生四起搶案
(D) 傷勢是由罪犯所引起的

164. In which of the positions marked **(1)**, **(2)**, **(3)**, and **(4)** does the following sentence best belong? "**As to the second bank, four criminals shot a citizen.**" (A) (1) (B) (2) **(C) (3)** (D) (4)	164. 以下這個句子最適合放在文中標記**(1)**、**(2)**、**(3)**、**(4)**的哪個位置? 「至於第二間銀行,四位嫌犯槍擊一位市民。」 (A) (1) (B) (2) **(C) (3)** (D) (4)
165. What can be inferred about the location of the larcener? (A) certain **(B) inconclusive** (C) predictable (D) reachable	165. 關於竊賊的位置,可以推測出什麼? (A) 特定的 **(B) 無法下定論的** (C) 可預測的 (D) 可達到的
166. Which of the following bank suffered from both the most monetary loss and personal loss? (A) The first **(B) The second** (C) The third (D) The fourth	166. 下列哪一個銀行受到最多的金錢損失和個人損失? (A) 第一間 **(B) 第二間** (C) 第三間 (D) 第四間

解析

· 第**163**題,最符合的是four major crimes occurring at banks,故答案為**選項C**。
· 第**164**題,可以依據序號順序協助判答,**(3)**最合適,故答案為**選項C**。
· 第**165**題,從This means they are still at large.可以推斷出是**inconclusive**,故答案為**選項B**。
· 第**166**題,第2間蒙受的財損和人力傷亡最慘痛,故答案為**選項B**。

According to the golden rule, he who first mentions the salary loses. Of course, during the job search, we are going to encounter different types of companies. Some large companies have a specific and fixed salary for every position, so you don't have much room for discussion. **(1)** And that's not within the range of our discussion. As for other companies, you don't have to mention the salary first, if they are really interested in you, it's highly likely that they are going to mention it or make a phone call and ask you about that. **(2)** You can totally escape the expected salary question by saying that you would like to know more about the role and job content to figure it out. **(3) Also, you are bound to encounter a situation that you have to write down your expected salary.** It's best that you write a range, instead of an exact figure, so that you have the room for further negotiation. **(4)** You also need to do your homework about the salary for the current position in different companies... and good luck...

Best Column

根據黃金法則，先提到薪資的那方是輸家。當然，在找工作的期間，我們都會遇到各種型態的公司。有些大公司對於每個職缺有著特定和固定的給薪，所以你沒有太多的討論空間。而那也不在我們的討論範圍內。而關於其他公司，你不用先提及薪資，如果他們真的對你有興趣的話，很可能他們會提及或用電話告知並且向你詢問。你可以藉由述說著，你想要更了解這個角色和工作內容才能了解薪資為何以完全避開期待薪資的問題。但是，你必定會遇到一個情況，就是你必須要寫下你的期待薪資。最好的方式是你寫一個範圍，而不是一個確切的數字，這樣一來你就有進一步的協商空間。關於不同公司給予這份職缺所核定的薪資，你也必須要做好功課...祝你好運...

倍斯特專欄

Questions 167-168

167. What is Not stated about the "Job Column"? (A) Mentioning the salary first can hurt you in some ways. (B) It's likely that you are asked to write down about your expected salary. (C) Writing a range is better than writing a fixed number. **(D) You have to be persistent in negotiating the salary with the larger company.**	167. 關於「求職專欄」的敘述，沒有提到什麼？ (A) 先提及薪資可能會以一些方式傷害到你。 (B) 你被要求寫下關於你所期待的薪資是可能的。 (C) 寫一個範圍比寫一個特定金額佳。 **(D) 在與較大型的公司協商薪資時，你必須堅持不懈。**
168. In which of the positions marked **(1)**, **(2)**, **(3)**, and **(4)** does the following sentence best belong? "**Also, you are bound to encounter a situation that you have to write down your expected salary.**" (A) (1) (B) (2) **(C) (3)** (D) (4)	168. 以下這個句子最適合放在文中標記**(1)**, **(2)**, **(3)**, **(4)**的哪個位置？ 「而且，你必定會遇到一個情況，就是你必須要寫下你的期待薪資。」 (A) (1) (B) (2) **(C) (3)** (D) (4)

解析

- 第**167**題，be persistent in negotiating the salary with the larger company.跟文章中的其他敘述不一致，故答案為**選項D**。
- 第**168**題，從It's best that you write a range可以推斷插入句的訊息要放置在這之前，**(3)**是最合適的，故答案為**選項C**。

To be honest, you don't have to say something that will be used against you during the job interview. **(1) Of course, you will need a great resume and a convincing autobiography to be invited to a job interview.** You have to craft your ability to talk, too. **(2)** There are times that you will be asking about your personal information, and it does matter. Everything you have said can be a consideration. Don't give them any doubts and instead clear the doubt. Sometimes you can sense that. **(3)** For example, if you are sensing that the interviewer has a concern about the expected salary you wrote earlier, you can instantly respond by saying you are willing to trim it down a little. **(4)** And you obviously don't have to reveal your plan to study abroad or other plans so you can only work in the company **temporarily**... be smarter than that...

Best Column

說真的，在面試期間，你不必說一些會被用於對你不利的話。當然，你會需要一份很棒的履歷和令人信服的自傳，讓自己能被邀請來參加面試。你也必須要精緻化你的談話能力。會有著你將被詢問關於你個人資訊的時刻，而這確實相關聯。每個你所述的部分都可能會是考量。不要給他們任何的疑慮並且取而代之的是清除所有疑慮。有時候你可能察覺的到。例如，如果你意識到面試官對於你先前所寫的期待薪資有疑慮的話，你可以即刻表明，藉由述說你會願意減低一些。而你顯然不需要揭露你的海外研讀計畫或其他計畫，所以你僅能短暫的替公司工作...放聰明點吧...。

倍斯特專欄

Questions 169-171	
169. What is Not stated about the "Job Column"? (A) One needs a fantastic resume to have a chance. (B) Personal information can be a deciding factor. (C) Be careful about the word that comes out of your mouth. **(D) It's ok to disclose your future goals.**	169. 關於「求職專欄」的敘述，沒有提到什麼？ (A) 求職者需要很棒的履歷以取得機會。 (B) 個人資訊會是決定性的因素。 (C) 小心關於任何從你口中所說出的話 **(D) 接露你的未來目標是可行的。**
170. The word "**temporarily**" in line 11, is closet in meaning to (A) permanently **(B) fleetingly** (C) increasingly (D) potentially	170. 在第11行的「暫時地、臨時地」，意思最接近 (A) 永久地、長期不變地 **(B) 疾馳地、短暫地** (C) 漸增地、越來越多地 (D) 潛在地、可能地
171. In which of the positions marked **(1)**, **(2)**, **(3)**, and **(4)** does the following sentence best belong? "**Of course, you will need a great resume and a convincing autobiography to be invited to a job interview.**" **(A)(1)** (B) (2) (C) (3) (D) (4)	171. 以下這個句子最適合放在文中標記**(1)**、**(2)**、**(3)**、**(4)**的哪個位置？ 「當然，你會需要一份很棒的履歷和令人信服的自傳，讓自己能被邀請來參加面試。」 **(A)(1)** (B) (2) (C) (3) (D) (4)

模擬試題（五）

模擬試題（一）

模擬試題（二）

模擬試題（三）

模擬試題（四）

模擬試題（五）

解析

- 第**169**題，文中有提到don't have to reveal your plan to study abroad or other plans，故答案為**選項D**。
- 第**170**題，temporarily = **fleeting**，故答案為**選項B**。
- 第**171**題，插入句放在**(1)**最合適，故答案為**選項A**。

The game of the ring toss has been intriguing for people of all ages, so it never fades. Recently, we have begun to include more incentives to lure more customers, and we have different geographical locations for adventurous people. For example, three gifts have been set in front of the huge waterfall. It's slippery in the place where you initiate a toss. The prize is actually money in a **translucent** bottle. You have no idea the amount until you toss the ring. Of course, nowadays people get to use the smartphone with 108M pixels to take a peek to decide whether they are going to play, and there are other geographical locations, too.

Setting	Number of tosses erected
Lake	5
Waterfall	3
River bank	8
High cliff	6
Volcano	9
Tunnel	10
Moving train	19

Note:

1. It's kind of hard to play ring toss game in a moving train, so the prize is going to be higher. Unlike other settings, it's a folded check in the bottle, so you can't take a peek at the amount written on it.

套圈圈這項遊戲已經引起所有年齡層玩家的興趣，所以這款遊戲不會退流行的。最近，我們已經納入更多的獎勵以引誘更多的玩家，而且我們有各種不同的地理位置的套圈圈提供給冒險玩家選擇。例如，三個禮物已經放置在巨大的瀑布裡。你進行投擲的地方是滑溜的。獎項其實是放置於半透明瓶子的金錢。你不知道實際的金額是多少直到你投擲到。當然，現今人們可以使用有1.08億畫素的智慧型手機以偷窺瓶中的獎項以決定是否要花錢玩，而我們還有其他地理位置的套圈圈可供選擇喔！

環境	套圈圈數的設立
湖泊	5個點
瀑布	3個點
河岸	8個點
高處峭壁	6個點
火山	9個點
隧道	10個點
移動火車	19個點

註：

1. 在移動的火車中玩套圈圈有點難，所以獎品也會更有價值。不像其他的地理環境，瓶中會是摺起的支票，所以你沒辦法窺見上面到底寫了多少金額。

Questions 172-175	
172. What is not mentioned about the game? (A) Different locations are used to attract adventurous people. (B) Three gifts have been set in front of the huge waterfall. **(C) The tunnel has the most tosses established.** (D) The checks will be put into the bottle in the moving train location.	172. 關於這項遊戲沒有提到什麼？ (A) 不同的地點用於吸引冒險型的玩家。 (B) 三種禮物被置於巨型瀑布的前方。 **(C) 隧道有最多的套圈圈設置。** (D) 支票會放置在移動火車地點的瓶子內。

173. The word "**translucent**" in paragraph1, line 7, is closet in meaning to **(A) semitransparent** (B) opaque (C) transparent (D) sparingly	173. 在第一段第7行的「暫時地、臨時地」，意思最接近 **(A) 半透明的** (B) 不透明的、不透光的 (C) 透明的、清澈的 (D) 節儉地、愛惜地
174. Which of the following is related to players' resistance to heat? (A) Waterfall (B) Lake (C) High cliff **(D) Volcano**	174. 下列那項與玩家抵抗熱有關聯？ (A) 瀑布 (B) 湖泊 (C) 高聳峭壁 **(D) 火山**
175. Which of the following prize has been kept invisible? (A) Waterfall **(B) Moving train** (C) Tunnel (D) High cliff	175. 下列哪項獎品一直是隱蔽的？ (A) 瀑布 **(B) 移動的火車** (C) 隧道 (D) 高聳峭壁

解析

- 第**172**題，tunnel的並不是最多的，故答案為**選項C**。
- 第**173**題，translucent = **semitransparent** 半透明的，故答案為**選項A**。
- 第**174**題，resistant to heat令人馬上聯想到volcano，故答案為**選項D**。
- 第**175**題，it's a folded check in the bottle, so you can't take a peek at the amount written on it.= **what has been kept invisible**，故答案為**選項B**。

Dear CEO

Thanks I'm finally getting the bonus and the raise. I was **passed over** when the company cannot afford to lose Cindy Lin as a CMO. The second time, it was the new recruit who had the information that could be used against the rival company. He did not want the money. He just wanted the title. The scandal between the CFO and the advertising manager cost a place for my promotion. The fourth time it was because of the economic downturn, and we were in a difficult time. We had a hiring freeze, let alone having a promotion thing. Luckily, after a **circuitous** route, if it's yours then it's yours. I eventually got the position. I'm going to the HR department to change the new ID badge. It's quite worth the wait.

Jack

親愛的執行長

謝謝，我最終獲得了獎金和加薪。當公司無法負擔失去身為CMO的辛蒂時，我被公司掠過。第二次的時候，是一位新進的員工，有著能用於對抗對手公司的資訊。他不要錢。他只想要頭銜。公司財務長和廣告經理的醜聞也讓我的升遷無期。第四次是因為景氣蕭條，而我們處於艱困的時期。我們經歷著冷凍期，更別說是升遷這種東西了。幸運的是，在迂迴的路途後，如果這是你的，那麼這就會是你的。我最終獲得了升遷。我正要去人事部門更換新的員工識別證。等待真的相當值得。

傑克

Dear Jack,

Again thanks for having great faith in the company. We have been working so hard since the start of the company... that means working here for 20 years. You have shown your loyalty, and you are quite admired by coworkers and subordinates, and that's kind of the rare quality that we are looking for as a leader. You didn't make a job hop. Not once. That surprised me. It's great that you didn't accept the offer from ABC Cosmetics. The Marketing Director had a plane accident last July. It was **hijacked** by some mobs who were unsatisfied with the government... to cut to the chase... good luck with everything...

CEO

親愛的傑克

再次感謝你對於公司的信念。從創立公司開始，我們一直都非常的努力...在這裡20年的工作時光。你已經展現出了你的忠誠，而你在同事和下屬間也受到相當的欽佩，這樣罕見的特質也是我們希望領導人所該具備的。你也未曾跳槽過。一次都沒有。那讓我感到驚訝。很棒的是，你並未接受ABC化妝品公司的聘約。去年七月，他們的行銷總裁發生了飛機失事的意外。飛機被一些不滿於政府的暴民所劫持...言歸正傳...祝一切好運...。

執行長

Questions 176-180

176. The word "**passed over**" in paragraph1, line 1, is closet in meaning to
(A) disconnected by
(B) dialed down
(C) penalized by
(D) left aside

176. 在第一段第三行的「掠過、忽視」，意思最接近
(A) 被分隔開來
(B) 調整...回
(C) 受到...懲罰
(D) 擱到一旁

177. What is Not stated about the letter written by Jack? (A) He finally gets the perks. (B) The new recruit had confidential documents. (C) The company went through the hiring freeze phase. **(D) The HR Department refused to renew the ID badge.**	177. 關於由傑克所寫的信件中沒有提到什麼? (A) 他最終獲得獎金。 (B) 新聘成員有機密文件。 (C) 公司曾經歷雇用冷凍期。 **(D) 人事部門拒絕更換新的徽章給他。**
178. The word "**circuitous**" in the letter 1, line 8, is closet in meaning to (A) circled **(B) meandering** (C) relinquishing (D) conflicting	178. 在第1封信第8行的「迂曲的、繞行的」,意思最接近 (A) 盤旋、旋轉、環行、流傳 **(B) 迂迴曲折、蜿蜒** (C) 放棄、撤出 (D) 相矛盾的、衝突的
179. What would have happened to Jack, if he had taken the MD position? (A) have the desired title **(B) get killed** (C) get the perks (D) earn a great fortune	179. 如果傑克接下那份MD工作,會發生什麼事情呢? (A) 有理想的頭銜 **(B) 被殺死** (C) 獲取津貼 (D) 賺取一筆財富
180. The word "**hijacked**" in letter 2, line 7, is closet in meaning to (A) unimportantly menaced (B) proudly imprisoned **(C) unlawfully seized** (D) influentially captured	180. 在第2封信第7行的「劫持、攔路搶劫」,意思最接近 (A) 不重要地威脅 (B) 得意洋洋地禁錮 **(C) 非法地逮住** (D) 有影響力地抓住

解析

- 第**176**題，passed away = **left aside**，故答案為**選項D**。
- 第**177**題，並未提到The HR Department refused to renew the ID badge.
- ，故答案為**選項D**。
- 第**178**題，circuitous = **meandering**，故答案為**選項B**。
- 第**179**題，因為他如果有接受該挖角的職缺，可能會因此而喪命，故答案為**選項B**。
- 第**180**題，hijacked = **unlawfully seized**，故答案為**選項C**。

Statement from the company

To be clear, our company does not **condone** sexual scandals. Therefore, we have to make the painful cut for our employee, who was accused of the sexual harassment and possession of recordings of several minors a month ago. We are a company that has built our name on our integrity and honesty. We have to caution all employees working in the company to remain vigilant and be responsible for their actions, and we don't accept any **misconduct** that may damage the reputation of the company. From now on, the hiring process will be lengthier and involve the scrutiny of me and other CEOs.

2022 0504

公司的聲明

為了澄清，我們的公司不會寬恕性醜聞。因此，我們必須要忍痛裁掉一個月前被控訴性騷擾和持有幾個未成年視頻的員工。我們的公司將名聲建於正直和誠實的根基上。我們必須要警示所有員工以保有機警和替他們的行為負責，而我們不接受任何會影響公司聲譽的行為不端。從現在起，招聘的過程將會更為冗長且包含我和其他執行長的審視。

2022 0504

Recruitment of the CFO

Experience: at least working in the car industry for 5 years
Degree: university or above
Recommendation: from the previous boss
Talent: great with numbers and accounting
Self-introduction: 500 words in English
Languages: Spanish or German, and English

Note: Candidates must use the on-line application form and fill out all the necessary details on the website. Send the document to the HR department before 2020 July 1. Selected candidates will participate in the first and second interviews in Europe. Finalists will be attending the great exhibition of our car in Japan. We will make the final decision in our headquarter, California. The new CFO will start their new journey in our branch office (South America) to get familiar with every part of our business.

財務長的招聘

經驗: 至少在汽車產業有5年的工作經驗
學歷: 大學或以上的學歷
推薦: 前東家
才能: 對數字和會計擅長
自我介紹: 500字的英文
語言: 西班牙文或德語，英語

註：候選人必須要使用線上申請表格並且於網站上填好所有必要的資訊。在2020年7月1日前將文件送至人事部門。獲選的候選人必須要參加在歐洲的第一次和第二次的面試。決賽者們會參與我們在日本的最大型展覽。我們會在我們的加州總部作最後的決定。新上任的執行長會在我們的南美洲分公司熟悉我們每個部份的事業。

Questions 181-185	
181. The word "**condone**" in paragraph1, line 1, is closet in meaning to **(A) tolerate** (B) concede (C) conclude (D) conduct	181. 在第一段第三行的「寬恕、赦免」，意思最接近 **(A) 忍受、容忍、寬恕** (B) 讓步、承認失敗 (C) 結束、推斷出、斷定 (D) 引導、帶領、實施
182. Who most likely can be the person that got the accusation? (A) CMO (B) CEO **(C) CFO** (D) The boss	182. 誰最有可能是當時受到控告的人？ (A) CMO (B) CEO **(C) CFO** (D) 老闆
183. The word "**misconduct**" in paragraph1, line 6, is closet in meaning to (A) decorum **(B) misbehavior** (C) misunderstanding (D) miscommunication	183. 在第一段第6行的「不規矩、不端行為」，意思最接近 (A) 彬彬有禮、合宜 **(B) 不禮貌、品行不端** (C) 誤解、不和 (D) 無法適切地溝通
184. What is Not stated about the qualification? **(A) Chinese** (B) familiarity with the industry (C) diploma (D) autobiography	184. 關於資格的部分，沒有提到什麼？ **(A) 中文** (B) 熟悉這個產業 (C) 文憑 (D) 自傳

185. Where will the new CFO be working at, if hired? (A) Europe (B) North America **(C) South America** (D) California	185. 如果受到聘用，新的財務長將會在哪裡工作？ (A) 歐洲 (B) 北美洲 **(C) 南美洲** (D) 加州

解析

- **第181題**，condone的意思就是tolerate，故答案為**選項A**。
- **第182題**，被控告的人為CFO，因為公司接續要招聘的人也是CFO，且也因為此事件而更慎重看待人選，故答案為**選項C**。
- **第183題**，misconduct = **misbehavior**，故答案為**選項B**。
- **第184題**，familiarity with the industry = experience，diploma = degree，qualification中並未提到**中文**，故答案為**選項A**。
- **第185題**，從The new CFO will start their new journey in our branch office **South America** to get familiar with every part of our business，故答案為**選項C**。

Day 73

We've decided to celebrate for a day and called the food truck to order some food and drinks. After some wine, I began to feel dizzy and tried to get some water by the river. I got two buckets of water. When I got back to the tent, some of our teammates yelled "They are still in the box", right? That scared the hell out of me. It turned out those pebbles weren't stolen. Imagine my relief. I opened the box and it hit me out of nowhere that I wanted to clean the surface of the pebbles to make it striking and stainless. After a moment, I regretted the action that I had done. The color on these pebbles **obliterated**. I couldn't believe it and thought I probably got drunk and mistakenly.... until my teammates all verified that. All gone. We've got nothing. And the person who wrote the letter played us... and big... but who did that?

第73日

我們已經決定要於今日慶祝一番，並且呼叫餐車點一些食物和飲料。在飲用一些酒後，我開始覺得有點暈眩並試圖要去河邊取些水來喝。當我回到帳篷時，我們有些成員大喊，石頭還在盒子裡頭，對吧?這把我嚇了一大跳。還好最後證明那些石頭沒有被偷走。可以想像我的如釋重負。我打開了盒子，而我的腦海中不知道從哪兒靈光閃現著，我該清洗下石頭的表面，讓這些石礫看起來更為耀眼且無汙點般。稍後，我就對於這個行為感到後悔了。這些石頭上的顏色消退了。我感到不可置信，而儘管可能是我喝醉了且誤將...直到我們的隊友都證實這件事情。都沒了。我們一無所獲。而是誰寫那封信把我們耍得團團轉呢...且耍得很大...但是到底是誰呢?

Day 74

We were completely **blindsided** by that, and couldn't think of what to do next...**(1) Then one of the monkeys handed a box to us that included a letter as well.** Should we trust what's written on the letter? **(2)** But since we didn't know what to do next... we followed the instruction given and went to the other side of the bank. A tall bush and then a forest. We were all wet. **(3)** Fortunately, things in our package didn't. We set up a tent and was ready to rest. **(4)** My instinct told me that something strange was going to happen. Then I woke up some guys, fearing that a wild beast was lurking in there. We walked several miles and there was a cave... I was like no... a giant spider? We could all get killed.

第74天

我們已經全然被那樣的事情攻其不備，且也想不到下一步要做什麼...然後其中一隻猴子遞給我們一個盒子，也包含了一封信在其中。我們應該再次相信信裡所寫的內容嘛?但是既然我們現在也不知道接下來要幹嘛...我們遵照上頭的指示並到了河岸的另一端。長灌木叢，然後接著是個森林。我們全身都溼透了。幸運的是，我們的包裹沒有。我們搭好了帳篷並且準備要做休息。我的本能告訴我，接下來可能有些奇怪的事情要發生了。然後我叫醒一些成員，唯恐有頭野獸潛伏在那裡。我們走了幾哩，然後發現那裡有個洞穴...我心中浮現了...不會吧...是巨型蜘蛛嘛?我們可能都會被殺害。

Day 75

A guy in our team would like to quit, and of course I said no... there is no quitting... and we have to find who's behind this. **(1)** Then all of a sudden, another team arrived at the scene as well, which increased our confidence to check if there actually was a giant spider in there, and of course we have to evenly split the credits with them... but fine... some of us were ready to ambush and some of us were ready to strike with the weapon. **(2)** We stayed **motionless** for a moment and decided to toss a coin to decide which team went in the cave first. Our team members lighted the torch and went in there. A giant spider horrifically stood there and we yelled loudly. So ten of us v.s the giant spider. **(3)** We threw several knifes and it remained undamaged. Then I threw the torch out of my hands for no reason... perhaps because I was too nervous... so the fight ended... the spider was fake... and we found boxes of heavy stuff in the cave...**(4) oh my god it was gold**... we are going to get rich...

第75天

我們隊上有位成員想要放棄，而想當然的...我反對...沒有放棄這種事...但我們必須要找到背後的主謀。然後，突然之間，另一個隊伍也抵達此地，此舉增進了我們的信心，如果在裡頭真的有隻大型蜘蛛的話，不過我們理所當然的要與他們均分這些分數...但是還好就是了...我們之中有些人準備好要埋伏，而另一些人準備以武器進行攻擊。我們維持靜止不動一陣子，然後決定要投擲硬幣來決定哪個隊伍要先進到洞穴裡頭。我們的隊伍成員點燃了火炬，然後進了洞穴。巨型蜘蛛恐怖地靜候在洞穴裡頭，我們則大聲喊叫著。所以這會是我們十個成員跟巨型蜘蛛間的戰鬥。我們丟了幾把刀子，而蜘蛛則維持毫髮無傷。然後我沒來由地丟擲了我手中的火把...或許是因為我出於太緊張的緣故...而戰鬥也因此而結束了...蜘蛛是假的...然後我們在洞穴裡頭發現了幾盒沉重的東西...我的天啊！這是黃金...我們要變富有了...。

Questions 186-190	
186. The word "**obliterated**" in paragraph1, line 8, is closet in meaning to (A) strengthened (B) emerged **(C) disappeared** (D) surged	186. 在第一段第8行的「擦掉……的痕跡、沖刷（掉）、消滅、忘掉」，意思最接近 (A) 加強、增強、鞏固 (B) 浮現、出現 **(C) 消失、不見、突然離開** (D) 激增
187. The word "**blindsided**" in paragraph2, line 1, is closet in meaning to (A) do something in blindfold **(B) do something in an unexpected way** (C) disturbed (D) enraged	187. 在第2段第1行的「出其不意、攻其不備」，意思最接近 (A) 以蒙住眼睛的方式做某事 **(B) 以出其不意的方式做某事** (C) 干擾 (D) 激怒、使憤怒
188. In which of the positions marked **(1)**, **(2)**, **(3)**, and **(4)** does the following sentence best belong? "**Then one of the monkeys handed a box to us that included a letter as well.**" **(A)(1)** (B) (2) (C) (3) (D) (4)	188. 以下這個句子最適合放在文中標記**(1)**, **(2)**, **(3)**, **(4)**的哪個位置? 「然後其中一隻猴子遞給我們一個盒子，也包含了一封信在其中。」 **(A)(1)** (B) (2) (C) (3) (D) (4)
189. The word "**motionless**" in paragraph3, line 7, is closet in meaning to (A) molested (B) counterproductive (C) flexible **(D)stationary**	189. 在第3段第7行的「不動的、靜止的」，意思最接近 (A) 妨礙、干擾、騷擾 (B) 產生不良後果的、適得其反的 (C) 柔韌的、有彈性的 **(D)停著的、停滯的、固定的**

| 190. In which of the positions marked **(1)**, **(2)**, **(3)**, and **(4)** does the following sentence best belong? "**oh my god it was gold**"

(A) (1)
(B) (2)
(C) (3)
(D) (4) | 190. 以下這個句子最適合放在文中標記**(1)**, **(2)**, **(3)**, **(4)**的哪個位置?
「我的天啊!這是黃金」

(A) (1)
(B) (2)
(C) (3)
(D) (4) |

解析

- 第**186**題,obliterated的意思其實就是disappeared,故答案為**選項C**。
- 第**187**題,blindsided的意思是do something in an unexpected way,故答案為**選項B**。
- 第**188**題,以letter為關鍵字和上下文敘述,可以推斷最適合插入的地方是**(1)**,故答案為**選項A**。
- 第**189**題,motionless的意思就是stationary,故答案為**選項D**。
- 第**190**題,從heavy stuff和we are going to get rich...,可以推斷最適合插入的地方是**(4)**,故答案為**選項D**。

Day 76

It was as authentic as it could be... because I even bit the gold.... it was real...**(1)** Since day one... I couldn't say I hadn't had the slightest doubt about the program thing. **(2)** Now without finishing all goals here and went on to find the real treasure on the island. We hit the lottery by finding it first. We were so happy and were so angry at the same time. **(3)** The fake spider was **inflamed** due to the torch I threw at it a moment before... we had to move boxes of gold outside before the fire was too big. The smoke was so unbearable. **(4) The fake spider must have been made by a harmful substance**. We could have died here by inhaling too much deleterious gas. We had to retreat and find something to extinguish the fire.

第76天

這真的在真實不過了…因為我甚至咬了黃金…這是真的「黃金」…自從第一天…我不能説我對於這個計劃沒有任何絲毫的疑慮在。現在，都還沒完成所有的目標，而卻發現了島上實際的寶藏。我們就像中樂透般地最先找到寶藏。我們都樂此不疲，而與之同時感到飢腸轆轆。蜘蛛贗品也因為我前陣子所丟的火炬的關係而燃燒著。…在火勢盛大之前，我們必須要把盛裝著金子的盒子都移到外頭。煙霧令人感到如此難以忍受。假蜘蛛可能是有害物質製成的。我們可能會因為吸入過多的有害氣體而喪命於此。我們必須撤退且找些東西來滅火。

Day 77

Miraculously, the fire was put out. And we all knew that boxes of gold had to be equally split between 10 people. Still it was a great fortune, enough for any of us to use for the rest of our lives. Of course, I didn't want any confrontations with others. I gathered everyone here and told them that each of us would get his 1/10 share of what we found. All of them agreed. We moved all of the boxes outside the cave and decided to **calculate** the amount of gold in those boxes. A real giant spider approached. Some of the guys said run... hurry... ran away... what a coward? Without a weapon, I had to run, too.

第77日

奇蹟似地，火勢被撲滅了。而我們所能知道的是盒中的金子要均分成10人份。而儘管如此這仍舊是很大量的財富，足夠我們餘生使用綽綽有餘了。當然，我不想要與隊友們有任何的爭執。我把每個人匯聚於此，並且告訴他們我們每個人都將會獲得所找的金子的1/10份。他們所有人都同意此事。我們將所有的盒子都移至洞穴外頭，並且決定要計算在那些盒中金子的數量。一隻真的巨型蜘蛛卻在此時迫近。他們之中有些人說道…跑啊!快點….逃跑!?…多麼懦夫的行為啊!…沒有武器在手，我也必須逃跑。

Day 78

We decided to regroup and launch an attack. By the time we got back to the original place, the giant spider was gone. So were boxes of gold. Who did that? The spider couldn't do that right? The ten of us went back to where we camped and were too exhausted. The wealth was just within reach, and now it was all gone. We had to start somewhere. We weren't in the mood to call the restaurant car. Then we saw several ostriches chasing by the cheetah and we grasped the chance to take a closer look at the nest. No golden ostrich eggs could be found, but there was something else. We moved several ostrich eggs to our jeep and then we found that it was like a floorboard thing. It's a gateway to the basement. Another new finding... good for us...

第78日

我們決定要重組且發起攻擊。在我們回到原處時，巨型蜘蛛不見蹤跡了。而幾盒金子也不見所蹤。是誰幹的?蜘蛛沒辦法將它移走，對吧!我們十個人回到露營紮營處均感到筋疲力竭。財富就近在咫尺，而現在又都化為烏有了。我們必須要從某個地方重新開始。我們都沒有心情去叫「餐車」了。然後我們看到幾隻被獵豹追逐的鴕鳥，於是我們抓緊機會要進一步地觀看巢穴。沒有看到任何的金色鴕鳥蛋，但是卻有些東西。我們將幾顆鴕鳥蛋搬到我們的吉普車上，而之後我們發現了像是地板之類的東西。這是通往地下室的入口。另一個新發現...對我們來說是件好事...。

Questions 191-195

191. The word "**inflamed**" in paragraph1, line 6, is closet in meaning to (A) terrified (B) lit up (C) led to (D) unaware of	191. 在第一段第6行的「使燃燒、使極度激動」，意思最接近 (A) 使害怕、使恐怖 (B) 點燃 (C) 被引至 (D) 未查覺到

192. In which of the positions marked **(1)**, **(2)**, **(3)**, and **(4)** does the following sentence best belong? "**The fake spider must have been made by a harmful substance.**" (A) (1) (B) (2) (C) (3) **(D)(4)**	192. 以下這個句子最適合放在文中標記**(1)**, **(2)**, **(3)**, **(4)**的哪個位置？ 「假蜘蛛可能是有害物質製成的。」 (A) (1) (B) (2) (C) (3) **(D)(4)**
193. The word "**calculate**" in paragraph2, line 6, is closet in meaning to (A) profuse (B) capitalize **(C) compute** (D) calibrate	193. 在第2段第6行的「計算、估計、預測」，意思最接近 (A) 毫不吝惜的、十分慷慨的、極其豐富的 (B) 利用 **(C) 計算、估算、推斷** (D) 測定......的口徑、校準
194. What is Not mentioned about discovered gold? (A) The gold was authentic. **(B) They eventually knew who took the gold that they miraculously discovered.** (C) The gold had to be evenly distributed to all attendances. (D) It was stashed in different containers.	194. 關於所發現的黃金，沒有提到什麼？ (A) 黃金是真品。 **(B) 他們最終知道誰奪取了他們奇蹟似找到的黃金。** (C) 黃金必須要平均分配給所有參與者。 (D) 它儲藏在不同的容納空間裡。

195. What is Not indicated about the team during and after "the spider incident"?

(A) **They were now professionally trained, so they were gallant enough to tackle the real spider.**

(B) They couldn't stand the gas generated by the burning of the counterfeit spider.

(C) Their hope shattered because the gold unexpectedly disappeared.

(D) The appearance of ostriches led them to another new adventure.

195. 關於團隊在「蜘蛛事件」期間和之後，沒有提到什麼？

(A) 他們現在都是專業訓練過的，所以他們都勇敢到能夠應付真正的蜘蛛。

(B) 他們無法抵抗由燃燒假蜘蛛所產生的氣體。

(C) 他們的希望破碎了，因為黃金突然地消失了。

(D) 鴕鳥的出現引導他們朝向一個新的冒險旅程。

解析

· 第191題，inflamed的意思就是lit up，故答案為**選項B**。

· 第192題，從前、後句The smoke was so unbearable.和We could have died here by inhaling too much deleterious gas.和插入句的關鍵詞組a harmful substance可以推斷插入的部分應該要在**(4)**，故答案為**選項D**。

· 第193題，calculate其實就是compute的意思，故答案為**選項C**。

· 第194題，這題也要注意關於gold的相關敘述，他們還是不知道是誰將黃金拿走了，故答案為**選項B**。

· 第195題，這題也是跨篇章的出題，不過在選項A就可以看到描述錯誤的地方，儘管他們後來又受過訓練，但真正的蜘蛛出現時，他們是拔腿而逃，故答案為**選項A**。

Day 79

We lit several torches and found several paintings on the basement wall. A guy on our team boldly removed one of the paintings on the wall. **(1)** What was hidden behind... golden ostriches' eggs. Miraculously, we got these. **(2) When we were about to move these eggs back to our jeep, the gateway closed.** Let us out... who did that? I assumed it was the person from the beginning. **(3)** The person on the ground ignored our crying for help. Fine, then we destroyed all the paintings. We removed all paintings and found something intriguing. We assembled all the paintings on the ground, and surprisingly discovered that it was the map of this island. We got the map without costing a cent. Remember the company tried to sell the map to each of us. **(4)** That gave our team a leg up. Then I heard the voice of people on the ground. Were they coaches? That's...

第79日

我們點燃了火炬且在地下室的牆上發現了幾幅畫作。我們隊上一個成員膽大包天地將其中一幅畫作移開。藏在後頭的是...金鴕鳥蛋。奇蹟似地，我們得到這些金色鴕鳥蛋。當我們正要將這些鴕鳥蛋搬回吉普車上時。入口被關上了。讓我們出去...誰幹的呢?我假定這是從一開頭的那個人。在地面上的那個人忽視著我們的呼救。算了，那麼我們毀掉所有畫作吧!我們將所有的畫作移除且發現一些有趣的地方。我們在地上拼湊所有畫作，驚奇地發現這其實是幅這座島上的地圖。我們沒花費一分錢就得到了地圖。記得一開始的時候，公司試圖要向我們販售這張地圖嘛。這真的是給了我們一臂之力。然後，我聽到在地面上的人們的交談聲。是教練們嘛?...那真的...。

Day 80

I took out the pen and drew exactly the same map on the paper. While I was drawing the map, other guys either broke all golden ostrich eggs or tried to find the exit. There was a tunnel that could lead us somewhere. Great. And we grabbed all the keys on the ground. They came from the breaking of these golden ostrich eggs. It could be useful in the future... great... no I kind of like this adventure... hopefully, we would all be safe and back to the training center. In the very end of the tunnel, we found some light. That was great. Based on the map, we would be arriving at the peacock valley... I was sure more amazing things were to be revealed...(to be continued)

第80日

我拿出一枝筆，於紙上繪製了一張一模一樣的地圖。當我在地圖上繪製時，其他隊員將所有的金鴕鳥蛋摔碎或試圖找尋出口。這裡有個隧道可以將我們引導到某處。大棒了。然後，我們將地上所有的鑰匙拾起。鑰匙來自於這些黃金鴕鳥蛋。在未來這可能會有用處...太好了...不...我有點喜歡這項冒險事...希望，我們最終都能安然無恙地回到訓練中心。在隧道最底端處，我們察覺到一些光線。這真是太棒了。根據地圖，我們將會抵達孔雀山谷...我相信還有更多驚艷的事情會揭露出來的...（待續）

School Newspaper

"During 80 adventures" is actually a **shortened** version of what we found in our school library. There are three theories accounting for the story. The first one was backed by an archaeologist. It actually happened 50 years ago... about an adventure and the author wrote the diary to record all the information. The second theory indicated that this was an AI game created by a game company... and it was so believable that during the trial time... the government shut it down, fearing that it could be detrimental to our health, and once you were in the game, there was no turning back. Even if they unplugged the electricity, the game player's body might have suffered severe injuries. The third theory revolved around a promising young college student who wrote the story in cursive writings on the old paper hoping it could eventually get published... and he wrote it on and off. Only 80-day diary remains.

學校報紙

冒險80日期間，實際上是我們在學校所發現的一個縮短的版本。有三種說法來解釋關於這個故事。第一個說法是由一位考古學家所支持的，認為這實際上在50年前發生過此事...關於一項冒險和作者所述的日記去記錄所有資訊。第二個說法是，這實際上是遊戲公司所創設的一款AI遊戲...而在試玩版時...這真的太逼真了...政府決定要將其關閉，懼怕這可能會對於我們的健康造成危害，而且一旦進入了遊戲中，就無法回頭了。即使拔除電力，遊戲者的身體遭受嚴重的危害。第三個說法圍繞在一個前景看好的大學生以英文草寫將故事書寫在古老紙上，期盼有一天最終能將其出版...在這期間，就這樣斷斷續續地僅有80天的日記僅存著。

Questions 196-200

196. In which of the positions marked **(1)**, **(2)**, **(3)**, and **(4)** does the following sentence best belong? "**When we were about to move these eggs back to our jeep, the gateway closed.**" (A) (1) **(B) (2)** (C) (3) (D) (4)	196. 以下這個句子最適合放在文中標記**(1)**, **(2)**, **(3)**, **(4)**的哪個位置? 「當我們正要將這些鴕鳥蛋搬回吉普車上時。入口被關上了。」 (A) (1) **(B) (2)** (C) (3) (D) (4)
197. What is Not Mentioned about the map? (A) The map can give the team an upper hand. **(B) Because they were locked under the basement, they had no choice but to purchase the map from the company.** (C) They extracted all the paintings from the wall. (D) The guy imitated the map to sketch an identical one.	197. 文中沒有提到什麼? (A) 地圖可以讓團隊佔上風。 **(B) 因為他們被鎖在地下室,他們不得不購買公司所販售的地圖。** (C) 他們從牆上取下所有畫作。 (D) 那個男子模仿地圖繪製一幅相似的地圖。
198. What is Not True about golden ostriches' eggs? (A) They were concealed behind these paintings (B) Keys were in these eggs. (C) They were shattered by the guy's teammate. **(D) They were carried back to the jeep successfully.**	198. 關於金鴕鳥蛋的敘述,何者不正確? (A) 牠們藏匿在這些畫的背後。 (B) 鑰匙在這些蛋中。 (C) 牠們被男子的隊友摧毀了。 **(D) 牠們被成功地搬到吉普車上。**

199. The word "**shortened**" in paragraph1, line 3, is closet in meaning to (A) summary (B) adaptation (C) descriptive **(D) abbreviated**	199. 在第一段第三行的「縮短的」，意思最接近 (A) 摘要 (B) 改編、改寫 (C) 描述性的 **(D) 縮短的**
200. What is Not indicated about three theories? (A) The first theory stated a story entirely based on the diary of the writer. (B) The third theory was about a story that never got printed. **(C) The first one is more believable than the other two since it was backed up by a scholar.** (D) The second theory revolved around an incredible experience in an AI setting.	200. 關於三種說法，文中沒有提到什麼？ (A) 第一個說法陳述了一則故事，全然基於作家的日記。 (B) 第三個說法是關於一則故事並未有出版見市的機會。 **(C) 比起其他兩個版本，第一個說法比較可信，因為他是由一位學者所背書的。** (D) 第二種說法圍繞在AI環境下的驚人體驗。

- **第196題**，挖空的地方出現let us out所以剛好是接續插入文字敘述中的the gateway closed，故答案為**選項B**。
- **第197題**，文章中並沒有提到他們有向公司購買地圖，故答案為**選項B**。
- **第198題**，這題是詢問金鴕鳥蛋，在兩個篇章都有出現，所以是跨篇章的考題，文中並未提到將金鴕鳥蛋搬回吉普車上，有搬回的是普通鴕鳥蛋，故答案為**選項D**。
- **第199題**，這題要注意的點是shortened是形容詞，問的不是version，儘管這個很容易看成是adaptation等等，但要選同義的形容詞，**abbreviated**，故答案為**選項D**。
- **第200題**，這題是詢問關於三種說法，直接定位在第三篇段落，選項A的the author wrote the diary to record all the information等同於a story entirely based on the diary of the writer，選項B的原文段落hoping it could eventually get published對應到a story that never got printed，選項C是描述關於兩種說法的比較，但是段落中並未比較這三種說法哪種較可信，只是講述有這三種流傳的說法，選項D是原文提到第二種說法的濃縮式表達，故答案為**選項C**。

新多益聽力模擬試題 答案表

模擬試題（一）

PART 5

101. D	102. B	103. C	104. D	105. C	106. C	107. D	108. B	109. C
110. C	111. A	112. B	113. C	114. B	115. C	116. C	117. D	118. B
119. B	120. B	121. C	122. D	123. D	124. D	125. B	126. B	127. B
128. D	129. C	130. C						

PART 6

131. B	132. C	133. A	134. D	135. D	136. C	137. C	138. B	139. D
140. D	141. B	142. A	143. C	144. D	145. D	146. A		

PART 7

147. C	148. B	149. D	150. A	151. B	152. C	153. C	154. C	155. C
156. A	157. C	158. C	159. C	160. D	161. B	162. D	163. C	164. D
165. C	166. C	167. C	168. A	169. B	170. A	171. B	172. D	173. D
174. D	175. D	176. C	177. D	178. A	179. C	180. D	181. A	182. D
183. A	184. A	185. C	186. A	187. C	188. D	189. B	190. C	191. C
192. A	193. C	194. B	195. D	196. C	197. D	198. C	199. D	200. B

模擬試題（二）

PART 5

101. C	102. B	103. D	104. C	105. D	106. C	107. A	108. D	109. C
110. B	111. B	112. A	113. B	114. B	115. B	116. C	117. C	118. C
119. B	120. A	121. D	122. D	123. B	124. C	125. A	126. C	127. C
128. D	129. B	130. B						

PART 6

131. C	132. A	133. C	134. C	135. B	136. C	137. B	138. D	139. D
140. B	141. D	142. C	143. B	144. B	145. D	146. C		

PART 7

147. D	148. D	149. C	150. D	151. D	152. A	153. A	154. C	155. D
156. C	157. A	158. D	159. B	160. C	161. D	162. D	163. A	164. D
165. C	166. A	167. C	168. B	169. A	170. D	171. C	172. C	173. A
174. D	175. C	176. C	177. C	178. C	179. C	180. C	181. C	182. D
183. B	184. D	185. C	186. B	187. C	188. A	189. A	190. C	191. C
192. D	193. C	194. C	195. D	196. A	197. B	198. D	199. C	200. D

模擬試題（三）

PART 5

101. A	102. C	103. C	104. D	105. B	106. B	107. B	108. D	109. C
110. A	111. C	112. D	113. B	114. D	115. C	116. D	117. C	118. D
119. A	120. B	121. D	122. B	123. B	124. C	125. C	126. C	127. B
128. C	129. C	130. C						

PART 6

131. C	132. B	133. A	134. D	135. D	136. C	137. B	138. C	139. B
140. B	141. D	142. C	143. D	144. B	145. C	146. A		

PART 7

147. C	148. D	149. C	150. C	151. B	152. C	153. B	154. B	155. A
156. D	157. D	158. C	159. C	160. C	161. D	162. B	163. D	164. B
165. C	166. B	167. C	168. B	169. D	170. B	171. C	172. A	173. C
174. B	175. C	176. D	177. C	178. C	179. A	180. D	181. D	182. C
183. D	184. C	185. D	186. D	187. C	188. B	189. A	190. B	191. A
192. A	193. B	194. A	195. D	196. C	197. C	198. C	199. C	200. D

模擬試題（四）

PART 5

101. C	102. A	103. C	104. D	105. C	106. C	107. B	108. D	109. C
110. B	111. D	112. A	113. D	114. B	115. D	116. D	117. A	118. D
119. D	120. D	121. B	122. A	123. C	124. D	125. A	126. A	127. D
128. C	129. A	130. B						

PART 6

131. C	132. D	133. B	134. D	135. C	136. B	137. C	138. A	139. A
140. B	141. C	142. D	143. A	144. D	145. C	146. B		

PART 7

147. A	148. C	149. B	150. A	151. C	152. C	153. A	154. D	155. C
156. D	157. B	158. A	159. A	160. D	161. D	162. B	163. C	164. C
165. D	166. A	167. B	168. A	169. D	170. B	171. B	172. D	173. A
174. D	175. C	176. A	177. D	178. A	179. B	180. C	181. C	182. C
183. A	184. C	185. B	186. D	187. C	188. B	189. D	190. C	191. C
192. D	193. B	194. B	195. C	196. B	197. B	198. A	199. C	200. C

模擬試題（五）

PART 5

101. B	102. C	103. A	104. B	105. D	106. D	107. A	108. D	109. B
110. B	111. A	112. C	113. D	114. D	115. C	116. B	117. D	118. C
119. C	120. B	121. D	122. B	123. B	124. D	125. D	126. B	127. D
128. D	129. C	130. B						

PART 6

131. C	132. C	133. B	134. A	135. B	136. D	137. C	138. D	139. D
140. B	141. A	142. C	143. D	144. C	145. A	146. D		

PART 7

147. D	148. C	149. B	150. C	151. C	152. B	153. B	154. A	155. B
156. C	157. D	158. C	159. B	160. C	161. B	162. B	163. C	164. C
165. B	166. B	167. D	168. C	169. D	170. B	171. A	172. C	173. A
174. D	175. B	176. D	177. D	178. B	179. B	180. C	181. A	182. C
183. B	184. A	185. C	186. C	187. B	188. A	189. D	190. D	191. B
192. D	193. C	194. B	195. A	196. B	197. B	198. D	199. D	200. C

國家圖書館出版品預行編目(CIP)資料

新制多益閱讀滿分：神準5回全真試題+解題
策略 / 韋爾著-- 初版. -- 新北市：倍斯特,
2020.07面；公分. --（考用英語系列；25）
ISBN 978-986-98079-5-1
1.多益測驗

805.1895   109008865

考用英語系列 025

新制多益閱讀滿分：神準5回全真試題+解題策略

初　　版　　2020年7月
定　　價　　新台幣620元

作　　者　　韋爾
審　　稿　　Christine Etzel
出　　版　　倍斯特出版事業有限公司
發 行 人　　周瑞德
電　　話　　886-2-8245-6905
傳　　真　　886-2-2245-6398
地　　址　　23558 新北市中和區立業路83巷7號4樓
E-mail　　best.books.service@gmail.com
官　　網　　www.bestbookstw.com
總 編 輯　　齊心瑀
封面構成　　高鍾琪
內頁構成　　菩薩蠻數位文化有限公司
印　　製　　大亞彩色印刷製版股份有限公司

港澳地區總經銷　　泛華發行代理有限公司
地　　址　　香港新界將軍澳工業邨駿昌街7號2樓
電　　話　　852-2798-2323
傳　　真　　852-3181-3973